A Crafty and Devious God

"...a great read..."
"Weirdly excellent"
"[The] writing is very natural, loose and easy, yet deep and thoughtful."
"...an engaging character study... a tale of a man who's lost, looking for his way, and a girl who knows she is destined for great things and is determined to achieve it at all costs."
"I gave it a try. And kept reading, and reading, and reading. Just very well-written, scattered throughout with concepts that made me think (which I occasionally like to do)."

|

After

...short stories of New Yorkers trying to make sense of their changed world in the immediate aftermath of 9/11."
"These stories are emotionally impactful but they are not grim. Each character finds some measure of hope or understanding or, at the very least, adaptation to their circumstances."
"...a masterful job of depicting the surreal dream-like state that trauma survivors inhabit..."
"Intricately woven stories of despair and ultimately hope..."
"...a tender tribute to the survivors of 9/11."

Also by Ted Krever:

A Crafty and Devious God
Howling at Wolves
Green
Mindbenders
After

Praise for Ted Krever's books:

Mindbenders

"...a storyline that takes hold in the first few pages and doesn't let go..."
"...really fast paced...I found myself unable to put it back down."

"...dialog that left me breathless."
"...[a] global, international conspiracy of corporate and governmental politics, mind control, murder and intrigue."
"OMG!...finally crawled into bed early hours of the next day."
"This is that rare piece of fiction based on fact in such a way as to make the two seem to blur."
"Mindbenders...will make you wonder if your mind really does belong to you."

Mindbenders 2: The Fiery Sky

"...a more than worthy followup to the 1st book, fast paced, well written and exciting!"
"...takes me places that were only in my imagination - I feel like I have been to that island in the South Pacific living on the water, and I've been parched in the Aussie desert - it's all real."
"...A complete thrill ride from beginning to end...great style and substance."
"...intense, memorable scenes..."
"...seamlessly weaves multiple storylines together, delivering a powerful punch of an ending."

GREEN

"…not your typical romance…
"…a unique look into the mindset of men, rather than the typical romance, which is told from the woman's point of view."
"… a smart, witty and wise look at love later in life…"
"I found myself laughing aloud more than once, only to shortly thereafter find myself deeply touched."
"The descriptions…of Ireland are alone worth the price of the book…"
"If you like reading about horses, Ireland, friendship, love in any form..."
"Part a love story, part a political thriller, and part a satiric commentary on life and politics…"
"Green is a charming book."

Howling at Wolves

"This book, simply put...is funny!"
"Keep your tissues handy as you won't stop laughing."
"Nothing is sacred..."
"…like Garp on steroids (or maybe Viagra?)

Mindbenders 2:
The Fiery Sky

~~~~

A Max Renn Thriller

by Ted Krever

Little David Publications

www.tedkrever.com

Author's Note:

This is Book Two of a series. Just in case you haven't, it usually makes sense to start with Book One. I'm just sayin'....

~~~~

'Mindbender' face photo by Jack Cowley

(contact me, Jack, I owe you money)

~~~~

~~~~

ISBN: 978-1-7327865-1-6

~~~~

To Claire

Ted Krever

Book One

reunion 1
december 2008

Darwin, Australia

The man tied to the slab means nothing to me.

He's about my age, muscled, dark hair and eyes—and they're cutting him open right in front of me, two L Corp flunkies, a big blonde lumberjack one and a smaller oily one with an Asian tattoo at the base of his neck. Tat Man is holding him down while Blondie slits into him with a razor.

The poor jerk keeps looking from one to the other, screaming "What do you want? I'll tell you! What do you want?" They don't answer, don't seem to want anything—unless it's just to get at me. And, since L Corp is the McDonalds of mindbenders, I suspect that's just the thought they intend me to have.

If I could look away, close my eyes, hum real loud and drown out the screams, maybe I could just not care. I don't know this fucker from a doorknob. It should be easier watching someone else get tortured—there but for the grace, etc. But I know better. Because of Iraq, I know better.

All those guys on the far side of the gun sight, we didn't like their attitude or their wardrobe, we called them rude names in loud voices. It shouldn't have been an issue forgetting them since we never knew them in the first place. But they came back to us, took vengeance on us, later, in our dreams. Some of them have lingered a thousand times longer and more vividly in my memory than they ever did in my life.

And now, here's this guy right in front of me crying for mercy in English— clearly, I'll never get rid of him unless I do something.

Which is a challenge, what with me being tied to a chair.

"Tell me where Renn is!" Straw Hat, who seems to be the L Corp crewboss, yells at me. "Then we can avoid all this." He's a natty little fuck—neat handlebar mustache, baby face, straw hat with a feather in the brim, jacket and pants tailored and fitted a size too small. Everybody else in the requisite blue L Corp jumpsuits and he's out of *LA Style*, hipster edition. "Tell me and we'll patch him up before he's useless to everyone."

When they dig the razor into the prisoner's leg, I *feel* it. It's like his cries are coming from inside my head. It's so vivid—realer than real. Why aren't they slicing *me* open? Wouldn't that work better? It makes me wonder if *any* of this is real.

There has to be at least one mindbender in the bunch. I'm confident that I'm blocking them—that they can't read my thoughts—but that didn't stop them from pulling me off the flying boat from the islands and dragging me out to these warehouses on the edge of the city, jetliners whooshing overhead every thirty seconds.

"Duuude, make it easy, for Christ's sake!" Straw Hat says, like I'm upsetting his plans for a pleasant afternoon. "Next, we'll have to start cutting things *off!*"

The razor digs in and I flinch at the screams. I'm not going to be able to do this for long.

"Why do I need to *tell* you anything?" I demand. "Why don't you just read my mind?"

Tat Man smacks me upside the head. But I see it coming just far enough ahead to go with the blow—it glances off without really biting.

"Shut up and answer!" he bellows. A moment later, I feel the closed-air heaviness of a mind probe. Somebody wants inside my head. But who? Who's the boss? Who's the mindbender? I toss a bone and wait for a reaction.

"Max Renn's dead!" I blurt. "He died in Nepal three days ago."

Blondie and Tat Man immediately look at Straw Hat. Okay, *he's* the mindbender.

"You don't know that," he says but the probe instantly gets thicker, more powerful. Which tells me a) my blocking is working and b) he's no surer where Max was three days ago than I am.

When they're probing, Max told me, they're searching for your mind in the here and now. So don't be here and now. Get inside a memory that takes you out of yourself, out of the moment. For me, that means back to Fallujah. Back to the tinbox popping of automatic weapons, the shrieking of twisted metal, the smell of smoke and haze, burning rubber and gasoline. I can make the switch in my sleep - I do, in fact, all too often. That fucking memory is more real to me than anything happening in my life is, ever—and so, once I learned how to drop into it while wide-awake, nobody could ever force their way into my head. At least, no one has so far.

"Okay," I yell, like he's dragged it out of me, "I'm not sure. I haven't seen him in six months!"

"Since Rome. Since the G8."

"Right."

"But you're here to meet him—right?"

Straw Hat is pressing, making me think in the here and now, feeling for a way to squeeze inside my head. He's powerful and relentless - it's like someone wrapping a blanket tight around your face. Either I break this probe quick or he'll have me.I can't risk a lie while he's probing. *Stay as close to the truth as possible,* I tell myself, *and see how far along you can string him.*

"Maybe."

Tat Man smacks me again, on the temple this time, but he's over-eager and catches me at an angle instead of square to the cheek. The guy is hopeless— I let out a cry just to encourage him. If you're going to get tortured, this is the guy to ask for.

"What's 'maybe' mean?"

"It means when Max Renn gives you directions, you never know if you're following them right. He told me *Follow the Sounds.*"

"Follow the—?"

"Follow the Sounds. Travel 'til sunrise. I'll meet you there."

"Meet you where?"

"Wherever I ended up, I guess."

"That's stupid."

"Tell me about it."

Straw Hat looks positively amused. "How did he tell you this?"

The truth, as much as possible. "In a note."

"Where'd you get the note?"

"He gave it to me."

"So you *did* see him!"

"He gave it to me six months ago."

"The note that told you to come here today…"

"Well, it didn't say that when he gave it to me."

"You expect us to believe that?"

"If Max Renn ever gave you directions, you'd believe it. *All* his directions are like that."

"Enough!" Straw Hat yells. "Show him what we do!"

Blondie pins the guy to the table; immediately, he starts writhing and shrieking. The sound of a grown man screaming and crying for his life is a pathetic and terrible sound. When Tat Man raises the razor to his eye, it's too much for me and I just fade away.

night of the G8
june 30, 2008

six months earlier

~~~~

Trastevere, Rome

It was the walking on water that broke the spell for me.

We ran uphill through thick panicking crowds, away from
Tiber Island and the wreckage of the G8 Concert, away from the
sirens that said L Corp and G8 Security were right on our tail —
and all I could think about was the sight of Max Renn kneading
the air, changing its molecular structure (or maybe the magnetic
field; I'm a soldier, not a geek) so it thickened into a shield he set
hovering over the river.

We clattered across that spongy shield, from the tip of Tiber
Island onto the south bank and the G8 guards fell into the water
seconds later when the shield dissolved under their feet as they
tried to follow.

After all the crazy shit that had already happened, *that* somehow put me over the edge.

A lone *caribiniere* appeared around the corner of an ancient church (it's Rome, they're everywhere). Kate Crowell, sprinting to my left, flicked a shield that smacked him hard across the forehead and flattened him against the wall, unconscious. She'd done the same thing a hundred times in the last hour, fending off a platoon of L Corp guards and the white-haired assassin Marat, who shot lightning bolts from his fingers.

How did I let *that* detail go by without crying 'Foul'?

The sirens howled real close for a moment—I went twitchy, looking over my shoulder—and then, all at once, turned eastward and waned in a hurry.

"Max has a whole neighborhood calling the emergency line," Kate chuckled. "'Who are those people running through my garden?'"

And, as soon as she said it, I could see blocks of people jumping up from the kitchen table or out of bed, complaining of phantoms in the backyard, intruders who were actually half a mile away and headed in the other direction. I wondered if the images were my imagination at work or the real thing, Max channeling the vision of people he was influencing and sharing it with us. I'd been with him long enough to know it could be either.

We walked out of Trastavere six minutes after we'd entered it, past three *carabinieri* and a BND German intelligence officer, all of whom looked sharp and on-guard and all of whom totally ignored us going by. Ignored us like we were invisible.

By the time we clomped onboard the *Cerberus*, a fishing boat heading out before dawn, scrounging for anchovies and sea lobster, the strangeness of it all was finally clear to me.

The crew wanted nothing to do with passengers until Kate went to work and they suddenly decided it was their sacred duty to smuggle us away from the Nazis.

"None of these guys was born the last time there were Nazis here," I told her. "And wasn't Italy their ally?"

"They watch a lot of movies," she replied.

The waters near Fiumicino were salted with police boats but our crew knew the cops by name—they bantered about *futbol* and fussed with the nets while we puttered slowly away. By afternoon, we were south of Sicily and safe to go on-deck.

"When do we land?" I asked.

"Tomorrow night—in Tunisia," Max said.

"That's a long time in the open, isn't it? Isn't there a faster way?"

"That's the point—they're watching all the fast ways out of town. By the time we surface again, they'll have decided they lost us."

I was leaned half over the rail but it wasn't the choppy water, it was the memories flooding over me. Three tours in Iraq, a year in VA hospitals and then Dave Monaghan's PTSD halfway house in the Everglades. Until Dave got shot dead in the bathtub and his friend Max showed up looking for information Dave had hidden, only to find—when I started spouting the names and addresses of people I'd never heard of—that Dave had hidden it all inside my head.

After that, we were riding the wave and I just got swept up in the moment. We picked up Mark Tauber, the American mindbender in Savannah, almost got captured by his old teammate(?)(!), Miriam Fine, in Durham, actually got captured by Marat and Pietr Volkov, the L Corp head and Max's old comrade from Mindbender High School in Novosibirsk, Siberia.

Oh yeah—by that time, Max had explained to me not only that he was a mind control agent, but also *not* one of ours. Bred to be a Soviet spy but still in training when the country collapsed, now out of early retirement because he was as determined as I was to find out who killed Dave.

Volkov did, was the short answer—at least, he ordered the shooting, the same way he sent agents to run over Kate's father, one of the only other remaining American mindbenders. After we escaped by way of Max setting the air on fire, we found out that L Corp was going after Aryana Singh, the Indian Prime Minister, champion of nonviolence and nuclear disarmament. Because that's what L Corp does, using mind control to get people to buy SUV's even though they never go off-road and vote for politicians who work totally against their interests.

Still hung out over the rail, watching the cruise ships and our fishing net picking up a couple strays, I ticked off the list of weird shit that had happened to us and marveled that I'd gone along without demanding a rubber room and one of those suits with the arms that tie.

But I hadn't. I made it all the way to Rome, to the Concert on the opening night of the G8, where Max held off Volkov long enough to save Singh, where Marat killed Tauber with a lightning blast and where Max and Kate turned on Marat simultaneously and...

Kate was staring at me with an expression I wanted to bottle. Every time she brushed against me, I got an erection—she insisted this was coincidence. "What did you do to Marat?" I demanded.

Her face went a shade of green. "How do I know? What did you see?"

"He killed Tauber and you and Max just gave him a stare like—like death..."

"And he disappeared!"

"Well, he burst into all those nice twirly spirals in the air," I said."At least he died pretty." It wasn't funny but I wasn't really feeling funny. Tauber was my Max-translator when we first started rolling together. He kept my feet on the ground and now he was gone. We'd stopped L Corp, which was payback for them killing Dave but it still didn't feel like victory.

On the North African coast, we were met by a couple of very shy individuals who didn't seem to know how they'd gotten there. Max said a few words and they handed over a bunch of really-convincing passports, credit cards and stacks of currency — Euros, dollars and yen. Max distributed them among us at Tunis Airport, by which time we'd acquired suitcases and a couple changes of clothes, lack of baggage being a dead giveaway. He told us to stick the money inside our clothes, suitcase sidewalls and socks.

"The money's good?" Kate asked, grinning.

"It might not always be real," Max said, "but it's from the finest local forgers. They've funded wars, Presidents and even peace between nations. I'd use up the dollars first, all the same." He led us to the middle of the international terminal.

"They're looking for three of us," he said, "so the smart thing to do is split up for a while." He handed us each a hand-written note, folded in half. "Don't open them until you're on the plane," he said, "then follow the instructions to the letter." And just like that, he was gone at a sprint, heading for his gate.

Kate and I turned to each other, awkward as ever. "I—I—" I've always fumbled for words with girls but it was a million times worse when she knew *everything* you were thinking.

"I feel like we barely know each other...for a thousand years," she said and, just like that, nailed the thing. We embraced and I checked my tickets as she walked away. Dubai and Singapore!

I breathed an involuntary sigh. Singapore felt right, a long way from everything.

I'll slip away, I remember thinking, *find some peace and quiet, figure out what 'normal' means.*

And, for a few hours, that almost seemed possible.

~~~~

Amsterdam, Netherlands

This was an Amsterdam homie if ever there was one.

Grass-green and egg-yellow polka-dot shirt, flaming orange pajama pants, beard to the chest, hair graying at the temples and flaring out behind him—one look and Landau would have said 'Amsterdam' without a beat. Landau favored a hipper look—handlebar 'stache, tightly-tailored jacket and slacks, colorful striped socks and a straw hat with a feather in the brim. He was at home in New York, LA, London, Tokyo, anyplace. This geezer would get arrested in an instant anywhere but here, Utrechtstrat just off the Prinsengracht, pirouetting past Landau's favorite coffee shop to a tune only he heard.

But I hear it too, Landau thought. Werner Tomas, 52, arrived in the Seventies for the pot and the hookers and never found his way home. There were lots of him here, growing seeds, making connections and selling harder stuff at the edge of the Dam.

But I hear it too. Werner's head echoed with wobbly memories of thirty-year-old songs rendered in his own (slightly pitchy) singing voice. Landau had a good connection with dear ol' Werner and he was feeling the mischief this night—exercising new muscles, finally giving them free reign. What's the point of a good new trick if you never tried it out?

A moment later, Werner stopped at the edge of the sidewalk, turning in wonderment along with the rest of the street traffic, seeking the source of a funny-sounding version of *The Low Spark of High-Heeled Boys,* now drifting over the block. It was a bizarre sound, barely music at all, fluttering between keys and finally stalling in atonal noise. A moment later, a hummed version of *All the Young Dudes* followed and this time, Werner recognized it as the music inside his own head.

How—? I didn't take anything extra-special this morning, did I? Could he be sure? Werner changed the tune in his head to Count Basie and then to his memory of Werner's sister playing the one horrible tune she'd learned on the piano—and each piece filled the sky, passing heads turning and grimacing (the music *was* bad, no doubt about it—he was just used to it), looking at upstairs windows in vain. Only Werner knew where the music was coming from. The car horn blared at the same time his mother's voice began singing 'Happy Birthday' out of the sky.

Landau pulled out his phone. "A man's been hit by a car," he reported, giving the address. "Not sure if he's injured or dead. He wandered into traffic." He rung off before they could ask his name.

When the car hit Werner, a huge cacophonous chord rang his end, horns and bells and industrial sounds, airplane engines and clothes washers, church organs, handsaws, elevator doors and the string section of the London Symphony Orchestra, a chord that rippled and wavered in the air for three long minutes before fading into a deeper dream.

Stupid dick didn't have to get himself squashed. Bloody waste— Landau was almost upset. You made connections with people, even fleeting ones like this, you almost developed an affection for them, like pets. But you had to let go. What was important was, it showed how far Landau had developed his touch. It was not the first test but each success was a milestone in its own way.

Landau had heard voices his whole life. He'd known early that, when wound-up or angry, he could bend strangers to his will—and as he got older, Landau found himself angry a whole lot. It came as a shock when he heard whispers of a company searching for people like him, one that promised to develop those skills.

This was followed by another shock when it became clear that L Corp didn't think as highly of his potential as he did. The assholes clearly had no idea who they were dealing with! He wasn't one of their sheep, to sit lotus-style in a group and brainwash stupid stockholders to vote for a hostile takeover they didn't want or invest in a development in Arizona that would never be built.

L Corp paid well and the place had lots of pretty boys and girls for Landau to flirt with. But pretty quickly, he was bored again.

And when Landau was bored, he went hunting for thrills.

In this case, the thrills came from hacking into L Corp's computer network. Defense contractors had the money and expertise to build elaborate security networks, which was just the kind of challenge Landau enjoyed.

He found his way into forbidden documents detailing the connections between Jim Avery's *Your World* empire (*Be Your Own Best Self!* Self-help advice videos, classes, cruises and personal appearances, hyped on Avery's cable network 24 hours a day, 7 days a week) and Pietr Volkov's L Corp security contractor, of which only a tiny trickle of information was known. Both corporations used the same methods and sometimes the same employees, first, to make customers feel hooked on empowerment, second, to rig governments and corporate elections and other, murkier dirty tricks.

The more he dug, the more irritated Landau got about being left out of the inner circle. So now he combined hacking with spying, the kind only a mindbender could employ—locating vulnerable co-workers with admin access, pulling their passwords right out of their heads and discovering the location of a critical file buried in a subdirectory of a subdirectory. Eventually, Landau found what he'd been looking for—the advanced-level mindbender training courses, the stuff they taught to the snots in the advanced ranks who kissed up and passed the stupid psych eval.

Of course, after a little while, that wasn't enough either, so he ferreted out the names and addresses of the instructors who wrote the courses. They had the real dirt, the tricks and strategies no one ever wrote down, only disseminated on a one-to-one, need-to-know basis.

When he needed to put all this knowledge to a real-world test, his guinea pig was handed to him in the form of the one job L Corp decided he was qualified for: the NATO research scientists he'd been assigned to babysit.

Simple job—just establish a mental connection with them and report on his work progresses. As if! Landau found far better uses for the pair, concocting an extremely entertaining sideline for them to work, on their own time, without anyone else knowing—hell, without the scientists themselves even knowing!

After a few months of this, Landau realized he'd outstripped anything L Corp would ever let him do.

So tonight he'd reached the crossroads. Landau wasn't one to watch the grass grow. The new gadget would pay off big-time on the open market. Time to start peddling it. So now he was coming in on a day off to tender his resignation. As the elevator rose to the sixth floor, he thought with satisfaction, *Goodbye, L Corp, you've served me well.*

And then the steel doors opened and deposited him into the middle of a raging fuckfest and those thoughts disappeared forever.

"Are you seeing this?"

"Get me a clean line!"

"All bureaus worldwide report in! Security Status—NOW!"

"Who *are* these guys?!"

L Corp grunts stood at their screens, banging on keyboards or, in more than a few cases, just staring open-mouthed like overfed sunfish. And who could blame them? Onscreen and under attack, the Major Dudes, the instantly-recognizable Leaders of the Industrialized Nations, huddled in a swoopy Plexiglas viewing box at the tip of Tiber Island, watching a Symphony Orchestra frantically playing Holst's 'Mars' while chaos erupted all around.

Lightning bolts flew, security forces ran in every direction, musicians with panicked looks held their positions like the band on the deck of the Titanic. PA's wandered the room aimlessly, carrying now-meaningless reports that nobody would ever bother to read.

It was the G8! Half the Amsterdam staff—not including Landau!—had been shipped off to Rome for support. *G8's gonna be the big moment for us,* the Boss said. *It'll put us on the map.*

Landau could see, staring at the screens, that this wasn't a map you'd want to be remotely associated with.

Smack in the middle of the chaos was the Boss himself, Pietr Volkov, hovering just outside the Plexiglas box. Landau had only met Volkov once on a stupid office inspection. But even he could see the man looked shaken.

"Who the hell's THAT?"

Some girl hurtled across the screen, bounding across the front of the orchestra. Lightning bolts burst around her—was she *shooting* or deflecting them? How would you even do that? Four or five beefy security guards rushed her and were sent flying— *flying!*—with a swipe of her hands in the air.

Almost unnoticed was the skinny dude in the corner of the screen with a concentration-camp haircut and wild eyes, crouching in the girl's shadow. He and Volkov seemed to know each other; gesturing back and forth in a sign language only they understood. While the rest of the room stayed riveted on the girl, Landau focused on the dude. And when the next lightning bolt lit up the scene, he realized why.

"It's *Renn!*" he exhaled.

The whole clattering room went suddenly, jarringly silent, as though every member of the team had choked at the same time.

All eyes focused on the historic relic at the edge of the screen. Max Renn, the great Soviet experiment, the mindbender of mindbenders. Landau had read the name twenty times, heard it spoken in hushed tones fifty more—now here he was in the flesh!

Renn and Volkov faced off like grizzlies over a dead stag and, suddenly, a seam opened in the air between them, a pulsing line of energy from fingertip to outstretched fingertip, taking them as much by surprise as the rest of the world watching.

Any semblance of order vanished—spectators stampeded screaming from the bleachers on both sides of the river, the police abandoned any attempt to control anything. Renn and Volkov tugged back and forth, prisoners of their writhing connection, until the seam glanced off the Plexiglas dome and shattered it into a million fragments.

After that, it was over fast. The security guys dragged the World leaders away to safety. Volkov was tackled by one of the intruders into the Tiber. A concluding exchange of lightning, killing one attacker and one defender. Someone shouted Marat had been killed! And then, Renn's team escaped, with unnecessary drama, across the surface of the Tiber into the twisting Roman streets.

Silence followed. For about three seconds.

Then, pandemonium. The officers start barking orders all over the room at once:

"Where'd they go? Find out!"

"Get us somebody in Rome! Anybody! What's our status? What's Plan B? Or C?"

"Monitor police traffic! Report every promising lead!"

"Get the train stations, airports! I want open feeds! Cut off all the escape routes!"

Landau grabbed a terminal and started working his connections.

The breathless pace continued until three in the morning, when word came to stand down. The team slumped over their desks, finally soaking up the attack, which continued playing an undying loop on the news channels.

By now, the report had been confirmed internally—Marat, Volkov's fearsome white-haired enforcer, was dead and the leaders of the G8 were alive and well. It was clear from the faces of the top brass that this was not the plan. An air of gloom emanated from the corner office where a loud teleconferenced debate could be overheard concerning the best way to spin what at least one manager termed 'a shrieking disaster'.

Landau was anything but gloomy. He'd come in planning to end his career at L Corp, convinced the company had no forward path for him. In the last four hours, instead, he'd watched, astonished, as the world reoriented itself to put him at the center of L Corp's future.

Whatever else came out of this night, Volkov would need new weapons.

And Landau had them. At very least, he had a prototype for the perfect step forward.

And he was the only one on Earth who knew it even existed.

Now that things had calmed down, he checked, naturally, on his charges, De Jogt and Saminov, the babies he was supposed to have been sitting. Landau threw them a lazy probe, expecting to find them sound asleep—and went white, taut in his chair, then bolted for the door.

As he hit the street, Landau realized he was facing a choice between the job he'd been hired to do and the one he'd made for himself.

A day earlier, that might have been a difficult choice. But in the new world, the one in which Landau was the central component, there really was no choice at all.

~~~~

Amsterdam

Vlad Saminov was gliding through the 23rd mile of a marathon when the phone on his night table went off. He was still in the midst of the dream as he held the receiver to his ear.

"I've had a epiphany," De Jogt's voice crackled through the speaker.

Vlad glanced at the clock. "It's half-three. *Now*?"

"Very good!" De Jogt replied like it was Vlad's suggestion and hung up.

Stacia kicked him as he rolled out of bed and nearly tripped over the covers.

"Vlad! Where are you going?"

"Work."

"At this hour? Get back to bed! It's cold!"

Vlad shook his head—he had to go.

Literally, he felt *compelled* to go.

Hazily pulling clothes from his closet, Vlad realized this compulsion was nothing new. He'd been under for—what, weeks?—without knowing it. Only the accident of the phone call interrupting a powerful dream had allowed him to catch on. More importantly, he recognized this particular type of compulsion from experience, years ago and half a continent away. *Keep it light*, he thought. *No sense worrying her yet*.

"Einstein's assistant's wife probably thought he was crazy too."

"She was *right*!" Stacia laughed and pulled the sheets over her head.

He carefully pieced together other memories now, other suppressed memories. This wasn't the first time he'd gone to work this late recently—why? And who the hell was De Jogt? He knew they were working together, knew it as soon as he picked up the phone—but he also knew he had no idea who the man was.

Somehow he also knew not to drive. *Take the tram*, said the voice in his head. The voice wasn't familiar, which didn't surprise him. He slit his eyes and mumbled a nonsense phrase to himself over and over, an old mechanism, remaining in the drowsy half-consciousness that knew what he was expected to do next.

The night was warm; an oily film remained on the street after the evening's rain. As his tram wound its way through the Centrum, Vlad changed lines, doubled-back on himself and hopped off between stops to wander alleys and canals rather than streets, as if in a trance.

But, unlike De Jogt, Vlad *wasn't* in a trance. They might share this half-sleep but Vlad had the advantage of knowing what was behind it. The mindthread not on autopilot was plotting his next step.

The neighborhood loomed with heavy stone buildings and morning mist—barely a soul out at this hour. Vlad took the back door, hidden behind a wall of trash containers, and up a staircase behind the labs to a storage room he'd have sworn he'd never entered before.

"I've really got something!" De Jogt exclaimed. "I was on the phone to you before I'd even come awake." He peered through square glasses that were too small for his face. "You came the safe way, yes? The tram?"

Vlad nodded.

"Why do we do that?" De Jogt asked.

"Because he wants it."

"That's right, of course," De Jogt muttered. "*Who* does?"

The answer was on the tip of Vlad's tongue, but he knew he'd never get any closer. You weren't even supposed to know you were being controlled, so the name of the controller, what they wanted and why? He shrugged helplessly.

De Jogt didn't seem surprised. The Dutchman lifted a deep silver case onto the table and flicked three metal catches. It opened with a *sproing!* and a cloud of dry ice. Pulling on rubber gloves, he pulled out a human arm, elbow to fingertip. Vlad's forehead went clammy.

"Where'd you get *that*?"

De Jogt placed the limb in a makeshift cradle on the counter. "You wouldn't believe how hard it was to get two of them," he said, pulling another arm from a second case and placing it in an identical cradle so the fingers were touching. "Hands, I can get - but with the arm attached? It's highway robbery!"

"You *paid* someone? Out in the open?"

"It's what we needed," De Jogt said, as though it was obvious. "*Do what's needed* – didn't somebody say that?"

Those *were* the instructions—Vlad recognized them immediately. He also knew buying body parts was a disaster, totally off-program—even if he didn't know what the program was.

Where was the keeper? Drunk? Dead? Distracted somehow? Something was wrong, or he'd have long since squelched this unplanned meeting. They'd be on their way home without the slightest memory of it—at least, that was the plan. Vlad was instead salvaging every hazy memory he could of previous meetings, after-hours, for weeks, improvising on a project that...the possibilities made him shiver.

De Jogt pulled a metal coil over the extended index finger of one arm. He fastened the attached wires to a black-box on the table. "Stay back—it's still erratic." He must have been working at least an hour jury-rigging—in his sleep—before calling Vlad. They moved to a closed-off control room, De Jogt checked a blinking switch on the panel and threw it.

Vlad flinched at a burst of light so overwhelming he couldn't pinpoint its location, sparks in the air and a sudden burning smell. When they came out of the control room, both arms were blackened, singed with a spidery pattern like lightning from finger to elbow.

"Well, it needs tuning—but it works!" De Jogt exulted. And as he said it, Vlad realized how much he knew of the plan—and what De Jogt had made of it.

"We have to go! Now!"

"What are you talking about?"

"This is bad. All this—"

"It's brilliant, really. I'd never have thought of it myself."

"No, you don't get it." And looking into De Jogt's eyes, Vlad could see he wasn't going to. Not yet. De Jogt was solidly under suggestion, without the tools or background to know how to break out.

He grabbed the Dutchman by the shoulders. "How long have we been meeting here?"

"I don't know."

"What are we working on?"

"Ahhh…"

"You can't say it but you know. And you know what it can do."

De Jogt's eyes retreated as he tried to string several thoughts together—and failed.

"Listen to me," Vlad was feverish. "Some morning soon, you're going to catch voices in your head, voices not your own. You'll realize you've been hearing them for a while, like music in the wind—and when that happens, you'll have just a few seconds to break away. You'll need a memory of some place, some other time in your life, that you can dive into, dive so deep you won't know for sure where you are. Can you do that?"

De Jogt nodded, though there was no way to tell if he really understood. Vlad threw a couple of the coils into his bag.

"Where are you going?"

"To someone who'll know what to do," Vlad said, stomping out the door, hoping it was true.

~~~~

NATO Intelligence Headquarters
Brussels, Belgium

Scott Cornwell elbowed his way through the crush, angling for the Control Center, dreading every step. After twenty-five years in the service, he knew his own reputation—he'd worked hard for years to beat back the whispers. Now he was on his way to fan the flames again.

Younger colleagues darted around him as he neared the door. Someone had finally brought some food. After five hours of checking airports and railway stations to cut off escape routes, of monitoring NATO facilities all over the world to ensure there were no further attacks, the greasiest burgers in the world looked like steak. And home.

Gretschmer stood surrounded by his kids, the wave of the future. If you could learn everything you needed to know from electronic research and surveillance, Gretschmer was king of the world.

The Chief saw the tall black man coming. "What is it now, Scott?" he asked in a tone of bereavement, removing the pickles from his burger.

"Can we talk privately?"

Gretschmer returned his eyes to the monitors, the RAI Italian television footage of the concert, now bolstered by hundreds of amateur cellphone videos that kept appearing on YouTube as daylight loomed. "We're trying to catch a few terrorists at the moment. Can it wait?"

So much for discretion. "You're not going to catch them."

"They're in Trastavere, right across the river. We had two hundred Italian cops locking up the place and the sewer exits closed within ten minutes after they disappeared. We'll catch—"

"Six minutes was too long and you know it. And if they took longer, they walked right past the guards and nobody'll remember seeing them."

"And how did they do that?"

"'These aren't the droids you're looking for,'" Cornwell quoted.

"Oh, for Christ's sake!" Gretschmer slumped in his chair.

"You don't have anybody out there who can stop them."

Gretschmer rolled his eyes. "Scott, I thought you'd given that stuff up." The man sighed. "Seriously? Either you've got proof or get back to work. I've got better things—"

"The proof is right in front of you," Cornwell said, pointing to the monitor above Gretschmer's head. *"That* is Pietr Volkov—"

"That's Jonathan Tapir, he's the COO of L Corp, a security contractor with many very very influential friends on Capitol Hill. He turned back the assassination single-handedly, if you believe the news."

"Good for him," Cornwell said. *"Before* he was Jonathan Tapir, he was Pietr Volkov, of what we called Project NIMBUS in the good ol' Soviet Union. Any of you guys ever look it up?"

"Grade Five Classified," one of Gretschmer's Eager Beavers called from behind his monitor.

"No shit - I wonder why? It was the Soviet mind control program. Volkov was one of their top agents when the Soviet Union collapsed. Now he's found the light of capitalism and started security contracting."

"Scott, this whole discussion is above the clearance of several people in this room. Actually, it's above *your* clearance, isn't it?"

"That," Cornwell continued, pointing at the screen, "is Mark Tauber, a veteran of Stargate—"

"—the American mindbender program," the Eager Beaver said. "It's been declassified."

"Don't believe what you read in the files," Cornwell cautioned. "We bent the auditors pretty regular."

"We got Tauber's record hours ago," Gretschmer said. "He's an alcoholic, long out of service, blew his pension — "

"He saw things people weren't meant to see," Cornwell said. "We all did." Pointing again, now at the girl blasting through the guards, "And how about *her*?"

"College student - no record."

"You don't see lightning bolts? Coming off her hands? You telling me that doesn't get your attention?"

"Don't give me shit, Scott—"

"That is Kate Crowell. Once I realized who she was, this all started to make sense. She's Ruben and Marjorie Crowell's kid. They were the Stargate sweethearts, the only mindbender marriage that didn't just explode." He paused a moment, taking in the group around Gretschmer. "Doesn't anybody see a common thread here?"

"Are you listening to what you're saying? Lightning bolts? Disgraced projects? You want to go crazy on the record? Really?"

"Really? Just explain what you see on that screen *without* sounding crazy. And while you're at it, explain *him* - the guy having a finger war with Volkov."

"Max Renn—he's a known anarchist."

"You know better than that."

"Don't cross the line, Scott."

"Max Renn was number one on our hit parade in the late 80's. The most legendary mind control agent the Soviets ever produced. Except the place collapsed before he ever made it into the field. I interviewed him for weeks after 9/11 when he wanted to come in. Powers off the charts and a belief in America that we knocked out of his system but good."

"Phone call," Eager Beaver said, dangling a receiver in front of Cornwell.

"Later. Let me sum up."

"Not necessary, Scott."

"I think it is, since you're trying so hard to ignore it. Every player on the field tonight is a mindbender with ties to the American or Soviet program."

"How about the guy tackling Volkov at the end?"

Eager Beaver: "Greg Hirsch, three tours in Iraq, First Battle of Fallujah, honorable discharge, PTSD screening at Homestead CBOC, released to a halfway-house nearby a year ago."

"Fine—no idea. Who cares? The others are all connected." Cornwell raised his shoulders theatrically. "Gretschmer, there's a consistent story playing out here—the only story that actually fits the facts, by the way. You really want to ignore it? I'm giving you a chance to be a hero."

Gretschmer sighed hard. "Okay. Write me a report and I'll pass it along."

Cornwell pulled the rolled-up pages from his back pocket. "Please," he handed them over as Gretschmer and his entourage moved on.

"Phone call," Eager Beaver said again, this time almost begging. "Line Z."

"Line Z?" Z was reserved for agents or other assets in trouble. "They asked for me?" Cornwell said—he hadn't worked that line in years. Eager Beaver nodded.

Cornwell grabbed the phone.

"Do you know who you're calling?" he demanded and, for the first time in twenty years, felt a mind probe. He blocked it instinctively, old training kicking in out of habit.

"Oh, I've reached the right person," an eastern-accented voice said. *Jesus, the old soldiers are all coming out of the woodwork tonight.* "We have to talk. Rome is just the beginning."

"We have to meet someplace safe," Cornwell said.

"There might not be anyplace safe. There's a dangerous weapon being developed, right under your nose. I have information and not much time."

Cornwell dropping his blocking for a moment and sent out an address. The voice said, "I've got it."

"The key is in the flower box directly across the street. Take the basement steps. Turn the lamp at the bottom of the staircase counter-clockwise—"

"Anti-clockwise?"

"Anti-clockwise, yes." *Brit English and Russian accent,* he noted. "A wall panel will open. It's a panic room. Get in, shut the door and wait."

"They can't be far behind me," the voice was jittery.

"Just get to that room. It'll survive nuclear explosions and hurricanes. They can't think you to death," he said, hoping that was true. "I'll be there as soon as I can."

He handed the phone back to Eager Beaver, who replaced it in the cradle. The rest of the room had returned to roadblocks and airport security as though he hadn't said a word. The kid, however, was staring at him expectantly. "Now what?" he asked.

"You don't think I'm nuts?"

The kid's face went clamlike. "I'm open-minded," he said. "I read all about Stargate." Was he Gretschmer's spy? Did it matter? Cornwell had nowhere to go but up at the moment.

"What's your name?"

"Carl Dardenne."

"Carl, get us a car. There's a canary in the coalmine."

~~~~

The safe house stood at the apex of a curve a short distance from the Commission headquarters, offering a clear view in both directions and a short drive to two different highways to Antwerp. With a massive gable protruding from the tile roof and a saucer-shaped window like a huge eye inset into the brick front, it was a hallucination at 5:15 am.

Dardenne parked around the corner and they approached on foot, watchful, Cornwell probing in all directions but not necessarily trusting his abilities after such a long layoff. Was mindbending like riding a bicycle? The question sounded idiotic.

The woman's voice echoed from around the curve and then, before they could react, there she was, wandering and wavering, gargling and gagging, cackling and choking back tears all at once. Her forearm hung at an odd angle, dripping blood onto the sidewalk. "It's a feast!" she snapped, voice cracking. "Love and sausage, with onions."

Cornwell backed away from her. "You need help?" he asked half-heartedly but she danced away and he grabbed Dardenne by the arm and pulled him to the bushes at the side of the road. Dardenne reached into the shoulder of his jacket and Cornwell saw the glint of a pistol. "Whoa Nelly, let's not get ahead of ourselves," he said. Dardenne's hand was trembling.

"What happened to her?"

"Driven insane, axe murderer, bit by a dog, hit by a car, or her husband—we don't know yet, do we?" Dardenne nodded but the movements were taut, twitchy. "You ever *use* that thing?"

"On the range," the kid sputtered.

"Okay. Leave it parked unless you *have* to pull it. I only want you returning fire and only after you've taken cover and a breath. Okay?" Dardenne nodded, stretched as tight as a wire. "I'm going in the back way. You loiter at the store windows on the corner and then drift vaguely down the block. Check your Blackberry, look tipsy and bored. Do not draw your weapon or take action unless someone else starts it. If I don't come out in ten minutes, get yourself to a safe distance and call for help, okay?"

Cornwell ducked around a blocky apartment tower and into the trees lining the curved driveway on the far side. He pushed through the brush to a shoulder-high wall cutting fifty feet through the brush behind the safe house. There was a gate on the far side but who knew if it was manned and time was ticking away. Cornwell gulped a breath, pulled his pistol and dragged himself over the wall (*Note to self: getting too old for this*).

He found his way lightly through the moonlight to the recessed basement door. A single light shone in the kitchen above—the place was occupied. Popping the hidden panel alongside the back door revealed an LCD screen showing only one entry, seven minutes earlier. He slid the key into the lock and slipped inside.

The Agency didn't spend money on safe houses. Cobwebs wagged in the corner, the place smelled of musty concrete and stone. Cornwell sensed no other presences in the house but they might be cloaked. Or, for that matter, his senses might be for shit— it had been a long time.

He moved methodically to the front, clearing each doorway and each room in turn before opening the front door for a tetchy-looking Dardenne.

They descended the front steps. Dardenne took a textbook position, where he'd have a clear shot through the panic room door once it opened.

"What smells like bacon?" the kid asked.

"When you're hungry, *everything* smells like bacon," Cornwell answered. They'd missed the burgers at HQ. He turned the light anti-clockwise and a panel in the wall popped open. He punched in the response code and stood back, pistol at the ready.

The door opened on a heavyset man lounging in a chair facing them, eyes open, three-days growth of beard and a thick V of dark hair splitting his forehead. His posture was alert but his eyes were vacant.

There was a pause before Cornwell put up his gun and walked into the room. Dardenne followed, wide-eyed.

"Is he—?"

"Dead as the past."

The kid turned white. "You said only one person came in."

"That's what it said."

"And anyone else—"

"—would need both codes, outside and in. Yeah, it doesn't make sense."

Cornwell pulled a phone from a cradle on the wall. "Get me Ezra Dean—tell him it's important!" he ordered. "Hi, Deacon. Ring House. A locker job with the trimmings. Now would be good." He hung up and immediately began digging through the man's pockets. "Vladimir Saminov, Dutch resident, not citizen. Amsterdam address—not a long trip, if he felt compelled."

Dardenne was recovering now. "Is there another way in? For emergencies?"

Cornwell shook his head. "This place is *only* for emergencies. You lock that door, the world blows up outside and you're alright—that's what it's for. You can't get in without the codes, the codes change every day and anyone who wants them has to sign for them."

"So either he came in alone or he gave the code you sent him to someone else."

"That's logical. The world isn't always logical." Cornwell dug back into the man's pockets. "Credit cards, all Vlad Saminov. €350 in cash, mostly Dutch bills, two French, a KLM ticket, short notice, paid full rate." Replacing a credit card, he hit a snag. Feeling carefully inside, he found another card hiding in a sleeve at the back of the compartment. He pulled the card halfway out before recognizing it, shoving it back inside and slipping the sleeve into his pocket.

"Gas!" the kid gulped from the far corner. "That's how they killed him. They piped gas in."

"The gas, air and water here are recirculated, totally self-contained. Not reachable from outside - and the place is sealed, so if somehow he brought it in with him, it would have gotten us when we opened the door."

"It does smell like bacon."

"Bacon takes longer than seven minutes to kill you."
Cornwell opened the kitchen cupboard and began removing the
cups and plates from the shelves, placing them in somewhat
organized rows on the floor.

"So he just walked into the room, sat down and had a heart
attack?"

"Let's see." Cornwell had finally emptied the cabinet. He
undid a few latches under a shelf, lifted it out of the enclosure and
laid it on the table. Withdrawing the wall panel behind revealed a
video monitor and recording equipment. He ran the time ribbon
back seven minutes and let it play.

On screen, Saminov entered the room, followed by a
younger woman. "It's her," Cornwell said. "The one we saw on
the street."

"No way—she looked crazy older."

"No, she just looked crazy. *Driven* crazy."

On screen, Saminov heaved a sigh of relief and settled into
the chair. The woman wrapped her arms around him for just a
moment. They swayed back and forth in embrace and then she
disappeared offscreen and a red light came on in the upper right
corner.

"You said he came in alone."

"The readout said one entry. The door opened, they came in together. She must have shoved something into the doorway and exited before the door closed, so one entry."

They waited. Onscreen, Saminov remained in the chair.

"Is he moving?"

"No."

"I think he just did."

"I don't think so."

A minute went by and another. Cornwell pushed fast-forward 2x and then 4x. The minutes passed until they saw themselves coming into the picture. Nothing else changed in that time.

"Where does he die?"

"I have no idea. Nothing happened." *They can't think you to death*, he'd told the voice on the phone. Was it possible? Was that what Renn and the others were trying to do to Singh in Rome? Was Vlad, whoever he was, somehow connected with that?

They heard a door open upstairs. "It's me," came a voice through the speaker and Cornwell entered the code to unlock the panic door. A waspish man with a bowl cut and a dusty suit two sizes too big came in carrying a heavy suitcase.

Ezra Dean sniffed the air. "What the fuck are you cooking?"

"Bacon."

"He died of trichinosis?"

"Can it kill you in seven minutes?"

"No."

"Then it won't do."

"What's the tale of the videotape?"

"He walks in with his wife, girlfriend, whatever, sits in the chair, she hugs him goodbye and seven minutes later we get here. Somewhere in between, he gets dead."

"That's it?"

Cornwell shrugged.

"Don't you ever call me for easy ones?"

"You *love* shit like this—don't tell me different."

"Let's have a look at him." Dean said, un-rolling a cloth bag in a clatter of metal—Dardenne saw scalpels sheathed in plastic, a power saw, several grisly-looking pincers and a very long thermometer. Cornwell motioned Dardenne to grab the corpse under the arm. "Okay, UPPPP!" They lifted Saminov onto the table.

Dean tugged off the man's shoes, jacket and shirt, concentrating on several long white scars that radiated like veins along Saminov's arms. Next, he tugged the pants off, sniffed the air, pulled on a pair of latex gloves and plunged the thermometer up the body's anus. Dardenne nearly swooned before Dean checked the results and whistled.

"You weren't kidding," he said.

"What?"

"Bacon! He's been dead long enough that his skin's cold."

"No kidding."

"But inside? 450 degrees!" He gave the body an echoing smack. "This boy's been cooked. From the inside."

conference call

Hong Kong/Rome

Jim Avery skimmed the edge of a gleaming mahogany conference table, gesturing at the rising lines on the graph filling the wallscreen. "SUV's that go offroad though you never go offroad, fast food salads with more calories than a burger, energy drinks that are water with caffeine and sugar—these weren't just stupid ideas, they were unsellable ideas that didn't have a single argument in their favor! Now they're major growth industries, all because of *Your World's* methods of persuasion! How many millions do you spend on advertising methods with a 5% ROI? We routinely return 40-65% conversion rates in target audience! Totally off the charts!"

Turning his expansive glow on the sleek business suits and freshly-peeled faces around the table, Avery slumped. "Miriam, they're not talking. What good is it if they can't talk?"

Miriam Fine turned to the two-way mirror, speaking to the team of mindbenders on the other side. "Simpson, you're clamping. Relax. Ten per cent less, everybody—we want to open them up, not lobotomize them."

Three seconds later, the eyes around the table—a collection of CEO's, Presidents and Board Members of fabled corporations— lost their milky haze and their equanimity.

"Jim, cut the crap, please. What's 'methods of persuasion' mean?"

"It means we can directly induce the consumer to buy."

"'Induce?' That sounds a lot more like 'force' than 'persuasion'."

"Which do you prefer, Richard?"

"'Persuade' sounds nice—'force' sounds like money."

Avery smiled. "Right. It's not persuasion, it's coercion."

Another president squirmed a bit. "You're being very plain-spoken here, Jim," she said, looking around the table. "Is that wise?"

"You mean, Joan, you don't trust the people around the table to keep it secret," Avery mirrored. "They're nasty, petty, competitive snakes who've sabotaged their best friends and sued family members into poverty to get what they want. You don't even like being in the same building with them, much less the same room, talking openly about the strengths and weaknesses of your business."

"I haven't said anything about my business."

"You will."

"I seriously doubt it," Joan said.

"Okay friends, let's understand how this works," Avery stalked the front of the room. "None of you would have come to this meeting if invited and certainly not if you knew who else was coming. We dragged you here against your will and when this is over, you won't remember any of it—at least, you won't remember any of it as it actually happened. You won't remember being in the same room, you won't remember the details of what I've said or you've said or any of the others have said. You'll go back to your office with a fat portfolio of graphs and metrics and anecdotes to justify the inducement campaign you're about to hire us for. If anyone asks questions—and that isn't likely, at least not to your face—you can trot out an intricate series of explanations so full of jargon that nobody else can possibly understand, much less argue with."

"That's a good thing?"

"Tim, it's the best possible thing! What's your nickname? The one on your book cover?"

Tim smirked. "'The Magician.'"

"Why? Because nobody can explain how you made your success. Where'd it come from? That meteoric jump from sales geek to Executive VP and eventually Chairman of the Board?" Avery glanced at Miriam Fine, who shot a piercing glance in the man's direction. Tim grabbed the back of his head as though it had suddenly gone hot to the touch. "C'mon, Tim, share with us."

Tim clearly had no desire to share anything with this audience. He scowled and squirmed in his chair, issuing a series of hacks and throat-clearing growls. Finally, his mouth opened and he said, "I bribed a member of the State Planning Commission to give me the route of a new interstate highway extension while it was all still deep and dark. I went to contract on a package of real estate that would be right off the planned exit routes. I didn't have the money but I brought the package to the Chairman of my company. He would make me VP—with a bonus large enough to cover the purchases—and I would sell them to the company." Tim's eyes widened as he spoke--clearly, he was stunned to hear the words coming out of his mouth.

"So you got them really valuable land—and insulated them in case charges were ever brought—in return for your executive job."

"Right. But I earned my promotions after that every step of the way."

A few snickers echoed around the room. Avery spun in his tracks. "Is that so funny, Jean? What got *you* started?"

"I offered to 'lose' some negative research—I was staff on a Congressional pharmaceutical probe—in return for a VP job with the company. I was bluffing—nobody on the committee wanted to find anything anyway!" Again, the woman seemed stunned to hear the story she was sharing.

Avery proceeded around the table, pulling—compelling—a string of similar stories out of the other executives at the table.

"Okay," he said at the end. "So you all know from personal experience that you can't play by the rules and win. You have to have an edge. Moving forward from here, *we're* your edge!"

"But we're not going to remember any of it?"

"You're not going to remember any of it *accurately*. You'll have believable placeholders for your memories."

"What the fuck does that mean?"

"We're putting ideas in your mind, Al."

"I don't like that."

"We're just doing to you what we'll be doing to your customers—for your benefit."

"It's totally disrespectful."

"Exactly. That's why it works."

"Okay, I'm in." Then, gesturing across the table. "As long as he isn't."

"Well, no, that's not—"

"I can be in too if I want."

"No way, I'm not doing anything if he's involved. We're competitors."

"Not in the markets we're working on. We only choose one client in any particular market." Avery sighed and leaned over the front of the table. "People, people, I'm offering you unlimited domination of your markets, all you have to do is take it."

"I'm not working anything with him. I don't even know why he's invited."

"I was invited to show you how to handle things graciously," his competitor said, flicking paper clips at him across the table.

A moment later, the two were up, confronting each other across the desk. Fine stepped between them, clapping her hands in the air. Both men stopped dead and turned to the wall, their faces up against the wood paneling.

"Okay, we'll deal with them later," Avery said, ignoring the stares and open mouths of the rest of the group at the table. "Who's smart enough to take advantage—"

Five seconds silence.

"I'm in."

"Me too."

"Okay, let's get some contracts on the table here, please."

~~~

"Jesus H!" Avery burst as he and Fine paced down the corridor to another conference room. "I thought we could make people do *anything*!"

Fine shrugged. "There has to be a little blood flow between their ears."

"These are not stupid people, Miriam! I swear they aren't."

"Of course not. Not stupid. Jealous and petty. There's so little sense to it, it's like trying to trap water."

"Well, what did it take, thirty mindbenders for a week to get them together in the first place?

"College kids at minimum wage," Fine said. "Training costs us peanuts."

"I don't care—we've got to find a better way," Avery concluded, opening the door to another suite. Inside, a big screen and technician stood waiting. "Are we on VPN?"

"Yes, sir."

"Good—go outside and wait." Once the tech left, Avery turned to Fine, "Make sure he hears nothing." She followed the man outside. Avery clicked on the screen and Volkov's face was there waiting. No surprise there—but he seemed surprisingly relaxed. Avery found that irritating.

"Hello Jim."

"Pietr." Avery's voice was clipped. "I expected, the next time we spoke, there would be, at minimum, two or three world leaders in the hospital, at least one hopefully dead, stock markets in free-fall and widespread panic. That *was* the plan, wasn't it?"

"It was," Volkov replied. "We just got lucky."

Avery's eyes narrowed. "Okay, Pietr, I"m listening."

"We talked about it—the weakness of the original plan was we might over-reach and end up with uncontrollable chaos. We now have a manageable crisis, with actual terrorists at large after attacking world leaders—a real face to put on the threat. Max Renn, radical ex-KGB agent who thinks he's a mindreader." Volkov was watching him weigh this thought. "Because, of course, there are no *real* mindbenders."

Avery felt obligated to play along, though he was far from convinced. "Jedi warriors!"

"The thought is farcical, of course—but just disturbing enough to drive hordes of unsettled civilians into the arms of *Your World*."

"*Your World's* mission is to soothe the troubled soul," Avery recited the line from habit. He offered it four to six times a week to audiences by the thousands, in amphitheater stages, on cruises and his 24-hour-a-day cable television network. "A way to surmount the turmoil of the outer world and the inner."

"The added bonus is, the old guard at the top of intelligence services worldwide *remember* Max Renn, the Soviet mystery spy. And now here he is, in the flesh—and L Corp the only organization with a track record of stopping him."

"When did you stop him?"

"In Rome, earlier tonight. Singh is alive, isn't she?"

Now Avery was smiling. "Of course, of course, I'm sorry, his plot was to assassinate her, I forgot. And you foiled his evil plan. Is that it?"

"It better be. I've just given twenty interviews saying so."

Avery couldn't hold his laughter.

"That's pretty good, Pietr. This could have—should have—been a disaster. I underestimated you. Really quite good."

"'Leadership isn't always the best plan; sometimes it's just making the most of opportunity'—you taught me that, Jim."

"I'm sure I stole it from somebody." Avery tapped the desk. "It wouldn't do for the Italian police to catch him, would it?"

"I've been laying false clues and trails for the authorities—by now, I'm confident he's out of Italy."

"And any other lingering issues for us?"

"I'm taking care of them tonight. Something else that will be laid at Renn's feet, to make him yet more mysterious and frightening."

"After this all sorts itself out, I still want him working for us, Pietr."

"You mean, intentionally."

"Exactly, yes. I still think he's the overwhelming weapon, the last nail."

"Well, then I have to make sure he really has nowhere else to go, don't I?"

Volkov's eyes sparkled. Avery would have loved to read his mind at that moment but he wasn't the mindbender. Volkov had promised not to read him in return. "We're partners. You want to know something," Avery had said, "Ask me. Don't just pluck it out of me." It was a measured trust between two untrusting souls that had worked so far. It might, Avery thought, just a little longer.

reunion 2
December 2008

Darwin, Australia

When I come to, dripping with water from a bucket, Straw Hat has taken over at the table, short blade poised over the victim, who is still lashed to the slab, slashed to slivers, blood streaming and animal cries filling the room or my head or whatever makes this seem so fucking *real*.

Blondie and Tat Man stand around watching and pulling a living wage. "We can keep doing this all day," Straw Hat says. "How about you?" But there's an edge to his voice. He doesn't seem to be enjoying himself and if you're L Corp and don't enjoy a little torturing, something's wrong.

Tat Man fills a paper cup with water and holds it out to me. Instead of drinking, I grab it with my teeth and swing my head around, throwing it at the poor son-of-a-bitch on the slab. The water passes right through his body and the torture table and splatters onto the floor below.

"Fuck you!" I spit. "The whole thing's a fucking illusion! That's the best you've got?"

Before they answer, the door flies open behind me, I feel a rush of air and the sound of footsteps clattering in. The Torture Team snaps to attention. A second later, somebody picks up my chair and turns it around and there's Pietr Volkov sitting behind a metal desk.

"We haven't broken him yet but we will," Straw Hat reports. "All we've got so far are some bullshit directions he says Renn gave him—"

"Which were?" Volkov snaps.

Straw Hat, sniffing at his notes: "*Follow the sounds. Travel till sunrise. I'll meet you at the end*—"

Volkov smiles the typical creepy mindbender's smile. "That sounds like Max." His face goes dark. "Did I say I wanted him broken?!"

"You tasked me to find Renn as soon as he hits Australia," Straw Hat doesn't wilt. "Where this one goes, Renn's nearby."

Volkov steams. "Renn's a trained agent like you are." He starts counting on his fingers. "Superior numbers, superior firepower, superior position, surprise—a trained agent doesn't confront an opponent without at least one of those. You expect him to just barge in here stupidly?"

"He did in Rome."

"He had surprise in Rome—we weren't expecting him—and, with the girl, he had equal firepower. You expected him here, Mr. Landau, and he didn't show. Now it's my turn." Volkov motions at a soft tubular case on the floor. "Set up."

Blondie and Tat Man jump to it, unzipping the bag, pulling out a skeleton of metal braces and Plexiglas panels trailing a spaghetti cluster of wires. In three minutes, they assemble a rickety metal box with Plexiglas windows, maybe four feet by three, with a rubberized floor and little fibrous antennae sprouting from the top. From a second bag, Tat Man pulls a turbine-like power supply and attaches it to the spaghetti connectors.

"Bring her in," Volkov orders—does the guy ever just ask? The door squeaks open, hot air blasting in from outside and a chair scrapes past me, carrying a bound and evidently drugged woman. Brown like a nut, hair cropped short and streaked bright red. It's only when she blinks and I see her eyes that I realize it's Kate, our warrior princess and moral compass, our only viable connection to Planet Earth.

"*Everyone,*" Volkov sneers, "is hiding out in Australia these days."

the enthusiast
July 2008

Dubai, United Arab Emirates

The airport lobby was the closest thing to the Imperial Senate in *Star Wars*—the new *Star Wars*, not the old, good ones. The walls looked like a plastic model kit, not a nail or screw or seam in sight, plastic textured to look like plaster, chrome and glass. We glided on a moving walkway between a double line of three-story palm trees, a simulation of a natural world that existed exactly nowhere. The view outside was totally unnatural too, unless you figured natural for 350 degrees.

The walkway dumped us out in the middle of the Mall, where LED lights tracked the balconies and a shiny aluminum palm tree sprouted from the center of a bar with leaning room for fifty. Surrounded by ACRES OF SALES! TV's, luggage, stereos, vacation deals, even cars—the kind I'd only seen in magazines—all for sale inside the terminal.

I had a thick wad of cash split between my pockets and socks and carry-on; no reason I couldn't buy myself a toy. Maybe not a car, but a watch or something else I could carry with me.

While I was thinking about it, a pale kid in a Linux penguin t-shirt and a laptop case fit for World War III or at least the zombie apocalypse—extra batteries, a portable wifi hotspot, over-ear and in-ear headphones—wandered up to me and stared in a way that gave me the shivers.

This was forty-four hours after escaping Rome in a fishing boat and four hours after Kate and Renn and I split up at the airport in Tunis. "Read the note on the plane," Max had said. "Follow the instructions explicitly. You'll be contacted."

"By who?" I asked but he was already halfway across the courtyard and disappearing into the crowd. After a quick hug from Kate, I was on my own, searching for the gate.

In-flight an hour later, I read the note: *Take the slowest ship you can from Singapore to Pulau Patang. Find a room on the second floor with a view of the beach. Drink tuak. Walk the beach twice a day. You will be contacted.*

The note made me laugh. It didn't tell me where Pulau Patang was, how to find the slowest boat, how to choose one second-floor room over another, why I was supposed to walk the beach or what the fuck tuak was, much less why I should drink it.

Should I drink *only* tuak? Was I supposed to eat anything? What if I was allergic? Not to be ungrateful or anything, but if you want me to follow directions precisely, how about giving me precise directions? In the Army, they call this a bad attitude.

And now, at my first stop, here was Linux Boy. Wherever I went, he showed up pretty quick. I wasn't getting any mind probes from him and he didn't have the Masters of the Universe swagger all the L Corp shooters flaunted. But I couldn't have missed him and I took that eventually as a sign that he wasn't a pro. I actually smiled at him, just to see what would happen and he smiled back, without doing anything else. Visibly nervous, no visible social skills but definitely not a spy. Which just made him confusing.

At one point, I slipped into a cell phone store and bought one of the new smartphones—there's my toy—complete with international service and all the accessories that would fit in my backpack. I slipped out the freight exit into another section of the mall, picked up a new coat and a floppy hat and parked myself at a terminal at an Internet café. I wanted to check out Pulau Patang but the monitor opened to a news site and instantly blotted out every other thought in my head.

Because the headline news picture was *me*, larger than life.

Me, Max, Kate and Pietr Volkov, to be precise. Volkov facing the camera, Max facing him, me next to Max pointing to the energy field connecting the two of them while Kate deflected a lightning blast in the foreground. The headline read:

ATTACK AT THE G8

ROME - The G8 Summit came to a sudden and contentious end yesterday, after members of a radical anti-globalization sect penetrated a summit-related concert Saturday night, shattering a protective dome housing world leaders and causing minor injuries to members of G8 Security. One member of the sect was injured during the altercation and died later at the hospital.

A G8 spokesperson blamed the attack on 'unreasonable expectations' raised by Indian Premier Aryana Singh, whose pledge to advocate worldwide nuclear disarmament had already made this one of the tensest G8's in a series that has rarely lacked tension.

Singh protested the abrupt cancellation of further events and thousands of demonstrators took up her message in the streets of Rome, while planes carrying the rest of the world's leaders headed home.

The dead man was identified as Mark Tauber, most recently of Savannah Georgia.

"We were familiar with Mr. Tauber," Savannah
Police Chief Leonard Boyle stated. "I wouldn't
have thought him capable of radical political
thinking. I wouldn't have thought there were
enough recyclable plastic bottles in Savannah to
buy him a flight to Rome either.'

I read that much in a gulp, without a single conscious
thought. I should have realized we'd be headlines, but up until the
Concert, it was just the four of us running—Max, Kate, Tauber and
me. Dave Monaghan got shot in Florida, Max took me out of
Dave's halfway house just before it blew up and then we were
running, finding the old mindbenders and then trying to figure
out what they were up to. Every crazy thing that happened—and
everything that happened was crazy—felt like it grew out of our
little group, our little lives. Newspapers and websites and TV
networks paying attention just felt *rude.*

Volkov and the police, G8 Security and the governments
had all proclaimed us terrorists and that was good enough for Big
Media. Somebody dredged up some old picture of me from Iraq,
pushed the contrast and processed it until I looked like Manson's
spawn. It was everywhere.

I never liked that picture.

And then I looked up from staring at it and there was Linux
Boy again. If the look on his face before was that he wasn't sure,

now it was that he'd decided. All he had to do was yell "Terrorist!!" and the crowd would have torn me to pieces.

Except, he didn't look terrified—it was more like I was strangely fascinating. I like myself okay but fascinating I'm not.

"You...you were there," he said, a voice full of tremors like he was talking to Jesus or something. "I saw...the videos."

"There are *videos*?"

In ten seconds, he had six YouTube windows open, clicking back and forth like a meth machine. Kate and me pounding the banks of the Tiber, her throwing guards around like twigs in the wind, Max and Volkov battling by the Dome, Tauber catching a fatal blast from Marat.

RAI television—Italy's Public Broadcasting—had cameras all around the orchestra and VIP box, I remembered almost colliding with them six or seven times. And at least fifty spectators had already uploaded cell phone clips from the stands on both sides of the Tiber. The RAI stuff was super-sharp but too close to the action; the cameras kept wagging back and forth, never getting anything clear. The shots from the bleachers were fuzzy and almost always a beat behind the action.

But Linux Boy kept clicking video after video and, as he went along, I began to realize that the whole terrorist thing got shaky if you were actually paying attention.

The raw uncut video had only appeared on RAI's site for about an hour before being yanked without explanation and replaced by an edited version.

But once online, always online. The raw feed hit the torrent sites and from there, reappeared in a hundred versions and twenty languages, complete with commentary from bloggers, 'patriots' and even 'Rome Three enthusiasts' (that was a scary thought), re-edited to Radiohead and Skrillex, Arvo Part, 'Face the Face' and 'There's somethin' happenin' here.'

Some anti-globalization group 'took responsibility' for us - their videos had Stevie Wonder's *Superstition*. Other pages linked us to MK Ultra, Stonehenge, 9/11, Vatican conspiracies and Elvis. We even had a nickname—The Rome Three. Catchy.

One video was titled, **ATTACK—PROVOKED?** It was zoomed-in and digitally-sharpened, with slowed-down video, boosted contrast and endless (contradictory) commentary:

> Look! The security guy fired first!
> Only one guerrilla fired and he was
> aiming at the security guy with the
> beard (Volkov)!

We weren't terrorists, this guy said, we were freedom fighters against globalization, without really explaining what that meant. The clip ended with a clear shot of me tackling Volkov into the Tiber.

It was a relief to know there was pushback against the official story—of course, it would have been more encouraging if the doubters hadn't got all the details equally wrong.

But what rolled over me at the kiosk, Linux Boy finally pausing between clips, was that I was now a major terrorist, sitting at the wide-open counter of an Internet café in the busiest airport in the world, thousands of people passing who had to have read a newspaper or seen a picture or a news flash in the last twenty-four hours. I got chills and palpitations—it wasn't fun.

I was afraid to stand up—it would only have made people stare at me who were ignoring me at the moment—but then I saw Linux Boy wasn't done with me. He had a new clip on the screen, this one of us running across the Tiber to escape.

"H—how?" he stammered and I couldn't blame him. How do you question someone you've just seen walk on water?

I didn't have time to answer.

"You with the cause?" I asked and he nodded like his head was hanging from a string. "I have a mission for you. I've got tickets on (*What's the farthest gate I can see?*)...Emirates...in ten minutes. Check out the boarding area for me. If you see somebody in...a checkered coat and...a red beret—turn your shirt inside out where I can see you."

He nearly jumped out of his shoes, spurting away and then right back again, holding out his fist for me to bump. "Strike without demands," he said. "Bomb the IMF. And legalize marijuana."

And then he was gone.

I quickly ran my search ('pulau patang': 14,373 hits in 0.17 seconds) mapped the place and printed it, bought an oversized sweatshirt at the gift store and meandered off in the other direction, toward my flight to Singapore.

files

Brussels, Belgium

The cell phone rang twice and then stopped. Cornwell grabbed it off the desk, checked that it was 'Number Unavailable', then hustled down the hall and out of the building.

His last day in Brussels, so of course, it was gorgeous. Clouds like trumpet flourishes cut through purple-gray skies on a brisk wind, their shadows flickering over the frippery of Flemish architecture and the curved steel of the new United Europe.

Two minutes after the first call, almost to the second, the phone rang again. Cornwell picked up the line without saying a word.

"We're clear," Dardenne said from the other end. "I've messed with the encryption and looped this thing through a couple of servers, including a Chinese military one."

"Now you're showing off."

"Did you just want to see what I could do—or is there a reason for this crazy shit?"

"There's a reason. How are you getting on with the Masters of the Universe?"

"Won't have to get on with anyone much longer. I'm being transferred—to Fairbanks."

"Alaska?"

"There's another Fairbanks?"

"Sorry about that."

"You should be. Everyone says it's because I'm associated with you, though no one knows why. In the meantime, they're giving me courier shit. Back-of-the-hand, making it clear they don't trust me. Also making it obvious they don't really have anything on me or else they wouldn't be giving me courier shit."

"Well, if they find out you're talking to me now, that's the *best* you can expect for eternity. So if you want to bail, I'll understand."

"I can't turn you down until you make an offer," Dardenne said. "That's how business works."

Cornwell sighed. When he'd started in the secret world, nobody ever thought of it as business. "What I'm proposing is some real spy work."

"What makes it 'real' spy work, as opposed to what I used to do before I got scheduled for Fairbanks?"

"It'll be freelance—unsanctioned. You'll be in danger of censorship or court martial, right up until they pin the medals on our chests." He took a breath. "That's the worst of it."

"Does this have to do with what happened to Saminov?"

"Hopefully."

"Then that *isn't* the worst of it."

"What do you mean?"

"Because, the worst of it is, we'll be spying on our own people."

Silence for a long moment. Cornwell realized he was now holding his breath. "Meaning, some of us are involved?"

"Meaning, *Saminov* was one of us. Worked for a NATO defense contractor in Amsterdam, Forus Technologies. Exotic metallurgy, supposedly. Even to me,that reeks of cover story. I couldn't get near any of their files."

"And the woman?"

"Mrs. Saminov. No surprise there. Don't ask what happened to her—or to your friend Dean either."

"What about Dean?"

"Both of them disappeared. Dean's been transferred someplace way too hush-hush for me to know—nobody even gossips about him, which is real unusual. As for her, I was told point-blank not to ask questions, like a Bogart movie or something."

"You know Bogart?"

"Sure, I know the Tyrannosaurus Rex too."

"So, who's telling you not to ask questions, Company people or L Corp?"

"It's getting harder to find the dividing lines. There's a couple new guys around —they've got security badges but no Company ID. They shouldn't even fit in the pecking order but you get all these awkward silences from ranking officers when they're around."

Cornwell shivered involuntarily. Was that a scan? He scanned the edges of the square but there were too many cars, too many windows, too many passersby.

"Are you practicing what I taught you?"

"Blocking? Hell, yeah. Why aren't you reading my mind, by the way, instead of using the phone?"

"When Stargate disbanded, most of the agents left the Service. I wanted to stay. Part of the deal was to promise I wasn't ever going to use my abilities around the office—or in the field unless I had specific instructions to do so. I'm just a regular guy and by now, my abilities are spotty at best."

"Well, the other side has no such limitations. At first, I thought you were nuts—sorry—but I woke up in the middle of the night hearing voices once and found myself in a square without any idea how I got there."

"And, since you haven't hit sixty yet, you guessed something might be wrong."

"Fuck you too. I felt better as soon as I started blocking—and it seems like they're watching me closer. So I got the old-time religion now."

"Welcome. So we don't buy that Forus Technology is about metallurgy?"

"Every file that isn't PR gas is totally locked up, way beyond Top Secret. The first thing I noticed was a weird classification on his dossier—his security clearance was DX3."

"Never heard of it."

"Nobody has. Haven't seen it used anywhere else but I found it in a Freedom of Information Act search, buried way down."

"So?"

"It means Vlad didn't have security clearance for the things he was working on."

"Huh?"

"It sounds like he brought in for some technical expertise they needed but it wasn't considered safe for him to know the results."

"That's a queer little arrangement, even for us."

"There were 'concerns' about his background."

"Am I going to be thrilled?"

"This was big digging. I had to get a friend to let me look over his shoulder—"

"Fine, he's in my will. What's Vlad's story?"

"His previous work background was at something called the Institute for Visual Measurement and Calculation—"

"—in Novosibirsk!"

"Yeah! How'd you know?

"That's my old stomping grounds! The Soviet mind control program! That's good work. What did he do there?"

"Good luck with that. I've used up my favors."

"It's got to be in the files."

"Those files are *way* above my clearance—now. Somebody reclassified them 'Need to Know' in the last two weeks."

"Hmmph! Well, that demands looking into. Okay, there's a girl in Research, Betty Olinsky—"

"Brunette, glasses, the tall one?"

"Yeah. She loves peeps, you know those marshmallow things?"

"Sure."

"There's a store in the train station in Halle that sells them. Get a box, eat them while you're passing her desk. Start a conversation. Buy her a drink. Suggest with your eyes that you're smitten and will love her forever—"

"I've got a girl, Scott."

"This is national security research, my man, you've got to learn to sacrifice for your country. I said 'suggest'—don't say anything that could be used against you in divorce court. Those papers were totally available two weeks ago. Get the girl to roll the

clock back four."

renn returns

Rome, Italy

Teo Russo crowded the dark marble walls of Ciampino airport, diligently scanning the filtering crowd with a growing sense of futility.

Idiota! Lucarelli, the chief of Airport Security, had placed Russo and some of his best men in the Arrivals Area this morning—for what? Two days after the attack on the G8, the odds of capturing the Rome Three *arriving* were nonexistent.

The passengers were finally paying attention to the posters and PA announcements. *Give them mobs of soldiers with assault rifles and watch them focus*, Russo sniffed. But to a professional like him, it was obvious the chicks had long since flown the coop.

Russo sighed. His job was to defend his airport—you made the best attempt you could in life, despite the pointlessness of it all. Two thousand years of post-Roman civilization rested on that concept.

The face passed him in a flicker, just the barest glimpse—but Russo changed direction immediately. He had a natural instinct for details. That quirk would make him Chief of Airport Security someday.

He searched the crowd off...the Tunis flight, searching for that face again, for a second, longer look. The man's hair was wrong—red instead of brown and sporting a three-days-growth goatee, though he would have had just enough time for such a change. Russo ran over the Interpol profile in his mind: Former Soviet asset, disappeared after collapse of the Soviet Union, unconfirmed involvement in arms trafficking or drug trade, deranged claims to mind control powers.

This man was slim, almost fragile, with horn-rim glasses, a flashy Milanese suit and expensive briefcase. Very new shoes. He kept moving in and out of view, which only cultivated Russo's curiosity.

A glance at a reflection in the bank window and Russo pulled the walkie-talkie from his pocket.

"Parte Verde!" –the signal for Rome Three—he whispered into his mouthpiece. "Entering Concourse from Arrivals Area. Block off the Exits *Subito!!*" and added a description.

How had the man cleared Customs? The face wasn't *that* different from the flyer.

Russo lost track of him for just a moment and picked him up again between two tall Swedes, wearing a blue hooded sweatshirt instead of the fine suit jacket. That was as much as proof!

His men were jockeying into position by the kiosks that split the floor a good twenty meters from the doors. But they were hovering there, eyes glazed, not alert. *What is wrong with you?* Russo thought. *What are you staring at? You don't see him?*

He turned to point out the target and couldn't find him in the crowd. Not because he'd disappeared but because Russo suddenly couldn't remember what the man looked like. How was that possible? He'd been all over him ten seconds earlier. He had…a picture on…a piece of paper. Was that right? Where was it? Why was his mind moving so slowly?

Struggling against the fog quickly enveloping him, Russo found the security briefing in his hand and waved it at the dark-haired tourist. "You're under arrest!" he yelled and his men moved in, over screams from the now-scattering crowd.

Mussina, his youngest, snagged the perp by the shoulders and dragged him down while the others swarmed him in seconds. Russo slipped the handcuffs on and patted the man down on the floor. When they lifted him, kicking and protesting, to his feet, Russo's stomach sank.

It wasn't the same face. It wasn't even close. Russo knew just enough French to understand the man's repetitive claims of abusive treatment.

Tombo and Mussina swore they'd checked the face before taking down the Frenchman—they'd seen the same face as the flyer, except for the goatee. They were adamant, despite the Frenchman looking nothing like the photo. By the time Lucarelli arrived, however, a fog had descended over the entire group. Suddenly, none of them, not even Russo, could remember what they'd seen, why they'd done what they'd done or even who they thought they'd been looking for.

Two blocks away, Max Renn dumped the blue hoodie into a trash compactor and hopped a bus to the Termini railroad station.

Renn's head was filled with voices, as always. The thoughts of every living soul in a three-block radius fought for space in his head. The woman in the seat in front of him was frantically searching her pockets, bag and wallet for a scrap of paper in, the address of the hotel where the insect who left her for that stupid Romanian waitress was hiding. When she found him, she'd...

The rest of the passengers were reading, listening to music on headphones (a lot of French rock n' roll on this bus, not to Renn's taste) and longing for their hotel room, the hotel bar, the train departing for fill-in-the-blank or to go back where they'd come from instead of continuing this trip to fill-in-the-blank. The driver was spending much too much time worrying about a growth he'd discovered in his armpit that morning. As the bus crawled through clogged Roman streets, Renn heard people singing songs in their heads (sometimes on-key) and thinking about food (the most common thought), money (second) and sex. The usual scrum of complaints, worries and daydreams; he struggled to maintain some thoughts of his own at the forefront.

When the bus pulled up alongside the angular station and the crowd emptied off, Renn loitered at the back of the crowd and paused to tell the driver, "It's just a cyst, nothing to worry about."

"What?"

"What you're worrying about. It's a cyst, not cancer."

The lumpy-looking man leaned way back off his chair. "What do you know about it?"

Renn sighed, looking at the license posted over the driver's head. "I know Luciano Boltone is not your real name. I know you saw the baker across the street put his head in the oven last month and did nothing because you were afraid of the police identifying you. Did you tell *anyone* about that?"

"What — how — ?!"

"Okay, so I know things, yes? In that same way, I know you don't have a tumor."

"You're an angel from up above! It's real what they say!"

"Ha! I'm no angel."

"You *must* be! No other way you know!"

Renn regretted starting the conversation. He descended the steps to the street.

"Wait!" Boltone yelled after him. "How do you treat a cyst?"

"Hmph! I guess you *will* need a doctor," Renn said, leaving the man stupefied in his chair.

Starting moments after the Concert showdown, all the while as he was escaping with the others from Rome and ever since, Renn had heard a voice in his head that somehow stood clear of the chatter, that seemed to issue from somewhere deep inside him, a voice he felt as much as heard. The experience was both comforting and profoundly unsettling. Listening to its disturbing message had led him full-circle back to the Eternal City, back into harm's way.

Now he slipped across the street to the shadows of a lush cemetery. Cedars towered over terraced stone walkways, shafts of late-day sunlight cut through the deep green. A pair of cats curled on a gravestone that read: *Here lies One Whose Name Was Writ in Water*. Renn settled onto a shady bench along a high red-clay wall. The spot suggested a serene afterlife for which Renn felt nostalgic without really believing. On the other hand, it also offered a clean view, across the street, of L Corp's Rome offices.

After leaving the others in Tunis, Renn had slipped into an Internet cafe and caught an interview with the hero of the G8, Pietr Volkov, that mentioned he was remaining another day in Rome "to resolve any further threats" before returning home to the United States.

The phrase had resonated like an off-key note in a symphony. The only remaining threat to Singh was L Corp and Volkov himself. Why was he still hanging around?

The sun blared out its final rays. Renn closed his eyes and began to hum, slipping into a deep open state, stretching his consciousness out to the marble-and-glass building across the street.

Volkov's vibrations were as familiar to Renn as his own; they called to him as soon as his mind went silent. His old comrade was holding court in a second-floor conference room, across the table from two other trained mindbenders—Renn could sense three distinct magnetic fields and the separately-pitched blank spots of each man's blocking.

Renn dubbed the silent mindbender 'The Assassin'—he recognized the type immediately, having grown up in a training school for them. Cold, watchful and paranoid, a simmering temper, a bully, thug, brawler, action hero and warrior in his own mind. Casually vicious, all feeling capped, coiled and bottled-up until it was time to blow. For the moment, he was casually taking in the conversation between the other two.

The second—the one Volkov was addressing—was not the usual type. High energy—ADHD? Amphetamines?—reckless, baiting, rebellious. And talented, clearly. Volkov didn't allow this much discussion. He tasked you and you did what he ordered; when he was questioning you—as he seemed to be doing here—he expected respectful deference. This kid deferred to no one—he was casual, almost mocking. A satirical bent that spoke of unpredictability and imagination, a truly dangerous combination. 'The Careerist'? No—'The Entrepreneur'. Renn would have paid good money to actually listen in but the risk was too great. As it was, he could sense Volkov's dissatisfaction. An exchange followed round-robin—the two shooters clearly coordinating something—and the meeting broke up.

The Entrepreneur, liberated, hopped down the staircase to the street. Renn wandered to the gate for a glimpse and nearly got bowled over as the man briskly crossed the street through the cemetery and out the other side to the Termini. Hipster mustache, slacks and jacket a size too small, striped socks and a straw hat perched at a precarious angle. In L Corp? Justin Timberlake playing for the New York Philharmonic? Renn fixed the image in his memory for future use and returned his focus to the conference room.

Volkov and the Assassin had a few more comments once they were left alone. Pointed, weighty comments, was how it felt to Renn. Details not to be shared even with the Entrepreneur, who was given a job but not entirely trusted. A minute later, Volkov was in the elevator and down to the street, a car pulling up as he exited the building. Renn remained in the shadow of the clay wall and watched the car pull away, channeling the thoughts of a taxidermist and writer of (awful) Romantic poetry standing a few feet away to ensure Volkov didn't recognize his mental signature.

The Assassin, left for last, descended the steps at a langorous pace. Renn moved to the arched gateway, continuing to channel the German plumber (*But ah! Olde Cedar Tree, if you could but see, the fever that steeps in a thing like me...*) and watched the tall black man with flopping dreadlocks and a wooly multi-colored coat emerge through the electric doors and saunter away around the corner.

...a Jamaican guy with dreads and the best weed in the world, Jesus. He gets his own room 'cause nobody can think once he lights up. Renn had learned of the Jamaican from Jim Avery's majordomo Samantha, what was her last name? She had called him one of L Corp's most dangerous assassins. *He might keep a lit spliff in his room*, Renn thought, *but he doesn't smoke it much.* The man's consciousness cut like a knife. There wasn't a dulled edge—or a relaxed muscle—in him. Tracking him would be tricky—he was entirely paranoid. For a spy, it was an essential survival skill.

Renn grabbed his briefcase and adjusted his glasses, pulled himself erect and stepped stiffly onto the street. Just a businessman heading to a dinner meeting, another interchangeable tool in the wheel of Commerce.

The Jamaican turned into an alley a few blocks up. Renn ditched his jacket, briefcase and glasses in a dumpster and paused for almost a minute before continuing, following the Jamaican's base frequency from a distance, the way any mindbender spy would be trained to do.

Because that's what I am now, a spy. After a lifetime resisting, I am what they trained me to be.

The Jamaican stopped suddenly, awkwardly, admiring himself in a shop window and it was all Renn could do to keep moving, to keep himself from reacting. A quick look measured the angle of the Jamaican's glance. Had he caught on? No, the eyes weren't on Renn, they were farther up the block—the German plumber! Renn must still have been channeling the poor guy; he was towing him down the street without realizing it.

The plumber, cast adrift, turned into a side street and disappeared. Renn instantly shifted his channeling to the young man passing him. The Jamaican scanned the block again—if the plumber wasn't following him, was someone else?

Renn quickly put his arm around...Curt, Curt Mulder from Essen, 36, older than he looked, an electrical contractor who moonlighted playing jazz saxophone in local bands. Poor Curt went under the instant Renn touched him. "To me," Renn confided, as though continuing a long conversation, "Coltrane is perfect; the problem is that, after him, less talented players felt they had to go further—and further was chaos."

As Curt unleashed a stream of invective at fans and club owners favoring lounge-music over passionate art, Renn felt the Jamaican contact their mindstreams, scan them briefly and pass on. Renn herded Curt around the next corner and away, continuing up the side street until he felt the assassin relax (as much as he ever did).

Renn released Curt, who stopped dead, staring around, trying to figure out where the hell he'd gone—he had to stop daydreaming! An old man came out of a doorway in a cheap black jacket and cap. Three seconds later, Renn was wearing them and trotting back toward the Jamaican. He could still read the assassin's base vibration—the man stuck out of the crowd like an electric guitar at the symphony. Finding him again would be no challenge. Cracking him open would be.

Renn had a good idea what was coming—*how* and *when* were the important questions. And, based on what he'd gleaned from the meeting, the only ones who knew the whole picture were Volkov and the Jamaican. Which meant, he had to pull the details from the Jamaican, hopefully without giving himself away.

Just a little waver of concentration, that's all he'd need to slip inside the Jamaican's head. But for two blocks and then three, Renn followed at a respectful distance and the Jamaican's concentration never wavered. He glanced once at a shop window (expensive leather jacket), twice at a pair of young women passing and then, finally, lingered over restaurant menus and bakery windows.

Food! Renn augmented the aroma coming from the kitchens. *If that's your appetite*, he thought, *let's work with it.*

A minute later, the Jamaican dove into an open-front, noisy café, tables nestled between indoor palms against a marble wall that had probably cooled Crusaders drinking mead. The Jamaican bent the maitre d' senseless to get a table in the corner facing all the action—and tipped him anyway. Renn smiled. Tip or no tip, the Jamaican would have to keep the maitre d' under suggestion until he left the place—split focus. *He's impatient and reckless*, Renn decided, *wasting energy on a fancy table*. He filed the information away for future use, the way a spy had to and nestled on a stool at the far end of the oak bar. He could just make out the top of the Jamaican's head over the crowd, whose thoughts, as always, filled his head:

-I said the same thing a second ago! He doesn't listen to me at all.

-'The fountain was badly in need of repair when Fellini arrived. The crew needed to repair stonework at the base...'

-Soy is down six in New York; what next?

The kid sitting next to him at the bar was fiddling with his fingers obsessively, so obsessive and relentless that Renn couldn't ignore it. But his thoughts, when he tuned in, totally belied his behavior.

A swing set, that would be fun and maybe I could paint the shed—no, even better, a TREE HOUSE! She'd go crazy! Just a few pieces of timber and move her tea set up there and she'll—

The kid's thinking came in a torrent, clenched and terrified, the feel of it totally at odds with the content. And those crazy hands! Fingers flying, rubbing, pulling violently at one other.

Renn, digging, broke through to something deeper, a smaller and much younger version of the kid's voice, several layers below: She won't notice, it's just a ring, I could have left it anywhere. It didn't fall off—I must have taken it off. That's all she'll think about—why did I take it off? When was the last time I had it—Thursday? Is that possible? The torrent about the tree house was his best attempt to drown out this terrified, repetitive monologue. When the ache in the kid's stomach finally made him sick, he wouldn't even know where the stress came from.

It didn't matter! Renn shut out the rest of the world, the way he'd done for years and focused again on the Jamaican. Focus was everything in this craft—why was he suddenly getting sidetracked? The Jamaican was scanning his menu—this was a classic opportunity for him to *lose* focus. In the assassin's mind, he was already eating everything on the page. The zuppa de mare and scungilli were already laid out on the table in front of him, he could smell the tangy red sauce and taste the oregano and basil on the spongy shellfish. He hadn't decided what to order yet but his senses were already aflame. Appetite—sex, hunger, drugs—were the regular disruptors of blocking. There was the famous case of the Serbian mindbender who triggered World War I because of a soufflé. But the Jamaican considered every dish on the page without faltering.

If there were no disruptions inside him, Renn would have to find some outside.

Son of a bitch! Tells me to meet him and doesn't show, doesn't text, doesn't...!!

Lita Essen of Hamburg sat directly across the bar, furious at the Swedish boy who'd promised to meet her there and failed to show. She was casting about for a way to salvage the evening.

Renn guided her attention to the dangerous-looking black man in the multicolor coat and boosted her attention so the Jamaican couldn't miss it. Their eyes met. Renn would have made certain Lita didn't look away but in the end, he didn't have to.

He felt the Jamaican's interest instantly. The dreadlocked assassin ordered Lita a drink and, as soon as it arrived, she surprised all of them by leaving her seat and walking right over to his table.

Renn had prompted her and now her feelings were clear and explicit, both to him and now to the Jamaican—and the assassin latched onto them and matched them and then outmatched them in seconds. Suddenly, Renn had what he wanted—the Jamaican's thoughts came clear to him as he stared into Lita's eyes, taking control of her and glancing at the clock on the wall: Twenty minutes, maybe twenty-five but no more. Last chance to put the genie back in the bottle accompanied by Singh's face, a vision of a very familiar handgun and then a string of explicit mental pictures of what he planned to do to Lita in the available next twenty minutes.

She was already turning toward the back of the saloon, eyes glazing, as Renn realized the sacrifice he'd made of her, what would become of her if he didn't act immediately. He couldn't fight the Jamaican's suggestion without betraying his presence — but he could slip around it. He sent a flash of thought, a quick and dirty shock, directly to her motor center and the girl went white and limp in three seconds. The Jamaican caught her in mid-fall from simple instinct and then, as the crowd turned to ogle and wonder, poured her into a chair and left her in the care of a passing waiter as he committed immediately to the exit.

...only one chance to put the genie back in the bottle... The phrase had come in Pietr Volkov's voice, accompanied by two images — Singh's face and a very familiar pistol.

Renn was out of the restaurant in seconds.

Where is Singh right now?

A Web search at an Internet café down the block showed Singh recovering at the home of the Indian Ambassador and scheduled to testify at a judicial hearing about the attack the next day.

So what's the genie in the bottle? Is that the gun?

How to find this on the web? A search for 'Singh's gun' came up empty. 'Singh in Viewing Box' brought up several video clips, with Singh transfixed, her hand movements unclear to the cameras—but several posters noting she was on her feet and fumbling nervously with her bag more than a minute *before* the disturbances outside the box. 'Concert Attack'—nothing new. 'Concert Aftermath'—a half-serious sidebar mentioned the German Prime Minister's handbag being confiscated, along with all the heads of state's personal effects, by G8 security after the Concert. Antonio Villarobos, the G8 security chief, had assured the paper that the effects would be returned tomorrow, Monday, 'after a routine inventory.'

So Singh's gun was still in her purse, which would be inventoried tomorrow. *Genie in the bottle.*

L Corp's original plan was to force Singh, the advocate of peace, to shoot the other leaders in the box, paint her as deranged and discredit her mission of peace and disarmament. But now that plan had failed, L Corp had switched gears completely and painted her the saintly, innocent victim, the target of Renn's terrorist assassination plot. How would that play if a gun was found in her bag—the bag she was clutching a minute *before* the fighting started?

L Corp had to make sure that gun disappeared before the inventory.

And there was something more, something that became clear to him only now.

The voice that had been bubbling in the background of Renn's consciousness for days, the voice that he'd felt inside as much as heard, that had called him back to Rome and into harm's way again—now he recognized that voice as Aryana Singh's.

When Renn first connected with Singh at the Concert, Volkov had almost complete possession of her, his powerful suggestion bolstered by fifty low-level L Corp mindbenders brought in to subdue Singh's will.

Singh knew none of that at the moment. She was stunned and terrified by what she saw as her own impulse to draw a gun, by the inexplicable compulsion she felt taking over her mind and body.

But Singh's humane, respectful pacifism wasn't a pose—it had arisen from the deepest parts of her being. She was an Indian woman and an Indian woman mathematician—she knew how to resist what didn't feel right to her and now she resisted fiercely.

Renn arrived at the Concert with grave doubts. He and Volkov had been raised together in the Project in Siberia. They had been raised in competition, to work in tandem and opposition, so that, if one failed in his duty to the Soviet Union, the other would naturally find a different path to success. Their psychotronic suggestions grew from different roots and took different neural paths—their suggestions came from different directions and neither ever had any success at breaking the other's.

In that moment, with Holst's *Mars* roaring out of the orchestra three feet behind and Singh in peril twenty feet ahead of him, Renn realized he didn't have to break Volkov's suggestion—all he had to do was strengthen Singh's own instincts and help her defend herself.

He gave himself up, surrendered his will and his mindbending skills to her—and the two of them made a connection unlike any he'd ever experienced. A connection that had continued ever since.

So now, he felt her reaching out to him and suddenly understood why. She was scheduled to testify about the attack tomorrow and had only the murkiest understanding of what had happened. So far, all her memories had been clouded by Volkov's suggestions and her mental efforts, merged with Renn's, to defy them.

Volkov, Renn realized, couldn't allow those memories to come clear.

~~~~

An hour later, Antonio Villarobos arrived in his office near the Spanish Steps. His next official function—the inventory and return of diplomat's effects from the concert—wasn't due until morning but somehow, he'd felt an urge to drop by the office tonight. He'd rushed through dinner with his wife and daughter in order to return, though, now that he'd arrived, he couldn't remember why.

Hand twirling a lock. What lock? Lock on the safe. Knows the combination—who the hell's hands on the handle? Oh hell, mine. My hands pulling out a handbag for inspection. Check the condition of things, make sure there's no problems with anything before the inventory. Don't want any diplomatic kerfuffle. Mmm, lovely night out, ought to enjoy it a bit before it's gone. Is there something wrong? What am I doing? Of course not, nothing wrong, just going for a walk, of course.

Julian Landau sat waiting in a rented Alfa Romeo across the street, eating Panini from a plastic container. He hated eating in the car—it just wasn't *healthy*.

Amsterdam had selected a different man to go to Rome for this job. When Landau arrived instead, the supervisors knew what was up.

"Where'd you learn that maneuver?"

"What maneuver?"

"Rucker called in sick—when we contacted him, he thought he was in Tahiti on vacation."

"Which only proves I'm better for this job."

"This organization runs on military discipline," said the gray suit across the desk. But Landau sensed (he was a fast learner) that the blue suit next to him was more open-minded.

"There are jobs for soldiers," Landau said, "and jobs for commandos. This is a commando job."

"You don't get to decide—"

"What's the difference?" interrupted Blue Suit.

"A soldier goes where you tell him and does exactly what he's told. So as long as you foresee everything that happens, he'll do fine," said Landau. "But if one thing goes wrong, you're screwed because your orders no longer fit the circumstances and he depends on orders. A commando understands the objective and finds a way to get it done, regardless of how the circumstances change."

"You've no experience for a job like this."

"The guys with experience are on other jobs or making sure the judges at tomorrow's tribunal stick to our story. Your other choices are weak minds keeping the media on the 'Renn the Assassin' narrative. That's why you ordered a solo player out of Amsterdam."

"You're not privy to our personnel decisions!" said Gray Suit.

"I got it anyway. Just more proof I'm the right guy for you."

After a recess and a short, stern meeting with Volkov and another shooter, here Landau was, in the action where he belonged. Now he threw his dinner aside, because it was time. He'd made preliminary contact with Villarobos that afternoon. A simple suggestion had gotten the cop in on his night off. Another had him opening his safe and pulling out Singh's bag. Now it was time to cash in.

Villarobos was on his way down the stairs, Landau could feel him coming. He had the man locked solid. He checked the angle of his hat in the rearview mirror, hopped out of the car and headed for the side staircase. *Just meet me at the doorway, dude, hand over the gun and put the bag back upstairs where it belongs.*

Except that, when Landau reached the doorway, Villarobos wasn't there. He pushed open the outer door and a guard at the desk inside sat up straight and demanded ID. Landau paused for just a moment, searching for the guard's mindstream. A moment later, the guard's eyes glazed and he buzzed the door open.

Landau dashed up the staircase to Villarobos' office. The Spaniard was behind his desk, looking dazed.

"Where is it?"

"What?"

"The purse! You were supposed to bring it. Where'd you stash it?"

"Stash what?"

"The purse! Do you not understand me?"

"Understand who?"

Landau reached for Villarobos' mindstream—he'd have sworn he was in contact with it a moment earlier but what he found was completely different, a different frequency running in circles, phrases and questions recurring endlessly.

He bent to the safe—locked solid. And no chance of getting the combination from Villarobos, not in the shape he was in.

Rushing back to the car, he drove Rome's chaotic streets as fast as he could without drawing attention from the *polizia*. The meeting point was five blocks from the Indian embassy. The Jamaican was waiting for him in the shadows.

"Where is it?"

"Locked in his safe and his brain scrambled." The Jamaican threw him a suspicious look. Landau shook his head. "Not me," he said. "Somebody got to him." He pulled a pistol from his pocket. "Use this one."

"It's got to be hers."

"Then just scramble her mind altogether," Landau offered. "A touch to the temple, they'll ask her about Rome and she'll tell them about Malaysia. They'll ask her about her bag and she'll answer about peanut butter sandwiches. Nobody will ever take her seriously again. And nobody will care about the gun."

The Jamaican considered. "It's not the plan."

"It's the objective—that's more important than the plan," Landau answered and the Jamaican disappeared into the trees.

~~~~

The Indian Ambassador's residence was magnificent—rust-colored plaster and a vaulted black-tile roof from the Renaissance, marble steps staring down a sloping lawn to the security fence and guardhouse added at street level centuries later.

The Jamaican sat in his car under a grove of towering cypress trees half a block away, soaking up the place and the mindstreams of its inhabitants, for the sixth time in the last twenty-four hours. He liked the lines and color of the place—in his quiet moments, the Jamaican considered himself an architecture lover. It was comforting knowing his assault on Singh would not result in property damage. Just another proof that mindbending was the perfect weapon for a materialistic age.

The Jamaican blanketed the compound. Nobody was blocking or showing any unusual awareness. The mixup with the gun unsettled him but Landau had probably bungled that all by himself. Too damn many new people—expansion just diluted the talent pool.

He renewed his psychotronic connection with the guard at the gatehouse. As his car approached the checkpoint, instead of a black man with dreads and a wild-colored coat, the guard saw Villarobos, the G8 Security Chief, at the wheel. He hesitated briefly and asked, "Forget something?" before waving the Jamaican through.

Singh's bedroom was upstairs in the North Wing, overlooking a walled-in garden. The guards at the top of the staircase also saw him as Villarobos and jumped to attention as he approached.

Inside the suite, the Jamaican moved warily past ornate plates and tapestries, suits of armor and swords from the second century, trappings that proclaimed, in the midst of Rome, the age and power of India's culture.

The bedroom door wasn't locked. The Jamaican turned the knob from a distance and watched the door drift inward.

Moonlight filtered through the drapes, floating lazily on an unfelt breeze. The trees in the garden beyond seemed to swim back and forth, in and out of focus. There was Singh, tossing and turning in the low enamel bed. An unnatural sheen traced the rim of a gong in a corner, a corner that should have been dark.

Something was wrong. He could feel it.

Reaching for the bed, his hands found fabric instead of skin. The Jamaican reached left and right—Singh was right in front of him but all he felt were blankets.

"Enough playing," he announced, standing tall. "Come out and fight."

"I like playing," the voice came from the window. "What's the point of fighting?" Now it was in the doorway. "She's long gone." Now, by the suspiciously glowing gong in the dark corner.

"If she was long gone, you wouldn't be here," he replied.

The Jamaican jumped swiftly to the gong but—it wasn't there. Throwing his arms in front of him, he felt heavy embroidery, the drapes parted and the light streaming in on him through an open windowsill.

Which meant the gong would be...*this* way!

He jumped quickly, straight into a huge standing clock...that should have been behind him.

He'd studied the room obsessively for twelve hours, planning this attack. He knew where every piece of furniture was—at least, where it was *supposed* to be.

Next to the standing clock should be an armoire. He turned to his left and found...a tall planter. Which should have been to the right.

His head was swimming. Which direction should have led him to the clock? The exact opposite of the gong.

He walked away from the window...and found himself at the window. Jesus! The whole place was mirrored...no, surely he was mirroring the place himself, in his mind, perceiving Left as Right and vice versa. He struck off in the opposite direction from the gong...and there it was.

Ha! He'd licked it! He'd figured it out!

"Very clever," he exclaimed angrily. "But you can't hide forever!"

As if in response, the lights came on all over the suite, suddenly packed with security guards, their weapons drawn.

"Hands in the air! Hands—!" several yelled, followed by a long stunned silence. Their confused faces showed the Jamaican's suggestion still held sway on them. "Signor Villarobos—?"

"What are you waiting for?" he belched, grabbing the opportunity with both hands. "Where are the people who turned in the alarm? Have you seized them?"

"But—it was *you*. You alerted us, just now...in the hallway. You said there was...an intruder," the lead guard stammered. At that, they all heard the Jamaican's car starting in the lot downstairs and watched it pull out the gate and away. The Jamaican felt his cheeks flush redder than the carpet.

~~~~

Renn made a series of quick turns onto small roads, each leading in a different direction, until they were a good distance from the embassy. Eventually, he reached a particular corner near a particular intersection. He slowed down and pulled into a discrete grove of trees obscuring the car from the road. Singh sat up in the passenger seat.

"You're real," she said. "They tried to convince me I'd made you up. They tried to make me forget—"

"It would be safer for you if you did."

"I won't be safe, one way or the other, will I? No one is safe with those people around. What do they want? Do they *know* what they want?"

"I don't know," he answered. "It might just be 'More'."

Singh nodded. "We all want," she said. "But some people, it's an empty hole that keeps getting bigger." She hesitated for a moment. "Thank you for saving me."

"You saved yourself. I assisted."

"At the Concert, I thought I was battling myself, something awful inside me—when you appeared, I felt you believed in me, in what I was doing. And once I felt you there, I felt *him* too, the other one, the one who's been on the television ever since. And that was crucial. Fighting yourself is terrifying. Fighting someone else? I'm a woman in politics; it's habitual." She took in their surroundings for the first time. "What are we waiting for?"

"There is a Mr. Hindi who was part of your security detail. He was arrested at the airport on a narcotics charge."

"I remember…"

"The charge was trumped up, to separate him from you."

Singh's eyes narrowed. "He is not highly thought of among my senior people."

"I'm not surprised. Mr. Hindi is one of the last members of your government's *Samadhi* program, your government's attempt to work with…people like me. Like me and the people who tried to make you forget. He could have protected you at the Concert, which is why they separated you. I recommend you make him a permanent part of your security detail from now on."

"What about the narcotics charge?"

"Leave Italy within twenty-four hours. I have cultivated...an influence over the police chief, but it's temporary. As long as you're gone in that time, you'll be fine. Hindi will be here in a few minutes. You must go into hiding under his protection. Do you understand?"

She eyed him in a way that made him uncomfortable. "Will you...be with me...inside...like the last few days?"

Renn drew a sharp breath. "That would be dangerous for you."

"Dangerous for me? Or uncomfortable for you?"

Renn just stared, unwilling or unable to reply.

Singh's gaze was sharp. "I'm not going into hiding. I'm going to testify tomorrow."

"It's not wise."

"I'm going to tell them everything I remember." She arched an eyebrow. "I have the suspicion I could remember quite a bit more than I do." Her expression demanded a response.

"Again, it's safer if you don't."

"I think it's time other people stopped deciding what's safe for me."

Renn sighed and reached for her forehead. "Remember *everything*," he said. He watched her eyes widen; he could hear her putting together bits and pieces of memory, hammering sensation into patterns like people did. After a minute, she said, "Why? What was the point?"

"I'm still not sure. Clearly, one way to gain power—and maintain it—is by scaring people. Instability is good business for those who promise security."

"This is *business*?"

"They say *everything* is business. It's the way of the world now." She nodded, tightly, that she understood. "So now you understand the danger you're in. Mr. Hindi can protect you long enough for you to testify. But he will eventually have to sleep and I have to disappear."

"My testimony—won't that clear you?"

"There are very powerful interests who are building a narrative here. Anyone who challenges that narrative will be, in their view, dangerous or crazy. If you're truthful, you will just give them enough detail to prove it."

She was quiet for a long moment, her thoughts reduced to a sort of distant music.

"I want to make a difference," Singh said finally. "That's all I've ever wanted. You understand that—I know you do."

"I never thought that was possible for me—I felt all my gifts were perverse."

"And now you know differently."

"The world is perverse. In such a place, my gifts can be useful."

She rose up in her seat. "The game may be stacked against me but I don't play games. The only honorable thing is to show up and tell the truth. Your job will be to show the world that it was the situation that was crazy and not me."

Renn's discomfort only increased at this but he didn't get a chance to sort through his feelings. A blue Citroen pulled off the highway, blinked its lights twice and switched off. A tall, shaven-headed man stepped into the moonlight. The two mindbenders acknowledged each other with an almost imperceptible nod.

Singh took Renn's hand. "I won't forget—" she began and he cut her off.

"I—I know," he said, tapping his forehead.

She smiled, tapping her own forehead in return. "I think I'm *not* leaving you. I think you're going to stay in here. I don't think you have a say in it."

Renn returned the smile. "We'll see," he said. "This is new to me too."

And then she trotted to Hindi's car and the Citroen pulled away onto the autostrata.

Renn sat quietly, listening to the gathering of nighttime voices, the tumult of arguments, prayers, curses, crushes and bad jokes. For most of his life, those voices had been noise to him, static he did all he could to repel and ignore. Unquestionably, that had now changed. Renn was queasily uncomfortable with this new depth of involvement but there was no denying it. With Singh's quiet music bleeding through the hum, the voices were alive to him now, in a way that was wondrous and terrifying all at once.

Renn put the car in gear and drove off into the crowded night.

a bigger world

Australia

Keep the piercings and tattoos all the way to Darwin, Kate read Renn's note. *Buy some blonde hair color, the cheaper and brassier the better. Buy a ticket to Sydney on a regional airline for the next morning, just in case someone's watching—but don't use it. Take a hotel room, then 'persuade' the desk clerk to give you the key to a different room on a different floor instead. Dye your hair again, change clothes, leave through the back entrance and take the first bus south-east. About an hour out of Darwin, you won't be able to sit anymore. Live off the kindness of strangers. You will be contacted.*

The piercings and tattoos had been Renn's idea in the first place. Everyone will look at you but all they'll see are the piercings. Seven on her ears, the nose ring to intimidate and a nipple ring just for her to know about. Sure, they were all fake but, by the time she reached Mumbai, she no longer had any desire to remove them. On the contrary. The chopped-off hair, the raccoon eyeliner and the piercings—they were her armor. Back off world. She fell in love with the new Kate while she was just an idea.

Daring, brave, angry, powerful. Free. Whattaya want? Whattaya got? That was a line from a movie, wasn't it?

She was brimming with feeling, bursting with it. That was the revolution inside her. The woman racing across the grass on Tiber Island with the orchestra shrieking behind her, blocking Marat's lightning bolts with a flick of the wrist and blowing them back in his face, was someone she didn't recognize, someone she couldn't have imagined living inside her. How can you be something you can't imagine? The only sensible answer—'You can't'—didn't fit the facts.

She dejectedly followed Renn's instructions, ditching the piercings, going blonde and getting out of town without triggering a probe or disturbing a living soul. Twenty minutes out of town, the natural world began to crowd out the world of men. The clustered homes felt like outposts being returned, bit by bit, to an all-enveloping garden.

Time slowed. Numbered highways split off the main road; Kate watched a tree sway on a distant bluff for fifteen minutes without it ever seeming closer or farther. In all this time, she'd moved barely an inch on the map.

She'd moved a million miles from home, or anyplace that felt like it.

Clattering across a metal-skeleton bridge over a water hole out of Eden, palm and mango trees, deer, eagles and a small pack of foxes, the thought that kept recurring was: What next? What now?

You will be contacted—how? How would anyone contact her in a million miles of Outback?

An hour into the journey, the bus stopped for food. She was down the aisle and onto the dusty roadside in a blink. Nothing could have kept her tied to that seat.

"Where you going, pretty girl?"

Now he was a dream. Beautiful and knowing it, dark and long-faced, aboriginal features 10 million years old, slouched over an ancient Triumph cycle, black on black, glinting in the sunlight. He appraised her like an auctioneer, smiled like the devil himself and that wild feeling brimmed over inside her again.

"What's around here?"

"Nothing if you're going someplace."

"What if I want to get lost?"

"Welcome home," he smiled and slapped the back seat of the bike like a lover.

This definitely isn't what Renn had in mind, she thought. But this was the new Kate, the one who took big chances and trusted her instincts. She gulped hard, climbed onto the seat and clapped her arms around his midsection.

His name was Rafael and he lived in the back of nowhere, in the midst of everything. Ten miles of rutted dirt path and a thousand more with no path at all, past thickets of reeds and trees that were saplings when Jesus was a boy. His home was cinder blocks under a tin roof, a potbelly stove and three windows with chicken wire instead of glass, each looking out on a different world.

The night was a million crickets, a tangle of netting over a sleeping mat with a billowing comforter—and thunder and lightning.

In the morning, she saw the river glistening through the brush and moved toward it like a compass to true north. She plunged into bulrushes over her head, so thick she could barely see daylight.

Just before she bent to dip the pitcher in, Rafael grabbed her from behind and pointed to the two unblinking eyes bobbing on the surface. The eyes moved, after a pause, smoothly to the other bank. There, a heavy tail flicked from the water, stunning a large crane just long enough for the seven-foot crocodile to leap from the river, grab it by the neck and drag it beneath the surface, water foaming and frothing for almost a minute before returning to its indifferent calm.

On the way back uphill, Rafael stepped lightly, eyes everywhere. He pointed out three snakes, six or seven feet long, sunning on rocks a few feet from the path. Kate paid attention to everything after that—the way he walked, the way he observed detail, eyes scanning what was ahead with respect for a world full of unpredictable—and threatening—life.

The trees formed leaf curtains over waterholes clotted with wildflowers, the fish arcing out of the water like fireworks. Flocks of gulls and hawks swooped across the sky. Endless space surrounded them but she never felt alone nor wanting privacy.

She could have probed him, measured his intentions and sincerity but, in truth, she didn't want to. She resisted knowing more, was thrilled to ignore her gifts, to live surrounded by mysteries.

Before, with boys, she always seemed to be rushing to the end of the story; now, she was content to roll with the river, learning to be herself in the midst of a bigger world.

That night, she awoke to a song she'd never heard before, not birdsong, not a wolf howl, something long and sharp and melodic and she followed it outside into moonlight like the rocks and rushes were glowing from within. She felt Rafael behind her and sensed another presence through the rushes, bulky and moving on spindly legs and, a moment later, there it was, insect-like but ten feet high, covered in paint, ochre and luminescent green and yellow stripes around its stick-like appendages, both the ones it walked on and the ones sprouting besides its ten thousand eyes. Not uniform stripes, mind you, but hand-painted smears, blobs of paint smudging at the edges and dripping as the thing moved, taller than the trees, eyes fluorescent and lighting a path ahead...

And then there were other travelers, as the land dried out and the hills grew sharp and barren: a skinny boy Rafael's age, squinting and hiding his face in his hands, mouse-like; a coven of old women giggling and singing; an older man in a loincloth and bandana carrying a long stick, dancing heavy-legged in circles, leaving a glowing trail on the clay plateau floor—and a bulky woman in a sheath dark as infinity and shining a moment later with vivid splashes of color, under a sky lit up with stars, millions of stars shooting messages back and forth across the sky. The woman's voice chanted sounds that weren't language, not any human speech Kate had ever heard and yet she could feel the whole group gathering within the drone, adding their voices to it.

It was an odd dream and odder yet in that she was aware of it as a dream.

A lizard as tall as Rafael's shack clomped around leaving splotches of color moving like clouds across his broad back. And when an otherworldly song broke through the drone, she was shocked and embarrassed and then proud to find it coming from her own mouth.

She came to a moment later, Rafael beside her and realized they were dreaming together, that somehow he was manipulating the dream for both of them.

"Are we awake?" she asked, stretched against the damp sheets, the cicadas like a drilling army outside.

"What's the other choice?"

"That's it's another dream."

"Why would you want to know?"

That afternoon, he led her up to the hills and showed her the paintings. The birds and huge bugs, spiders and rainbow snakes, the huge mantis and the lizard—all of them were in the dream. Now they were painted on the hillside and in the caves, in outline or skeleton or covered with elaborate patterns and designs.

"Oldest paintings in the world," he said. "More than 50,000 years. The spirits that created the world back in the Dreamtime. When the Earth was born. Born of dreams."

"Like last night—or however many nights that was?"

"Our dreams are just dreams, not like theirs."

"What can you do with dreams? Obviously more than most."

He shrugged. "It's just a way to fool around."

"That's not all," she said. He flinched; that momentary interruption was enough to allow her to slip into his mind and make sure he understood she could do it while they were awake. "You speak through them. You can do things through them you couldn't do yourself." She barely knew what she was saying until she heard it come out of her mouth. But he knew—and was fine with her knowing that much. Kate relaxed—if he'd had a sinister intent, he wouldn't be so relaxed about it.

"It's something the shamans teach," he said.

"So it's not just a really manipulative way for you to get girls."

He flashed his wicked grin again.

"The world is the product of our dreams, millions of years of them, some more pointed and powerful than others. Dreams are the back door. People don't resist them. Shape the dream, you shape the world."

This is why I'm here, Kate thought bitterly. Renn sent me here to learn this. Her whole world turned upsdie-down, anger welling at Renn for manipulating her so brazenly—and subtly. Rafael and Renn suddenly seemed childish to her, playing with people's heads without concern for the consequences. Could Renn have known that she would understand the dream's power better than Rafael did? Did he make me want him? Did he know I would?

The next day, he led her across the grassland to a village enclosed by the river on three sides. Dogs wearing bandanas were the first sign of drawing near. Simple cinder block constructions like Rafael's with outhouses, a few chickens and pigs running loose, some residents friendly and bantering with Rafael, some eyeing Kate warily. A few seemed familiar from the dreams, which only added to the incongruity.

"Ten, twelve families here," Rafael told her, buoyant. "We've got a generator, electricity three, four hours a day."

"For what? Washing machines? Freezers?" she guessed.

"Oh, sure," he laughed. "Soap operas and Internet, the necessities."

"Are there jobs?"

He laughed. "Everybody's got something. Organic eggs and livestock, tours of the cave paintings—not the prime shit I show you, the touristy ones—and we've got our art and jewelry."

He led her up a hill to a red house.

"What's this?"

"Mama's place. Biggest in town."

"Big family?"

"Patients."

The front room held ten people in distress—children with broken bones and sniffles, old people stooped over with arthritis.

Dolores was a big woman with a long pony tail and a loose floral housedress, tending to several patients at once. They joined her in a small room where an old woman sat moaning, hands clasped to her skull. "Migraines," Rafael said.

Dolores rotated her hands over the old woman's forehead and astonished Kate by unleashing a guttural drone that shook the walls. It was the drone from the Dreaming but she realized now that she'd heard a sound like that once before, coming from Max Renn. Five seconds of it removed the tension from the old woman's face. After ten, she was smiling. Dolores took several gasping breaths, then kissed the old woman on both cheeks and sent her on her way.

"Who have you brought me?" Mother growled at son. Rafael grinned like a pirate.

"A helper."

Dolores was suddenly, literally, in Kate's face, staring directly into her eyes. Her first impulse was to pull back but instead, she stiffened. *I've got nothing to hide,* she thought, denying the truth, and stared right back. Five seconds later, Dolores turned to Rafael.

"She's too good for you."

"Don't tell her."

"She'll figure it out." Dolores hugged her and held on a moment longer than Kate expected—and there was a curious look on her face when she released her.

Dolores delivered babies and taught new mothers to care for them, made poultices and ointments from local roots and berries. Kate helped make treatments, organized files and histories. She found herself anticipating Dolores' needs. If she was reading her mind, she wasn't aware of it. It was as though they had an effortless connection.

And then she was ushered into a more delicate part of Dolores' world, curing muscle aches and cranky joints by laying on hands and generating a healing vibration. In the most serious cases, three older women—Minerva, Alda and Mama Bill—assisted. This went on in a back area not open to anyone else. Then, with no warning, Kate was pulled in.

She watched as they chanted and droned into a shared dream state, working on a seriously arthritic woman. Kate knew immediately that this was what they'd been doing for several nights together in their sleep.

They stood in the examining room and suddenly, at the same time, in a clearing, reeds waving over their heads, the patient turning in mid-air like a rotisserie, sections of her body changing to a subtle yellow or orange as Dolores droned and passed her hands over. The droning changed notes with some kind of feedback, back and forth, from the body.

Now Kate anticipated Dolores again, her hands setting sections of the body glowing. She had no idea what they were doing but knew, somehow, how to do it.

When they were done, Dolores dragged her to another examining room. An old man hobbled in on two canes, throwing his legs around with each step. He settled on the bench near the window, eyes fixed on Dolores. "Nestor comes every week. He wants to walk like a young man and I can't help him—I don't think he ever walked like a young man. I massage his legs and give him my best remedies and nothing happens."

"He's seen a doctor?"

Dolores snorted. "Last time a doctor came out here—six months ago—he said 'He's old', like that's an answer."

Kate waited until the silence became unnerving. "Okay— and me? What can I do for him?"

"Exactly," Dolores said and left the room.

contact

Singapore

The bomb went off during Morning Prayer, glass fragments erupting from black smoke like sparklers and a booming bass note rippling in multiple echoes off the surrounding buildings. The blast drowned out the *muezzin's* wails in the mosque next door, the Presbyterian hymn across the street and the Buddhists droning down at the end of the block.

I ran the checklist, like every other bomb I've heard—takes less than a second. Still alive. Standing upright on my own. Not dizzy; can feel and see my hands and feet. Okay, take a breath, look around.

A thick blood stain, more black than red, ran down the face of a three-story Buddha across the street. I exhaled—and a charred Toyota Corolla dropped out of the sky and slammed onto the street right in front of me.

We—the whole crowd in the marketplace—started tearing for the outskirts.

I got six feet through thick smoke before almost stepping on him.

He must have been a small man to begin with—now he was even smaller, shriveled and seared down his left side. He reached out to me—on instinct, I grabbed and pulled and his hand came apart in mine.

He crumpled forward and I caught him on the way down. It felt like the next breath would split him wide open. I wasn't sure what would be worse—laying him down or picking him up—but I couldn't do nothing.

A crowd was clustered in a vestibule halfway up the block. I carried him like Grandma's crystal. It was a clinic and he was on a gurney rolling down the hallway before I could say 'Thank you.'

It wasn't till the next corner, fighting the crowd, that I noticed the charcoal in my hand. And before I could chuck it, I felt a probe.

I'm no mindbender. Max and Kate, Tauber and Dave Monaghan, Volkov, Marat, all of them, sure, but not me. I got kidnapped into the whole thing, at least at the beginning.

I only spent a week in Max Renn's world but it was enough so I could recognize a mind probe in my sleep, that echo-chamber feel of somebody knocking on my door, checking if it was locked and then if they could pick it, in that order.

If they'd followed me from Dubai, why didn't they seize me on the plane? And if not, I'd been a day-and-a-half on a boat leaving Rome and almost another day in the air since then. What were they waiting for?

Too damn many possibilities. I had to get away now and fast.

I drifted up an alley but the probe had locked onto me and was still banging away, trying to get in. Which meant my blocking was working but who knew how long I could keep it up.

And then there was a fly in my face and I swatted at it and the probe *vanished*. Gone. Totally out of mind—in the middle of a pulse. Whoever it was hadn't quit, those guys just don't, once they've got the scent. Somehow I'd shut it down, all by myself. How? I looked at my hand and saw the charcoal stick still in it.

Except it wasn't a stick. A stick doesn't have fucking knuckles.

It was his finger, the guy in the street, long and delicate and fragile as charcoal. I breathed in and a wave of nausea rolled through me.

It was the *smell*, that familiar stench—burnt flesh, tires on melting asphalt and high explosives—one sniff and I was back in Fallujah, back in Iraq, where no sane feeling ever had a home. Fallujah was the oldest memory I could muster and who the fuck needs 'em? I'd forgotten everything before the war when what I really needed was to forget the fucking war.

But the finger was a keeper. I took a long sniff and let it carry me away. Singapore's soggy damp faded to dry sheets of air like a furnace. My shoulders sagged from carrying full pack, sixty pounds of armor and helmet, ammo belts and rifle, goggles on my forehead while, all the while, I knew they weren't really there.

The panicked crowd finally reached the next intersection, pouring into traffic like October leaves on a river. Dodging trucks, honking cars, scooters buzzing like mosquitoes and squadrons of bicycles, I nurtured the Fallujah inside me, scanning rooftops for snipers, eyeing postboxes and street lights for IED's. Singaporean faces took on hajibs and burqas, street signs morphed from the squiggly local Tamil and Malay into Arabic and English. I lost myself in the dream, one toe in, one toe out of the real world. It wasn't any more sensible there than it sounds here—but after my week in Maxworld, I knew it *worked* and that, if the probe was L Corp, my life depended on it.

My job was to get to the docks, to find *the slowest ship you can from Singapore to Pulau Patang. Find a room on the second floor with a view of the beach. Drink tuak. Walk the beach twice a day. You will be contacted.* Max's gonzo directions—I'd read them so often (trying to make sense of them) that I could recite them.

There was no slowest ship to Pulau Patang; there was *one* ship to Pulau Patang, the *Babu*, and it sailed in two hours. Either I was onboard when it sailed or stuck in Singapore for most of a week, waiting for it to come around again.

So now I scanned the area, trying to look like one more hysterical bystander instead of a guy trying to pick out the guy who was trying to pick his mind.

That's when I saw the skinny guy in a floppy hat pulling up his bike in front of a nail salon. No reason to focus on him but when he reached under his shirt with a particular gesture and a particular expression on his face, the world went into slow motion and the alarm started screaming in the back of my head.

I dove into a weaver's shop. In the States, the place was a closet; here, it was somebody's life's work—at least, it was for two more seconds, until the *big* bomb went off.

Not that I remember any of it. I came to with my ears ringing, under a pile of shattered display plates and twisted hub caps, shredded tablecloths and a tall black man with a series of nasty new cuts on his back and shoulders. He pulled himself off me and I instantly felt a heavy weight nestling against my crotch. I glanced down at a very serious pistol in my happy place.

"If I feel a *hint* of a probe," he said, "you'll be singing notes only dogs can hear." I didn't know him from Adam but I knew instantly that he was the one probing me.

"I won't if you won't," I said. It was intriguing that he was worried about *me* probing *him*. Two buff guys came out of nowhere and grabbed me under the arms. I could hear the hiss from their earpieces—white-noise headphones to cancel out any mind control I might be throwing. The phones were an L Corp specialty, so I *knew* who I was up against.

I blocked another probe. "I thought we just agreed no probes."

"That wasn't me," he said and I felt a chill up my back. Who the hell *else* was out there?

They dragged me through the stampeding crowd, which was trampling its occupants in the rush to Anywhere Else. Body parts littered the street. Sirens wailed in every direction so there had to be more bombs going off in other parts of town.

"Is this you guys? This attack?" Burly Man demanded.

"I just about had my fucking head blown off twice in the last five minutes. Of course, it's not me."

"It was you at the G8, attacking Singh—"

"Save that shit for the office," I cracked and he raised an eyebrow. "The only one we attacked in Rome was your man Volkov and he's not people, as far as I'm concerned."

His eyes narrowed. "Who do you think we are? Where do you think we're taking you?"

"To the black cube. We got Tauber out of one of your little sweatboxes last week. I'm not going back."

"The Black Cube? L Corp headquarters?"

"What do *you* call it? Xanadu?"

"You were in L Corp headquarters last week? What were they doing to Mark?"

"Mark?"

"Tauber," he said and the way he said it changed my whole attitude in a heartbeat.

"You know Tauber?"

"I knew all those guys from the old days." He looked around at his posse. "We're not that old crew, that's for sure—but we're not L Corp either." I must have looked at him cross-eyed, because he continued. "Government issue, your taxpayer dollars at work."

"CIA." I said it like a statement but he knew it was a question, a question those guys are trained not to answer. "I'm Army," I told him. "Fallujah, three tours, two voluntary. We're on the same side." There was a look on his face now. I can't read minds but again, I could read leverage for me in that face. "You need information."

"That's the job, yes."

"I can give you a shitload." His eyes widened. "But we've gotta work out the terms."

~~~~

We ended up at some rundown dive along a canal. The sign read 'Tapas' but all they knew about tapas was that it was a word on the side of a restaurant. Burly Man bought a bottle of really cheap booze to justify the table but nobody touched it. His boys staked out the doors while we sat.

"So? Where do we start?"

"You got a name?" I asked.

"Scott Cornwell," he said. "Recently of Brussels, soon from locales Down Under."

"Congratulations."

"Yeah, that's what they tell me."

"Is Cornwell your real name?"

"Shit, son, I've been doing this a while. They're all my real name. My home town is Philly, Wichita, New Orleans, Ojai, Glenwood Springs and Milwaukee. You want to know all the shit I know about Milwaukee, having grown up there?"

"Not really."

"Good, I can't remember it anyway. So what's your story?"

"Ask me a question."

"Fuck you, you're going coy now?"

"Fuck you too. We're talking the price of information here. I'm a useful source of information—you don't throw me in jail or haul me away for interrogation."

I saw him glance at the mirror on the wall behind me, checking out his guys, minding the street and the back door overlooking a canal. "I don't completely control my fate here, y'see? These guys are taking my orders for the moment but they're really here to make sure I report to my new job without incident."

"Why is this supposed to matter to me?" I asked, trying to hide the fact that it very much did.

"Because I started asking questions. Like how come half the known mindbender population of the world suddenly decided to hold a reunion in Rome—along with a few previously-unknowns." He was nodding at *me* there. "I've been exiled to the Outback for my trouble. Bringing you in would put me back in good graces." He poured some water from a pitcher on the table, lifted the glass to look it over, then poured some of the wine into the other glass and sipped that instead. "You've got intel that's worth more than that?"

Now he had me. I worked things over in my head ten times but they always came out the same.

"Never mind. If you want in their good graces, you'll *run* from what I've got." As soon as I said it, I saw the light in his eyes. He was interested, good graces or not. Maybe even *more* if not. "What'd you think of Mark Tauber?"

"He was a unreliable cranky bastard."

"Well, yeah, okay," I couldn't deny it. "But an assassin?"

"Hell no. I loved the man. He was an information-gatherer, not a shooter."

"And on *our* side. A patriot."

"A cracked one, but yeah. So you, Mr. Army and Mark and Max Renn, all cozy. How'd *that* happen?"

"L Corp killed Dave Monaghan." If he knew 'all those guys from the old days,' he knew Dave. His eyes went hard and I started thinking there just might be a person inside. "Shot dead in the Everglades ten days ago. "

"How do you know it was L Corp?"

"I was in his house when it happened. Max was Dave's friend, I didn't know who he was at the time. We tracked the guys who did it right back to L Corp."

"Oh, don't tell me that," he whined. "L Corp's one of us — our security contractor."

"Congratulations."

"Why would they want to kill Dave?"

"Because of Jim Avery."

"From *Your World? Be Your Own Best Self?*"

"Yup—24/7 cable network, self-help videos, seminars, lectures, vacation resorts and cruises, hell yeah. Avery's the money behind L Corp."

His eyes went silver-dollar-sized. "Avery was an aide to the Intelligence Subcommittee years back; we both helped debrief Renn when he came in after 9/11."

"That's where Avery got the idea for a mindbender business—"

"Business?"

"Two, to be precise. *Your World* has an army of low-level college kids, massing their pea-sized brainwaves—rigging elections and stockholder votes, selling SUV's to people who don't need them and making them believe their local politician really cares about the working man. Whatever'll pay. That's Avery's baby. L Corp is Volkov running Marat, Miriam Fine and six or seven other serious spy-assassin types. Overthrowing governments, undermining economies, assassinations, you name it."

He was getting more and more confused and I couldn't blame him. "So..in Rome...?"

"We weren't trying to kill Singh." I told him about the gun in her purse. "*Watch* the videos. When the dome shatters and they pull everybody to safety, *we're* the ones celebrating."

"How does Singh shooting up the world help them?" He wasn't arguing, he was gathering information.

"Chaos. Governments in disarray for L Corp to 'influence', crowds of frightened civilians willing to pay for the reassurance *Your World* offers."

He bent back like I was carrying an infection. "So that's it? The bad guys are tearing up the world to make a buck?"

"Hard to believe, isn't it?"

"Well, no, not really—they're security contractors, that's what they do. How reliable's your sourcing on all this?"

"Avery and Volkov."

"What do you mean? They *told* you?"

"At the Black Cube. They were trying to recruit Max, just before he set the air on fire and we escaped."

Awkward pause here—I guess I shouldn't have expected anything else—but not a long one, really. "And what about Vlad Saminov?" he asked.

"Who?"

"Vladimir Saminov—from Amsterdam. He knew all about the mindbenders. He was one, apparently."

"Never heard of him."

Cornwell got up and traipsed back and forth. I'd completely forgotten the tapas place. Then he sat down and laughed. "Son, as a source, you're worth a load of nothing."

"Why? I just gave you—"

"Yesterday, I get hauled into an interrogation room and there's Pietr Volkov, straight from his guest appearance on all the morning shows, wanting to know where I get off casting aspersions at his fine organization, which just saved the Western world. He threatens my job and pension and asks if I want to spend the rest of my life in a sanitarium. I don't give in but it's five hours of my life I'll never get back.

"And as soon as I get upstairs, my station chief calls: 'Congratulations! Your transfer came through! Sun, surf, shrimp on the barbie!' I didn't ask for a transfer. I'm in the center of the New Europe, in the middle of the action; why would I want to get exiled to the south of nowhere? With two guards to make sure I actually show up? 'Here's your hat; what's your hurry'?"

"Well, now you know why."

He wasn't happy. He even jiggled the bottle of booze again, which was proof of desperation. "This is a tough sell, son," he told me. "L Corp is the favored child and you are a dangerous terrorist, certified by all the networks. Washington *loves* their dangerous terrorists and their favorite children. They get to protect Mom and Pop from the terrorists and reward the favorite children, who reward them back when they run for re-election." He wagged a finger. "But they only love you as long as they can stick a scary label on you and be done with it. They do *not* want to have to explain to the public that the terrorists can read your mind and move the refrigerator to the other side of the house without touching it. So your information is worthless." He took a breath. "Officially."

I'm Army—I knew what *that* meant. "What about *un*officially?"

He glanced at the mirror again. "Right now, L Corp is in the driver's seat and I'm in exile. Not to mention their chief screwing me to the wall the other day. So if you had information that could, oh, lets say, nail *them*, I could make sure it reached the right pair of ears." He gave me the stare—I felt the back of my head get warm, not hot like Max made it but at least summer's-day-warm. "But that means *proof*. Not Mirandized court-of-law evidence but something that proves that they're breaking the trust about something crucial, something national-security important. You haven't got that at the moment, do you?"

"No."

"And you've never heard of Vlad Saminov?" By now, I figured this was a trick question—I just shook my head. "Well then, I'm still taking the paycheck and swearing the oath." He read the puzzled look on my face. "Which means I have to take you in and hand you over to the Agency for debriefing." He handed me a business card—just his name and a phone number—and his voice dropped. "Unless something happens that makes that impossible, of course. But you're gonna have to figure that out on your own."

My turn to check the mirror. Guard One was only a few feet away, staking out the front door, eyes up and down the road out front. Guard Two was watching the rowboats and barges moving up and down the canal behind the kitchen.

The building, now that I was paying attention, surely wasn't built to be a restaurant. The canal in back would have been a great view but almost the whole back wall was covered with cabinets holding shelves and plates. The only light that way came from below—the stairs the cooks used, carrying bags of flour and bowls of vegetables up and down to the kitchen, were bathed in shimmery, watery sunlight. I leaned around in my chair and made out the hulls of two or three rowboats tied up behind.

"Was that a sound out front?" I asked Cornwell mildly. "A menacing sound?"

"What kind of sound would that be?" he asked lightly back.

"What kind of sound would spook your boys?" I asked. "Just for a second."

His eyes said he understood and a second later, I heard a thump against the front wall that made me flinch. I saw his boys come to attention instantly.

"What was that?" I said, jumping to my feet. Cornwell pointed out a side window. "Over there!" and Guard One jumped to check it out.

I grabbed a bottle of disinfectant off the kitchen shelf and chucked it as hard as I could through the front window the guard had just vacated. It shattered with a crash and startled cries from passersby.

Guard Two came running from the back. Everybody saw the windows explode but nobody understood yet where the blast had come from. The guards dove against the front wall, pistols out and eyes scanning the street for attackers.

I slid down the kitchen steps full-speed, feet in mid-air, burning my hands on the rails. I heard Cornwell and the guards yelling (*What do you see? That way! Where are they?*) while the staff started barging down the stairs behind me and squeezing through the back windows to the boats in a panic.

I climbed into a boat alongside the cook, cast off the line and pushed away, ducking low under the rail. It occurred to me from his expression that maybe I wasn't the first guy he'd seen on the run—maybe not the first one that week.

As we hit the middle of the canal, I sneaked a peek and there was Cornwell sticking his head out the back window. I heard him yell, "He's not here - he *must* be out front!"

I stuck to the floor until the current took us through a veil of reeds, then lifted myself up onto the seat and took over rowing, pulling for the harbor and the *Babu* and Pulau Patang, wherever that was.

aryana singh: the interview

The following is a transcript of an interview conducted yesterday by our reporter Billy Szymczyk with former Indian Premier Aryana Singh at a sanitarium outside New Delhi.

BS: How goes your recovery?

AS: I'm afraid my diagnosis would differ from my doctor's. I feel alright most of the time. I've been through a shock and I don't deny it has unsettled me. But I don't believe I need to be held against my will.

BS: Is that happening?

AS: Absolutely. I've asked to be released for weeks. I demanded it for four or five days. Now, I've given up. No one answers me. No one even speaks to me, really. I'm surprised you were allowed inside.

BS: I'm not sure I've been 'allowed.' We'll find out the next time a nurse comes by.

AS: I see. Well, take my story out of here because I have no belief I will get out any other way. I am quite sane, that is the first and most important point. That said, I am not entirely clear what happened to me.

BS: What do you remember? We know you were the subject of an assassination attempt; that had to be diff—

AS: I was not. This is incorrect. I found myself standing in the Head of State Box at the concert with a pistol in my bag, being told to kill the other leaders in the box.

BS: The doctors say you're hearing voices.

AS: That is also entirely incorrect. The day of the concert was the one and only time I have 'heard voices' in my entire life. It was a chorus of voices; it appeared the morning before the concert. It told me—ordered me—to shoot the others and was accompanied by a repetitive image of me in the box, pulling the gun from my bag and firing wildly in all directions.

BS: The gun that was found in your purse, that was yours?

AS: I don't own a gun.

BS: Well, then where did it come from?

AS: I've no idea. (Pausing) I see your point. That is interesting. (Thoughtful for a moment) Actually, I'm not being entirely accurate about hearing voices. I heard that chanting chorus beginning the night before the concert, telling me to shoot. And then there was another at the concert, a voice that resisted, that strengthened my resolve not to. And that voice, I will admit having heard for years.

BS: Whose voice was that?

AS: (laughing) My own. We all hear our own voice, speaking to us, don't we? There may have been another, mingled with it, making it stronger. (shrugs) What I know is that I did not wish to hurt anyone. I'm not crazy. I should not be here.

BS: The doctors say—

AS: The doctor's aren't making the decisions here. At least not where I'm concerned. Hang around a bit after we talk and see for yourself. They ask me questions but they don't listen to my answers. I watch what they're writing—I can read upside-down, it's a useful skill for a politician. They write down answers I don't give them.

BS: You think the doctors are conspiring against you? Why would they do that?

AS: Listen, I understand how crazy this sounds. I don't think they're against me—they're doctors. I think perhaps they are also hearing voices, telling them what they're hearing and what they should be writing down. Possibly those same voices I was hearing the day of the concert.

At this point, the conversation was interrupted and our reporter ejected from the grounds. The facility deny he was ever present there. This newspaper, however, stands by its transcript, which is available for screening by any responsible authority.

reunion 3
December 2008

Darwin, Australia

This isn't the way I want to see Kate again.

Goldie and Tat Man place her in the cage and Tat Man gives her a shot. She coughs and twitches and wavers in the general direction of conscious. Before she can do anything, Straw Hat throws a switch and sparks fly from the turbine. The air charges and the hair stands up on the back of my neck. The cage purrs with the power of this magnetic field and I see the field envelop the cage, the skeletal bits tighten up and lock into place and suddenly the rickety thing looks like it was carved out of stone.

Kate revives—she flexes against the energy field but it doesn't budge. She tries to stick her hand between the braces; the field warps and sparks and she pulls her hand back in a hurry.

Volkov drags a chair around in front of her, wearing his white-noise sunglasses. He has a fancier pair than the other guys—it's good to be king.

"I'm very disappointed seeing you two again," he says to the pair of us, like the teacher supervising detention. He glances at his watch. "I've got ten minutes. Let's talk about the future. At the moment, you don't have one. There's no place you can go on Earth without being recognized, hounded, arrested or murdered. If I shoot you here and now, no jury would convict me." Dramatic pause. "On the other hand, you might find my situation interesting. A man arrived in Darwin this morning. We've been looking for him for several days. We should have had him a week ago but someone took their eyes off the ball."

Straw Hat shoots him a dirty look. "He's close, I can sense him. He's carrying information that could endanger people around the world. We will find him, that's not in doubt. But time is an issue and it turns out he's blocking us—and successfully. We have to find him. You could help."

"You killed Dave Monaghan, you killed Tauber, you killed Kate's father. Why would we help you?"

Volkov's no fool—he ignores me and focuses on Kate.

"You've had six months to think since Rome. Here you are, with very few options and where's Max? He told Soldier here (gesturing at me) to meet him—I assume he told you the same. So where is he? You're a smart young woman. I'm offering you a way out of the prison he's put you in. Maybe you're—wisely—coming to the conclusion that Max serves his own agenda and that what serves him does not serve you. "

"We don't need you," I jumped in. "We've stayed out of your clutches for six months."

"You've stayed out of my *way* for six months! You showed your face for thirty seconds today and here you are, tied to a chair!" He turns his attention back to Kate. "I run a major multinational corporation, with interests and projects—and powerful friends—all over the world. We can shelter you from the troubles of the world."

"Like you," Kate says. "You're trouble" and I have to smirk.

Volkov doesn't blink. "It's your choice," he says blandly.

He motions and the door behind us opens again. This time, they drag in a bulky Aboriginal woman in a flowered housedress and an Aboriginal guy around my age, a little shorter but real muscled.

Kate straightens up so fast, she hits the ceiling of her cage. "Dolores! Rafael!"

"Of course," Volkov continues, "in real life, the choices you make have consequences." He pulls a gun from under his jacket and shoots Rafael at point-blank range. Kate gasps and a moment later, swarms of bats slash down from the ceiling, swirling through the air overhead, while snakes slither out of the floor tiles and wrap themselves around the guards' legs.

"Stand your ground! They're illusions!" Volkov yells—easy for him to say. The old woman tries to reach Rafael but the guards hold her back.

Volkov leans into Kate's cage. "I was careful about shooting him. Help me—and don't waste time—and we'll patch him up before he bleeds to death." She stares without answering and he shrugs. "Landau, do nothing until you hear from me." He points at me. "This one's yours. Let's go." The guards grab the cage and carry Kate away. She looks fierce and the cage trembles, though I don't see her moving inside. The door closes behind them and the place settles into quiet.

Straw Hat—Volkov called him Landau—surveys the mess he's been left. The old woman stares bullets at him but he ignores her. Instead, he advances on *me* with razor in hand.

I've been in combat—I'm over the whole bravery thing. I'm tied to the chair but I'm pulling way back into the cushions. The blade gleams bright as it darts straight for my eye and I close it instinctively, not that it'll make any difference in the end.

And then I hear that sizzling noise I remember from Florida and when I look up, Blondie is sprawled over the table, Landau is twitching on the floor and Tat Man is cutting the plastic ties from around my wrists. A familiar voice says, "Get into Blondie's jumpsuit. I'll take care of Rafael."

I look up, startled by the sight of Tat Man's brown eyes flickering, going blurry and refiring grey a moment later. Those grey eyes look awful familiar...

His face now somehow morphs, changing shape, until, all at once, I'm staring at Max Renn. All the clumsy missed hits and bad arm angles Tat Man threw at me suddenly make sense.

"You were shit for a torturer," I tell him.

"You're welcome," he says.

that man
July 2008

South China Sea

The Butcher was the first one I knew for sure.

Peeking around the door of a butcher shop, a lot more of him reflected in the mirror behind than I saw head-on. Long thin face, Shiite beard, mole on his cheek. I saw the bullet come out the back of his head just before the mirror shattered.

The Baker was next, not that I really know what he did for a living but Baker follows Butcher and, in my dreams, the two of them always come together. In my dreams, in my dreams, every night in the red skies and hazy clouds of my dreams.

He was a doughboy so maybe that's why he's the Baker, doughy and waddling between burnt-out cars and bits of crumbling wall. At first, we thought he was just another raghead with a rifle so we took a couple shots and missed him out of indifference—there were lots of higher-priority targets at the moment. Then somebody called out he had an RPG—could he have had one stashed under a car in the street, who knows? Soon as anyone sees an RPG, the whole squad stops squawking and starts shooting.

But it was my shot that got him. I saw it in the scope. I felt the kick in my shoulder, saw him twitch and then the splatter. I can see it in my head right now. There are plenty I don't know for sure but him and the Tailor, I know.

And the Artist, him too, a boy's face and wide-open eyes, twitchy scared and awestruck in a real battle, scraggly hair on his chin and wearing a beret, who knows where that came from? He had a girl's shoulders.

All three of them lingered. I saw the light go out of their eyes as I ran over to take their positions or sometimes even before I pulled the scope down. It was only seconds but they saw the future, knew what was coming. Thank God they were dead before I had to move on—I didn't want to have to finish any of them off while they were watching.

Tauber's eyes were like theirs. When Marat's lightning found him, as he dropped to the ground in front of us, all the life in Tauber got trapped in his eyes. I saw them flare up real strong just before they went out for good.

How could all those eyes look so alike, the raghead rebels and the alky mindbender? Am I just mashing them together in my dreams? Do I not want to remember the difference—or is it that Dead overwhelms whatever kind of alive you once were?

I'm not going out that way. I'm not fucking flaring up one second before I die. I'm going to be a fucking fireball for whatever's left. There's a million ways to live, but only one kind of dead.

Over. Done. The End.

~~~~

I came to in a blur, in an unfamiliar place, haunted by green, deep green, ocean green, moss green, dappled and mottled, shiny and porous like the skin of a whale, like I'd been swallowed by a great fish. Water slapped at the sides, the smell of brine leeched in from everywhere, the walls bobbed and squirmed as my eyes tried to focus. You could feel ponderous momentum fighting some endless deep friction. I'm fucking Jonah, in the belly of the beast, kidnapped to prophesy to people I don't want to save.

And then I rolled over and felt the bedroll below and the ship came back to me.

Not that you could really call the Babu a ship—it's sorta like calling McDonalds a restaurant. The Babu was a filthy scow, groaning and leaking at every rivet, cabin doors that couldn't shut proper because the whole boat was out of frame, coughing and spitting between spurts of power, ferrying dirty laundry, the finest counterfeit electronics and radioactive chicken feathers around the South China Sea on a twice-weekly basis, manned by a crew who failed the audition to be pirates.

I pulled on my clothes and backpack and clanked up the narrow metal steps to the foredeck. Endless sunrise, water in every direction and nothing else. Well, almost nothing else—a toothpick with a parasol rose from the horizon dead ahead.

I heard it long before I could see it—headbanger music, heavy metal, power chords and shrieking vocals. Metallica. Whitesnake. Twisted Sister. Plus Tupac, ludacris, Outkast. All this at the same time, mind you, blaring out of speakers set every three feet across a quarter mile. From the middle of the sea, it sounded like:

%XZT$!Y!!!ZGRWLX*#XXRZ!!FFX#XZ%!!SS*M^@!Z$!%!!XW!!!!

It took an hour for the parasol to reveal itself as a huge tree looming over a leafy-topped island still way in the distance, with a sharp cliff on one side and jungle on the other, a steroidal pineapple popping out of the water.

I fingered Max's note: *Take the slowest ship you can from Singapore to Pulau Patang. Find a room on the second floor with a view of the beach. Drink tuak. Walk the beach twice a day. You will be contacted.*

As we got near, it became clear Patang was hell on stilts. The island remained wildest jungle—no one had tried to tame it. The town was a forest of tiny houses jutting out into the water on three jetties, thrown together from loose timber and sheets of tin, connected by narrow plank walkways with no railings, the whole works as rickety as a Louisiana toolshed. The place looked thrown together in three months and built to last as long.

Unwashed children of three or four dangled out of windows over a two-story drop to the sea. The plankboard walkways were jammed with bicycles and families with their every possession stuffed into shopping carts. It was a Dickens-slum-on-the-sea, at least it would have been but for the cellphones at every ear and the full-zoot satellite dishes sprouting like mushrooms from the rooftops.

A lineup of tankers waited at anchor for the privilege of tying up to the dock. Trylon Energy—the World Runs on Us, a sign proclaimed over a gate separated from the town by steel pillars and razor wire. On the far side, a tall complex of chemical tanks and suspended pipelines rose into the inland jungle. An unruly mob crowded the gate, clamoring for work, though no hiring seemed to be going on at the moment. Guys kept jumping out of line to detour to the bars or the happy ending houses (plenty of both close by), returning with bottles to be shared with three or four friends—all this at eight in the morning.

I sat a few hours in a coffee bar, taking the gist. Helicopters fluttered off an octagonal pad on Trylon's side of the wire, derelict boats puttered out from the smaller jetties to the big ships at anchor, returning with food, booze (contraband in nearby Muslim countries) and other, even more slippery commodities. Packages openly circulated that, in size and handling, suggested contents smokable, snortable or injectable. In broad daylight, guns and explosives were shipped and received in ones, twos and stacks. Friendly women in accidental wardrobes climbed onto the ships and returned to dock with pathetic speed.

Well, if you literally had to get lost—and surely that was the plan—this was the place for it. If you wanted to work, you could, but if you preferred to hang out for months at a time with no visible means of support, nobody was asking questions. You didn't have to worry about flouting the law—there didn't appear to be any law to flout.

So now what? What next? *Find a room on the second floor with a view of the beach. Drink tuak. Walk the beach twice a day. You will be contacted.* The upstairs rooms didn't seem any different from the downstairs but the note was explicit. When the third apartment I checked out looked exactly like the other two, I offered dollars— hard currency—a month in advance and didn't haggle the rent. The owners kicked out their ground floor tenant on the spot and moved their few belongings downstairs in order to give me the second floor. I almost felt guilty until I watched the old tenants take up residence in an empty apartment three doors down—and work out the rent when the owners returned home that evening, chattering in several unfamiliar languages.

I stuffed packets of money in the walls and floor and, while I was at it, Max's note spilled out of my pocket and I stopped dead staring at it: *Drink tuak. Walk the beach twice a day. You will be contacted.* Not a word about the second-floor apartment! If I hadn't had such trouble finding one, I would have wondered if I'd made up the whole thing. So Max could not only read minds, he could move ink around on a page at a distance. I suppose it was a superpower but not one that would make it into the movie trailer.

I walked the short stretch of beach a couple times. It wasn't exactly thrilling—dirty sand piled with garbage, out to the end of the bay. I went back later for a spectacular golden-ball-melting-into-the-horizon-over-the-dirty-sand-and-garbage sunset. It was the first moment I'd had since Dave died to relax and take my own temperature.

Once you'd intentionally gotten lost, what came next? Was it naïve to think there even *was* a next?

When Max and I started traveling together, I was, like the song says, comfortably numb. I didn't speak to anyone, I couldn't remember anything before Iraq. Max brought me back into the world, in the same way that a hurricane comes into the world. Now the hurricane was over and I was alone with all the doubts and fears I'd carefully numbed out. What I really feared was that, without Max around, they'd take me over again.

Which made the next of Max's commandments easy to take: *Drink tuak.* I sat in what was supposed to be a coffee shop, filling styrofoam cups out of a dark brown bottle that looked like slime off a roadbed. I repeated *alcohol kills germs* to myself with every sip like a mantra.

And then I got lost for several days. It might have been weeks maybe, I stopped counting. I'd wake up, crawl into a bottle and stay there until I passed out. And do it again the next day. There may have been a few chemistry experiments mixed in at the beginning but not for long. I saw two guys get rolled and carried aboard ship with no ability to fight back and after that, I stuck to bartenders I knew and paid well for bottles opened in my presence.

I renewed my hair dye and let my beard grow and after a few days in that sun, my skin was as red as my hair. I called myself Donal, not that it mattered. Pulau Patang was a place where names weren't used much and you never expected the ones you knew to be real.

I was feeling sorry for myself, basically. Max was a loner when I first met him, preferring the company of herons and crocodiles to people. Dave's murder brought him out of hiding and, now that I knew who he was, I couldn't blame him if he just wanted to go back into hiding now and stay there. He'd done right by me, found me a place where I wouldn't be noticed. But it left me feeling abandoned, afraid of who I would become, left alone with myself for too long.

My answer was to do my chores and bury my fears. He told me to drink and walk the beach so I made that my job and went at it serious. It got pretty comical at times, cataloguing the hypodermics and shell casings that came in on the tide every morning, along with wallets, underwear, toupees and the slime that could have been discarded food or evidence of homicide.

A large part of the island's population basically lived under tin roofing propped against a tree on the beach for weeks at a time. Every once in a while, someone would hit a winning streak at one of the gambling dens and move into a floating apartment until the money and/or the luck ran out. The rest of the strip functioned as a kind of ever-changing flea market and the whole village—even well-off folks with their own shack on one of the jetties—stopped by regularly to check the place out. Who doesn't love a bargain?

There was a guy with a George Foreman grill turning out real good fried dough cakes and dangerous homemade booze (I had a sample, for scientific purposes). There was the guy who sold "Love in the Age of Cholera" in twelve languages—I never found out where he got the books but he never ran out of them and he never had any other title to sell. There was a Buddha seller—brass, plastic and jade Buddha's, solemn ones and happy ones, fat and thin ones, along with statues of Ganesh, a Hindu elephant head with multiple arms who specialized in clearing obstacles (a really useful god on an island full of people high as a kite, trying to remember what identity they were using today). There was a guy who sold pieces of things—outboard motor shafts, windshield wiper arms, steering wheels, cinder blocks, plastic tubing, doorknobs, shower heads—just the sort of thing to elevate your shack on the jetty in this pretend city.

I was hanging on the beach, in an entertaining haze, when the first battleship dropped anchor.

It wasn't a big ship by military standards, just way bigger than anything I'd ever seen, a serious cannon on the front deck and a rotating gun platform in the rear. It was alarming at first but, even in my condition, I realized nobody was sending a battleship to get me.

"Fucking Vietnamese," grumbled the Buddha seller, a wiry coot with a bit of white hair, a Jimi Hendrix t-shirt and black pants a little too short for his legs.

The crew marched off the ship in white uniforms that had never seen a day's work and stood at attention for maybe five minutes, raising their flag on the pole in the middle of the jetty. While they did, everything stopped. Nobody moved on the beach, the talking and music from the bars died off. I could actually hear the birds, which proves I'm not making it up. It was like the clock was ticking but no time passed.

Of course, the minute they were back out in the harbor, hip-hop blared from the speakers, booze flowed like water and all was right with the world. For about ten minutes. That's when I spied the other battleships—bigger ones.

"They're coming back?"

"Fucking Chinese," the Buddha seller spat.

Three ships in this convoy, though only one actually entered the harbor. Way more destructo-looking than the Vietnamese, yellow-tipped missiles on swivel mounts sprouting from every deck. The thing docked with sailors standing by the ropes, showing they didn't intend to stay long. A party of marines in steel helmets and blue-and-white camo swept onto the dock to tear down the Vietnamese flag and run their own up instead. Then they stomped down to a fishing barge tied up at the end of the jetty and grabbed three crewmen by the neck. The youngest put up a stink until a marine shoved his rifle butt into his stomach. They dragged the three of them onto the ship, which sailed into the channel between Pulau Patang and Narua, the only other chunk of land in sight, ran a Vietnamese fishing boat aground against the reef and raised their flag there, too.

"Can they do that?"

"Who fucking stop them?" the Buddha seller said.

"Isn't this Indonesia?" Indonesia was all around us on the map.

"This nothing. Nobody fucking owns."

"Nobody wants it?"

"Everybody fucking want it! China, Vietnam, Brunei, fucking Phillippines—everybody want!" He threw his hands up and motioned for me to follow. We climbed a little rise and he pointed out over the sea. It took a while to pick out what he was showing me. Maybe two miles out to sea sat a pair of rocks just breaking the surface of the water, about half a mile apart. Somebody—the Chinese flag was flying there at the moment but it was flying everywhere at the moment—had built a landing strip on a steel mooring, joining the two rocks.

"That's ridiculous," I said.

"Not ridiculous—Money. Power. Oil."

I flashed back to Iraq. Amazing how oil always seems to connect the dots.

Patang was returning to its usual tumult, having used up a days worth of real-world tension. I resumed my mid-day walk, trudging to the end of the beach and back for the fourth or fourteenth or four hundredth day in a row. I wore sandals, having learned that shoes or even sneakers were impossibly heavy in the sand but I was clomping in the sandals all the same. Not that it mattered—I was just putting in my time. What was there to see that I hadn't seen already?

The Buddha seller was packing his statues into big oilskin bags. "What fucking with you?" he demanded.

"What do you care?"

"Walking back and forth, morning and night—where you fuckin' going?"

"Nowhere fast, that's where."

He mirrored my prune face. "There a right way to go nowhere," he said, "but you don't know it."

I turned to start another pass but those words just kept echoing in my head. I reached into my pocket and pulled out Max's note, knowing somehow exactly what I was going to see. It now read in total: *You have been contacted.*

BOOK TWO

alpha test

Sclessin, Belgium

This was the place to send someone to hell, Landau thought.

A cement factory, a blast furnace and twelve rail lines converged along a mud-brown river—in late July heat, it felt and smelled like war, or at least Landau's conception of what war might smell like.

And here were his hellions, a scrum of homeless men who lived under the trestles and made a bit of a living collecting scrap metal and reselling the waste chemicals that gathered downwind of the furnace.

Landau switched off the pickup and waited until he found two who worked as a team. They had a bleary banter he could tune into, focus relentless focus on the sound of the voices, riding the sound until he isolated the shared frequency and suddenly they were walking over to the car all friendly-like, more than a little confused as to why.

Skeevy-looking dudes up close, greasy-haired in clumps and old scars on cheeks and foreheads that hadn't healed properly; one lumpy and long-haired (the Lion) and one long and bowing at the waist and matted (the Weasel).

Landau got out of the car and waxed eloquent about the significance of Jay Z as an entrepreneur. The Lion returned a gravel-throated harangue offering him a deal on the chemicals, which apparently could be sold to the store under the trestle and warning him off the scrap metal, which they intended to sell themselves. Landau spoke English and the hellions spoke Flemish, rendering the entire conversation absurd—particularly the fact that the two locals never seemed to notice.

Which proved Landau had them both dialed in and under control.

"Why don't you dudes load your bags into the back?" he told them, gesturing at the bay in the back of the pickup.

"We do no such thing—not without being paid," said the Weasel, grabbing the end of the bag and helping the Lion hoist it into the bay. "We do nothing unless we get paid first. Thinks he's getting the best of us!"

"And the scrap metal too," Landau told them.

"Not a chance," Weasel continued, all this in Flemish, as the two of them began throwing the scrap metal in over the side rails.

"This is our territory. You want something from here, you pay, big-time, you pay before we pick up one a bottle cap!" He said this while helping the Lion load a car fender that made the tiny rental truck sag under the weight.

Without Landau doing anything more than staring at him, the Weasel said, "That's more like it!" and mimed counting out bills into the palm of the Lion's hand while the other man looked on, mystified, knowing something was wrong and somehow unable to say so.

Landau held to the frequency, humming the damn thing to keep himself on-target. He sighed as the Lion turned to him, awaiting further instructions. Just for safety sake, he willed the other man to pull off one of his gloves and chew on the end of a finger.

They were like marionettes, standing there, will erased, thoughts silenced, nowhere to go and nothing to do, waiting for an animal purpose to be set toward. Landau's breathing quickened. He knew how fast the worm could turn if his control lapsed—both of them outweighed him by fifty pounds or more and the street had left them mean and hungry.

Now was the time. Landau pulled De Jogt's coil from his pocket and slipped it over the Lion's right hand. The pug watched him do it without argument. Landau slipped the control box over the man's belt and connected the wires to the poles on the end of the coil.   The air crackled and Landau's hair stood on end.

Shit! He'd caught them both on the same frequency—how did he send a message to the Lion without sending it also to the Weasel, who wasn't going to like this one. He sent orders—*Move your right hand up! Wink with the left eye!*—and both obeyed. This was no good.

He decided to take a chance. He settled into the driver's seat just in case but left the door open to get a clear view. Then he focused on the two men and imagined a moment of true camaraderie and brotherhood, the kind he'd seen many times in the movies. He visualized the way it looked—the way they looked, the marionettes on this shrieking, stinking hellish stage in front of him—and the way it would feel to feel that way about someone else. He did his best to approximate that kind of feeling, until he could see in their eyes and expressions that he had gotten through.

And then he nodded and the Lion turned to his friend and put his arms around him.

It was hard to understand how there could be a bright flash in such a fiercely bright place but somehow, there was. The sky went so white as to render all else dead black and a smell like burning rubber filled the air. Landau heard the crackle in the air and there must have been some heat but it was already too hot to know for sure.

A moment later, the Weasel was on the ground, twitching wildly. The Lion trudged around screaming, blood spurting from a bloody stump where his right hand had been. The blood pooled into the clouds of chemicals floating off the furnace and the Lion, remembering just enough, cried out in grief and guilt at the sight of his murdered friend.

Landau tossed the bag of chemicals and pushed the fender from his trunk, dropped into the driver's seat and pulled away. He flicked on the recorder on his phone and dictated:

"Okay, this didn't do it. This one gave a flash of light and a bang you could hear all over town. And it still blew the shooter's arm off—let's see if you can't solve that. I like the way you had it the first time. Stealth. Spooky. Why can't you just go back to where you were?"

in dreams 1

Dreamland

Renn knew this room all too well, low-ceilinged, a maze of pipes and conduits painted over a hundred times, odd assemblages of test equipment and forgotten toys and games, the light looming perversely at odd angles, shadows in all the wrong places. He recognized familiar voices murmuring in Russian, close enough to be heard, far enough away to elude understanding. The scene was as familiar as his own breathing—the training laboratory in Novosibirsk. He'd spent a decade and more in the stunted air of that place.

He turned and stretched out his senses, seeking confirmation of something he shouldn't have known—that it was all a dream. He slept so little that his dreams came mostly in fragments, disjointed surreal feints of memory—but there was something different about this one.

Where were the thoughtstreams, the buzz of voices that filled every room? What happened to the smells—paint, formaldehyde and urine, constant companions in the lab and nowhere to be found here. There were no motes of dust in the air, the odd white patch of light that always showed in the far corner wasn't there. The whole thing was static, dead…a picture of a space instead of being in the space.

Underneath it all, a cold chill told him these were not just memories, not just a dream—and not solely his.

Someone else was out there watching.

He could make out a voice, just barely, somewhere way below the surface, a murmur that called to him. And somehow, even though he couldn't make out anything it was saying, he knew that whoever it was, they had never been in the lab. That was why the air was dead, why all the smells and some of the details were off. They were making it up from a photograph or someone else's mental picture—and not doing a particularly brilliant job of it.

He shifted and found himself tangled in the sheets and retreated back, willingly, to the dream—but this time with his own agenda.

Was he leaking thoughtstreams? Had someone defeated his blocking? If so, why hadn't they attacked? Who would find a way to break into his consciousness—even if the consciousness was the farthest they'd gotten—and not finish the job?

A moment later, he heard the voice, the subterranean voice, speaking directly to him: *Everybody has a place they call Home.*

Everything was upside down now. Renn was swimming in the bed, grasping for control. He had to know—how could he find out?

A moment later, he populated the lab with a crowd of teenagers, kids he remembered from the Project, a few who had died before the place crumbled, the whole group circulating in giggles and asking questions and packing the place the way he remembered it—and immediately, he felt uncertainty and discomfort at the other end. That in itself was half an answer. *Pick out the survivors*, he thought—but just to himself, just a private conversation.

He waited almost a minute without receiving an answer and sighed with relief.

It meant: 1) while there *was* a two-way connection with his visitor, 2) whoever he was, he wasn't reading Renn's thoughts. He had seen the kids Renn added to the dream but hadn't been able to read their identities or their significance to him. He hadn't heard the question Renn has asked himself.

Who *was* this kid? It was a kid, he was sure. Something in the voice and something in the approach spoke of recklessness, daring without judgment. He was formidable, that was certain— but spottily trained. He'd contacted Renn at a distance by inhabiting a dream—those techniques were deep knowledge, but he couldn't create a true two-way connection, apparently. Could he be from Pietr? Volkov would have been more thorough, if only out of paranoia. But where else could he come from?

Now Renn sent a thought in the clear, actually flashed it openly to his visitor. *You think I'll talk to anyone who creeps into my dreams?*

Isn't that exactly what you're doing? the voice answered and disappeared.

Renn kicked off the sheets and sat up, drenched in sweat. The squirming sensation of another mind inside his own lingered. Invasive. Seductive. Creepy. A taste of your own medicine, he thought. I've certainly dished it out enough times.

But there was no comfort in his drenched t-shirt and scattered sheets, in the moonlit room still teeming with ghosts. This kid was good and he hadn't come on a whim.

Whoever he was, he'd be back.

the secret in the silence

Reykjavik, Iceland

"Arthur, you're full of it! If you hadn't said—"

"I didn't say any such—"

"I have a vivid memory of you, standing right there, saying—"

Renn couldn't stand another moment.

"Nonsense!"

"Excuse me?" The face was young, British, upper-class surely, very well-educated without necessarily being terribly bright. Raymond, sixteenth Earl of Whatchamacallit, the half-wit brother. One-eighth wit, more likely.

"It's complete nonsense. Memory doesn't exist, not the way you're thinking of it. Memory is a story we tell ourselves over and over."

"I'm sorry but—"

"It changes over the years and with circumstances, depending on what you need to hear, whatever spin you're putting on prior circumstances or future hopes. It's a filter and a buffer. Your memory being vivid carries no certainty of its being accurate."

"Is this scientific?"

Based on thousands of hours of listening to boobs like you think. "You can't even agree on her eye color," Renn concluded, walking away.

"Green."

"Blue!"

The world was full of ghosts, ghosts everywhere among the living.

Annika, who sold diamonds and expensive watches in Copenhagen, was staring at the boy at the waffle stand, in the plaid shirt and shaggy hair: *He's so like Marco, the one who wouldn't leave.* Suddenly, she was at her bedroom window again, Marco banging at the bolted door downstairs as she threw his things, one by one, out the third-story window. He had great taste—she admired the shirts as they unfurled in the wind and fluttered down among the passing cars.

Jules from Manchester pulled the guitar off his back and strummed a tune for a young woman from Adelaide, a redhead who kindled memories of the bus driver last summer—his head filled with the bus driver's laughter and her (slightly off-key) singing. Even when Adelaide here joined in, he held onto the sound of the bus driver's voice mixed into the chorus—he would never hear that song without her.

The sun slid through purpling clouds just above the horizon line—it would return in less than three hours. Twenty-one hours of sunlight a day, July in the Arctic Circle.

If not for a broken strap on his backpack, Renn would already be gone, hiking into the barren interior: tundra, moss, rivers and ice floes, even in summer. After the first twenty minutes, the riot of voices in his head would fade into one of the few accessible places on the planet where the only thoughts he'd hear would be his own.

Here and now, the crowd did what people do in crowds—they worked hard at having a good time. Every open door blasted music into the street: trance, Eurotrash, hiphop, disco. Renn hated disco: *bum bum bum bum*. The dancers gyrated out the doors and across the cobblestones as though the center of the tiny city was a continuous parquet floor. And the music made a mashup, mulching the usual cacophony of drunken, happy, lost and hungry voices in his head:

Maybe that dress—Dave'd LOVE me in that dress. Hell, Billy wouldn't have left if I'd had that dress.

That one's got potential - Armani jacket, seriously plastered, wallet in right back pants pocket, iPhone in upper left jacket. First time he leans over the bar, I'll pick him clean...

Look at that chin. I'm getting old. I'll never find anyone...

No moment arrived self-contained. Every experience trailed associations, sounds, smells and images, the present a mere veil over all that past. Einstein said time was not linear—travel was not forward or backward but in depth—and Renn heard the proof all around him.

Loss was the glue, the bass note under every emotional chord, a drone that lingered after the high notes faded. *God, I'm fucking morose*, Renn thought and looked for any diversion.

She passed him the first time coming out of a doorway, stepping down the high steps of the Eurotrash club with two girlfriends, squabbling merrily about the best espresso place in Buenos Aires. Squabbling in French. They wobbled down the block, three thirtyish-looking women dressed for business, not tourism.

Renn took a few steps in the other direction before realizing something was very wrong.

He whirled and followed like a cat stalking a light on a wall. He'd missed her face the first time, so he rushed past them and ducked into a doorway for a second look—but, when they passed, her face was bent the other direction. On purpose? Was she aware of being watched?

Why didn't he *know*?

The distance to the corner was one of the longest walks of Renn's life. Each step, he checked and rechecked and checked again, a thousand times in half a block. By the time they stopped outside the bright crimson houseclub booming retro-disco, there was no doubt what was happening, though Renn couldn't account for it in any way.

He read no thoughts from her. *Nothing.*

She wasn't blocking him—he'd have felt the empty space. She simply issued no thoughts he could hear.

Her girlfriends thought in English, while arguing in French—he read *their* thoughts without difficulty, not that it helped in the least:

Look over the Investment instruments when we get back—

These shoes hurt—

That boy is cute (is he looking at me?)—

One last meeting with the client tomorrow afternoon—afternoon, because the whole group figures to party the night away...

His senses functioned normally—except for the girl at the center of the group.

Was it some kind of ploy? Was she toying with him? Was she even aware of the effect she had on him? This was like being handicapped, dumb and colorblind and tone-deaf.

They stepped brightly into the dim club at the corner. The *Disco* club. Renn, who *hated* disco, had no choice but to grit his teeth and follow.

Inside, he strained against the pounding bass, the strobe lights and the unrelenting static of mindstreams, trying to locate a small pocket of quiet. *I can hear everyone else without trying—how do I go about finding nothing?*

The floor was wall-to-wall dancers, grinding and strutting. Walking just didn't work, resulting in collisions and attention he didn't need. So Renn danced, or made his best approximation, which was none too good. Wagging his arms and butt, hips twitching nearly to the beat, he waddled the dance floor, scanning for a glimpse of that woman.

He did not go unnoticed. His dancing drew impolite snickering from all across the room.

He'd have paid millions to stop reading minds at just that moment.

Finally, Renn boogied to the shadows at the edge of the floor and let the crowd find other amusements.

As they did, he spied her with her girlfriends, nursing a drink at the edge of the bar, chatting up two men a bit older and surely duller:

Should I tell her I'm leaving town tomorrow?...

He's just like Richie, that scumbag. I wonder where he's staying...

Where'd he get that haircut?...

I should have worn the green blouse...

Good God, she likes Coldplay and she's just like my mother...

Everyone's thoughts but hers; Renn could hear her voice through their ears but—again—not a jot directly from her. He watched in fascination, a silent movie without title cards.

She was bewitching. She argued fiercely, laughed without inhibition and there was a kind of sad mystery to her face. She reminded him of someone, he didn't bother to figure out who — here were his own associations and suddenly he couldn't scoff at their potency. Was she world-weary or just plain tired? What did that expression mean? That shrug? *What was she thinking?*

He had to break through this wall before she disappeared. If she was a threat, he'd have to deal with her — but it didn't feel like that. Something in her beckoned to him, made him uncomfortable in the nicest way. He blundered across the floor straight up to her. The cluster of friends stopped talking, all eyes turned to him and he realized suddenly that he had no idea how to begin.

"Uh, uh—I—" was all that came out.

The girl's eyes opened wide (they were wide to begin with—and deep green). "Yes," she said immediately, standing at her stool. "Of course I will."

~~~~

Outside, it was just past midnight and finally fully dark. She navigated the narrow streets for them both, herding him between clusters of college kids and tourists looking for a second (or fourth) wind, keeping up a constant chatter the whole time.

Renn was astonished. He hadn't uttered a sensible syllable. Had he somehow taken control of her *without* reading her thoughts? The silence between them—the silence he'd longed for his whole life—was terrifying.

She'd come from London with several colleagues for an emergency conference. There was some crisis, local banks overstretched or something. It was so funny, her being in finance—Renn missed her explanation of why it was funny. He was lost in the sound of her voice, and the realization of how little attention he'd paid to such things in the past.

She made him uncomfortable but not in any way that felt sinister. She was young, which was to say, he felt old in her company. She even seemed to be having fun—maybe that was what made him so uncomfortable. *I'm the child of psychics, mystical rabbis, radical atheists and revolutionaries*, he mused. *I don't trust pleasure. And I'm fucking morose.*

At one point, he tried to break into the stream of consciousness and she shushed him to silence immediately. At that point, if there was something past Red Alert, he was there, senses stretched to the limit, checking everywhere for the stray observer, the tourist out-of-place, the too-quiet corner.

The streets grew ever quieter until she led him to a bench alongside a huge fountain, the three-story metal ball in its center spouting streams of mist. It was a reckless move, wasn't it, leading a strange man to a deserted park bench blocks from the crowds—

was she crazy? Was it a trap? He scanned every direction, searching for blocking, a hint of danger and finding nothing.

When he returned to her, looking her in the eye, she was waiting for him.

"Do you hear anything?" she said, in a way that sounded like she knew what the words meant to him. "Why are you here? What are you doing in Iceland?"

An intense wash of longing, almost nostalgia, broke over him. What was going on? These feelings were totally out of proportion to anything that had passed between them. *Had* anything passed between them? Why did he feel as if something had?

"I'm heading for the interior in the morning," he said, treading water.

"To get away from someone?" she asked and Renn shivered, a total-body quake. She was talking to him in *Russian!* His defenses went to bursting but still he felt nothing threatening—except the girl he inexplicably couldn't read.

"Just to get away," he answered. "Solitude."

"Well, that makes sense," she said. "It's the perfect place." A geyser shot comically from the center of the globe, like a whale spouting from a goldfish bowl. "I should take the bankers out there, though their stress level is nothing to yours."

Renn sat up against the bench. "What do you know of my stress level?" he demanded. "Why are you speaking to me in Russian?"

"Max!" she shrieked with laughter. The sound of his name in her voice blanked out the rest of the world. "How can you not know?" she asked, shocked and no words had ever frightened him so. "It's Zoya, Max."

Time stopped. Renn struggled to reconcile the prim banker with a mischievous little girl (with the same eyes) carrying a stuffed bear through a drab living room a million years ago.

"Zoya? That's not possible," he said. "You're—you were—"

"I was eleven. Max, the Project—the Soviet Union—ended twenty years ago." A shock of dark hair, the same eyes—the details smacked him on the forehead. "Maybe I wasn't very memorable."

"No one was memorable to me in your sister's company," Renn mumbled and saw her whole demeanor change in a second. He flushed red and retreated, as always with memories of Elena, to a state of helpless bereavement.

"I'm—I'm sorry," he stammered. "I shouldn't have mentioned her—it's thoughtless of me..."

She cut through the mood instantly. "Who are you talking to, Max? Our lives *revolved* around her. Every time we ever saw each other, we were worshiping at the temple of Elena."

He was flummoxed, suddenly tongue-tied, no idea how to respond to this. Those memories were as sacred as any he had. They were, as ever, convulsive, disruptive to any sense of peace. Elena forever threw him totally off his game.

"What?" she said. "What did you expect—a reverent mourner, all these years later? I loved her, Max, she was my big sister, you loved her, Pietr loved her, everyone who knew her loved her and wanted her. I miss her every day."

"You *resented* her," Renn said, as though he had standing as an accuser.

"Not while she was alive," Zoya admitted. "And not now — she can't take anything from me now I idolized her—who didn't? I've just come to realize over the years how much easier it is, how much freer my life has been, without her. I'm sorry—I know how that sounds."

"No—no, I—"

"Look! Look what she did to you! You're supposed to be the most dangerous man on the planet! Here you are, cowering in fear of her memory!" She shook her head. "You've never been in therapy, have you?"

"I—I—"

"Oh no, of course—you can't because you can hear everything the therapist is feeling! Another reason I'm glad not to be a mindbender!"

Renn gave up any attempt at speech. He not only had no idea what to say, he had no idea if he ever wanted to say anything to anyone ever again.

Zoya stared at him. "Right—you've been mourning her for twenty years? Now I *am* sorry."

It was almost impossible to get the words out of his mouth. "Zoya, I—I *killed* her. I have to at least—"

"God almighty! You *believe* that?"

This was too much. "I made her love me. I didn't mean to but I did—and she felt violated so she killed herself. How do I not take that seriously?"

"Says who?"

"Says...everybody."

"No, not everybody. Who told us all this story? Who was the author?"

"Well, Pietr..."

"Volkov."

"Yes."

"Who you believe everything he says because he's such a trustworthy fellow."

"I don't believe him," Renn said, finally on firm ground. "I believe her. She killed herself. That tells me everything I need to know about how she felt."

Zoya was up now, pacing around the bench. "You're amazing, the two of you."

"Who?"

"You and Volkov. The two masterminds, the center of the universe. I saw the pictures from Rome, the two of you still trying to outdo each other, just like the old days. When she died, you—both of you!—knew it had to be about you." She plopped down on the bench again, inches from him, fuming. "Elena was a sick girl. She was cutting herself and hurting herself before she ever met you. You made her as happy as anyone could. She really loved you. I was there—I knew her. She loved you, Max.

"Pietr Volkov is and always was a dick. He made up the story about you forcing her. The ones who believed it wanted to hate you anyway. But it was the story itself—the humiliation she felt from it, the judging—that's what made her kill herself."

"I—I only felt happiness from her when we were together."

"That's what she felt! If you'd been older and together all the time, if you could have set up house somewhere, maybe it would have been different. If you'd been older, maybe she would have told them to go fuck themselves, *blyad*!"

"If only I hadn't been so stupid!" Renn cried. "Blind! Egotistical! What should I have been?"

Zoya smacked him hard across the cheek, hard enough that he saw stars. "You shouldn't have been *seventeen*!"

She grabbed him by the elbows and forced him to look her in the eye.

"Max, she was my sister. My daughter is named after her. We loved her more than the rest of the world. The next time either of us sees Pietr Volkov, we'll balance the scales. But for now, *let her go*. After twenty years of therapy, I'm allowed to say that. Make a new memory. Sing a new song. Throw the world off your fucking back. Let it be *over!*"

She was in his face, fierce. "Forgive me for letting her go — and I'll forgive you for not being able to."

She bent over and kissed him on both cheeks. "Like the fucking Queen of England with her sword," she said. "I grant you dispensation for your sins, whatever the hell they are."

And suddenly, Renn's mind filled with her thoughts. He heard *everything*: her life in London, the crisis that brought her here, the husband she'd left a year earlier — and Elena. Elena was everywhere, the valiant, vain, self-dramatizing, sensitive, deluded, glamorous bitchy older sister, a role model and a warning all in one — *Elena, the root of all that I am, please don't let me go the same way.*

Everything Renn remembered — and more.

That's why I couldn't hear Zoya's thoughts, he realized. *Her mindscape, her vibrations, are so like Elena's… I blocked her out. She was something I couldn't bring myself to feel again.*

She led him out of the park now, through a cluster of modest brightly-painted homes. At the corner, she held out her arms to him but he backed away, somehow unable to take them. They moved in separate directions, as though a tide was sweeping them apart, she receding towards the crowd and the city and *life*, Renn in the other direction, tracing the edge of the bay, shielding his eyes from the ribbon of orange growing along the rim of the mountains across the bay.

Sing a new song, Zoya had said. Could revenge be a new song? Wasn't it the oldest song there was? It felt new to him at the moment, new and powerful and endless, a perennial Top Ten Golden Oldie.

Renn needed no other songs. This one fired his imagination like nothing he'd ever heard.

tribunal

Australia

Cornwell knew he'd arrived packing a warning label.

Duncan, his new station chief, had kept him at arm's length since the day he arrived, offering busy work and reducing even routine contact to written memos and group meetings. So when he cracked Cornwell's office door, all by himself, it was a bad sign.

"You've got visitors," Duncan said, motioning down the hall.

Internal Affairs—these two had the smell. The department was the ruleskeeper for a bureau of risktakers and it had a long memory. When convenient or necessary, they had the means and leisure to find an infraction on which to hang *anyone*. A lifetime of bad behavior passed before Cornwell's eyes before he had time to sit down.

"This is an informal inquiry," Thing One said immediately.

"I didn't take those chocolate bars - they jumped into my pocket," Cornwell joked without effect.

"No notes will be taken and no report will be issued," Thing One continued, putting one legal pad and two pencils (!) on the desk in front of him and the room went positively gloomy. An Internal Affairs audit was automatically serious but none so serious as the ones that never happened. "We have a report from the early morning of July 1, signed by you, concerning a deceased civilian found in a safe house."

"Not so safe, as it turns out." Was *that* what they were about? Saminov?

Thing One went on as though reading a script. "It says you discovered the body."

"That's correct."

"You notified the Station and they collected the body."

Cornwell drew a deep breath, collected himself and made a decision.

"No, I brought him in, along with Medical Officer Michael Dean. We delivered the body to the secondary holding office and called the duty officer in charge."

"You're saying the official record is a lie?"

"Not completely. We did find a dead man in the safe house." *Fuck it*, he thought. *Tell the truth, it might confound them. At very least, it'll confuse them.*

"Well, then where the hell did *this* story come from?"

"The story was concocted, as far as I can tell, by Gretschmer, the Station Chief and a couple of contractors from L Corp."

"That's hearsay," said Thing Number Two, who apparently could talk all on his own.

"Gretschmer handed me the report and ordered me to sign it. That was after five hours in an interrogation room with the two contractors, who tried to browbeat me into it first. I kept asking them for ID, which they never provided. Midway through the proceedings, we were joined by Pietr Volkov, the COO of L Corp and hero of the G8, in case you're keeping score at home."

"The COO's name is Jonathan Tapir. There is no Pietr Volkov—"

"Call him any name you want. Just don't tell me it's hearsay." Cornwell snapped. Okay, so Thing Two was L Corp. *That* was interesting, because he was pretty certain Thing One was Agency. Duncan was watching the two of them with equal disdain.

There were twelve ways Cornwell figured he could hang for the events of that evening. But he was beginning to feel that his demise (career-wise) might not be inevitable and so the old instincts came flooding back: he wasn't going down without a fight. He'd survived, more or less, the Vietnam War, the Cold War, the Grenada war, the Gulf War, the Bosnia war, the Falklands War (just coincidentally in the neighborhood at the time, of course), the Afghan war, the Iraq war and the never-ending War on Terror. He was damned if he was going to end up a casualty of the never-ending Bureaucratic War. So now he listened carefully.

"They pushed you into an inaccurate story?" Thing One asked.

"That's putting words in his mouth," Thing Two said immediately. "You went to the safe house, found a dead body and reported it to your Station. That is correct, isn't it?"

"Yes it is."

"But you brought him in yourself for a reason, I assume," Thing One followed.

"The circumstances...were...unusual," Cornwell began. *Hang back, don't offer, let them lead you. C'mon boys, tell me where you want me to go. Or maybe, tell me where you* don't *want me to go.* The tantalizing thought arose that they might not actually be after him.

"The circumstances are the circumstances. Maybe things got glossed over in the official record, that happens all the time," Thing Two said.

"We have a missing body, one operative transferred to Australia and a medical officer shipped off to Antarctica—that's a lot of gloss," Thing One answered and Cornwell suddenly glimpsed the exit door through the smoke. This was an in-house fight; all he had to do was get out of the way and let them have at it.

Two: "You can still talk to him in Antarctica."

One: "Sure, in three-minute bursts when we can arrange complete privacy and there's nothing of scientific significance happening, which is to say, never."

Two: "This is not the place for this. (returning to Cornwell) So, you know nothing about this man except that he made you an offer of information and then died in the safe room, is that right?"

This was the moment. Cornwell calmed his nerves and leaned across the table. "This is a closed hearing with no notes, right?"

"That's what I said."

"Well, in that case, I found out that Vlad Saminov was doing hot-shit project work for NATO in Amsterdam." He looked directly at Thing Two and lowered his voice. "And he had special skills you guys would particularly appreciate." As he leaned back, he felt the probe he was expecting and blocked it—and saw the look of recognition on Thing Two's face.

"Where did you get that information?" Thing One asked, trying to suppress a smirk with only middling success. Duncan, on the other hand, looked distinctly like he wanted to make travel plans.

Cornwell pulled a leather sleeve from his pocket, removed the card and dropped it on the table. "This was in his wallet: a boilerplate NATO-contractor entry card from Forus Technologies for one Vladimir Saminov, hired January 17, 2007. Clearance Level DX3, which, as a lifer, I'd never *heard* of. After a bit of checking, I found out it's a very obscure clearance for people used in top-secret research but not trusted with the clearance to know the results of their own work. Well, why would that be, I wonder?"

Thing Two was looking distinctly uncomfortable here. "Maybe because Vlad got his basic training in Soviet Intelligence, Scientific Division, in Novosibirsk back in the day."

"Wait a minute!" Thing Two sputtered to life now. "Where does this information come from? You don't have documentation to prove any of this!" Thing One was sitting up taller in his chair than before and his blood pressure seemed to be spiking as well.

"Which might be," Cornwell said, "why no one wants his untimely death to look anything but routine, even in internal agency documents."

He leaned back and took in the gloomy faces across the table. The tension level was wonderful. Duncan glanced back and forth between the two Things as though following a tennis match, but neither of them moved a muscle. Cornwell waited until they'd both thought through the implications of what he'd said before continuing.

"So the question when you walked in here was: What happened? *Now* the question is, do you really want to know? I've been in this Agency long enough to know that when they stomp on your face and ship you to Australia, you say 'Thank you very much' and stop asking questions." He turned to Duncan. "Have I mentioned any of this to you?"

"Not a word."

"I have no intention of doing so. I know what I know and you two (gesturing at the Things) don't know what you don't want to know and, I suspect, that's how we'd all like things to remain, right?" Duncan's face went sphinxlike. Cornwell nodded at the Things politely. "Anything else you need?"

"I think we can work something out," Thing One said; the two men stood and walked out.

Duncan sat staring at the table for a long moment before speaking. "Is there anything else I shouldn't know?"

Cornwell burst out laughing. "That's good!" he said, taken unawares by the man's sense of humor—and belatedly realizing there was no humor involved. "Uh, no, excuse me, nothing."

"Fine," Duncan said, exiting. "We won't talk about it anymore."

Cornwell grabbed his jacket and went for a walk. He had no awareness of where he was going, only that his legs were moving. He walked carelessly, taking no precautions against being followed. He was, however, careful not to be probed. It was a breezy day but he was sweating like a pig on a spit.

He'd dodged the bullet. He hadn't had to mention mindbenders. He'd made his point obliquely to the only other man in the room who knew what was really going on. He had retained his pension and position and all he'd done in return was promise that he'd finished investigating Vlad Saminov and had no intention of going any farther.

Which is to say, he'd lied.

the buddha seller

South China Sea

Irfunya was the Buddha-seller's name.

"Not my fucking real name," he said. "My name now."

"Vietnam," he continued, spitting. "That where I learn my fucking English, from Yankee soldiers. Work for Americans there. Then they go home, cut us off. North attacks, we got no bullets." He showed me a long welt along his back. "North kills whole family. Think they kill me too. Fucking losers. I steal a boat and paddle. Man keep moving, he don't get old."

That first night, he bundled me into the middle of a long outrigger canoe stuffed full of his statues and figurines and motioned at me to paddle while he steered with an oar at the rear.

"Where the hell are we going?" I asked ten minutes after my arms started to fall off.

"Where the hell I live," he motioned to keep paddling so I did.

I'm too damn trusting. I trusted Max Renn because he was Dave's Monaghan's friend. That worked out okay if you don't mind ending up a terrorist on every front page in the world. Once I met Irfunya, Max's note said *you have been contacted.* So now I kept paddling because Irfunya said so, even though he swore he'd never heard of Max. Max Renn's arrangements felt like other people's accidents.

Twenty minutes after I'd devised pet names for every tendon in my arm, I glimpsed lights on the horizon. I kept waiting for the land they were attached to but it never showed up. Eventually, I realized they were just bobbing on the water.

It was a floating village, about twenty huts on pontoons, lashed together and anchored in the open sea, with a coral reef that was invisible to me (I'm Army, not Navy) acting as a breakwater protecting them from the currents. Once we tied up, he introduced me to a rowdy, loud group in bright dirty clothes, broiling fish on a makeshift spit, roasting some scrawny vegetables in the ash bed below, adding rice and an abundance of tuak and we all sat down to eat together.

The meal was full of raucous laughter, some of which I could actually join in on, the conversation jittering between Tagalog, Cebuano, bursts of Portuguese, French, Dutch, and a little English. Their English was pretty approximate—they learned most of it bartering with tourists on passing cruise ships, so numbers and names were precise but not much else. Irfunya's attempts at translating were worse than guessing.

Five-year-olds were introduced to me like respected members of the community, which didn't stop them from swinging from the rafters and launching themselves into the sea like flying squirrels. And nothing stopped the sixty-year-olds from joining in to show them a thing or two, either. I drew blushes and laughter just glancing at the younger girls and watchful smiles from the older ones.

When things broke up, it turned out we were partying right alongside Irfunya's hut. It was a one-room bamboo-walled cube with a thatched roof. A pot-belly kerosene stove stood right beside a sliding partition door. A cheap-looking rack of colored beads above the stove swayed in the breeze. In the corner, a beat-up old dresser somebody threw out years ago sat on the plank floor. Waves lapped noisily at the pontoons four inches beneath the floor.

Irfunya threw the partition doors open and a breeze blew through like we were out at sea. Well, I guess we *were* out at sea but out at sea at home, if you get my drift.

I pulled my smartphone out of my pocket to check the time and found it blank. No signal, no time. Which is pretty much what it felt like out there. I'd had good bars in Pulau Patang, so if that was the last place on Earth, this was an hour and a half further.

In the morning, Irfunya held up the remains of the rice and fish, offering it for breakfast. I decided to have a look around instead—I'd have killed for toothpaste.

The village was filthy by any standard, even Patang, which is saying something. The toilet was a screened-in spot on the far end of the deck where you could hang over and do your business.

On the other hand, these people lived a totally self-sufficient life. A big metal bucket collected rain water for drinking, they caught their own fish and traded them for vegetables, fruit, rice and goat's milk on nearby islands.

When I'd returned from my five-minutes reconnoiter, Irfunya offered the same bowl of rice and fish and gestured toward the outrigger. I knew what that meant so I ate.

Twenty minutes later, I was paddling, this time middle in a crowd of canoes, two or three guys paddling in each. Boys of eight and ten I'd been introduced to the night before were now crammed between the adults and given the same responsibilities.

It was uncanny, paddling fast for at least an hour without seeing a blessed thing, not an island, a tree, a bush, not even a wave. Sea as smooth as glass and the sun pounding relentlessly overhead. You got to understand what mirages are about—after a while, you just desperately wanted to see anything at all, just so you could believe you'd moved.

And then, all at once, for no reason I could figure, the whole group stopped rowing and, three seconds later, were all in the water. The look on Irfunya's face said *C'mon, what are you waiting for?*

"What if the boats drift away?"

"That what fucking rope is for," he said and disappeared under the surface. As he went down, I saw the rope trailing him out of the boat. Apparently, he'd tied it to his waist to help him get back. From where?

I'm a good swimmer. I don't remember how or where I learned but I'm pretty cocky in the water. I dove, dove as far as I could, saw nothing and nobody, waited and waited and came back up. And waited and waited and waited for them to join me. I had time to notice the water was really clear a long way down. The boats were mighty still on the silent water. Not a soul in sight.

Nothing nowhere.

They had to come up soon. They had acted way too routine for this to be dangerous. Of course, they should have come up *already*. Already quite a while ago. Or be in big trouble. The whole group of them? They couldn't *all* be in trouble.

"Hey!" I shouted.

"Hey!" came a reply and I saw Matapang, one of the oldest in the group, pop up in a canoe a few feet away.

"Where are they?" I said, pointing all around.

He pointed straight down.

"They can't!"

He just kept pointing. Of course, Matapang was a loon. He'd spent the night before leaning against the wall with his lifeless legs, swiping at the taunting, giggling kids who kept racing around just beyond his grasp. It would be just my luck to end up stuck here with him and no idea of where the next anything was.

Then I caught a few bubbles breaking the surface. Dark shapes appeared through the haze below. They were drifting politely toward the surface, no flailing around, not much motion and a whole lot less bubbles than I expected. Were they all breathing? The bubbles seemed to be coming from just a few but they weren't always the ones moving either. Was this the mirage? I looked over at Matapang and he seemed real relaxed but that didn't mean a thing.

And then the first one breached, jerked his head upward and sucked in a couple hard breaths—not desperate, not gasping, just pulling one in after another and after about ten seconds scrambling, full of energy, over the rail into a canoe. The others followed, all of them following the same routine. I ended up the last to climb onboard, weak and faded by comparison, even to the ones I thought sure were dead. I had no idea how long they'd actually been under—I didn't start paying attention till they'd been gone way too long.

Irfunya called a tally and each man dropped a handful of coins, jewelry and coral into a heap on the floor of their canoes. By the time they were finished, the boats were heavy with loot. And then we were on our way again. As we paddled, I demanded, "How'd you do that?"

In response, over the next few days, Irfunya retaught me something I thought couldn't be taught: how to breathe.

He taught me to lie like a corpse on the surface of the water, filling my lungs with six or seven breaths, then rolling over and letting myself sink down without the exertion of swimming. *Breath quick, release slow*—that was the trick. That, plus a gargle that pumped up all the extra oxygen around the edges of the lungs so you could put it to work.

At first, it was hell. Every single stroke felt like I was going to die right *now* and I had to prove to myself over and over that it wasn't true. It wasn't easy making progress that way. Finally, one day, Irfunya just sighed and said, "This not for you. Got to be fucking made for this."

Well, you don't tell me I can't do something. I will die rather than let you be right. And that, of course, was when I started making progress because every day I survived to eat fish heads and rice again was a triumph so I started feeling good about myself. By that time, a month had probably gone by, I was at least ten pounds lighter and really needed a haircut but I was holding my breath for five minutes at a clip. Which meant I could dive about sixty feet and get back in one piece. Sixty feet is the difference between blue and black water, between seeing the surface above and having no idea if you're swimming up or down because you can't see *anything*.

I flat-out panicked once, early on, where Irfunya had to grab me to keep me from resurfacing too fast. Paddling home later, he told me that that's what happened to Matapang—he'd come up too fast and lost the use of his legs. He said it right in front of Matapang, who nodded pleasantly—nobody saw it as an excuse to feel sorry for the guy, just as a demonstration of why it wasn't a good idea.

So I was diving okay but that didn't make me productive. The other guys brought up handfuls of coins and jewels and trinkets, instead of dirt with a little bright coral glinting through. We all dove to the same place but they found the good stuff in the dark and I found nothing except scaly things that kept wanting to bite me.

"How do you see down there? Why does everyone have the magic but me?"

"No fucking magic," Irfunya replied. "You don't fucking breathe when you get here, either. Got more to learn."

"Like what?"

"Wait," he said. "Learn to wait. Learn what things *are*. Learn *that* first."

That didn't make a whole lot of sense to me but at least it suggested I'd be moving on sometime soon, which was all I had to hope for.

When we got back to the village, three very fast-looking motorboats were tied up on the open dock, two of them with very aggressive-looking bundles under wraps on the back deck, the other with a very impressive satellite dish in the same spot.

"Guntar!" somebody called out.

Guntar was a short, barrel-chested man with a big grin, several gold teeth, an Ozzy Osbourne sweatshirt he'd worn until it had become part of his chest and a hyena laugh that was more menacing than merry. Guntar had arrived bearing unimaginable riches — several colors of silk for the women, rubber flippers and goggles for the men, chocolates and nuts, soap (!) and a case of expensive cognac.

So, of course, a huge spread was laid out in Guntar's honor — any excuse for a meal — on the deck between the huts. The huge spread started with the same rice and fish we'd had the previous 67 days, but Guntar added sausages and real vegetables, coffee and several different beers. As we dug in, Guntar's boys — seven strong and rather nasty-looking guys — filled one of the corner huts with rice and molasses, canvas, rope, sealing wax, steel chain and a solar-powered boom box blasting some Filipino Dr. Dre wannabe. Then they joined us for the festivities.

The whole village lazed around on the decks, eating and drinking to their heart's content, while Guntar offered gifts to everyone, including me — apparently he brought extras because the place was used to passing strangers. Radios, flashlights, hair clips and simple picture books to help the kids learn to write and read (most of the adults couldn't).

In the middle of the party, Guntar lapped it all up. He seemed like the irresponsible younger uncle, the ne'er-do-well and casual rule-breaker who came home prosperous, proving their society wasn't really all that different from ours.

'Uncle', like all family titles, had a fuzzy meaning here. Apparently there was a constellation of these villages stretching several thousand miles in every direction. The water people, as they called themselves, considered themselves a brotherhood and apparently, the brothers in particular got around, traveling from village to village with the seasons and whims. Almost everybody in the village was related, often in several different ways—first cousins by one reckoning; third by another.

"The old man says you're learning to dive," Guntar got around to me after a few rounds, howling laughter.

"Yeah and teaching me to see in the dark," I answered.

"That's a useful skill in this part of the world."

"What's your work?"

"I'm a pirate," he said, like it was a job category on LinkedIn.

"There's a hundred thousand miles of ocean out there and it's ours. We live all over, move all over. We know where the fish are and when they're there. We know where the good reefs are when somebody needs good coral, we know where the safe harbors to dock and to live are—and we know every ship that's passing through,where it's going, what it's carrying—"

"And what they can steal!" Irfunya jumped in. "Big thief with boats and guns!"

"It's not theft, it's *taxation!*" Guntar yelled back. "You use the Jersey Turnpike, you pay the toll. You use our waterway, you pay us. Just because we don't have a flag doesn't mean we've got no rights."

"Got no *law*, so you got no rights," Irfunya grumbled.

"You've gotta have a *country* to make laws, old man. We've got no country."

"Why need a country?" Irfunya asked. "Who says? *Countries* say."

"We're the world's orphans, that's the fact of it."

"Not facts!" Irfunya bellowed, which was his normal tone of voice anyway. "That game—*their* game."

"So what would you have me do, uncle? Ignore reality?"

"Don't play! Make own game!"

Guntar rolled his eyes, daring me to say something, anything at all.

"You know the Jersey Turnpike?" is all I came up with.

"Two years at Rutgers. Thought I was going to study law. Now I'm a pirate." He laughed again, flashing his shiny teeth.

I knew some fearsome people in Iraq—people who we suspected kidnapped buddies of ours, kidnapped and raped and beheaded people we'd heard of. These were guys who were supposed to be on our side, by the way, at least for the moment. Guntar wanted to be a tough guy but tough guys didn't worry about taxation and access rights. They just took what they wanted. Guntar was thoughtful in his own way, he just seemed to resent his own thoughtfulness.

"How do you pirate?" Like asking a dentist how he filled cavities.

"Nowadays? With difficulty. The tourist ships didn't used to have guards," he answered. "You just surrounded them with a couple machine guns and they'd pay for safe passage. Two cruise lines kept me on retainer for a while—I got paid regular, white man's job. No more."

"What happened?"

"Maybe they wised up. Maybe I got greedy. Maybe somebody else did. I'm not sure."

"So what now?" I asked. It was the next question but I wasn't sure I wanted to know the answer.

"Now? I move stuff around. Move a little rice, a little sugar, some coffee, whatever pays. Manalea got more rice than they can eat but the fish don't like that stinking hole—so I bring fish from Katchapilapu, where the fish grow but the rice don't."

I giggled like a kid at the sound of the name—I don't know why; it just struck me funny—and his eyes flashed. All of a sudden, I saw the pirate, the guy who really might shoot you if you didn't pay him off.

"Hey man, that's their names!" he said, fierce. "You look on Google Earth, it says, like 'Island R-37288' or something! That's bullshit! They got fucking names!"

Irfunya leaned across the table and corrected him for cursing—in a surreal day, that was a Top Ten moment. Guntar found this just as funny as I did.

"I coulda stayed alive here begging, like the rest of 'em. Oh, you haven't seen that yet? They hang out by the cruise ship lanes, paddle up when a boat comes by, like monkeys in a zoo and the tourists throw coins to them. Except most of the time, they throw 'em off to the side so they can see the cute islanders dive for them. And they do—they dive to the bottom of the sea, which is something those fat assholes couldn't do if their life depended on it, just to get a nickel or ha'penny."

I looked around the table. Nobody seemed embarrassed by this description but somehow it made me defensive.

"You're right, they couldn't do it," I said. "I've been down there; you can't see a thing. It's magic."

Irfunya went red. "There's other ways to see!" he burst. "The world *full* of magic!"

"Oh, everything's magic to you, old man," Guntar taunted. "Let's thank the fish for letting us eat them…"

"That right! Fish fucking spirit! Water fucking spirit! Air alive! You my dinner, I thank you. You give me life, I thank you!"

It smelled like an old argument—a familiar scab Guntar liked to pick at. But the pirate turned to me after a long moment of waiting and I swear I saw a trace of envy in his eyes.

"Now you'll get his little magic show" he said and wandered off to his boat, toting a bottle of local tuak and leaving behind the brandy.

Irfunya slapped me on the shoulder and said, "You not fucking snob."

"No," I shook my head. I didn't think I was, though I wasn't sure what it had to do with anything.

He poured some of the tuak into a pitcher and placed it on the kerosene stove in the middle of the room. It heated the room a bit, which was all you needed in that climate.

As the pitcher warmed up, he closed his eyes and began to chant. "We thank the fish," he said to me, though surely it was aimed at Guntar. "We thank the sea, we thank the air, everything what give to us. We in Everything. Everything in Everything." He repeated the chant in whatever language it came in and motioned to me to repeat it so we did, slowly and repeatedly.

I had no idea what we were chanting, all I knew was that the sound was hypnotic—the air changed somehow, texture or density or something. I was suddenly super-aware of the air rushing in and out of my lungs and the sheets of warmth radiating off the oven, like they might disappear if I stopped participating in them. That's how I put it to myself, without ever really having a clue what it meant.

I could feel the villagers settling onto the deck outside, paying attention while pretending to be real casual about it. I felt Irfunya focusing on the cheap beads hanging over the oven so I focused there too.

And, in a moment, my life changed.

As I fastened my eyes on those beads, they expanded, amplifying, gaining detail and texture like I was getting closer and closer to them by the second. There might not have been anything more to them than a moment before—but suddenly I was seeing *everything* that was there.

Each bead was own totally unique, blonde wood rubbing against onyx, jade against ivory and ivory against glass. The tiny spots where they rubbed together were dull, glaring, like a flat spot on a mirror—except the mirror was the size of a fingernail.

The night breeze stirred and the beads swung like the hands of a symphony conductor. A couple knocked together, scattering bright flecks of water vapor, splintering into a million particles, each the size of a basketball, each with its own shiver and arc and glimmer, impurities in each forming whirlpools, sucking in the particles within the particles within the particles.

All at once, the whole world was particles.

They taught us in school that water vapor evaporated. I never took it as anything personal until suddenly I could *see* it happening right in front of me—water particles mingling with air particles, all the little bits swirling at different speeds and patterns. The water wasn't liquid and the air wasn't gaseous—everything was everything. At this level, all the bits were identical, it was just that water particles danced a different dance than air particles and both of them different from the particles forming the bamboo ribbing in the roof.

The water vapor came shimmering off the stove, particles a millionth of an inch tall, sheets of heated air pushing up, distorting the heavier cool air above like rippling a sheet. I actually watched the waves slurrying through the bamboo of the thatched roof and out into the night sky, watched the air particles become part of the bamboo particles and vice versa as they passed and exchanged.

And then I went blank and a second later, the roof was gone and the sky stood naked above us, a billion stars in Southern constellations, the stars just more bright particles mingling with the billion luminous bits drifting upward from Irfunya's little fire, everything the same, a piece of another piece, mingling and sharing, competing, collaborating, colliding, connecting and conniving together.

Max had described it all to me the night after Dave was killed, the night after it all started—about how thoughts were a physical force like the water and the air, like the fire and beads in the breeze, just another bunch of particles with their own dance, their own constellation that could be molded and distorted, heard and sent at a distance, where a thought particle could unravel a steel cable if you knew the right vibration to play. I'd seen him put it into action a hundred times since but a little part of me always held out for him being whacko, right up to now, when suddenly here it was, all laid out right in front of me.

And then we were back in the dirty little hut and Irfunya was pouring from the warm flask into two small cups. He handed me one, lifted the other in a toast and said "Drink. And then tell me who's this fucking Max Renn guy."

reunion 4
December 2008

Australia

"What do you mean, 'Who's Irfunya?'—you *sent* me to him. *You have made contact*—your note said it! You *have* to know who he is!"

"Hey, over here!" says a voice across the room but Max ignores it, of course.

"I *don't* really have to know," he says, of course, because the laws of physics and logic got nothing on him. "We had to separate, I wanted you with someone sympathetic, who'd keep you growing. So I sent your base vibration into the Universal Field and—"

"Must be great to know what the Universal Field is," I mutter.

"Hey! I've got a man wounded here!" says the voice again, quite a bit louder and I feel a whole lot more uncomfortable ignoring her than I did a second ago.

Max glances over grudgingly. "Pietr knew what he was doing. The bullet missed the organs; he won't bleed out for at least forty minutes." He returns to me. "The Universal Field? Call it the Collective Unconscious, if you like. I found a match for you in a place you could hide for a while. I didn't bother with the details."

"Details? Like nearly drinking myself to death or diving to death or getting kidnapped—"

"It all worked out—here you are."

"HEY! Mindbender guy!" The woman Kate called Dolores— she looks like a wrestler and her voice explodes from inside my head now, the way Max's does when he's about to move a house with his mind. "I need you to work on him with me." 'Him' being the one she called Rafael, with way more emotion than makes me comfortable.

"Work on what?"

"Get the bullets out of him. Do it quick and I'll have him walking out of here in a few minutes, instead of needing an ambulance and an emergency room. That works for you, doesn't it?"

He focuses on her now, like he's really interested. This is not a common response for him. He looks different from what I remember—red hair and a goatee—and in an L Corp uniform.

"How do I know you're you?" I say.

"What?"

"I've seen Kate do illusions but not you, not like this. How do I know you're the real guy—maybe you're Tat Man pretending to be Renn. How do I know?"

"Hey! Hey!" says Dolores.

"Alright—one second," Max says. "An illusion is simple, a projection on the occipital lobe," he says. He starts fingering the back of my head near the neck (*how'd he get around there so fast?*) and suddenly I'm back in the Everglades in my rowboat and him and Dave, everybody's relaxed and smiling, our lines are in the water and the fish are jumping into the boat all by themselves. I see it, hear it, smell the water and the rot of the weeds and feel the heat on my back—it almost makes me cry because it feels so real and I know so strongly it isn't. "So—there you are," he says.

"There I am what?"

"There you are, I had a terrific illusion going and you knew it wasn't real. *It almost makes me cry because I know so strongly it isn't real.* When Tat Man's face faded into mine, you knew instinctively which face was real." He wags a finger in my face. "You have to *know what you know,*" he quotes himself.

"I didn't know you were Tat Man until your face faded."

"I didn't want you to know then."

"So how do I know you want me to know now?"

"It's fine," Dolores says. "I'll just tell the medics I was kidnapped by the Rome Three. That should get me good treatment."

"I'm coming!" Max says, turning sharply away from me and then adding, "Hertz—the one you call Blondie—he'll be coming through the door in a second. Knock him out, okay?'

Now he stalks over to Dolores, who's somehow keeping Rafael's bleeding down. Me take out Blondie? Blondie's a slab, probably snatches 1200 lbs and does five hundred reps of everything, every morning before breakfast. I'm two years past active duty and it's not like I spent most of that time working out.

"Once you've knocked Blondie out, put on his uniform, it should fit you." Max bends to Rafael as I hear footsteps just outside the door.

Zero time to plan. I pull the table lamp out of the wall socket. The instant Blondie bursts through the door, I smash him in the face with it. He staggers a moment until I kick out the back of his knees and stomp on his neck as soon as he hits the floor.

He's still breathing, wheezing a bit but that's okay with me. I start pulling off his uniform—he is way heavier than me.

"I need clean cloth!" she orders just at the right moment and I toss over my shirt. She lays it under Rafael's back and tells Max, "Get over this side, where you can help me."

"You've got him under control," Max says. "You want us to protect Kate, don't you?"

"When you catch up to her, you'd better be able to tell her he's stable or someone's gonna have to protect *you!*" Dolores says.

Max considers this for a second. "What do you want from me?"

"Visualize the bullet. Find the fragments. Force them out of him."

"Me?"

"You're the mindbender, right?" She glances at me. "*You* do this stuff?"

"No way."

Back to Max. "It's you, then."

The uniform's a little baggy on me but I get into it and start securing Blondie to my chair with plastic ties from his belt and six yards of gaffer's tape across his mouth and eyes. I get a little nauseous as the adrenaline drains but with the door still a little bit open and who knows what outside, I don't have time to get sick.

Max's eyes are closed and he's making his Ommming noise—it's like living inside an Oster. "There are four fragments— here, here and here," he says, pointing.

"How far from the surface?" Dolores demands.

"An inch, more or less."

"Okay, vibrate them."

"An ambulance would help you without an international incident. Why don't you—?"

"You lost somebody recently," Dolores says. "Old guy, drinker, probably not long for the world anyhow but you're carrying that injury around with you. You want that for her?" Max isn't used to getting argued with; he stares for a moment. She just says, "Make them move—but gently. You've got organs inches to right and left; we don't want anything nicked but we want them out now."

"You know this works?" he asks.

"Kate's the master of it. The two of you do things I could never."

Max's shoulders shiver, his neck muscles flex and the room buzzes—I see Dolores' eyes widen. Max puts his ear right over Rafael's chest, sampling different vibrations until he hears something he likes.

A moment later, Rafael's body levitates off the ground all by itself and we hear the click as the fragments drop onto the sticky floor. He settles softly down again and Dolores ties pieces of my shirt around his midsection.

"*This* is what Kate's been doing?" Max says.

"I've been teaching her."

"I sent her to learn Dreamtime from *him*," Max says, pointing a thumb at Rafael. "We need an offensive weapon."

Dolores laughs. "So leave her with us for another twenty years. Dreaming is a way of life, not a bag of tricks, though I'm sure she picked up a few things from this rascal."

Rafael suddenly seems to be coming around. "Where's Kate?" he asks Max. "What are you doing here? She's in danger."

"Not yet," Max says. "I've got a fix on them."

"They lured us from the village one by one to make her come searching for us, to flush her out of hiding."

Max shakes his head. "They're looking for a man with a package. They want her to help them find him." He bends over Blondie and Tat Man and gives each a zap from his finger. Their bodies hop into the air as the spark hits them and then drop to the floor like dead weight.

"There's one more outside," Max tells Dolores. "If we clear him out, can you two disappear for a while? They know Kate cares about you—you're a danger to her."

"They won't find us," Dolores vows. She stares hard at Max for a moment. "You could be a healer, you know. Better life than a killer."

"I haven't killed anybody in years."

"It's all you're thinking about," she says and he pulls his head back from reflex. I don't like the sound of that. "And it's not your nature. If you do the things you're thinking of, you're lost."

Max turns away from her and there I am. He looks thrown, which isn't real encouraging. "Zip up your jumpsuit," he says. "You've going out as Blondie."

"I don't look anything like him."

"The man outside will look at you and see him, I promise. Let's go—we've got to find a man with a package before they do."

tipping point
August 2008

Australia

Kate was not a 'nice girl.'

The words enraged her, sent her into the kind of fury that proved beyond doubt that they didn't apply. Boring stupid fucking boring boring boring!

It's what she'd been called, the box she'd been put into, all her life. It hadn't felt like a prison before. But now, after Rome, any kind of restriction felt intolerable.

"But you are," Dolores protested. "You're a decent soul, somebody who looks out for others. What should I do, pretend you're a witch to make you happy?"

She was accepted in the tribe now, respected and counted on. Nestor's legs hadn't regrown themselves straight but they were sturdy underneath him for the first time in a long life. Alda's migraines had faded from a constant trial to an occasional annoyance. Residents came to the clinic each week specifically for her treatment. And she had erupted with a fabulous fireworks display in the middle of the last Dreaming. She had found herself a magnet ever since, counseling tribe members during the nocturnal sharing who would never have felt comfortable seeking her out in the village.

The birds conducted a competitive honking, one group in the marsh below Kate's little house mixing it up with skittish little birds right in front and a pack of loud ones in a yard cluttered with scrap metal and tools half a mile away. She hovered away from the village, ignoring the voices in her head calling her back.

A big spotted cat bounded through a shop full of ornamental glass and silk drapes without a rustle and a macaw-like bird with thick jagged-edged woodcarving wings, right-angle talons and a jigsaw purple, lime and pink colorscheme flew over a river leaping with black grunters, glassfish and three species of catfish, parting in balletic patterns for the passing of crocodiles twelve feet long, beady-eyed operators intent on bigger game.

It was a dream, she knew, the dream that had surrounded her, engulfed her since she'd arrived, since she'd moved in with Rafael, since she'd become one with the village.

What had become clear only recently was that it wasn't just *her* dream.

They dreamed together, the whole village. It was some huge feedback loop, energy looping out through each member of the tribe, their energy feeding the dream and taking fuel from it. And the dreams didn't disappear when the sun came up, either. She passed between one state and the other without transition, without any clear demarcation.

That was part of what bothered her now. Hidalgo appeared in the Dreaming to have the dignity of a crane, long-limbed and limber—and he conducted himself during the day as though that was all there was to it. Meanwhile, half his teeth were missing and he accomplished little to nothing as village handyman without repeated urging. He took offense at every reminder without speeding up his response.

Benny, a coyote in the dark, was a joker and trickster, a thief of legends and a continual flirt—an adolescent spirit in the best and worst sense. He spent half the week in Darwin, returning with essential and whimsical items—how he paid for them, she didn't want to know. The others tried to keep him on a short leash but he wasn't reliable enough for it to work. For all the affection he drew—and it was plenty—he was sure to come to a bad end, no matter how much dream energy they all summoned to break his fall.

Rafael, also, lost luster in the light of day. In dreams, he was daring and powerful, a force of nature, leading the group from adventure to adventure. He was part of the land, the conduit of the deepest emotions and most vivid journeys. In daylight, he wandered in a marijuana haze, making his 'aboriginal' jewelry and theorizing about a better world he made no sustained effort to bring into being.

Minerva, Alba and Mama Bill were Dolores' Greek chorus, the witches from Hamlet and the town sewing circle, Dolores' mirror and amplifier and chamber ensemble, the drone that underpinned all strength.

And Dolores hovered behind it all, the strong melody that channeled the rest and gave the place structure and coherence. At least at night, in the moonworld. During the day, Kate saw her going gray, sighing and falling asleep at her desk, unable to manifest the transcendent powers she wielded in their collective story.

"It's all I can do to try to make something move forward," Dolores told her, "for us to find a way to accommodate the modern world without losing the magic of the world that never ends. It's always just a few—Benny!—that hold everyone back. The wolf pack, the kids you ran into. Everyone knows who they are and how they hold us all back—but there it is, what do you do? You're trying to find a way to a more compassionate life and maybe the only way to get there is to jettison them, eject them from the village or at least the Dreaming. But they're part of the family—and I don't know a family in the world that doesn't have one or two like that. Maybe that's what family is, who knows? Are you supposed to be tough and drop them, because they're holding everyone else back? Or, if you're trying to be compassionate, do you hold everyone back to wait for them, hoping they'll come along eventually? I really have no belief they will—at least, not before almost everyone is old and grey, not just me."

It was disappointing, watching Dolores have to water down a miraculous world so much bigger than any Kate had ever known. Maybe people just weren't meant to be that big?

When you dreamed in the First World, you were unconscious to everything. Dreaming in the Outback was lucid— she participated actively—but it was still wild, confusing and uncomfortably revealing. It showed her the tension that held underneath the 'nice' girl she'd always been.

That wasn't who she was anymore.

She was a terrorist now. It wasn't just a word or an image on TV screens and newsstands. The thrill of Rome was still inside her, still alive inside every moment.

Three days, that's all she'd spent in that vicious, reckless world. She'd counted those days over and over ever since.

So, the question was, now what?

What did she do now with all that feeling, all the passion and determination and power that had possessed her in those few days?

She wanted that feeling again, more than she'd ever wanted anything in her life.

And she was more terrified than she'd ever been of just how bad she wanted it.

tracking

Brno, Czech Republic

A 24-hour flight on a long weekend dumped Cornwell in Vienna and now he sweltered along the E461 to Brno in a mustard-colored Peugeot 107 with a stick shift and no AC. The car was a furnace even with the windows open. His mood was not helped a bit by the Mercedes and Porsches and BMW's on their way to Prague, flipping their headlights a half-mile back, leaving him barely enough time to get over before they flew by in air-conditioned comfort.

He hadn't kept Saminov's cellphone on purpose, at least not at first. He'd dropped it in his pocket out of force of habit and only found it exiting the next morning's tongue-lashing from Volkov. He'd held onto it after that out of sheer spite.

Settled into his new office in Darwin, going insane tracking Chinese shipping violations for the sixth day in a row, it finally occurred to him to check the call list.

The only calls Vlad made on his last evening were his wife and a number in Brno, listed to Elias Lazar. Cornwell perked up instantly at the familiarity of the name and dug hungrily till he found it in agency records.

Elias Lazar: 71 years old, Professor of Microbiology and Physics, University of Brno, previously Chief of Exploratory and Experimental Science, Institute for Visual Measurement and Calculation, Novosibirsk, Soviet Union.

Bingo! NIMBUS! Road Trip!

Lazar's home was the same color as Cornwell's rental car, teetering on a hillside overlooking center city. The sun played peek-a-boo with the clouds as he settled into a parking space and checked out the neighborhood.

The house was in a good defensive location, clear views and open backyards all around and several doors for escape *in extremis*. The windows were closed, so it was air conditioned— Cornwell considered surrendering immediately, just on that basis. Anyone covering the place effectively would need a team. But the management wasn't expecting trouble—the downstairs door hung slightly open and clothes wagged on a line like flags on a mast.

And a moment later, there she was: Mrs. Saminov in the flesh, emerging from the lower level, collecting blouses and sheets

off the line. Her right arm held the basket rigid against her body —
it ended in a stump just above the wrist. Cornwell traced the
spiderweb of jagged white lines up her forearm to the elbow.

It was as much of an invitation as he was likely to get.
Cornwell jumped the bolted gate, followed the raised walkway
halfway across the yard and dropped onto the lawn, heading
straight for Saminova. He got five feet on the grass before his legs
turned to mush. Blocking did no good — whoever had him kept
finding new frequencies. In a moment, he was rolling in the damp
grass.

A few words whispered in the distance — he struggled to
retrieve his Czech with no luck. Rolling over defensively, he was
confronted by a pair of legs in baggy corduroy pants and knew
somehow that they belonged to Lazar. He took Saminova by the
shoulder and ushered her back toward the house. A long knife
glinted in the old man's back pocket; Cornwell shivered helpless
on the ground.

His only chance was Saminova. "Remember me?" he called
out to her feet as they passed. "We passed in Brussels..." She
stared at him, as though trying to remember. "You said something
about love and sausages..."

"—and onions," she answered, the words blurting out as
though unexpected, eyes welling up.

"You were dancing — I wanted to help you."

"I was dancing," she repeated as though recalling some magical memory. Lazar's gaze moved from Saminova to Cornwell—he returned and rifled Cornwell's pockets, pulling his wallet and pistol and ID.

"Can you move?" he asked.

"Of course not. You've locked me down like a safe."

"So you understand, you're not going to be rushing her anymore, yes?"

"Yes."

"Hmph!" the old man sniffed, staring at the business card he'd withdrawn from Cornwell's wallet. "Ozark Folk Art Combine? You're in Brno collecting folk art with a pistol? This is clumsy, even for America."

"That's just improv," Cornwell said. "I'm not working—I'm here on my own."

Lazar's eyes widened. "Why?"

When a man has total control of your body, choose your words carefully. "Saminov called me his last night. He asked for me, I don't know how he knew I was at HQ, I don't know how he knew the phone number, I don't know how he knew who I was. He probed me over the phone, so I would know he was a mindbender. I sent him to the safe house—safe, ha! When we arrived, Mrs. Saminova was dancing down the street, babbling to herself and he was dead in the basement. Why do you think I'm here? I want to know what the hell happened!" Lazar took him in. "Can I get up, please? I'm getting grass stains on my clothes."

His legs came back, just enough to enable him to stagger to his feet. Maybe he really *was* too old for this. "So much for the grass-stain. You drink tea?" Lazar asked, leading him into the house.

The living room ran the length of the house, wraparound windows offering a grand view of the city snuggling among a ring of hills. A long table heaped with folders, file trays, black-and-white photos and sheafs of paper stood against a bamboo partition. Saminova took a seat facing the room and a pale young woman carried a steeping pot and china cups in from the kitchen.

"My daughter, Nicola," Lazar went around the room. "I am Elias Lazar and you are Scott Cornwell of the Ozark Folk Art Combine branch of the CIA.And this is Anastasia Saminova. I gather you two have met. He tried to help you?"

Saminova nodded, still shaky from the memory. "I was beyond help."

Lazar took a seat where he could watch everyone at once, the old spy's reflexes still at work. "So you say Vlad was dead when you got there? What was the cause of death?"

"We should be able to tell—we had cameras in the room, I had a medical officer ten minutes after we arrived. But your guess is as good as mine."

Lazar's eyebrows lifted. "That is the kind of result that always pleases the spymasters."

"In this case, there are people who will be happier if this just goes away."

"For what reason?"

"No offense, but if I knew, I probably couldn't discuss it with you."

"And what do you hope to learn here?"

"What happened to her arm, for starters."

Lazar glanced at Saminova but the look was more question than support. "Stacia is our guest; she decides if she wants to speak or not," he said. Cornwell attempted a probe but Lazar shook him off. *Too fragile,* he heard the old man's voice in his head and wondered if Lazar could be an ally.

"Did he tell you where you were going?"

Saminova stared a long time before answering.

"I—I wasn't there at the time. I wasn't there most of the night." She glanced at Lazar, who seemed in as much suspense as Cornwell. "Vlad got a call, in the middle of the night—he stayed late before but I don't remember him going in at such an hour. He called later, 'Meet me at the station, bring the emergency kit, we're leaving.' I went to the garage but as soon as I was in the car, I heard voices. I—it sounded like my own voice, truthfully, but I knew it wasn't. I grew up in Novosibirsk, I knew I was bent, but no idea who controlled me."

"Most people don't even know they're under," Lazar added sympathetically.

Tears began to stream down Saminova's face. "He was strong—I couldn't shake him. He put this tiny metal around my hand and slipped a little battery box in my jacket pocket, wires between them. I knew, the whole time, what would happen. He— the voice in my head—he let me know before.

"Vlad was going to meet me at the Martin Luther Kingpark, so we could jump on the A2 to Brussels. I remember sitting on that wide street waiting for him to come and—it was deserted, middle of the night—there was one light on in the apartments alongside, this middle-aged couple awake, in bathrobes, having coffee and clearly just having made love. And I started crying and Vlad appears on the sidewalk, 'Move over, I'll drive' and he drives and he never even sees me crying in the seat next to him and I can't speak a word, can't make my mouth move and all I think is 'You stupid fucking man, I'm going to have to kill you because you're not paying attention to details. He *never* paid attention.'" Lazar placed a small box of tissues on the table next to her but Saminova ignored them.

"And we get to Brussels and he opens the basement door and I hear the voice in my head say 'Block the door and say goodbye' and I know what it means and I can't cry anymore, nothing comes. I put my arms around Vlad and feel the electricity go through my arm and out my hand and my hand explodes but I can't make a sound. It goes through him and he falls back in the chair—"

"He didn't—he never moved," Cornwell said.

"Hmph! It felt like he did. And I went outside and there you were."

"What did it mean? 'Love and sausages—'"

"Sounds. Just sounds. I'd got the use of my voice back. I wasn't trying to say anything."

"You could have asked for help."

"For what? Vlad was dead, I felt it before I left. What help were you going to give me then?"

"So what killed him? What was the box?"

Her eyes flared. "I killed him—it was me saying goodbye. If I hadn't touched him, if I'd walked away, he'd be alive."

"The voice wouldn't have let you," Lazar said.

She settled back in the chair, impassive now. She held up her stump of an arm. "By the time I got back to the car, I was released. The voice was gone from my head. I could do anything I wanted—anything but the only thing I wanted to do, of course..."

The clock ticked. A cloud threw the yard into dusk for a moment and then passed. Cornwell spoke gingerly. "He told me someone was developing a weapon 'under our noses.' Did he say what he was doing?"

"The last few months, coming home late, he was...hazy, like I was after the voice in my head."

"Under suggestion."

"Of course, under suggestion. How did I not see it? It was right in front of me."

"He probably had you under control all along."

"Who?" Her voice snarled now, like an animal's sound. "Who did this? I know what we were raised for, what we were trained for. We were going to keep the others, the Normals, in line. Who could do this to us?"

"What was he working on for NATO?"

"You're not answering me." The anger reverberated through the room. "Who?"

"Maybe this man can find out," Lazar said.

"Vlad was a good soldier," she said bitterly. "He kept quiet." Her eyes welled up again as she stood. "I am grateful. You tried to help me. This is all I know." And then she was down the hall, Lazar's daughter following—he heard a door close a moment later.

Lazar pulled a pipe from his pocket and began filling it from a battered green pouch.

"Did this help you?" Lazar asked, striking a match and taking a few pulls. Could he confide in the old man? The old Russians were always inscrutable.

"What's your stake in this, Doctor?"

Another longer puff. "I have no stake but my concern for Stacia. I'm a professor who's trying to stay retired." And now a sigh. "No, that's not entirely true. You saw the Rome pictures?"

"I live on the planet Earth, yeah."

"This was a very close call," Lazar said. "It is very important we don't get closer."

"How so?"

"Look at the hysteria when someone yells 'Terrorist' in the United States, even though it's seven years since 9/11 and, so far, there hasn't been another attack. What happens when citizens discover there are people who can read your mind and force ideas into it? Can you imagine the witch hunt? The old woman who finishes your sentences over lunch? The man who picks three horses in a row at the racetrack? Whatever is going on, it has to end shortly and without creating this kind of panic. You seem a sensible and caring person."

"I apologize."

Lazar nodded. "Yes, we also saw this as a weakness. Be hard for the sake of Mother Russia. But now I see differently. If there is a way to end this without it becoming a public battle, that would save many innocents."

"Maybe," Cornwell admitted. "You're really in the middle of all this. You know almost all the players. You're going to end up in the middle soon."

"And you know the people who might blow this all up," Lazar answered. "We should keep in touch."

Cornwell nodded. "I see your point."

corporate strategy

Geneva, Switzerland

The meetings had become a symbol of influence; testimony to Jim Avery's entry into the top tier—business leaders and politicians filling the reception room after an Avery event, seeking encouragement and counsel and insider cred.

This night, however, was different and obviously so. Avery recognized the men arrayed in plush chairs across from them as soon as they entered the room.

"You know who we are?" The Foreign minister asked.

"Of course I know who you are," Avery said.

"You expected me to come alone," said the Investment Banker.

"I knew you were all coming, we found it out the other—"

"Cut the shit, Jim," said the Energy Company chief. "We have things to talk about."

"—in private," added the Foreign Minister—of a major power with 'interests' around the globe—as the door opened and Miriam Fine entered.

"I think I'll stay," Fine said. The Foreign Minister nodded to a security guard. "Oh yes, please do try to throw me out," Fine said as the ape took a step toward her and then froze—literally. The others saw him straining to move without success.

"How can I help you gentlemen?" Avery asked, to a moment of puzzled silence. The Foreign Minister gestured furiously to his ape, who raised his shoulders helplessly.

"Avery, I don't understand why but you've somehow gotten in over your head," the Energy Chief picked up, snapping his fingers. The door opened and two more apes escorted in a bulky middle-aged man with a flashy wardrobe, depositing him roughly in the one empty chair remaining. "You know this man?"

"Of course," Avery replied. "Mr. Hayadi is a respected energy broker on several continents."

"He's a scam artist and swindler."

Avery cleared his throat. "Today's scam artist is often tomorrow's captain of industry. There are people in this room—"

"There are matters of national sovereignty and international law being decided in this room," said the Foreign Minister. "Matters normally decided at the highest levels. You're in over your head with this game."

"What game is that?" asked Avery.

"Hayadi's got shell corporations buying up oil rigs; he's consolidated his holdings under different names across both sides of a very sensitive border," rattled off Investment Banker. "You'd think we never played this game ourselves. We know the players; when new names appear, we find out where they're coming from. And lately, the money's coming from you."

"We never grant drilling rights," the Foreign Minister said, "to anyone doing the same for the imperialist aggressor on our southern border. You know this. Hayadi hid his identity to get them. Those rights must be returned or sold. We will not contribute to the Imperialist Entity."

"You won't say their name," Avery said, "but you do business with them."

"When it suits us and never directly. This isn't politics. It's 3,000 years of history, religion and blood. It would be our lives and the suicide of our government if we permitted it."

"Your purchase agreements will be rescinded," ordered the Investment Banker. "Your funds will be transferred back to your account tomorrow, opening of business."

All eyes turned to Avery.

"Mr. Hayadi is our favored merchant," Avery said, deadpan. "He has the backing of *Your World* and its affiliated companies. Your best course of action would be to go forward with the deal as presently comprised."

A short pause before loud guffaws.

"You say that as though it matters," the Energy Chief snapped.

"I simply think this deal is in everyone's interest," Avery said.

"In what way? How does it benefit *us*?"

"Your Northern Pipeline is running into difficulty," Miriam Fine said quietly, heads swiveling at the sound of her voice. "You're counting on expanded distribution there but your neighbors have started grumbling—just this morning, in fact."

The Energy Chief sat up straight in his chair. "How do you—?"

"Someone told them your pipeline is 1/8" bigger than it's supposed to be, which means you're shorting them the transfer fee for thousands of gallons a week."

"It's nonsense! Their numbers are completely off-base!"

"Be that as it may, you've already had 'mechanical issues' at one transfer point that reduced your capacity by 30% this afternoon and—as you were walking in tonight—you heard about a rupture in the Central Valley that might shut you down for days."

"Where do you get this? It's sheer fantasy!"

"Would you like the latitude and longitude of the rupture?" Fine continued calmly. "Would you like the name of the foreman who'll carry it out if you don't agree to their terms by morning?"

Energy Chief's leather chair squawked as he tried unsuccessfully to find a comfortable position. "That isn't funny."

"No, it isn't," Avery agreed. "It's serious business."

Fine turned to the Foreign Minister. "You're being undermined by fluctuations in the currency market over the last twenty-four hours. They'll be much worse tomorrow morning."

"Are you *threatening* us?" the Minister burst.

"I'm simply reporting the facts—check Tokyo." She waited, motionless, for him to comply. He made it clear, remaining stock-still, that he had no intention to. An aide, standing against the back wall, did however and slid his phone in front of his boss to allow him to see the numbers drop.

"A panic is such an unpredictable animal," Avery said. "Once it gets started, there's no telling how bad it will get."

"You can make powerful people really angry with this sort of thing, Avery. This is extortion!"

"Not if you get a receipt," Avery replied with a smile. "Gentlemen, let's be real for a moment. His pipeline was oversized and his currency deserves to be unstable. If you each existed on your own merits, you'd be dead and buried long ago. Powerful people retain power by identifying their shared interests and becoming entangled, so that what hurts one hurts the other." He turned to the other players around the room. "That's why this is important to you all—if we can start a small panic over your currency, we can start a big one over bank security or online security or a new virus outbreak. A weakness here and a weakness there could eventually bring you all down."

"How would you accomplish that, Avery? Through your self-help weekends?"

"Our customers come to our weekends and cruises and events to feel confident and secure, capable of being everything they've ever dreamed of. They leave us and quickly discover they don't feel that solid anywhere else. So they keep coming back."

"You've created an addiction," the Energy Chief said admiringly.

"You should know. It's the point of big business, isn't it? Make them dependent enough, you're not discretionary spending, you're a necessity. And the same techniques we use to create that dependency are useful for rougher types of persuasion, when necessary."

"Such as?"

"Such as this gun in my hand," Miriam Fine said, advancing quickly on the Energy Chief and sticking the barrel down his throat. "Such as the way you feel the bullet," she added, firing. Energy Chief flew back onto the floor, thrown by the concussion of the shot, crying in pain and grabbing at his wound—until Fine held her hand up again, empty. Energy Chief lifted his hand from his chest, revealing—nothing. No wound, no blood, no powder. "No gun," Fine added, smiling.

"Why would she bring a gun?" Avery said. "We're all partners here, aren't we?"

Energy Chief rose and returned to his seat, trying to obscure the fact that he'd vacated his bowels in his pants.

"What's your point, Avery?"

"Jim, please. The point is that *Your World* hasn't 'gotten in over our head'—we're right where we should be, a player now on this level, with the ability to solve problems that might otherwise threaten the whole fabric of your collective success."

The Energy Chief was staring nervously at Avery. "And that's how you'll fix the pipeline? With a fake gun to the throat?"

"Not necessary. In this case, we simply convince your neighbor the pipe is exactly what it's supposed to be." A pause. "Yes, I know it isn't but I promise you, he'll see it that way."

He turned to the Foreign Minister. "The final oil field will be 42% on your land and 58% on the land of the Imperialist Entity. The royalties from the consolidated field, however, will be split equally. You can announce that billions in new social programs will be paid for by the swindle you carried out against the oppressor to the south. You may even be able to run for Prime Minister after that. And of course, you will have the gratitude of the other gentlemen in this room—and all that they influence—for helping prevent what could have been a cascading set of difficulties." The Foreign Minister took a look at the faces staring expectantly at him. "Because it's all for one and one for all, right? Success or hideous, worldwide infamy-scale failure together."

A few minutes later, Avery, Fine and Hayadi walked out of the building and into Avery's limo.

"I never thought you could pull it off," Hayadi said to Avery, wide-eyed.

"Well, I did—which kicks in our deal. Thirty per cent of everything you drill, on both sides of the border," Avery said.

"You earned it today."

"That's what I thought."

beta test

Amsterdam

It was amazing the things you could see from a first floor window.

Even the lunch crowd thinned out on this narrow street. A few tourists who'd probably gotten lost passed under the window, heading for the bay and the Science Museum that jutted out into it. Landau sat in the front window of his rented room, one floor up and a block inland, seeking targets of opportunity among the meager prospects.

The girl in the blue sweater coasted her bike to a halt on the *Peperbrug*. From the shelter of his window, Landau made out the pendant around her neck. A heart, simple enough. Landau's sister had had one just like it. How would she have felt about it?

It wasn't easy. He hated the bitch, sister or no. It was hard even to summon her memory, harder yet to find any sympathetic feeling towards her. But that was the way. The Soviet texts were as clear on this as they ever were: *Memory is permeable, impermanent, fluid. It is easily modified and manipulated and affords the opportunity for vivid connection with a subject.* Which meant: Find a memory that matches someone else's and you're in their heads, home free.

The pendant, the way Kris would have thought of it. Concentrate. He tried to make himself his sister or at very least some girl who loved her little locket. *C'mon, bitch, you were good at playacting once, you can do this one thing!* He forced himself to feel things he didn't feel, couldn't feel, until there was a glimmer, a connection and he seized it.

A moment later, the girl ripped the pendant from her neck and heaved it into the canal—and then burst into tears at the sight. She swiveled around, trying to find the despicable person who had done this, and, naturally, finding no one, ended up mystified and heartbroken.

Landau settled back into his chair—the only piece of furniture in the room. He looped a bass line he'd sampled in *Garageband*, editing it to fit the track he'd created. If the whole L Corp trip didn't work out, maybe he could produce. But for now, mindbending looked fruitful.

De Jogt's footsteps clomped up the staircase a minute early—Landau made a mental note. You could set them tasks but you couldn't reset their clock. As he came into the room, De Jogt's head was brimming with ideas and anxiety. Landau didn't have the patience to sort through the clutter.

"Boil it down for me, dude."

"I'm over my head here. This isn't my area of—"

"You're a wizard!" Landau cut him off. He'd been monitoring the man's progress almost obsessively since Vlad had gone. At first, he'd been concerned he'd have to find new talent but by now he knew better. "And you're getting results, aren't you? You love this shit."

"These are *much* better," De Jogt said, pulling a couple of coils and a plastic strip from his pocket. "I figured out how to damp the voltage so there's no flash and the sound is less than a light switch flicking. And no more box at the belt. You take the backing off and slap the patch onto the arm—it's got just enough power to trigger one blast and ignition consumes it so no evidence!"

De Jogt handed over five units. Landau pocketed them.

"You see? That's brilliant! This is just a sideline anyway. The main work is right up your alley. Do you really want to work with a partner?"

"Well, not really," De Jogt said. "But Lindevald brought me bills yesterday—he knew they were mine. He said he didn't remember authorizing them."

"I'll refresh his memory," Landau told him. Lindevald was becoming a pain in the ass—his suggestions required continual renewals. The sucker was going to end up with Alzheimer's. "I've been thinking—don't abandon the old coil," Landau told him. "I want to work two tracks at once. No, three."

De Jogt's eyes widened. God, what a geek! In love with creating, no interest at all in the results. Money, power? Naah. Give De Jogt a soldering iron, a circuit board and enough money for the latest games and he was a happy man. "Make sure we've got the new one solid—no flash, no sound, no evidence. Then go back to the old version and see how far you can build it up. A little flash and bang is okay—it's another option. It's not a bug, it's a feature." He glanced at De Jogt, just to make sure the geek was paying attention. "And for the ultimate, think big. How powerful can you make it, if you don't care how loud or bright it is? How destructive can it be?"

"Oh, I've been dreaming about that for a while," De Jogt said. Of course he had.

"Well, get to work on it. Let me know before you start testing—I'll refresh your boss just before you blow the wall out."

"Oh no, I'll need something bigger than a wall for what I've got in mind."

Now it was Landau's eyes widening. "Okay, let me know when you're ready. I'll find a target. Now—back to work!"

He smacked his hands together and De Jogt's eyes glazed. He turned neatly and skipped down the steps, leaving Landau with the keys to the kingdom.

As long as the damn things worked.

Of the six tests Landau had run in the past month, only two of the last three (with intermittent loud bangs and lightning flashes) had actually resulted in immediate death. The first two had acted only as a stroke, leaving the victim mute and addled. The third hadn't worked at all, succeeding only in burning the deliverer's arms and leaving the back of the control box melted into his stomach. In all those cases, he'd worked with homeless men, both delivering the voltage and receiving it, so the police had been initially baffled and then predictably uninterested. And, to give himself credit, he'd picked the right geek—De Jogt had improved the delivery system after each attempt.

Landau was confident this one would be a keeper. The point was not to kill—there was never a shortage of ways to kill someone. The point—of this version—was to kill in broad daylight without leaving a clue.

To really test it, Landau needed a target who mattered, someone whose death the police couldn't shrug off. And, in truth, there was no sense of accomplishment in killing homeless men— most of them would have been dead in a year or two anyway, from booze, exposure or just bad attitude.

It was time to think big.

He cast a wide net, a technique he'd never tried before and got immediate results. A face—an image in the mind of someone passing, a face he'd seen before somewhere, a face foreign, distant but somehow a known quantity.

Landau scrambled down the steps and out the front door, onto the long block before the *Prins Hendrikkade* and the waterfront. By the time he'd reached the water, he had already identified the mind with the vision, with the famous—for now he knew it was not just familiar but famous—face. He could feel the elation inside the young lawyer heading to Central Station for a quick hop to the Airport and then on his way to Central Asia to spring his famous client from prison. Several good suits hung in the garment bag over his shoulder, the definitive reprieve from the World Court in his carry-on, to sit under his seat the whole trip where he could keep an eye on it.

Landau had a pretty good fix on him now but this would still be a serious experiment. Not just checking out the new coil but his ability to sustain a suggestion at a distance. Taking risks. An awful pile of risk here on one play—Landau liked the feel of it. It was time to expand, to spread the wings.

"Nero!" he called out for that was the young lawyer's name. Nero turned and Landau bent him to see Landau as vaguely familiar somehow. It wasn't much, just enough to get him to hesitate, to hold out his hand. Once Landau had Nero's hand in his, the lawyer's mind was mush.

The coil went into Nero's jacket pocket and he touched his temple just long enough to feel the suggestion take root. Cars went by on the Henrikkade, boats passed, along with a few pedestrians—but who would remember this moment, two young men conversing along the water?

Landau turned and walked away along the Oudeschans, Nero continuing on his way to the Station. Nothing special, life rolling along in mundane fashion. Landau would return to L Corp, to his day job, and keep an eye on the papers, waiting for the obituaries, for the surprising death of the great man.

So many things could go wrong with this plan but somehow he felt nothing would. He hadn't planned. He'd let life bring the victim and the mechanism to him. This one just felt like it was meant to be.

in dreams 2
September 2008

Dreamland

The vision in the dark was the same as before, the same
pipes and gray paint and control room thick—paneled windows.
Renn heard the voice almost as soon as he stirred in bed:

So how is this place home? How could this be anybody's home?

He wants conversation? He figures out how to contact me
across continents—nothing about this felt localized—to ask about
home? Wary and untrusting, Renn nevertheless hears himself
answer: *You always come at me with a memory. Why is that?*

Because it's where you always seem to be.

That's new. I never used to think much about the past.

*I never do. Life is about the future. As soon as you start living in
the past, you're over.*

The future only comes to us through the past.

Sounds like the shit to me.

Okay - we meet in Rio. You take a first-class flight from Paris. I take a bus over the narrow roads, town to town, all the way from Guadalajara. You can tell me all you want we're in the same place; I'm telling you it won't feel the same.

Renn pauses, almost holding his breath. It's more of a conversation than he ever thought to have, more than he can remember having with anyone in a long time. The subject is meaningless, abstract—but he feels as though he's dropped his pants in class.

And then he hears the kid pick up the conversation all on his own: *My home sucked. They hated what I was. They were afraid of what I was, what I could do. At least they valued you in the Project.*

Valued? Renn surely wouldn't have responded if he'd had a chance to think twice. *Valued just enough to be lied to at every turn.*

That's how the world is. You're a hopeless dreamer, beyond hopeless, dude.

Maybe it was the hour or his somnolent state but the words stung. *How? That's asking so much?*

You believed in home.

I didn't—never.

You're still longing for it after all the proof in the world what a sham it is.

I don't know about longing. Confusion, maybe. What else was it, then? Why did the subject still come up? Why was he answering at all? The kid was fishing for information—maybe he didn't even know what he was fishing for but it surely wasn't for Renn's benefit.

What's confusing about home? My mother brought home five guys. 'This is your father, honey.' 'This one's really your father.' 'Remember what I told you? That wasn't strictly true. I was married to that one, sort of, but this one is your father.' By the time we got to the fifth guy, I just said 'Please don't tell me. I'll call him Dad without a peep if you just don't tell me a story' and she looked grateful. What's confusing about it? Family sucks but you know them for what they are, for the shit they are.

What was there to say to that? Nonetheless, Renn heard himself answering: *I grew up with a woman in my house who was supposed to be my mother—a father too, equally bogus. I knew before I could talk that they were phonies. Everyone's thoughts crowd into my head but somehow I knew I wasn't supposed to question that, wasn't supposed to know so I didn't. The biggest feat of mindbending I ever did was hide from who they really were. I kept the silence because I knew I was supposed to and I was trying to be a good son—to whom, I don't know.*

And then one day when I was thirteen or something, I yelled 'You're not my real parents' like any kid does in anger—and the look on their faces told me how literally true it was. And of course, I'd known what I wasn't supposed to know all along. They were actors, hired to play the part when the commissars figured out my real parents were unreliable, too radical. The actors were terrified that I'd out them — that I'd let on that I knew who they weren't. So I was a good son — I just shut up about and went back to pretending I didn't know. But this time, it was like hiding the refugees under the floorboards. I was an orphan in my own home.

A foghorn blew across the bay. Which bay? Where was he tonight? Better he didn't remember, Renn decided, just in case the kid was listening in—he wasn't listening, Renn could tell. He wasn't probing, wasn't even attempting to gain entry, at least not yet. That's why Renn left the channel open—at least, that's what he told himself.

What if that was what they wanted? the kid's voice said.

What does that mean?

Fuck, dude, where do they recruit spies? Orphanages, juvie homes, anyplace they can get kids who know betrayal, the mother's milk of effective agents. They've got to twist the knife, get you good and pissed—and then they give you a home in the Service where you can get back at everybody and do it in a good cause, not that you care if it is or not.

More silence, this silence even more empty than before. *So, not just a sham but a sham of a sham? Mirrors on mirrors?*

That's what they do, isn't it? Manipulate everyone to get what they want.

What about you? Renn asked. *Who are you doing this for?*

I just want to know you.

Why?

Because you're Renn, dude. You're it—the best mindbender there ever was, eleven on a scale of ten.

Renn didn't like the taste of this and shrugged it off. *And what about your mother and her five husbands? Where is she now?*

I torched her. Burnt her place to the ground with her in it.

Did you know she was inside?

I locked her in myself. Would I be merciful? Why? For what? All she ever did was lie to me. You want to be a saint, it's your call but I don't get it, dude. People have to get what they deserve.

Renn paused a moment before answering. *The funny thing is, I told myself they didn't matter a bit to me, that there just wasn't any point to exposing them. And then, ten or twelve years later, I was in Maine, just traveling around, trying to figure out where I fit in the post-Soviet world—and there she was, my 'mother', having lunch with two lady friends in some outdoor café along the water. I'm still surprised I recognized her, new hair and new clothes so yet another layer of fakery on top of what she always was. And all I wanted in that instant was to throw my arms around her and tell her what I'd been doing, to pretend to be her son. Just to have something to go back to.*

And with that, the connection ended. Renn felt it cut off and knew that he had cut it off, although it wasn't something he'd been aware of doing when it happened. His hands trembled in front of him in the darkness. The bed beneath him was soaked in sweat. He rolled over under the sheets, lay quiet a few minutes and then went to the window, trying to forget, to go back to pretending he didn't know.

bubbles

South China Sea

This time I was in trouble.

It was time to head back to the surface—but I didn't know where the surface was. I couldn't tell if I was upright or upended, upside-down, sideways or inside-out. I had to finger my own eyes to make sure they were open. Time stopped. Blossoms of color swam in front of my eyes but I knew they were inside my head.

And then I felt contact below the elbow, pushing me. I wasn't sure where I was going but at least I was moving and grateful to hand over the decision.

Pretty soon, I saw more color blossoms ahead but I didn't trust them because I also saw light behind me and if that was right, I was dead. I'd gone too far to turn around and make it back to the surface. Strangely enough, that calmed me down. Clarity—I had no choice but to keep going.

About ten seconds later, there was light—above, that way was definitely above—steady and brightening and heart pounding and so close but don't go too fast so you don't lose your legs and Good Lord how long past strangled am I for air.

"Fucking THINK TOO MUCH!" Irfunya slapped me upside the head while I was still gasping, trying to climb back into the boat. "Think takes energy, use up oxygen. Thinking make you fucking *dead*!" He glared at me like I should've known but if the Army hadn't knocked thinking out of me, it wasn't going.

Fine, I won't use my head, I won't wonder why everybody comes back up with better shit than me!"

"That right answer!" he yelled back—Irfunya's quietest tone was still yelling. "You want something good down there, put mind someplace else." That's when I got it.

"It's blocking!" I burst and he looked like I'd pulled a bouquet of flowers out of my ear. "When the bad guys want to read your mind, you send it someplace else so they can't connect. It's the same fucking thing!"

"No it fucking ain't! This shit, we get *money* for!"

So the next time I dove down into the endless darkness, I took a visit to the marketplace, mashing up a few from Iraq, the one I saw blown up in Singapore and the one on Pulau Patang— tropical fish and olives, mangoes and bananas, palm leaves and cheese rolls, flatbread and kefir, customers in burqas and sarongs and you could have anything cheap if you haggled, mujahedeen on skateboards and regular Army on surfboards and kids everywhere, including some I remember shooting before they might've shot us. The sea smelled like a Humvee, the market chattered with flocks of purple and yellow birds. I had a fine time imagining myself gobbling down the good stuff—other than the feasts on market days and when Guntar showed up, it was mostly fish heads and rice in the village, so I was *hungry*.

In the middle of all this, I realized I'd lost all track of time. I didn't feel in distress and knew by dropping stones which way was up—I decided to head back to the surface for safety's sake.

Seven minutes later, I was in the boat, pulling gems and watches, coins of twenty countries and a pair of very expensive-looking sunglasses from my pockets.

"See?" Irfunya gloated. "*That* how you do it!"

"I didn't know I was doing *anything!*"

"Don't have to know!" he bellowed. "Just go! Don't know!" He listened to the words playing back in his head and smiled, chanting 'Just go! Don't know!' all the way back to the village, grinning like an elf.

Of course, Max had said what sounded like the opposite: *You have to know what you know.* But somehow it felt like the same thing. I spent the whole trip back to the village trying to rig a counter-argument. Max had driven me crazy with that shit and now Irfunya was doubling-down.

So now I was productive, as useful as any average thirteen-year-old growing up out there. I still didn't fit in, really. When we went into Pulau Patang twice a week to trade in the things we'd found for vegetables or booze or batteries, they had me bargain. Irfunya said I made the sellers nervous because I looked like a cop on a TV show. And when they went out to the cruise liners, I had to keep my distance—whether this was to avoid questions about the white guy or preserve the indigenous flavor of the show, I never found out. But, when we were diving, I was one of the boys.

"You stop thinking, you find what you *know*," Irfunya said and it just proved Max sent me to him. You couldn't find two people in the world who made that little sense.

happy

Constanta,Romania

She was happy.

Not giddy, not delirious, just happy. But truly happy. Content, that was the word. Was that all happiness was—to be satisfied? No, there was something more, something *perfect* about this.

Renn and the woman he was involuntarily stalking followed the woman's tiny companion for three tree-lined blocks, blocks populated by Romania's new capitalist striving class, concrete-block houses barely justifying the swimming pool filling the narrow driveway and the copper metallic Maserati consigned showily to the street. The grandson was like a puppy, finding brilliant, destructive new purposes for every alcove, vase, garbage can, doghouse, planter—anything he could reach, he was inside or as close-to as he could shove. The grandmother was constantly extricating him from one disaster in time to watch him toddle off, delighted, in pursuit of another. But she and Renn followed with identical goofy smiles plastered across their mugs.

The boy was thrilled by every thing he saw and she just took in his joy and reflected it back at him—a perfect feedback loop. Prowling the streets like this, they blocked the whole world out. Renn had had to work to tune her in, simply because she wasn't thinking much. Why think when everything just felt so good?

A newspaper had published a small article referencing a man named Inyushin, a scientist who terrorized his neighborhood with loud angry dogs. This had been tolerated as a minor nuisance in the old Constanta but now as towers rose and newly-rich Russians came south for the Black Sea beaches, patience had run out. But the name and oddball description had drawn Renn to Constanta, to a dead end. There might be lots of oddballs in the Inyushin family but this one was not the one he'd had in mind.

And upon exiting the house, he'd encountered the grandmother and her little boy and, having tasted her joy just for a second, he'd followed the two of them helplessly for three blocks. He couldn't remember the last time his mood was this light. It came from the boy, who was delightful, but what he related to was the woman's response, her mirroring of his feelings—they carried a far richer, more complex tang. Around them passed the usual suspects, the litany of daily complaints and travails, the thoughts

Renn normally spent all his time analyzing but now, he didn't care. He was in a better place.

As they rounded a corner, there was another couple, a middle-aged couple, clearly much in love. Not passionate the way the young ones were, but content, happy, totally relaxed with one another, strolling, arms locked together, making a little banter, not thinking about a minute later, a moment later, now now now now.

It happened. People were happy. It might not last forever but it happened all the same. Why was it such a shock?

They turned into the supermarket and his run of luck ended. Renn lingered by the doorway as long as he could without drawing notice, trying to hold onto the feeling, then, in seconds, trying to preserve and finally, just to remember it, to turn it into a memory as he finally walked away, to store it in the back of his mind for the time ahead when he'd need it. But it was hopeless, gone within seconds.

Which made him lonely. Not sad, that would have made sense but lonely, empty, missing something that already felt like an illusion.

The difference, he realized all at once, was that he'd never been trained for happiness. He'd been trained to intercept thought, to monitor thought on a massive scale and identify anything useful or to pluck out specific details from a subject that might be operationally valuable. Plans, schemes, facts, fears—those were thoughts. Happiness wasn't a thought—if anything, it was the absence of thought, a deep well of feeling that made thought superfluous.

Why did it matter? Why had this suddenly become an issue?

Because he was becoming involved. Because the wall was cracking, the wall that had kept him separate, kept him safe.

Renn stared out at the Mediterranean and tried to remember where he was and why.

the blow-up

Australia

> The schooner *Zhou EnLai* left Nanjing Bay Sept 12, heading SSW on the usual meandering cruise through the Paracel and Spratly Islands. Sighted Sept 13 by asset on fishing boat near Shenhu Shoal, making approx. 20 nautical knots, sitting low in the water and doing targeting drills on nearby boats and rocks. Sighted again Sept 14...

Distraction, distraction, there had to be something else to do! Anything!

Cornwell had anticipated the job would be boring but the reality outstripped all his fears. There should never have been a CIA waterboarding scandal—why bother with torture when mindcrushing drudgery would bring any man to his knees? Set Al Qaeda to tracking Chinese vessels in the South China Sea and watch the whole thing collapse in weeks.

He switched to his newsfeeds. He'd set alarms online, pulling in certain phrases—'surprising death' 'unexpected stroke' and variations thereof—whenever they appeared in any of a hundred news sources worldwide.

So far, in two-and-a-half months, he'd seen nothing capable of raising his pulse above coma. Until now:

SHOCKING DEATH OF CHARISMATIC LEADER

By Rudger Payoart

(Waldawe) - This island nation was stunned tonight by the unexpected death of Martin D'aillard, the recently-deposed former President who had made the chain of atolls a major force in the international debate over climate change.

D'aillard was stricken by a heart attack at a celebration marking his release from three months imprisonment, following a ruling by the World Court in The Hague that his incarceration at the hands of the nation's military junta was 'without due process.' D'aillard had already called for prompt elections on his way out of prison.

Using websites, videos and speeches worldwide, D'aillard, 46, offered vivid illustrations of the complications of climate change. One of his innovations was an office to support Waldawean citizens with passports and consular support even after their physical homeland disappeared into the sea. When asked how his government in exile would pay for such services, D'aillard said, "To me, the obvious answer is to sue the governments most responsible for excessive carbon in the atmosphere, though I'm sure they will offer other suggestions."

Cornwell nearly ripped the phone off the desk.

"Mr. Payoart, my name is Daniel Carillo, I'm a project manager for TransWorld Integration in Darwin. We've been working with Mr. D'aillard's people on a big push for solar cells — we're very upset about what happened."

"Remember I'm only the messenger, Mr. Carillo."

"Of course. I don't know quite how to say this but — considering the situation, is there any chance it *wasn't* a heart attack?" There was no reply for a moment and Cornwell wondered aloud, "Should I call back on another line? Would you like to call me back?"

"No, no," the reporter answered, "I was just thinking. It's an odd situation. I think we all considered the possibility of foul play immediately but I'm truly convinced it isn't so. I've been in situations like that before and you get a quick and vehement and very clearly-worded denial from a 'responsible spokesperson'. Today? Chaos. Three different spokespersons from three different departments all called me separately, contradicting each other in details and clearly totally flustered by the whole thing. If it had been planned, the follow-up would have been much more focused." Cornwell was about to put down the phone when he added, "But then—?"

"Yes?"

"Well, there's the whole lawyer thing."

"What lawyer thing?"

"Well, it's just bizarre. His lawyer turned himself in for the 'murder'—except, of course, there is no murder. Poor man comes down from The Hague with the reprieve, gets the government to recognize it and has his client die in his arms."

"In his arms?"

"Yeah—I guess it would unhinge anyone."

"Anybody seen him?"

"The lawyer? I did, for like a minute maybe in the station, being handed over to the psychologists."

"He had long white spidery lines up his arm?"

"Yeah! How'd you know about that?"

"Any burn damage? Signs of explosion or fire on his body? Or D'aillard's?"

"No, the guy had a heart attack. His lawyer hugged him and he slumped over in his arms. No other signs. Nothing."

"Do they do autopsy's there?"

"Sure."

"You know the coroner? Well enough to ask a confidential question?"

"If it's got to be real confidential, I might need a plane ticket out of town before I ask. But I could ask."

"Book your ticket and then ask him if he took the internal temperature of the corpse."

dreamland

Australia

Benny was missing.

"It's not the first time."

"He could get lost going behind a bush to take a piss."

"He's probably in Darwin, he's just lost his way," Rafael answered defensively. *You have to have a way to lose it*, Kate thought but couldn't work up a rationale for saying so.

He'd only been gone two days and no one else was worried about it. Even Dolores shrugged it off. "Let him make himself useful to someone, then I'll worry about him," she sniffed.

But, to Kate, it was a warning, something ominous, like a rustling in the brush.

So she took matters into her own hands. The bi-weekly trip to Darwin was a chance to blow off steam, to hit the discount store Dolores and her pals browsed endlessly and generally without buying anything. Rafael would come along to trade weed for gemstones and supplies for his jewelry-making. Now she convinced Rafael to make the trip early. She needed to get away, to be able to be alone in her own thoughts for just a little while.

Dolores and what Kate thought of as the coven—Minerva, Alda and Mama Bill—packed the back of the van, tossing off snarky comments at the English world through the windows like a shrink minding his patients or zookeepers at the monkey house.

From the homeland to the highway was almost a third of the journey. In less than ten minutes, traffic ground to a crawl near the turn in the river, the place clogged with trucks delivering steel girders, sheetrock and roof tiles for the coming Miller's Superstore and the inevitable development next door, a Photo-shopped mirage of idyllic suburban split-levels, manicured lawns and cookie-cutter streets. Huge drills threw up dust clouds as a spidery metal frame rose against the blinding sun and bulldozers ripped away at the riotous tropical forest.

"That's it! Tear down the jungle so we can have a couple big lawns, y'know?" Dolores cracked.

"The concrete's so much nicer to sleep on in the heat!"

"You got just the crops for their back yards, Rafael!"

"That's so not happening."

"We'll see, we'll see!"

"Hold my hand?" asked Minerva, the deputy wise-cracker, in a bright flowered dress and hair that shone almost violet in the sunlight. Kate took it with a smile.

Minerva had brought a cracked hand to the clinic early in Kate's stay. Dolores had asked Kate to mind her while she set up, leaving Kate holding Minerva's hand between hers, humming while rubbing the surface, losing herself in the sound. After about ten minutes, Dolores had returned, examined the hand briefly and nodded. "That should do it," she'd said and waved goodbye to Minerva, leaving Kate speechless.

"Her hand's fine—what can you do for her brain?" cracked Alda, Minerva's sister, from the other side of the bench. Kate had cured her migraines.

"Kate can fix anything," added Mama Bill, a three-pack-a-day smoker rumored to be around 100 years old. She hovered in the back of the van, knitting and laughing at everyone else's jokes. Mama had only agreed to let Kate work on her after Kate relieved the pain of a brain tumor for Martin Dawes, a tribal leader. Martin was beyond cure but went to the end at peace. Now Kate was relieving Mama's arthritis to a degree even Dolores couldn't. "Anything but Rafael's driving."

The sun blazed over Darwin's skyscrapers and cast deep shadows beneath its palm trees. The streets were crammed with the lunch crowd and a few conspicuous refugees from the beach.

Rafael stashed the van in the ground floor of an enormous parking garage.

"I'm gonna check the spots, see if Benny's been around," he said. "No, alone—you would be...conspicuous. I'll be back in an hour, we can revisit anything that looks promising."

Kate didn't like it. She didn't feel any warning flags but it didn't feel right. But, without any solid objection, she could only nod and watch Rafael take off.

The store was shopping-as-therapy, getting lost in the abundance of nothing. Minerva and Alda argued over fine-woven cotton for dresses and Dolores abandoned her determination to live off the land and gave in to fresh strawberries, jalapeño peppers and ribs. Mama Bill sampled the brightest red L'Oreal lipstick at the counter, laughing uproariously while reapplying it in front of every mirror in the place. Kate grabbed a bag of Oreos and a Bundaberg Blood Orange pop bottle on her way to the supplement aisle. There, she picked out a box of Berry Flavor Iron Pills for some of the kids at the clinic and heard Dolores snorting— but not objecting—behind her. That was a measure of success— Dolores didn't accept any aspect of Western medicine without a fight.

She really did feel at home with them, as much as she ever had anywhere. Kate's passport was bogus, she'd traded her Canadian documents for Irish ones after joining the tribe. As long as no one stopped her for anything serious, maybe she could stay here for years.

She'd become aware of Renn lurking in the back of her mind, not often and never for long. It felt like she only sensed him as he was leaving or after he'd gone. At first, there'd been pangs of regret and then even anger—what did he want? When was he going to call them back? But as time went on, she lost any real belief that call would come. He'd put her somewhere she could get lost, really lost, away from the world and if she was practical and realistic, it was a good place to be. If she had to twist a few thoughts one last time to get legal, to make a home for herself, at least it would be for a reason. A new life was laid out in front of her and she was determined to meet it headon.

Reaching the check-out line, maybe they *were* a bit loud. The cashier, a stiff-looking older white woman, threw them a look of distaste. Kate smiled back, determined to be pleasant and drawing a condescending look in response. *I feel guilty about Renn's stupid bogus credit cards. It's still theft, even if it's CIA money or KGB or whatever*, she thought.

She handed over the card, as she had twenty times before. The cashier swiped it and her smile developed a little lemon around the edges. "Oh dear," she said, "it's been rejected. Can you wait right here just a moment?" She showed the screen immediately to the woman at the next window.

The room closed in on Kate all at once.

They know, she thought, the chill running through her. *They've been monitoring all over the world, waiting for one of us to appear on the radar. If they've canceled the credit card, they've canceled that passport. The other passport doesn't have an entry stamp. I'll have no way to travel, no way to escape. And Rafael and Dolores and the others will get sucked in after me.*

"Can I see the card please?" she said, voice quavering. "That magnetic strip's always been a little—"

"I'll just hold it for Security," the cashier said firmly, placing the card on the lip of the screen in front of her. Kate could feel her triumph as she waved for the guard.

The nasty old crone was just flaunting her position—she had no idea what she was into. Kate could force her to see differently—could make her see the code reversed, make her apologize, make her give back the card in a second.

If only it would do any good. The 'rejected' code was already in the records, stored in the company's servers. If Kate blanked out the staff here and in their headquarters (if she only knew how), it would still appear on the copies L Corp, ASIO, CIA or Interpol would surely demand later on. The images of the members of her party were on the video files taken throughout the store, those blinking little red eyes she saw everywhere now.

And there would be worse to come, surely.

In fact, it came instantly.

Multiple probes, not just local but converging from all over, detecting her rogue signal, triangulating her location, communicating with each other and calling out the alarm.

There were so many of them, coming so quickly, that it was all she could do just to block them. *Do they recognize me? Probably not, just an unidentified mindbender signal from an unexpected location. But as soon as they get to the security cameras...what if we're all held at the police station...?*

There was already a security guard near the door. Just her luck to draw the one body-builder-under-fifty store guard—and another ambling over in response to the cashier's call. If she bolted, they would just grab Minerva, Alma and Dolores, who were waiting patiently behind her, humming.

"I'll take the card—the whole thing's a mistake," Kate said firmly. All Renn had to do was talk to someone in that tone of voice and they did anything he wanted but the cashier didn't move—or even blink.

Literally—she wasn't blinking. Was she under suggestion? Or—was that a blink? Did she? *Have I just gone paranoid? How would I know?*

That's when she decided: *Just get out now, sort out the rest later.*

"Wouldn't you just try swiping it again?" she asked in her small-town Pennsylvania voice, the one she hated because it sounded so submissive—it was just about impossible to say 'no' to. "It's got to be a computer glitch."

"We'll wait," the cashier said.

"No, you'll try it again," Kate said and the voice that came out of her was a surprise—to her, more than anyone. It was quiet but commanding. There was no saying 'no' to it and this time, the cashier didn't try.

"We've never had that type of—" she said, swiping the card. The humming behind Kate grew louder; she felt it now through her toes.

As she swiped, Kate grabbed a peek at the terminal next to hers, showing that customer's credit card being accepted and fed that image to the cashier, whose eyes widened and cheeks flushed red. "Well, I'll—never mind Charley," she waved off the security guard, "just a glitch."

Annoyed, she reached clumsily for the receipt that should have been (but wasn't) printing out of the terminal. "It must be jammed again," she complained as Kate grabbed her shopping bag and bolted.

The automatic doors flew open as the group of women crashed out into the hot summer street. Kate led them at a feverish pace around the corner, then thrust her bags into Dolores' hands.

"Return this stuff to the police—now!"

"Daughter, it's—"

"Listen to me, Dolores. You don't know me, I showed up a few months ago and helped out around the village but you don't know who I am or where I came from. Just stick to that—and the rest of you, too!"

She left them open-mouthed and sprinted away. Six or seven blocks through thick crowds, she zigzagged from one street to another, changing directions frequently.

How could this be real? Could L Corp possibly monitor every cashier in the world for Kate Crowell sightings? It sounded idiotic but she knew what she'd felt. Within the next hour, someone would be plucking the story out of the cashier's memory and feeding it back across the ether to Pietr Volkov.

An animal moan escaped her throat. She felt trapped, helpless—the feeling was all too familiar and no feeling ever tore at her more. Sucking a deep breath, she turned the corner—and found the van idling there right in front of her.

"Come home, daughter," Dolores said from the passenger's window. "You're safer with us."

"You're not safe with me!" Kate argued. "The transaction never went through, they'll notice it tonight if they haven't already. And then—"

"And then they'll call the police," Dolores answered, "to look for four loud middle-aged Aboriginal women." She laughed. "Tell the police in this country you're searching for Aboriginals, they fill out the paperwork and throw it away because they know they can't find us."

"It's not the police," Kate said gravely. "There are...others who'll follow—much worse."

"From a credit card getting declined?"

"It's not a credit card, it's a red flag. I've told the bad guys where I am."

"We don't use the phone, no utilities, half the time we don't pay taxes—" It was Rafael leaning over from the driver's seat. "We're 50,000 years off the grid,"

"You *think*," Kate said in despair. "That's all they need to find you."

Dolores stared at her closely for a few moments. "If that's their game," she said, "we can play that too. Hide in the back—don't need passersby seeing you right now."

"They can see you."

Dolores grinned, pulling the door open. "Daughter, don't you know we all look alike?"

The workmen were laying roof beams into the three-story Miller's Superstore as they passed on the way back. The work blocked the way and several men held traffic signs and cones and looked over every car as it passed.

At home, Dolores had a huddled conference with Rafael and sent the other women packing around the village. "Go home," she motioned Kate to go with Rafael. "Collect the things you need. We're leaving."

"Who is?"

"All of us—we're moving the village," Rafael explained.

"We've used several sites over the years," Dolores added. "You'll figure out which is right and we'll join you."

"I dragged you into this—" Kate began, distraught and Dolores led her into the kitchen, pulling open a drawer brimming with recipes, ads for clothes she'd never afford and a stack of newspaper clippings she pressed into Kate's palm:

GUNFIGHT AT THE G8 CHORALE

read the headline on top of the pile. She'd seen the picture before: herself, bright in foreground against a dark sky, lightning bursting inches from her face; Renn and Pietr Volkov facing off behind her. There were three more clippings underneath.

"Recognized you the first day you got here," Dolores said.

"Why didn't you call the police?"

She received a Mona Lisa smile in response. "We try not to disturb the police. If you'd been a danger, we'd have dealt with you early on."

"You've taken enough risks for me," Kate said. "I have to go back out into the world."

Dolores fixed her with a steady gaze. "You like being in the middle of things."

"I like what I'm doing here."

Dolores shook her head. "You're great at it but the thrill isn't here for you, it's out there. You doing good or bad purpose?"

"Sometimes bad things done for good purpose?" Kate said.

"Hmph! Easier said than done," Dolores sniffed. "I decided you're okay that first day you came; I haven't changed my mind. Crazy world makes sane people do crazy things." She pointed at the newspaper clippings. "Those people with you—they crazy too?"

"I'm not touching that one," Kate said, surprised to find herself laughing out loud. "They're my friends. They're trying to do the right thing."

"They didn't abandon you here?" Dolores asked. It was a good question. Certainly, it's what Kate felt when she arrived. But now, searching through her feelings, she felt Renn keeping her company—not close by but somewhere, aware of her without intruding.

"I don't think so," she said. "If I need them, they'll come." She ached, saying it, feeling herself slipping back into the mindbender universe.

"Then maybe it's time you should need them. You're under our protection until they come."

"Your—what kind of protection?" Then the look on Dolores' face silenced her.

The next morning was spent moving to the new village. This entailed a long period of what seemed like wandering, with Rafael and Dolores pointing out features of the land that somehow suggested changes of direction to them.

They ended up on a long, flat rise with several old unoccupied concrete structures and the skeleton of the Miller's Superstore glinting through the haze below.

"This is where we want to be?" Kate asked Rafael.

"This is where we're meant to be," he nodded.

She'd felt probes as soon as they'd approached the place. She started blocking instinctively but they just grew more persistent.

Max. This is the moment, Max. Max. His grey eyes. Max Renn. Max the spy, Max the wolf, Max the unhappy mindbender-master. She'd caught intermittent traces of his voice mingled with her own, like a fog horn along the coast, a deep tone under her thoughts, ever since they'd separated. They'd never been totally out of touch, miles be damned. *Now is the time, Max. I need help, your kind of help.* As she called out to him, it felt inevitable. *Get back to me, Max. I'm ready to be a warrior—this is not my natural world. Tell me where to go.*

When she looked up at her watch again, twenty minutes had passed. She had no more information than before. *In the morning,* she decided, *I'm taking off on my own. I'll leave enough of a mental image to draw the bad guys away.* She wasn't going to expose the rest of them to this danger for no reason.

Between bouts of setting up their houses, Dolores, Mama and Alma kept returning to the cliff's edge all through the afternoon, watching the construction. Eventually, Dolores came up to Kate and said, "You know there's four of them down there, on the watch."

"I feel them," Kate said, surprised by the question.

"They don't know what they're looking for. They're like a conduit for someone else at a distance. It's not your friends?"

"No, not them," Kate said flatly.

She returned to Rafael's hut, setting up house. Calling it a hut was an insult—it had several chambers big enough for three or four to sleep, double-insulated doors and fine-mesh windows. She tried to keep to her work, both to relieve her nerves and make sure the probes found nothing worth paying attention to.

As the sky went red and began to deepen, a growl seemed to grow from inside her and then all around. She stepped from the tent to feel the air shivering, jittery. The sound grew in her feet and legs—and then a huge shudder rippled across the floor of the valley.

She ran, following the sound to the edge of the cliff. The whole construction site was in chaos—strong men crippled by sudden splitting headaches and ringing ears, electrical equipment malfunctioning, cranes stalling, generators running wild and exploding, tractor tires bursting without reason.

And then the superstructure of the Miller's Superstore teetered in mid-air, screeching and groaning, and folded right up, collapsing into a cloud of dust ten stories in the air. The roar rippled off the cliffs for seven minutes. When the smoke cleared, all that was left was a sinkhole where the store had stood and a slice of billboard, advertising antiseptically-safe suburban living.

Kate whirled to see Dolores, Minerva and Alda standing next to her, their humming finally dying away, watching the scene with satisfaction.

"Okay," Dolores sighed, "tomorrow we move again."

auld lange syne

Brno, Czech Republic

Brno was bounded by hills, soft-sloped like a woman's shoulders. The autumn clouds glided over tile roofs with curved cupolas and multiple chimneys, iron-grilled light stanchions and sleek trams tying the ancient patchwork together. The restaurants smelled of sausages and gravy, potato pancakes and fried cheese.

Renn traced the arc of a bending ridge, nursing a tender ankle and a grudge. Spindly trees poked through an early snow. He'd had another visitation, another voice whispering in the night—but this time, a familiar voice: *I own one or two of your secrets, Maximka. One or two even you don't know. I am in hiding now because of you. We should make a visit. Quickly.*

Lazar's voice was older naturally but he recognized it immediately. The whispers had led him to this derelict outlier's neighborhood, deep in afternoon shadow and plain as dust, stoic bungalows with boarded-up windows and appliance museums in the back yards, the house's barely a stone's throw apart. The few modest cars were run up on the sidewalks so as not to block the narrow streets. Renn inhaled, taking in the unspoken voices below:

Where's the cat? How'd he get out?

Another six bags and I can take a break.

She's cheating on me, I know it, she's with that fucking meth case up the hill. If I sneak around the far side, I could see...

Why do fools fall in love? Why do they si-ing so...

It's my knee again, I'm going to be a cripple. That doctor's a fraud...

Lazar was close, he was sure. *I am in hiding now because of you.* What have I done to him now? Renn searched for the old professor's prickly consciousness amidst the tangle of voices:

I should get the decent coffee next time, it's only a hundred koruna more...

The red wire attaches to the blue...

...bastard hides up there all day; she could come and go and I'd never prove...

Nothing. The old man still had his gift for elusiveness. *He contacted me—he wants me to find him. Or maybe he wants to find me.*

Renn stopped blocking, let his thoughts float free, surrendering to the man who knew his vibrations as well as anyone in the world. And heard a click, as if in answer, as the back door of a house directly below—two-story, paint crumbling, steps missing, broken windows in inaccessible locations—swung open like an invitation.

His antennae jumped to maximum. Had anyone else noticed the open door?

I could give her the best food in the world, she'd still wander all over...

How does anyone get TV reception in this gulley? Maybe a clothes hanger...

I'll kill the fucker if he's so much as looked at her...

All clear. Renn scrambled down the hill, kicking up a flurry of snow and clots of mud in front of him. He scanned the house from just outside the door—windows downstairs locked solid, heavy dark silence at the core of the ground floor. Deep electrical hum in the basement and dripping sink in the kitchen—the deserted-looking house had power and water service.

The door was still open, beckoning and dangerous. Renn vaulted up the steps and through the doorway, prepared for an attack but, inside, the place was eerily silent. Was that a light down the hall? He focused on the point of light and suddenly it sucked him down the corridor, which got longer and narrower as he moved faster and faster toward the end of it. And then there he was in a comfortable living room, clean and simple and relaxed, a good solid chair, shelves of books and good music playing—not music he recognized, not even a genre of music he knew, just something that felt comforting and familiar yet still a little edgy...wait, what was this about? He saw color in frames on the wall and they were retro and challenging—again, describing them but he didn't see them.

It's a trick. Despite being seated on a very comfortable couch with really relaxing cushions all around him, good for a snooze, he leaned sideways and immediately hit the wall—and the living room disappeared and he was back in the hall, hearing a familiar voice: "Oh, for God's sake, Papa."

Her face peeked out of the doorway a moment later. He hadn't imagined she'd still be with him. "Hello, Max. Come in, please. No more traps."

"Hello, Nicola," Renn answered. "It's been a long time." She met his smile without returning it.

They'd constructed a makeshift shelter within the confines of the living room, heavy rubber cladding and wool blankets hung from the beams to prevent magnetic interference. A few bulbs on metal clips threw a quavering light. A hot plate sat atop a small refrigerator, a large garbage can full of empty food packages nestled alongside. Old newspapers, liquor bottles and syringes were swept into a corner. "From the previous tenants," Nicola cracked, tapping her forehead. "We had to scare them off. They keep their distance now."

Elias Lazar lay on the settee, gaunt and shivering under a throw, eyes like a cats behind magnifying spectacles. Piles of books lay against the leg of the couch where he could reach them without moving, an old desktop radio close by on the nightstand.

"Either my traps are getting lazy," Lazar rasped "or you've developed your skills."

"Not intentionally. I'd hoped never to need them again."

"Yes, of course—the 'end of history.' That world didn't show up after all, did it? Where did you become such an optimist, Maximka? You should have known better."

"He did know better," Nicola said. "He knew enough to leave." The look on her face was an accusation and the room went silent for an awkward moment.

"I—I knew I couldn't stay, that's all I knew," Renn answered finally and Lazar seemed grateful to move on.

"We all move on as we need to," he said blandly, "and you certainly have. I saw you in Rome on...what is it?" glancing at Nicola.

"YouTube."

Lazar rolled his eyes. "I'm too old. There you were again, you and Pietr at each other's throats, like old times. It almost made me nostalgic. You were throwing lightning bolts."

"I was dodging them. Marat threw them."

"Marat? The assassin? He wasn't in the pictures. I remember you making electricity from your fingers. Electrocuting two of my assistants."

"I never meant to. I didn't know it was possible. They hit me and I responded before I knew what was happening."

"Well, it was a weapon. I thought maybe you'd developed that weapon also over the years."

"Don't be coy, Professor. What's the question you aren't asking?"

Lazar clutched the back of the couch and pulled himself upright. "You remember Vlad Saminov—one of my assistants you *didn't* kill?"

Renn nodded. "I remember."

"When the program disbanded, he went West. A week after Rome, his wife appears at our door —disturbed, disconnected. Here and not here, in a way we remember from the Project but none of the usual methods bring her out of it. After a week with us, she's still drifting away."

"And physically damaged," Nicola said, her face dark.

"Burns suspiciously like lightning up and down her forearm. We tend to her but I cannot put a suggestion on her to find out what happened, she's too fragile. A week later, a NATO man, Cornwell, shows up here, you know him perhaps?"

"Cornwell?"

"An American, tall black man—"

"I knew him, years ago, for a little while."

"That is what he says. Well, he's found me on Vlad's phone, somehow—"

"The call list on his mobile," Nicola fills in.

"Stasia remembers him from the night Vlad died, I can see it without having to bend her. She finally talks, she says, 'I killed Vladimir.' Vlad was taking her to Brussels to meet this Cornwell. On the way to meet Vlad, a man's voice speaks from inside her head and she is helpless. She meets him—young, not so tall, she tells me this later, a furry mustache and a silly brimmed hat."

"I caught a glimpse of him in Rome after the G8," Renn said. "He's L Corp—one of Pietr's men."

"Hmm—next time you see him, be careful. He places a metal spring around her finger and a box that hums on her belt, attached with wires under the clothes. She feels her hair lifting, you understand? From the magnetic field. And when they reach the safe house in Brussels, she puts her arms around Vlad and the current goes through her and Vlad is dead where he sits."

"What is it?"

"Cornwell tells me Vlad warned that some new weapon was being developed right under NATO's nose and he wants to know is this it?"

"How's NATO in this?"

"Vlad was working for them in Brussels. Some advanced project."

"And? What do you think?"

Lazar checked a teacup and, finding it empty, smashed it into the corner. "Vlad called me, that night. He discovered he'd been put under suggestion, didn't know for how long and was terrified someone was controlling his work."

"He was an assistant in a teaching laboratory—what could he know that was so terrifying?"

"What you taught us," Lazar said.

"Me?"

Nicola brought another cup of tea. Lazar stirred and sipped before answering. "We were a backwater, the three of us in the Research Department, myself, Inyushin and Saminov. We were nothing until you began electrocuting your instructors—"

"Not intentionally! And twice only!"

"Twice was enough! Qualified, security-cleared teachers developed serious respiratory ailments or petitioned for assignments in Yakutsk rather than teach Max Renn! However, to Moscow, this was a spectacular development—an agent who could not only read minds but electrocute the enemy with the touch of a finger! Suddenly we got funding, which was wonderful, but of course, for funding, they expected results. We had to come up with a safe way to teach you. You remember we taught you base frequency?"

Renn, reciting like a schoolboy: "One plus one is two, two plus two are four, base frequency is the frequency at which a person's—or a cockroach's or a desk's—electrons resonate. Electrons are electrons, base frequency groups electrons into a person or a donkey or a desk. In another person, it's the phone number to their consciousness."

"It's more like a chord—a combination of frequencies that have a harmonious or dissonant relationship," Nicola said. "Families work in the same 'key' with harmonics and overtones all over the place. With lovers, the shared frequencies strengthen over time. A person's 'chord' grows more complex with age and experience."

"Nicola's dissertation," Lazar, proud father, added. "Unfortunately, we're at the beginning of understanding and this information is most valuable to a type of person we no longer wish to associate with. The thing for you to know, Maximka, is that your base frequency is unique in the world."

"In what way?"

"You were our secret," Lazar smiled. "Not just from the enemy but our own people, even from you. No one knew but myself, Vlad and Inyushin." Renn's eyebrows rose. "Every person has a set base frequency. Everyone else ever tested. Yours changed every time someone else came into the room. You set up a harmonic instantly with whoever was talking to you, thinking about you. You juggled six different frequencies at a time—maybe more, that's all the people we could fit into that tiny room."

"It explains so much!" Nicola burst. "Most mindbenders read minds from outside, they have to establish contact—with you, there's no separation. It's as though you're inside them all at once."

"It sounds so *good* when you say it," Renn said.

"It explains also your ability with electricity. All human bodies carry an electrical charge but it's not concentrated enough to do any harm. In your case, when endangered or enraged, your base frequency swapped suddenly to your antagonist's polar opposite."

"And everything transfers at once. I fry them."

"Technically sketchy but it gets to the spirit of the thing," Lazar nodded. "Since you didn't have a static base frequency, we couldn't use it to isolate you, so we had to find another way to safely teach you. It took four months but we found an alloy that would suck the electricity out of the air—and you—and collect it where you couldn't set it off. We built an enclosure for you from this material, a safe space."

"I remember that stupid box. I had no idea what it was."

Lazar dropped a piece of coppery metal on the table. Renn picked it up.

"What is it?"

"It was in Stasia's pocket when she came to us, melted into her jacket. A piece of the coil that killed Vlad." Lazar's gaze was severe. "The same metal we used to protect ourselves from you."

"So Vlad was selling the stuff to NATO?"

"If he was just selling the alloy, he'd have long since made his sale and flown the coop. He was working on 'advanced weaponry,' she said."

"What kind? Did she know?"

"She didn't have the chance to tell us. A few days ago, Stasia was electrocuted right outside my classroom. She was feeling better, we were to have lunch. The killer walks up to her, scorches her to a crisp and walks away. People see but don't know what they saw. None of the hospitals admit anyone with strange burn marks up the arm, other than Stasia herself. I get three probes right after and my teaching assistant calls to say a man came by the office looking for me—young, furry mustache, straw hat. He leaves a card saying he is De Jogt but he is not De Jogt."

"Who is De Jogt?"

"Oh, I didn't say? I'm confused. De Jogt is Vlad's partner on this advanced weaponry in Amsterdam."

"For NATO."

"That's what Cornwell said. And since then, we're on the run, as you see. And I decide I must flash you a message."

"Why did you wait so long? You saw me fighting Pietr in June."

"We didn't know which side you were on," Nicola said drily. Renn stared, confused. "You left," she said finally.

"I'm sorry—?"

"You left. You took your money and your passports and went to America. When the Soviet Union disappeared."

"I—? What could I have done?"

"*Anything* would have been more than what you did." She began stacking plates, but they rattled and skittered in her hands until they almost spilled to the floor. "You and Pietr were the two at the top, oil and water or not. The teachers, the administrators looked to you—"

"For order," Renn interrupted. "To keep everybody in line, no deviating from the party-approved—"

"To keep the Project from falling apart, along with the rest of the country!" Nicola burst. "Max, Pietr held us together. He kept the Project going when everything around was chaos, when people were selling themselves and eating garbage and starving to death! He found backers with money, good foreign money that was worth something, even if we were mindbending to sell luxury condominium timeshares or foreign politicians. Where there was nothing, he made something. The world went capitalist, so Pietr became our entrepreneur. He made mindbending a business."

"Such an achievement."

"Fuck you, Max!" Nicola shouted, shocking herself as much as the others. "He kept us alive! He kept us together!"

"Ten years under Yeltsin," Lazar said, "we survived. Pietr makes sure the local government fears us, so nobody kicks us out of the building while he finds us work. Even the new KGB, the

SVR, they don't trust us but Pietr keeps watching and waiting. And he finds the man who sees how useful we can be."

"Papa—" Nicola warned.

"Daughter, he has to understand. We're out now."

"Litvinenko," she whispered. "There is no 'out,'" and the light dawned on Renn.

"He made Putin," he interjected.

"Not him alone," Lazar answered. "Pietr developed 'influence' on some of the old guard, a few who mattered. It's not the first time mindbenders were used this way—you might even say it was a tradition."

"The KGB *apparatchik* nobody ever heard of suddenly becomes Yeltsin's right hand and then his named successor. The old rednose turns over power and conveniently dies." Renn considered this for a moment. "So why aren't you with SVR?" he asked. "Surely Putin wanted you."

"This was Pietr's masterstroke!" Lazar actually cackled. "You know him, Maximka—he doesn't do one thing at a time, it's one thing doing while two things plotting ahead. He's made the connection with Jim Avery while working for Putin—big money, big connections and America! At the exact moment Putin takes control with Pietr's help, Pietr flies all of us, the whole operation, out of Russia. It's brilliant. Nobody is watching or if they are, they don't know who to report to. Those who want to stay in America get jobs with *Your World*/L Corp. Those who want to move on get severance and a pension, like good socialists. I receive a much-appreciated stipend from a holding company in Switzerland every month."

"I don't think you should count on that anymore. Okay, Pietr was a leader; I wasn't. Is that the point?"

"The point is, we're at a crossroads. Nicola and I have to make a decision. Pietr's organization is very impressive. Corporate security, government security, they have time to send a young man all the way here to execute a widow on a public street in broad daylight just to make a point." He rearranged himself on the settee—his limbs were frail, his movements careful and cautious. "The people you had in Rome—they're of your organization, yes?"

"Right."

"They seemed very capable, especially the young woman. I don't expect you to match the size of Pietr's group—" Lazar said and Renn understood all at once where the conversation was heading.

"We've—we've only been together a short while—" he stammered.

"How many agents do you have in total?"

"Me?"

"Yes."

"Right now?"

"No, last Thursday. Of course, now! Twenty? Fifty? A hundred?"

"At the moment—counting me—three."

Nicola blurted out a laugh like a seal. Lazar's face fell, the needle firmly in the balloon, followed by embarrassment for Renn and fear for his daughter. The old man settled against the couch and pulled a shawl around his shoulders.

"This is not good," he said finally, rounding on Renn with his face reddening. "You spent your entire time in the Project resisting everything we tried to teach you. Somehow you found that energy beam that locked up Pietr in Rome—"

"I—I have no idea what that was," Renn admitted. "I don't know how it happened."

"Well, you'd better FIGURE IT OUT!" Lazar thundered, shocking everyone in the room. It took him several moments to regain his composure; then he continued. "Pietr Volkov is not a romantic; he is a *professional*. He takes no risks without weighing the odds and finding them in his favor. If he is hijacking weapons meant for NATO, he's decided his organization has an advantage over the world's biggest multinational defense cooperative—this is hard to understand."

"They have influence over many of the leaders who fund NATO—and as a privately-held corporation, they're answerable to no one."

Lazar rubbed his chin. "Hmph! Better than the Soviet!" He eyed Renn up and down. "He has nothing to fear from you."

"We stopped him in Rome—and he tried a second time on Singh just after; I stopped him there as well."

"You can't be everywhere, with your three agents. He can." Lazar's face grew weary. "Maximka, you have more ability than all of them, you always did. If you are prepared to do what is necessary, you have a chance, despite everything. But—"

"But what?"

"I said it already—Pietr is a professional. And you are not."

"And?"

Lazar's eyes were cold. "An amateur acts from conviction or revenge, he acts out of feeling. He may do amazing things for a while but feeling will turn or waver, it will betray him sooner or later. A professional acts to achieve his objective, he is cold-blooded and single-minded; he is not distracted by feeling or passion or guilt. He does what is necessary."

"I'm not a killer."

"There will come a moment when it's kill or be killed. Facing someone you sympathize with—maybe more than they deserve—and if you hesitate, you will be the victim."

"I'm not a killer."

Lazar squirmed on the couch. "As one who has to depend on you, that is what worries me."

Renn listened impassively, lifted Lazar's tea cup and smashed it in the corner with the others.

"Too bad for you," he said. "There's nobody out there but me and Pietr. He's corralled the world's dangerous professionals and sent several of them after you. So, brilliant or fumbling, I'm all you've got. Better get ready to go." He moved out of the shelter to the front windows, peeking between the crossbeams:

Goose is better than the lamb but greasy...

What time must I leave? Am I late?

Maybe if I run wire out the window, I can get a decent picture. What time is the match?

...bastard hides in that place all day so she could come and go and I'd never be able to prove...

There was something out there—he could feel it. Nicola wandered over, not exactly friendly but needing reassurance, maybe. "Do you know someone with an impressive car?"

"Not that would loan it to me."

"They don't have to be willing."

He tracked the deep vibrations he'd heard before entering the house to the staircase. A gasoline-powered generator stood in the basement below. Renn returned to the front window.

"Where can you go?"

"We have family in—"

"It's safer with no family. They can trace—"

"Max," she whispered, suddenly close to his ear, "he'll be dead in four months, maybe less. Just get us out of here. I'll fend for myself."

"Not much of a life for you."

"I'll have a long life after him and soon enough—let me have what's left. If you can get us to—"

She's with that fucking meth case up the hill. If I sneak around the far side, I could see...

"Hush!" Renn snapped.

I could just jump-start it for a while...

If I wear the red, he'll notice me for sure...

...bastard hides in that place all day so she could come and go and I'd never be able to prove...

"What?" Nicola asked. Renn was tight as a wire, eyes slit open, eyeballs rolled up underneath.

"Who lives *there*?" pointing fiercely at the next house downhill.

"They come and go. Who knows?"

"I'm getting the same thoughts from a few minutes ago. *Verbatim*. It's a loop." He moved quickly into the hall. "They're covering themselves. They're on the move."

She was alongside as he reached the stairs.

"Does your father have a walker?"

"There's a motorized wheelchair in the shed out back."

"Is there more petrol?" She looked blank until he added, "For the generators."

"There in the corner—and in the basement, just under the steps."

He snatched two bottles from the stack in the corner where her father lay drowsy. "Fill these—quickly—and come right back."

"It won't leave much."

"You're not staying."

She returned with two half-full bottles, a twisted cloth rooted in petrol and protruding out the top. Renn nodded and took one. "Anarchy 101. Okay, we have six new neighbors. Two in the house right below, four coming from the house above." Renn pointed at the downhill house and then at her bottle. "Shooter Number One is in the window directly across the driveway—take him out with that. His backup is in the front window, watching the street—specifically, the blond across the street. As soon as Shooter One starts burning, you have to jump the driveway, grab his gun and shoot the backup. I'll take care of the four from uphill. Got it?" She nodded and began pulling nails so the window timbers would come off with a tug.

Renn moved back to the staircase. The basement door was opening, the vibrations of two intruders sounded inside and two more at the back entrance. He rubbed his fingers together until they sparked and set the cloth aflame.

He nodded to Nicola, who yanked the boards off the window and chucked her bottle. She was racing across the drive as the thing arced into the window opposite. The shooter screamed before the flame belched through the frame—a moment later, she was inside, grabbing for his weapon.

Renn tossed his bottle down the staircase. It smashed against the generator and spilled its contents over the floor and the gas canisters alongside. With a shudder felt through the house, the generator gulped and hiccupped—and the whole mess exploded.

Flames shot up the stairwell and shattered the basement windows; the howls of the shooters came from several directions at once.

Renn heard two gunshots next door as he lifted Lazar off the settee. He kicked through the front window timbers and carried the old man onto the front porch. Nicola came out of the window next door, rifle in hand to retrieve him.

Two shooters emerged around the side of the house, the first jumping onto the grass and rolling around to put out the flames consuming his coat. His partner ran up behind him to help. Renn kneaded his hands in the air to form an ion shield and flicked it at the partner. It caught him squarely in the neck and he went over like a tree trunk. Renn yanked the other up by his collar, the flames slowly flickering out.

"Is Volkov here?" he demanded. "Can you get him here?"

"I've never met him! Please—!"

A finger to the shooter's temple and he went rigid. "When you can move—in a few hours—you *find* him, you take a message to him. Tell him Max knows about Elena. You have that? Max Renn knows about Elena."

Ted Krever

"Max Renn knows about Elena," the shooter repeated, eyes glazed.

"You repeat that to Volkov himself—not an assistant, not on the phone. You understand?"

"I understand."

"Good." Renn dropped the man like a bag of laundry. Nicola had her father now in his wheelchair. Neighbors' faces hovered just inside their windows, checking out the commotion. Renn swept a hand slowly through the air and they drifted aimlessly away, wondering what had drawn them to the windows in the first place.

At dusk, an elderly man and his daughter flew first-class from Prague to Paris. From there, the trail became clouded as airline staffers reported transferring them onto flights to Jerusalem, Copenhagen, Montreal and Buenos Aires. The situation was further confused by the fact that they turned out not to have proper tickets for the Prague-Paris flight. The entire gate staff testified to seeing their names on the passenger manifest, though there was much confusion about what those names were. There was no luck in identifying their driver either, a thin dark-haired man whose license read Emil Vogel and who seemed to have disappeared completely as soon as the flight took off.

Book Three

reunion 5
December 2008

Darwin, Australia

The shooters carry Kate's cage out of the warehouse and stow it in the back of what looks like a laundry van. As they pull out into traffic, she can already read that someone—Dolores?—is taking care of Rafael's wound and her attention shifts to the oppressive climate inside.

"What have you got?" Volkov demands, prowling behind the front row seats.

"We've got a strong 16.5 mHz signal about ten blocks down, moving at automobile speed."

Kate tries rattling the magical cage they've shut her in—*try while they're otherwise occupied.*

"Remember," Volkov says, "De Jogt can block but he's not a mindbender. His signal probably isn't all that strong—I doubt he's anything over a .5."

The two shooters sitting behind the driver huddle over a cluster of monitors and sensor readouts. Listening to Volkov, they flip a switch or two and reorient themselves.

"Well, okay, now we've got about twelve possibles in the quadrant."

The wood framework is so flimsy, Kate feels she should be able to shake it apart. But the magnetic field around the cage holds the pieces taut.

"Where's Landau?" Volkov asks.

"Highway One, heading south."

Kate reaches for the crossbeams but the magnetic field thickens every time as she nears them so there's no penetrating.

"And what's that at nine-thirty?" Volkov asks.

"That's a false positive about half a mile away. Lutz bent a patrol cop—he pulled the guy over for an out-of-date inspection sticker. An electrician with an insane sound system in his car— three CD players, wave front speakers—he had a magnetic signature like a small reactor."

"Lutz knows what he's doing?" Volkov grills his lead man.

"He's thorough. If he had any doubts, he'd have told me."

"Alright," says Volkov and returns to prowling. "Take whatever target is closest to getting away and then the next." This is clearly just repeating normal procedure—the men up front exchange exasperated glances as soon as Volkov turns away.

A moment later, Kate sees Volkov retreating up the middle of the van, hunched-over. She stops probing the cage as he takes a seat facing her.

"You see my situation," he says, gesturing up front. "It's impossible to get good help."

"They seem competent."

Volkov throws his hands up. "Competent! We're on a mission and they're competent!"

"What's the mission?" Kate asks, knowing he'll ignore the question and he does.

"All of us here have a gift. You can't just go through the motions with a gift, you have to commit yourself to it. They expected a lot more from us when I was in training—"

"Your country was fighting for survival," Kate needles. "For these guys, it's a resume item and maybe a 401K."

Voice from up front: "He's a false positive."

"Jump to the next-closest profile fit."

"Yessir." Kate can hear in the voice that they knew this without asking.

Volkov's eyes flare. "It's a cause!" he rasps. "If I have to make that clear to them, I will." He makes an effort to slow down and reflect. "So, back in the warehouse, we were talking, you and me and the Soldier—"

"Greg."

"Yes, Greg. According to him, you're my deadly enemies, both of you. Is that correct?"

"You shot my lover right in front of me."

"Our business is persuasion. "

"I wasn't persuaded."

"It was a crude attempt. I've already abandoned it."

Is this his idea of flirting? she wonders, offended and curious at once. "You killed my father."

"You killed Marat."

"Marat was a hired hand. Don't tell me it's the same as my father."

"Don't tell me it's different. You don't know my feelings."

Now he's got feelings! Seriously, he's making overtures? Why?

"I could know your feelings—if you'd let me."

Volkov laughed. "You're much too powerful for that. There's no selective disclosure with you. I'm either wide-open to you or not. At the moment, the situation demands…caution, let's say."

"Wow, that sounds so reasonable. Like it's my fault—you'd be happy to open up if I wasn't so dangerous."

Volkov leans in, questioning. "You're still new to this, aren't you? I can tell you are. You can't understand the decisions I have to make. Max might, except he wants to destroy me. There are a few Young Turks inside my company who might, except they haven't the experience and the judgment and they want my job anyway. So it's true, I don't know who to open up to."

"It's lonely at the top. I can hear the violins."

"It's the truth—"

"Good for you. Your man ran my father over twice to make sure he wouldn't survive. Didn't run over him enough to kill him right away, of course. He lived long enough for the ambulance to arrive and take him halfway to the hospital, the EMT's breaking open his chest and—" her voice trailed off. "Maybe you ordered him to do it or maybe that's just the kind of people you hire— what's the difference?"

"It's a rough business."

"It's not my business."

"What business do you think it is?"

"I don't know—what business are the bad guys in the Bond movies in? Blowing up the world?"

"Who says I want to blow up the world?"

"You tried to force Singh to kill all those world leaders!"

"I never expected her to succeed!"

Kate almost chokes. "*What?*"

"She was in a narrow viewing box, surrounded by the best security money can buy. She was under suggestion. I had her totally under control until Max got in the way."

"Don't blame him. It was your plan—"

"Our plan was to get her to pull the gun from her bag. That would have been enough. She would then have hesitated—it was her natural inclination anyway—and the guards would have been all over her. Half those governments have us on retainer! We gain nothing killing leaders who are paying us! Our goal was simply to discredit her—and in the end, we managed it, no thanks to you."

Kate shakes her head. "Excuse me! I'm so ashamed."

"You think what you're doing is so different?"

"It's entirely different!"

"Because you're on the side of the angels." A disbelieving smile breaks across Volkov's face. "You and Max, you take it all so seriously."

"You don't?"

"Of course not! When we convince a government panel to approve a vaccine I know is flawed, fine, I lose sleep over that one. But when we 'persuade' some fool with more money than brains to buy a stainless-steel Bluetooth refrigerator or a $50 artisanal vodka with barley crushed under the hooves of Bolivian mountain goats—what's the difference?"

"It's fraud!"

"If they can afford such nonsense, it's a meaningless dent in the wallet, creating employment for people who grew up eating bugs and bushes."

"For God's sake!"

"Okay, maybe it's a bad example. But politics? Seriously? It's *all* window-dressing. They shuffle off the Western set with the sagebrush and the horses and bring out the big-city pinstripe suits and cool jazz. Meanwhile, the course of what we laughingly call civilization is decided in parlors and clubs, long before Election Day, by people you've never heard of."

Kate squirms. "That's what I said—the vast conspiracy to take over the world."

"Not so vast—only a few people. And people at the top don't conspire. They have shared interests. They want the same as the rest of us (a snort here from Kate)—they do! Life, liberty and the pursuit of happiness. As long as no one's placing obstacles in their way, the rest of the world can dance however it wants."

"Because most laws don't affect them—they don't care which way things go?"

"About what? The Right to Bear Arms? Affirmative Action? Gay Marriage? The Rights of the Unborn? Don't be absurd. At that level, it's all a circus—if you run it, you're responsible for the results. What sane person wants *that*? Let the politicians have their victories and losses, give us what matters—unfettered trade, deregulated markets. Starve out government so it can't gum up the works. Minimize taxes so the money flows."

"To you and your friends."

Volkov waves his hands dismissively. "It would anyway, we're just making the process more fluid."

"And the rest of us drive ourselves mad fighting over what's left," Kate muses and Volkov doesn't bother disputing. "So what do you need me for?"

"You have a unique skill set."

"Such as?"

"Such as the ability to sway whole groups at once, lay an illusion over them seamlessly without any preparation."

"Max can do that."

"He won't do it for me."

"You could do it yourself."

"I work for L Corp. You don't."

"So?"

Volkov shrugged. "Use your imagination."

A voice from up front: "Another false positive."

"You know the drill," Volkov answers back. "Just follow the protocols." His focus returns to her.

"You want me to work for you without officially being on the payroll."

"Correct. Why? Think!"

She tried reading him but he bounced her off rudely—he wanted her to work it out for some reason of his own. "To do work you don't want to admit you're doing."

"Exactly."

"Why would I do things even *you* wouldn't admit to?"

"To help bring about a more peaceful world."

Against all her best instincts, Kate laughs. The laugh skitters out of her like air from a balloon. "Peaceful for who?"

"L Corp is a contractor to the US government. That puts certain limits on us and —"

"Seriously? You can't spy on Americans, so you want *me* to do it for you?"

"It might be for a good cause." Volkov's showing all his teeth. He might think it's charming but Kate isn't even sure it's a smile.

"Might be? You're not sure."

"I can't talk about all the details."

"Forget that. I'm not interested in being used by —"

"Max used you, in his vendetta against me. He had no chance without you and the soldier —"

"Greg."

"Yes, Greg. His little army. But really, it's only you. Without you, he'd be a fly buzzing around our ears. Together, you're a threat to our worldwide enterprise."

"'Worldwide enterprise'—you're a gang of thugs. I'm sorry—a *corporation* of thugs. You boys get yourselves off on destruction!"

"We're a multinational entity, with worldwide interests and more power than most countries! And don't preach to me about destruction. Vanderbilt, Carnegie—why did they create their lovely charities? To atone for their sins. Ask the staff at

WordPerfect and Lotus about Bill Gates—oh, you can't, they're out of business! Business works because the superior idea destroys the inferior, superior execution destroys inferior, ruthlessness crushes goodwill. Evolution is destruction.

"The common person doesn't see it because history makes it seem inevitable—but that's because the winners write history." He smiles a steely smile. "You see? I don't pander to you. Max doesn't challenge you, doesn't even teach you. He's not a mentor." Volkov actually laughs or whatever his equivalent is. "Truth is, he's just trying to hang on. Kate stares sullenly but without reply. "You know it's true," Volkov concludes. "In our business, we can't be sentimental."

"I told you—I'm not in your business."

"What business are you in, then?"

"I'm a healer. I mend broken bones, dissolve tumors, close wounds—"

"With sympathetic vibration. Of course."

"Because that's what we can do that's *positive*!" Kate's voice rises in frustration. "If we're not obsessed with making people do what they don't want to do and exposing things they want to keep private."

"And that's what you want—to be positive. And helpful," Volkov says quietly, almost tenderly. "It must be satisfying, being so good." She feels the acid rise in her stomach but he continues before she can respond. "But that isn't what you feel, is it? You *love* the fight. It might be satisfying to do right but it isn't fun. It isn't wicked fun, is it? You enjoyed your fun, blowing away Marat's blasts, throwing my shooters into the Tiber, making them see statues fly and catacomb paintings come to life. That was impressive but more than that, it was being alive, far more than being the assistant to some tribal witch doctor."

"I'll put my life in Dolores' hands if I ever get ill, thank you very much."

"Alright, I pushed too far. But I'm right about the rest, I know I am. That's where I've got an advantage. Max doesn't have fun. Max doesn't know how. He *cares*. He wants to do the right thing. He wants the world to want to do the right thing. You and I, we know the truth—the world doesn't really want the right thing. People want to be bad. They want to win. They want everyone to be nice to them but they sure don't want to have to be nice to everyone else. I have opportunities for people who know what they *really* want. I can give you a chance to do things you'd never tell anyone—and get paid handsomely for it."

"That's not who I am."

"No, of course not," he arches an eyebrow, delight all over his face. "You want to go back to the bush and set bones and deliver babies or whatever. That's what your heart cries out for. The thrill I saw in your eyes in Rome, that was just a mirage, that was me just seeing what I wanted to see."

"That's right," Kate blurts a little too fast.

"Well, that's a concern," Volkov says. "Because, obviously, the most terrible illusions are the ones we tell ourselves."

The van suddenly lurches over and starts speeding through the park. Volkov wheels toward the driver. "What's happening?"

"Landau's got them—he's bringing them in!"

innocent bystander
September 2008

Copenhagen, Denmark

Rain swept the leaves into wobbly spouts, clogging the gutters and making slow-moving pools of narrow intersections. The spatter dimpled Thule's glasses until he could barely see. He pulled his wide-brimmed hat deeper over his face, leaned into the wind and pushed on. It was nasty weather but still just rain. This kind of water didn't give him nightmares.

Running torrents, the kind of river water that ran through this city every windy day, the kind Danes took for granted. Just the thought of that kind of water made Thule squirm, like some ancestral terror prodding under the skin. He veered instinctively toward the safety of the gray brick walls. *If I wasn't born in an island city, I'd never go near the water*, he thought.

"If you weren't born in an island city, dude, you wouldn't have ended up in the river in the first place." The voice came from just behind him, a soft, musical voice—but a cruel, mocking music.

He was a kid, for God's sake, maybe late-twenties, face unlined, a dense 19th-century gentleman's mustache and spiky hair under that ridiculous straw hat. Jacket a size too small, slacks rolled up above brightly-striped socks and calfskin shoes. Didn't he want a raincoat? He reeked of expensive display but what Thule noted most clearly was the cold mirror in his eyes. What did he want?

Childhood fear—if it's not gone by now, give it up, dude, it's got you. The voice came now from inside Thule's head—it could have been his own, though he retained just enough self-awareness to know it wasn't. *You were a strong swimmer, but that current was killer! Dragged you down, beat you up, like a china cup in a tornado.* The voice was darker now, whispering, provoking, intimate, every word pushing Thule farther back into that terrible memory, rekindling the terror he only now realized had never left, had remained fluttering just under the surface.

The old man lurched into a stone vestibule, clutching at any semblance of shelter. He huddled against the wall, panting, trying to collect himself. A streetcar slid past, spattering raindrops in its wake. *You struggled frantically, desperately, you grabbed at pilings and rocks until your hands were bleeding but all it did was pull you harder, farther down.*

The boy lingered on the sidewalk, regarding him lightly, nonchalant, as if ordering a cup of coffee. Thule, on the other hand, felt the air rushing hot through his lungs, his heart pounding. The river waves licked at his cheeks and rolled over his head as he gasped and fought for breath. It was all he could do to contain the panic. He'd thought sure these attacks had ended long ago but here was proof memory didn't fade, only deepened, waiting for the chance to pay back with interest.

"How could you know?" Thule begged.

"*You* know," the boy responded, as though that explained anything.

"What—what do you want from me?"

The cruel eyes widened. "To watch you *die*." It was the sound of a door slamming.

Thule burst from the arch into the spray, stumbling outward, moving for the sake of moving. Terror blurred his vision, the memory of the torrent clogged his nostrils. How to escape? How could there be escape when the terror was inside you?

And then, all at once, there was the bridge, the bridge he'd fallen from, nearly sixty years earlier, right in front of him and it felt almost laughingly obvious. The river beckoned behind an ankle-high chain.

Go on, the voice echoed in his head, *there it is. What could be more natural?*

Thule's feet were at the chain. Ten centimeters away, the wind whipped the white caps, the rain took its final, violent form. He realized now that this image had never left him, over all the years, his unending nightmare. Acknowledging this long-buried part of himself was almost comforting. This terror was home. He reclaimed it as an inevitable part of himself, in the same way the river was reclaimed by the sea.

Eyes wide-open, without another thought, he stepped over the edge.

everything is personal
October 2008

Tokyo Airport

"Why are you humming?" Avery demanded. Miriam Fine hadn't even realized she was.

"It's Haydn, actually."

"Why the hell are you humming Haydn?"

"I played the viola through college. You're lucky I wasn't humming Mahler. Why are you in such a foul mood?"

"Because I hate flying commercial!" Avery replied, muscling through a crowd of slow-moving tourists.

"Next time, buy a plane that never breaks down," Fine replied, picking up her pace to stay even and wishing she'd changed into sensible shoes.

Avery was not amused. His mood darkened further when he checked their status at the gate. Miriam took him by the arm and led him away from the desk as his face turned that nasty violet.

"They overbooked the flight," he muttered through clenched teeth. "They say they'll try to help but when they say it like that…"

"So you explain to the client our flight's been delayed. They've been through it. Just let me hear their voice over the phone and I'll make sure they're 'persuaded.'"

Avery shook his head. "That won't do it. There are a lot of people watching this one. One of my consults is desperate to acquire a piece of property—"

"'Consults?'"

"I offer a service for repeaters, anyone who's completed three *Your World* courses—for a not-so-reasonable fee, I'll call you once a week, give you a little pep talk and answer a question or two."

"That's a business?"

"Two college interns in my office lock onto the consult and bend him so he's energized and inspired by the time he gets off the phone. Once these guys start needing me for a regular mood adjustment, it's like any addiction—booze, drugs, pharmaceuticals, porn—the price goes up and the portions go down. Sometimes they call, desperate and the questions don't even make any sense. I swear even they don't know what they really want."

"They want your attention. They want to know you're focused on them for a few minutes. God, Jim, it's dating."

"Ha! It's not that personal."

"*Everything's* personal. That's the first thing you learn, reading people's thoughts. No irritation ever really comes from outside—it all ties into some lingering resentment from their parents or middle school or the boy who jilted them that summer in the country." Fine shook her head. "Every new idea, leader, every great company or piece of art and every war, for sure— they're *all* personal." She cocked an eyebrow. "What's your spur, Jimmy boy?"

"At the moment? My spur is that we're failing."

Fine arched an eyebrow. "You've got the spreadsheet upside-down. *Your World's* numbers are great—"

"Not enough. We're a cult. Thousands in this city, tens of thousands in that. We have power but I missed something—we're not known to have power. It's amazing how much influence in this world comes from influential people knowing you have influence on other influential people. You've been to meetings—you've seen how the elite guys treat me. I'm a sideline, a confidence man with a deluded following." Avery's eyes were fiery. "Those fuckers are going to snap to attention when I walk into a room—and soon!"

Several passengers turned at the sound of Avery's raised voice. Avery stared at the gate staff. "Make them give us seats."

"That's not a good idea—"

"And why the hell not?"

"I can make the agent rescind someone's seats and give them to us but as soon as I've physically left the location, the suggestion will slip—someone's going to remember what happened."

"I thought we could bend people's minds," Avery said, out of patience. "I thought we could force them to do whatever we wanted. Did I get sold a bill of goods?"

"Jim, we keep telling you there are limits and you keep ignoring us. Remember how many people Pietr had to pull into Rome just to make sure Singh stayed bent? Remember how many low-level kids we had to recruit to pull out the Arkansas Senate race, even after we narrowed the swing group to 5,000 in Hot Springs? Forcing people to do something against their will takes a huge amount of effort and then you have to keep up the suggestion until it hardens into memory, until they believe they did it themselves."

"Why? Why can't we just get on the fucking plane and let them get mad five minutes later? Who cares what they say?"

"The first time, nobody. The tenth time the same story comes up, maybe somebody starts paying attention."

"And?"

"And if mindbending becomes public knowledge, we're down for the count. Either you'll kick off a panic about *Muslim Mindbenders Who Hate Our Way of Life* or you'll kill the market."

"Huh?"

"Right now, you're benefiting from scarcity. You offer a service no one else can and setting your own rates. Once this comes out? Every palm reader and back porch psychic will be setting up shop, marketing apps and planning IPO's — and driving the price down. It'll be like every other commodity, a race to the bottom. Who needs that?"

Avery loosened his tie. "Okay, I get that part. I still have a hard time accepting we can't get a plane." He actually chuckled a bit. "You're humming again. Should I try it? Is it therapeutic?"

Fine was taken by surprise. "Am I—? Damn! It's Haydn again." She peered around the room, taking in the passengers. "Where am I getting—?"

Her eyes flickered for a moment and Avery saw her focus on a group huddled at the end of a row of seats, a mixed group of European and Asian musicians cradling their instrument cases and just now standing to join the line of passengers for boarding. He heard them chattering at each other in English.

"The gray-haired one at the end," Fine said. "Miko. She's got Hayden on the brain. That's where I'm getting it. Hmmm—?"

Fine closed her eyes again; her humming intensified—Avery didn't hear it anymore so much as feel it in the floor and the air around him.

"Musicians are sensitive to vibrations," Fine said finally, eyes flickering.

"Makes sense to me."

"All *kinds* of vibrations," she continued and Avery saw Miko turn to the others as if with a sudden thought. She mumbled a few sounds but nothing Avery recognized as words. A moment later, as if a switch was thrown, first one, then another, then another face turned to her, all of them mumbling in return as though answering a question—though no understandable question was ever asked.

Without further discussion, Miko walked to the counter and spoke with the agents at the gate, going back and forth, confirming her intentions several times. A moment later, Avery and Fine heard their names being called and went to the desk for their boarding passes.

After settling into their seats, Avery leaned into Fine's seat. "Okay, what happened? You bent all of them at once. You were just telling me that was enormously complicated—"

"I didn't. I didn't bend any of them, not the way we usually do."

"But—"

"*She* did it. Miko. When I realized I was humming the music in her head, I knew we had a connection. I started listening in and realized the whole group was playing that music in their heads — the same place in the tune, the same notes, they were all synchronized without knowing it. They've played together a long time; they're picking up each other's subconscious without effort. So I weaved a thought into the music, about staying over another night. I didn't force a suggestion, I just linked the idea with a pair of notes that resonated. I felt Miko pick it up immediately. And then, the same way the others picked up the music in her head, now they picked up the idea. Nobody was persuading; it just spread. I made Miko mumble some noises so anyone nearby would think they were talking but the thought went directly from her to the next person and the next." Fine's eyes widened. "And—I was listening in—each time it jumped, the signal got stronger. It was like they were amplifying the signal within their little set group."

"Because they were all on the same wavelength already."

"Exactly." Fine's face was taut, intense. "But listen, Jim—all kinds of groups get on the same wavelength. Families have the same base vibration to start with. Musicians in a group, players on a team, workers under pressure over a period of time—their vibrations converge pretty quickly. Women in the same house synchronize their periods." Avery looks ready to gag. "Oh, for God's sake," Miriam says.

"So you're saying—?"

"I'm not saying. I have no facts. So far, it's one experiment—but it's a really interesting experiment."

Avery weighed that thought for a long moment. "What's on your schedule for the next two months?"

"Following you around."

"I'll get a replacement. Follow up this project: Find out what happens when you make people think it's *their* idea. That's a brilliant insight, Miriam."

"Not so brilliant, Jim—I've spent my whole life dealing with men."

the man who didn't die

Copenhagen, Denmark

Max:

You told me, *just post to this blog and I'll see what you write.*
You don't even have to publish it, Billy, I'll see it, you said. Okay, so
here it is, I'm following your instructions.

And you told me it wouldn't be easy and you sure as hell
were right about that.

You told me to interview Singh so I did. I asked all the
questions you gave me. She remembered it pretty much the way
you said and okay, I got it exclusive. And then, she testified for the
Italians and they decided she was fucking bonkers, her party
threw her out of office and into house arrest, my paper laid me off
and said they'd throw me some freelance work here and there as
long as I stopped wasting their time on 'alternative angles' to

Rome. So understand, when it comes to your assignments, I'm on a very short leash.

But I went to Copenhagen like you asked. Don't ask me what I got, I don't have a clue.

Thule might've just cracked up, for all I know. He's a geezer, for Christ's sake, he smuggled Jews to Sweden during the war, they say. Smuggled them to the boats but wouldn't get on board, even when the Nazis came looking for him—deathly afraid of the water.

So it makes sense that falling into the river would unhinge him. When I met him, he was quivering and repeating himself, totally out of it.

Nobody can figure how he ended up *near* the water to begin with. His staff says he totally arranged his life to keep his distance. In Copenhagen, that takes some doing. Whenever he had to traverse a canal (I love the word 'traverse'), his staff would drive him. If he was walking anywhere, he would map a route to avoid the rivers. He knew every stretch of water in Copenhagen like I know every bar near the office.

When I saw him, there was food on the table that hadn't been touched. He didn't smell great either. He was trying to sit up in a chair and his assistant said that was a big step forward; he'd been hiding under the sheets since that night. "Don't take too long," she told me but I had the feeling she didn't know what day it was, once I said your name to her. Does it open Fort Knox, too? Just kidding.

"What do you want?" he said as soon as I came in.

"I want to talk about what happened."

"I went into the water. I hate the water."

I figure you had to be prompting me, because I certainly knew nothing about what I asked next: "Is that where you fell in as a boy?"

"I was a child. I...it was amazing I swam to the edge. I should have drowned."

"So you were always afraid of the water. You always stayed away from it."

"I—I told the police I didn't remember anything. They think I'm crazy."

"But you're not."

"I remember. I had to go. I didn't want to. My legs went without me. So I sound crazy—"

"Not really. Not if someone was making your legs do things you didn't want them to do."

His eyes widened again. "Is that possible?"

"Yes, it's possible."

As soon as I said that, he sat up like a champ. He came right up on the edge of the chair like he'd been running wind sprints.

"I didn't want to," he said. "I was scared. But I heard...things..."

"Voices." He looked afraid to answer me. "You heard a voice inside your head, not outside. Maybe it sounded like your own voice. It told you what to do but you were already doing it before you understood the words." His eyes opened even wider at that one. "You're not crazy. There are people who can do that."

"Did he send you?" he said, fearful. And then he got more alarmed: "There are others?"

"Brother, there's an army of them out there—and you got caught in the middle, somehow. You sell coffee, they tell me."

"Yes."

"You're not messing around on the side? Contraband, drug smuggling, arms deals?"

"No!" The whole idea completely confused him—I could see it on his face.

"No connection ever, no matter how distant, with NATO, national security, the secret world—"

"The what?" he asked and that was all the answer I needed. The guy's clean. Like I said, caught in the middle.

"So the voice in your head, did you see him?" I said and he coiled into a fetal position.

"He was walking with me for a while."

"Until the last block." He leaned back here, like I'd scared him. "I saw the tracks in the snow."

"The police thought I was crazy—I said he made me go."

"They decided you were crazy first and then saw whatever backed that conclusion. Cops." That calmed him down so I got to the point. "What was he after? You didn't have information he wanted, you weren't a threat, so why—?"

"To die," he said over me, like he had to get it out. "He wanted to watch me die."

"Huh? But you didn't—you're still here."

Up till then, like I said, he'd seemed lost. But not here. This part, clearly, he'd been thinking about over and over. "I gave up. I went over into the water and knew I was dead —and he knew, I could feel him inside my head, feeling it with me. I'm old and weak and *couldn't* survive. And once I'd had that moment, feeling everything freeze, giving up, ceasing to resist—once I *died*—he released me. He was gone, out of my head. And I was still standing on the bridge. I was able to step back and grab the pillars and I looked around and he was really gone, nowhere in sight. And then my knees buckled and I almost did go over into the water."

"'Almost?' Wait, so you *didn't* fall in?"

"No, I was still on the bridge, staring at the water. I thought I'd fallen did, I knew I'd fallen, I felt everything as though I had — but there I was, still on the edge, snow on my coat but clothes still dry." He shook his head. "He had to know how it felt to watch me die, I suppose—or he had to know how it felt to me dying. I feel like that's the answer but I have no idea what it means…"

After that, I couldn't get anything out of him for the bawling. He cried like a child, where no shame holds back the feeling.

So that's all I got. Mindbender (L Corp's?) finds him, has to see him die, like it's an experiment in a lab. Takes him to the edge of the bridge, the scariest thing in his world, makes him think he's jumped in, makes him feel like he's dying and then walks away. I don't even think the guy knew who he was. It feels like he was chosen purely at random, just happened along at the wrong moment.

I hear you in my head at odd moments, I know you're around. Can you give me a break around breakfast? I don't know shit in the morning. And is there some way you could reimburse me for the flight and the hotel? I didn't mention it but since you're a mindreader, you should already know I'm thinking about it.

This one showed up in the morning paper—it sounds like your kind of thing:

BIZARRE DEATHS IN AMSTERDAM

Diemen: Officials were baffled by two bodies struck dead by lightning in the Diemerpark section of the city this evening. The unidentified men were found on the ice of the canal in the midst of a snowstorm. According to meteorologists, such weather 'is extremely unusual under these conditions.'

I'll admit it sounds tempting—lightning in a snowstorm— but you're going to have to check that one out yourself, Max. I keep telling myself this is some juicy shit to write but I can't figure out what any of it means. Nobody wants to pay for it and my usual editors are beginning to look at me funny. If you can figure out how to help me in future, I'll be happy to return the favor but things have to get a little less one-sided.

Good luck,

Billy Szymczyk

(Marginally) Faithful (tenuously employed) Reporter

in dreams 3

Dreamland

What about the guy you offed? In the lab?

This time, he was waiting. Renn had felt the presence in the room—in his head—as soon as he'd awakened.

That's a bit personal, isn't it?

Dude, how personal could it be? It's famous. It's part of the fucking curriculum.

This was annoying. *What lesson are they teaching with that?*

'Don't get involved'. They say you lived through all the guy's memories—his life passing before his eyes—

That doesn't happen.

Well, his memories then, that you heard them all, lived them all, just before he stopped. And that's why you got so hung up on people.

I'm not hung up on people. I've been avoiding them my whole life.

C'mon, dude—if you weren't hung up on them, you could be running them around like puppets. You could be living among them without a second thought. You fucking worry about them.

This felt dangerous immediately. *I'm being set up*, Renn thought. But it was the complaint that had followed him everywhere, all his life. He couldn't keep himself from responding. *They exist. We're surrounded by them.*

They fascinate you. No point denying it.

Why not? Why no point? Can he read me? That fear curdled up Renn's spine like a needle. How is he finding me in my sleep? Why is he so confident about what's going on inside me?

More to the point, why had this started so soon after Rome, when they were suddenly no longer at a distance, when they started randomly penetrating him. Could that have been coincidence? After all, he'd attracted all sorts of unwanted attention since Rome.

What's the matter, Max? Can dish it out but you can't take it?

This was too much—he nearly threw his neck out, checking all around for visitors. There was no one there and he'd known there was no one there. The kid didn't even know where he was. For that matter, Renn barely knew where he was. Keeping on the move day and night, searching for answers, trying to keep out of sight but close enough to L Corp to hope to divine some sense of their purpose, one day merged into the next. Blue sky, rainy sky, wind, clouds, gabled roofs and crowned ones, steepled churches and domed ones. The kid might not be following him in real time but he still knew way too much. It was dangerous for…it would be dangerous for both of them.

And still, Renn felt the need to protest, to try to justify himself.

Our work is about them in the end, he flashed, feeling immediately that he was revealing too much. Revealing anything to anyone had always felt like too much. *Somewhere along the line, we're going to need more than specific facts out of their heads or making them follow orders—at some point, we'll have to understand how they think.*

You're a ridiculous romantic, the kid flashed back without a second's consideration. *THEY don't understand how they think. You've heard them a million times—they argue with their own best judgment, second-guess themselves, they're full of doubt.*

Aren't we all?

No. NO! Some of us attack! Some of us trust our instinct, find the weak spot and rip it open. You don't have to understand ANYTHING to do that. If I can't take them, use them or fuck them, what good are they?

Renn's cheeks burned like a child in school. He felt childish and naive; it was a familiar memory. He felt ashamed, while knowing the feeling was more than a bit absurd. Surely there was a counterargument but he was too downhearted to try to come up with it.

His life didn't pass before his eyes, he explained stubbornly, as though it mattered. *Quite the opposite. His own memories seemed entirely random, without quality. He had just enough time to be confused and angry about the fact that they gave no comfort. He died in frustration.*

That's it? That's all there is?

That's all there was.

Good for you, Max. I figured you'd demand to find some meaning in it all, at least pretend you found some meaning in it, even if you didn't.

He'd tried. Renn remembered trying for years without result and finally giving up. It still felt like a defeat. *I think I've had enough of this conversation,* he flashed.

For now, dude, the kid said calmly. *We'll talk again.*

I don't think so. I'm cutting you off.

You'll be back for more.

I don't think so.

You can't help yourself. No one's ever been as trapped inside himself as you are.

alone

Barcelona, Spain

No one's ever been as trapped inside himself as you are.

This time, he had no awareness of waking. He had no memory of having slept. It was just dark and hot and even the voices in the night wind were mostly silent.

Mostly—but not entirely. The voices arrived differently in the early hours. Instead of fighting for headspace, they were little grace notes at a distance that he could actually parse without a great effort to avoid being overwhelmed.

And sometimes—like now—the voices were ominous tones, rumbles, disturbance. Renn channeled one thread for a few minutes and found himself skipping down the wide marble steps to the street.

He crossed into the plaza and through a vaulted Gothic archway past an after-hours club. This was the old city—

blackstone streets that looked damp in the moonlight, medieval rooftops looming under a narrow rectangle of distant sky.

The child was alone in a fifth-story bedroom. The man across the airshaft had watched her for a week, worked out the parent's schedule; when they slept and how far their bedroom was from hers. Now he was on the fire escape, working his way across. He'd be in her window, clamp the handkerchief over her face until she was under, carry her back to his room and away to the docks before twenty minutes had passed. She was a beauty. She'd pay well.

Or maybe he'd take a little longer than twenty minutes. If no one cried out immediately, if he made it out of the courtyard without notice, maybe he could make a stop on the way.

Renn heard all his thoughts, all his plans. He pulled the insomniac butcher down from the second floor to open the lobby door, then ran through the butcher's apartment to the back window.

There was the scumsucking...on the balcony outside the girl's window. He watched her through the open frame. Renn had wished all his life to be able to stop reading other people's thoughts but never more than now.

Entering his mind meant harmonizing with the thoughts of a rapist, having to anticipate the vicious act, feel the thrill of it and the fear and impotence underneath, the feelings the rapist himself suppressed. Everything in him would be in Renn—it would be hell to lose later, to try to forget.

But that was later—no time to waste now. Renn quickly found the frequency and slipped through the man's consciousness. As the bastard reached for the window frame, Renn stopped him in place.

Now what? Up to this moment, he'd reacted. He'd heard the bastard's thoughts and taken action. But what next? How to handle this guy?

A few minutes later, the slightly-built red-headed man and his companion, fortyish and vaguely handsome, with a curiously glazed expression, left the building by the front entrance, the slight man's arm around the other's shoulder, seemingly holding him up against a thorough drunk.

As they walked away—that was the first goal, get him away—Renn's thoughts overwhelmed him. The bastard wouldn't bother her tonight—but what about tomorrow? What about the next pretty child he saw?

Should he have scared the parents? Would that have been better? Made them more cautious? Too late now. But what of this odious piece of shit? Sharing his thoughts for three seconds was more than enough—Renn had blanked out the man's thoughts for his own safety.

He stared at the face—narrow eyes maybe but good cheekbones and hair and a squared jawline. Like a film star—

children would trust him. His mood plummeted. "Let's go for a ramble, pal," Renn said, pulling him down the block, wobbly-legged and swaying.

The vertical walls and wood-shuttered windows were like bad dreams. Disorienting images jumped from paintings on the metal storefront gates—a giant eye swallowing a road, a naked woman on a rock clasping a telescope, watched by a Rousseau-like bull and Dali himself staring into the street through a dripping eye. The moonlight itself was a presence, a silent ambiguous judgment.

Kill the fucker. It was the obvious answer. Put your arm around his neck and snap it—he wouldn't resist. Or the Novosibirsk lab trick—a finger to his temple and let the sparks fly. Heart attack in the street overnight—it wouldn't even be considered a murder.

I'm not a killer. It was the only consolation Renn had. He hadn't done right leaving the Soviet Union, Tauber had died in Rome because of him while doing nothing to impede Pietr Volkov. And the rage he'd felt in Brno frightened him.

Tell Volkov Renn knows about Elena.

He'd nearly broken the fucking shooter's neck, jerking him back and forth on the lawn outside Lazar's hideout. He'd tried so hard to make the moment feel real, to convince himself of his own rage.

It hadn't worked.

His rage wasn't at Volkov, not really. His rage was at himself, at the fact that he'd believed Volkov without a second thought when he'd said Renn had forced Elena to love him. Volkov hadn't done a great job of selling the story; he'd had no clever stratagem to fool him. Renn had believed him because Volkov had said what Renn had always felt anyway. When had he ever believed he deserved Elena?

The balconies on the next block overflowed, moss hangings going yellow near the street lamps. A portrait of a saint—stern expression, severe cassock, under a cloudy sky—bore down from a second-story stained-glass window. A church? It looked like all the other homes on the block. The door was locked, like the others. Did they lock churches at night now? Or was it just that every door on Earth was blocked to him at the moment?

He could kill the fucker on his arm properly— professionally, without remorse, without attachment. But that wouldn't kill the things Renn really wanted dead.

I'm not a killer. He bent over his burden, brought the fucker's ear close to his lips and whispered, "The next time you even think about taking a child—or a woman or a man—against their will, you will vomit everything in your stomach and shit everything in your intestines instantly. This will continue violently without stop until the thought and intention leave you. Do you understand me?" The man nodded limply and Renn let him drop to the ground. Before he rounded the corner, he could hear the scumsucker beginning to wretch right where he was. He doubled back and pulled the man up off the street again. "You will seek serious psychological counseling and you will stick with it religiously until you are cured." He dropped the bastard again and left him, wondering if counseling could help at all.

He wandered the tiny streets of Gothic Barcelona. What of the girls outside his hearing? Who would protect them? If this one's parents were so careless with her window, how could she be safe tomorrow or next week? Or were they even careless? What was so wrong, sleeping with the window open in summer? Who could conceive of the blackness of this world?

In the last three blocks returning to his apartment, he heard couples fighting in rooms just above the street—fights just on the edge of violence—and a man planning his own suicide by gas. Renn tried to plant pleasant thoughts, life-affirming thoughts in his head and heard them rejected. He could not convince the man that life was worth living—his only choice would be to force him against his will.

By that time, he was back at his own door. Renn went inside and lay in bed, not even hoping for sleep.

the fiery sky

Manbolo, Zumbaya, Africa

Jomo Bakala hated bridges.

How to even tell where you were? Every stream, creek, every stinking drip of water in the country had the same Chinese bridge across it. He must have put fifty thousand miles on General Koto's diesel Mercedes in the past six months, half of them across those same stinking bridges. If he ever got out of the damn country for a vacation, he wasn't going to China.

"I told your boss he had to reckon with me!" Mombe bellowed from the back seat. "First he don't listen, now he sends his Mercedes and his boy to pick me up! What's the matter, Colonel? You don't got ears? You don't got a tongue to talk? Or you don't got a mind of your own?"

Bakala smiled blandly. "You're the leader of the Dobril. General Koto respects you and the Dobril nation."

Mombe spit out a laugh. "I'll *bet* he do! He respect his own soldiers that I kill and his own land that I take! He respect the ten cars full of guns following me!" When Mombe glanced out the rear window, it was with pride as well as to check that no one had pulled a switch on him. It had required protracted negotiations to get the man to agree to this meeting at all and the caravan of ancient trucks, vans and one lime-green bus that probably dated back before World War II was part of the price of making him feel secure. It would also be, if all went well, an audience to spread the word.

The sun was going down but the heat was still brutal, waves shimmering off the tarmac, plumes of dust billowing out behind them on the unpaved roads. They made a turn by the Hotel Paradiso, a grandly-named stack of shipping containers, doors and windows crudely cut out of the sides, ladders rickety against the stacks, patrons climbing to the upstairs apartments. As they slowed for the corner, Bakala saw the poet in the dusty parking lot, toes crabbing the edge of the road, declaiming loudly in the ancient language. He heard just enough to identify the old song:

> When I die, don't bury me under the forest trees,
> I fear their thorns.
> When I die, don't bury me under forest trees.
> I fear the dripping water.
> Bury me under the great shade trees in the market,

I want to hear drums beating

I want to feel the dancer's feet.

Bakala shivered. He didn't believe in much but he had an odd faith in the mutterings of poets and crazy people, assuming there was a difference.

"You respect us because we're *beating* you!" Mombe continued—did the man ever take a breath? "Three months, you going backwards! You got the capital and *shit* every place else! That ain't respect, that's fear and you right to be feeling it!" The man was a pestilence. And a loud one.

The amphitheater appeared at the end of the wide street, surrounded by an expanse of open land; no chance of anyone hiding soldiers or tanks or other odds-levelers, just as Mombe and several others had demanded. They bounced down the last few blocks.

At the end, several roads converged and another motorcade bounced onto the road alongside them, an identical Mercedes followed by a column of raggedy cars, vans and trucks, bristling with automatic weapons.

"Who's that?! Denabe? What *he* doin' here?"Mombe bristled.

"The General has invited you all to a conference—Denabe, Zuwinga, Nelebon," Bakala said smoothly. He rested his hand on his pistol and kept the rear-view mirror angled just the right way—if Mombe lost control, Bakala would do what he had to.

"I'm not talkin' to them!"

"That is up to you. But the General has a message for all of you and I think you will be impressed when you hear it."

Bakala could see the message take effect—Mombe swiveled to view the other caravans pulling up to the amphitheater in a cloud of dust.

"These clowns too? Your boss thinks I'm on their level? He got another thing coming!"

"You'll have a chance to tell him," Bakala said. "Soon. But for now, take your seats in section—"

"I'm not sitting no place here!" Mombe thundered. "This is a trick! Take me home! I'm not talkin' here!" He was still squirming in all directions, taking in the details of the circular stadium. "How do I know you're not serving me up to these fools?"

"Everyone who goes into the amphitheater will be unarmed—you see the metal detectors," Bakala answered quietly, soothingly and already, a few of the advance group were going through, with a few arguments but peaceably. "Each of you get ten members inside with you but you each have a hundred troops here, with their guns—the rebels here outnumber the General's staff by ten to one. Not to mention all the villagers watching, all these witnesses. No, the General has something to say to all of you and, as I said, I think you'll be impressed." He smiled blandly again. "Give us a chance—we're not pulling anything."

Mombe watched carefully as another of the rebel leaders stepped to the metal detector and then through, to take his seat inside the bowl of bleachers.

"How does Koto know somebody in the caravans don't shoot him when he shows?"

"The only thing you tribes have in common is hating the General. If someone shoots him, you'll all turn on each other, right here, right now. So, if I was you, I'd make sure all my men have their safeties on."

For the first time, Mombe didn't seem to have an answer. He nodded to his adjutant, who went running off to the caravan.

Finally, it was his turn. Mombe showily handed his pistol to his adjutant and stepped from the car, to a cheer from his men and jeers and catcalls from the other tribes. He passed through the metal detector and clanked up the metal steps to his seat, surrounded by five aides.

The leaders of the rebel tribes regarded each other resentfully across the bleachers. The troops assembled outside quieted as martial music cascaded from the bowl. The General's Fanfare, borrowed from some spaghetti Western—Bakala had seen it with the General, a few times, but strained now to remember the name. Officers cautioned their soldiers. A crowd of villagers pressed against the barriers manned by Army regulars and local police. A spurt of wind kicked the dust in little swirls around the edges of the open field.

Finally, General Koto appeared from under the stands, climbing to a platform at the open end of the amphitheater, facing the spectators behind Plexiglas panels. Stocky, acne'd, wearing a newly fitted uniform designed to camouflage his ever-increasing girth, he leaned into the microphone.

"So—finally—we are all together," he began, his deep voice rippling across the barren field. "You want my attention? Congratulations! You got it. You take a little here, a little there, I don't bother. But you call yourselves a rebellion—" Koto gazed out over the tribes arrayed before him. It became clear to all that at this moment he had no security detail, no guards on the stand or even around it. "You say 'Where does Koto get his nerve? What makes him Exalted Leader for Life? I got an army, I got some trucks, I can take a village or two! What's he got that makes him Exalted Leader?'"

The rebel leaders were standing now in the bleachers. A few were gesturing and shouting responses to Koto, though none of them could be heard outside, where the spectators clutched their guns, wondering if the whole situation was about to disintegrate into a mad bloodbath.

Koto raised his arms above his head and, as if from nowhere, they all saw the cloud—first a tiny black swirl in the air, then thickening and roiling, growing until it blocked the sun over the bowl.

"You got guns," Koto shouted. "But I've got God! God is on *my* side!"

Bakala's car rocked suddenly and he realized the engine had stopped. When he turned the key, nothing happened—but his hair was now standing on end.

Dead silence followed, for a long moment, only the sound of the swirling wind as the clouds continued gathering volume overhead. And then the laughter began, a mocking laugh up high in the stands and then, catching, a wave of derision, the laughter cascading from one end of the amphitheater to the other, the soldiers getting caught up in the sound of it, in the freedom and daring of laughing openly at Koto, at his bragging, chest-beating arrogance.

The laughter went on for more than a minute before anyone noticed that Koto was no longer on the stand, was retreating now to his Mercedes outside the amphitheater.

The sound of the first bolt came from nowhere, so sudden and shocking that the soldiers, hardened by years of fighting and privation, jumped at the sound. The other bolts followed so fast that it was all over before anyone could react.

Most said they came from the cloud, though this was disputed by a few with a different angle. What no one could dispute was the rolling fireball that looked like a lightning bolt and consumed everything within the amphitheater in seconds. The metal skeleton of the stadium melted and collapsed a few moments later.

The soldiers, the witnesses, long since used to the smell of burning flesh, ended up staggering, stunned, retching along the side of the road. When Koto's few officers appeared and began taking their guns, no one resisted.

How do you resist the lightning and thunder? How do you resist a man—a God—who can set the sky on fire?

razor's edge
November 2008

Amsterdam, Netherlands

The snow made a lace web, shivering in the afternoon air. De Jogt pedaled full-tilt, enjoying the cold sting on his cheeks, a tonic before hours in the lab.

De Jogt's parents had taught him to give back. For years, through a succession of jobs, he'd donated clothes and shoes to a charity spearheaded by a minister near his home. The man had passed on a few months earlier and the cause had been taken up by a church across the city, just past the Science Museum. De Jogt was on his way now to deliver a backpack's worth of clothes to the new location.

Why weren't bicycle video games a huge hit? People loved bicycling all over the world. Drop your real bike onto a stand in the living room and have at it! Project the image ahead, two-story jumps and sharp turns, narrow streets filled with stray tires, dogs and mattresses, like the favela races in South America—that would be the most popular version, surely.

Still lost in his videogame dream, De Jogt saw the familiar corner and made the left as he had so many times before. He was halfway down the block before confusion set in.

He didn't know where he was going...and yet, he did.

He knew the black doorway just off the next corner, alongside the café with the wraparound windows. He knew the way the door stuck unless you pulled hard, the squeak of the fourth step on the staircase and the view from the second floor window. His hand, instinctively, went grasping into his jacket pocket, searching for...the coil that wasn't there...

...because it wasn't the right time for him to be *here*.

Where was the voice in his head, the one that summoned him to these meetings. Meetings? Yes, they were meetings. The voice was missing... It wasn't in his head because it wasn't time.

And as soon as he understood that much, another voice appeared, this one from memory:

Some morning soon, you're going to catch voices in your head, voices not your own. You'll realize you've been hearing them for a while, like music in the wind—and when that happens, you'll have just a few seconds to break away. You'll need a memory of some place, some other time in your life, that you can dive into, dive so deep you won't know for sure where you are. Can you do that?

Whose voice was *that*? Vlad—who's Vlad? He saw the face murkily in the air in front of him. *My assistant. No, I'm his assistant. We work together—on what? On the thing that should be in my pocket. What is it?*

It was the coil. He could see it clearly in his mind and knew vividly how hard he'd worked to bring it to fruition—to bring the whole project to fruition. What project? Was he mad?

Somehow, with so much going on that he couldn't understand, he fell back on Vlad's voice, on what Vlad had told him. De Jogt located a memory, a strong one. His mother's funeral, standing in short pants in the rain under an umbrella while Pastor Villehauve—the one who'd just passed—spoke in a distant voice, mouthing words that had no connection to the mother he remembered. De Jogt could feel the rain on his face and legs right now, the spongy ground giving under his mud-splattered good shoes. He stood for ten seconds or twenty minutes or whatever it took until there were no other voices in his head, until he was in the graveyard and on the street near the Science Museum at the same time, until he knew that he could get away now, right now, don't dawdle, get away from the American whose voice was suddenly not inside his head for the first time in—how long? Months?

He turned the bicycle around and began pedaling back toward the *Prins Hendrikkade* and then left across a short bridge to the church. He dropped off his donation in minutes and turned back toward the office. He kept waiting for the American voice to reappear, to take him back under, to scratch that itch under his skull. He kept himself determinedly fixed on his mother's funeral - *thank you Vlad, whoever you are, for this.* He rushed into the office, right past the lab and into the storage areas at the back, a place he'd have sworn he'd never visited but now knew better, now he knew it the same way he'd know to turn left before reaching the church.

Don't think, don't think, just do, he told himself and some memory that remained just out of reach set his fingers on the right tabs to open the magnetic lock to the storage room door, a room which inexplicably looked totally familiar once he pushed open the door.

The latest coils were in the bin by the 3D printer—how on Earth did he get *that* in here without someone noticing? The sight lay on the counter nearby. He grabbed it, thought twice and picked up two slightly earlier versions as well, stuffing them all into his bag. He knew it wouldn't be long before his keeper, the American voice, noticed what he doing—once he did, De Jogt would have just minutes to get away.

The post office was on the corner. De Jogt maintained the image of his soaked feet standing by his mother's grave while he grabbed cardboard shipping containers and bought postage from a machine along the wall.

Half an hour later, he reached Diemerpark and his block of black stone, aluminum and glass attached houses. The voice was still silent, but now the silence felt ominous. There was a presence, unfamiliar, waiting for him to slip, waiting for a chance to slide inside and take him back. He sensed tension on the other side—and urgency. But where was the voice he'd expected? *Take the absence as a blessing*, he thought.

Racing upstairs, he stuffed the bare essentials into an overnight bag. The indicator light on the window alarm was out - not red, not green, just out. He flipped the light switch with no result. And when he pulled his mobile from his pocket, it was dead as well.

That's when he heard the click at the front door.

Any doubts he'd had were gone now. *The good die young—the paranoid survive*, he thought, hoping it was true. Were they opening the door or already inside, clearing the ground floor? No time to find out.

Slipping to the back room, De Jogt slid open the window and looked down on the roof of the garage. The car wasn't an option anymore—if they had the house, they had the garage covered. De Jogt gauged it as a four-foot drop—safer than the ten feet to the driveway, but still far enough to hurt. He was no action hero and these things didn't work the way they did in the movies. But the scratching was now on the steps. Grabbing the frame, De Jogt kicked out the window screen and hauled himself through.

Six seconds later, he was on the pavement and scrambling hard, offering thanks to whatever power bestowed shoddy garages on the world. The cheap tin roof had buckled under his weight and bounced back just enough to provide a broken arc onto the snow-covered lawn.

De Jogt made for the icy bay, weaving among the apartment buildings, pulling his collar tight against the wind. Only the Dutch would build a city in the middle of an inland sea. But now that frigid landscape offered a promising, insane escape route.

The goons weren't far behind. There were at least two—he could hear their calls. He skirted a tool shed, puffing by the time he crashed through the weed-lined banks. He was a decent runner and the ice should even the odds—nobody would be quick.

Out onto the slippery surface, De Jogt's shoes scuttered and scraped as he dug for the far bank. The lights were ten or fifteen minutes away if he didn't fall. There would be a pay phone, a police station, a bar with witnesses, something.

A moment later, the first of his pursuers broke into the open. What De Jogt saw gave him no comfort—a professional, very fit, in a dark heavily padded jumpsuit, a pair of very sophisticated night-vision goggles and what looked like a serious pistol (with silencer?) tucked at his hip. Why still tucked away?

He tried his mobile again with no luck. Scanning the far bank, he realized it was dark from end to end. No street lights, house lights, a few headlights moving tentatively through the pitch black. They'd taken out the whole area just to get him. *Who had? Who were they? The mind soldiers,* he told himself—*that's enough to know.*

He ran harder, which didn't mean faster, scrambling over an icy mound onto a section milled by gleeful schoolchildren in skates. The surface wasn't leveling the playing field the way he'd hoped—the jumpsuit was gaining rapidly while a second emerged from the houses ahead, moving at an angle to cut him off before he reached the shore.

The padding on the suits—was it rubberized? Did they know who they were after, sending out agents insulated against his touch? That's yesterday's news now, boys—no touch required anymore.

De Jogt placed the metal coil around his hand and the cap on his finger, giving the mechanism a few seconds to charge. The air around him began to tingle; his hair stood on end. The first jumpsuit was gaining—his time was up.

De Jogt pointed at the ice just in front of the jumpsuit and squeezed his fingers into his palm, completing the circuit. The surge ran across his forearm, his fingers erect, locked together with an insane force and the whole scene—weeds and ice, squared Dutch apartments and low-hanging clouds—went silver and black as the air between the two men sparkled, ignited and burst wide open. The light laid bare every follicle, hair, mole and discoloration on the jumpsuit's face; every crosshatch of his woven (carbon?) suit as it locked onto him.

The second jumpsuit stopped in his tracks—younger, fitter and reaching now for his gun. He was off the ice, on the weedy ground. No middle ground for this one. De Jogt raised his hand, pointed the index finger directly at the man's chest and let go.

the wrong man

Diemen, Netherlands

Correction: Yesterday's edition of this newspaper reported the death of two men from lightning in Diemenpark. That report was in error. According to police reports, there was one victim, apparently hit by a truck. He is in hospital in Diemen, still unidentified, in guarded but stable condition.

Every person on Earth hated his job on Mondays. Nic Osimandias faced proof of that hatred every Monday noon on a slab.

Sunday nights, pressure built to a boil, work loomed, the weekend's unresolved tensions came to a head. So being the assistant city coroner meant greeting the grotesque cadaver of the week almost every Monday—sometimes several excellent candidates for the title.

In three years, Nic had seen beheadings, slashings, disembowlments, poisonings, polite and ghoulish, limbs severed, eyes gouged out, angry phrases slashed across torsos, genitals shredded. Not that he didn't see those things the rest of the week but Mondays just felt a bit...edgier.

So he gritted his teeth opening the door this Monday—and still found himself taken by surprise.

The man standing between two open bays, both cadavers unzipped and exposed, was unhealthily thin, with a shock of scraggly red hair and a devilish goatee. He wore a blue windbreaker instead of a white lab coat, so he almost certainly wasn't an out-of-town official.

"What the—?"

"Ah—just the man I need!" the sallow man gestured over the bodies. "Come explain this to me, please."

"Who the hell are you?" Nic demanded. "How'd you get in here?"

"Emil Vogel," the man replied, answering exactly nothing. "Come have a look." Vogel—if that really was his name—wore no ID. Coroner, Police, Medical Inspector, State Security—Nic had seen them all and Vogel had none of them.

"I'm calling the police."

Vogel's eyes were gray and compelling. They locked onto Nic's and were bloody hard to look away from. When he did, Nic found himself staring at the phone in his hand, unable to remember why he'd picked it up.

"These two were brought in last night," Vogel said, flinging a stapled report at him. Osimandias scanned the coroner's notes — where'd Vogel get *them*? "It says they're homeless but that's absurd. Look at their teeth. That crown" — pointing at the cadaver on the left — "is brand-new. What happened? He went homeless on the way to the morgue?"

They were young men in very good shape, Nic noted, with military haircuts and body art. "I checked their clothes in the property room," Vogel continued. "Lightly worn only and not in the places clothes get worn first. Someone bought them in a thrift store. The boots are new — and expensive. Do you know the man who works the overnight?"

"Karl? He's okay, he works hard." He didn't love Karl but he was as good as anyone they'd had on that shift. Who was this guy to ask questions? Why was he answering?

"What's cause of death?"

Nic raced down the paperwork. "Uh — alcohol...alcohol poisoning!" He jumped to the next page. "Their levels were .4!"

"Look at the photos," Vogel continued, racing around the bodies checking — checking what? He clearly wasn't a coroner — what was he looking for? "See where they were found?"

"At the river."

"Right along the bank—you see their footprints? They were walking or running out to the middle of the river; then the tracks change. They're dragged the rest of the way," Vogel waved a finger around like a conductor's baton. "Explain it to me! Tell me how two men with a blood level of .4 managed to get even halfway across a frozen river in a snowstorm. With that much booze in them, they'd be lucky to crawl across the sidewalk to puke."

"This—this is—uh, you're sure these are the right pictures?" In the images, the snow had drifted up around the bodies. Three police deputies stood idly talking on the frozen river in the background—the tracks came from the far shore to the middle, just as Vogel said. Karl was a lazy slacker but he wouldn't have missed this. Couldn't have.

"It's not his fault. He had help misunderstanding," Vogel snapped. "Now look here." Nic was standing alongside the first corpse, without any awareness of having moved. Vogel gestured at the corpse's chest, at a rounded slightly raised mound of darkened skin. Nic would have taken it for a mole or growth but Vogel picked at the thing (*He shouldn't be doing that! Why am I letting him?*) until bits of charred skin flaked off. "Burnt to a crisp in one very precise spot," Vogel pronounced, lifting the sheet further to show a wild discoloration running nine inches toward the heart, a bright red line in the skin that branched like a tattoo of a lightning bolt. "And what's this?"

"Electric shock," Nic said immediately. Again, the answer was obvious. He hadn't seen that type of injury frequently, but there was no mistaking it for anything else.

"So not homeless and not alcohol poisoning. These are the men that were reported struck by lightning—in a snowstorm—the other day, until the story got retracted and turned into some idiot hit by a truck," Vogel said flatly. "The truck victim is in a bed in Rm 736—I've just visited him. His problem is six broken ribs and a collapsed lung. Is he related to these two?"

Vogel looked up suddenly, as though sniffing something unpleasant.

"You had a coat when you came in—where is it? Ah!" He skipped over to the coat before Nic could answer and returned a moment later, gesturing in Nic's face with something flashy he couldn't focus on.

"Where'd you get this pin?" Vogel demanded. It was the lapel pin, the ruby one he'd found the other—"Where'd you get it?"

Nic felt his mouth moving but no sound came out.

"It—uh—I don't—" he managed while the back of his head went white-hot.

"The Forger? Who's the Forger?" Vogel said next and Nic panicked. Nobody knew his pet names for the stiffs—people just didn't get the whole relationship thing. "What drawer is *he* in?"

"I—I swear I didn't—" Nic didn't want to remember, much less answer but he had no choice. "Drawer 23."

"Let's have a look," Vogel said and Nic followed him without any desire to do so. "You lifted his jewelry, Nic—it looked pretty, he had no family, nobody would know. Nobody cares. *I* don't care. Just tell me how he died."

Nic managed to answer. "Hit and Run."

"Where are the records? Anything suspicious about it?"

"I remember this—it was easy. Blunt trauma. Manslaughter, maybe, if they ever find the driver. Five witnesses saw him walk out of a store texting—the car came around the corner as he walked right into the street. Driver hit the brakes." Nic pulled out the crime scene photos—the skid marks were obvious. "Took off in a panic when he saw the guy go flying. Look, I've seen some crazy murders—this one's just everyday shit; sheer dumb bad luck."

Vogel took in the body, muscular like the two 'homeless' men. "Same kind of haircut as the two from last night—and the lapel pin." He turned to Nic with a hunger on his face. "Where are the rest of his effects?"

~~~~

Fifteen minutes later, Max Renn kicked through the drifting snow, regarding his prizes from the dead man's effects: a tiny coil of woven metal and a scrap of a business card with half a blotchy graphic torn down the middle. He paused at the corner, waiting for the light to change. The streets were filling with people rushing home from work. A tram approached around the corner, which would be useful once he figured out where he wanted to go.

The first body—the-hit-and-run from three days ago—was surely L Corp. The woven metal from his property locker was virtually identical to Lazar's sample and the ruby lapel pin right out of the L Corp dress code.

Was he the kid who killed Vlad, who'd been invading Renn's dreams? That voice had been silent for an unnaturally long time. Renn knew he'd have been better off with the kid dead—still, he wasn't sure if he wished for it.

Dave had been like this, back in the Everglades, the last time he knew peace. Dave Monaghan had known what was going on in Renn's head, without him having to share or block. The kid was dangerous—Renn had to be concerned about every single thing the kid had learned about him—but somehow there was such comfort in sharing, in company, that it made him second-guess the needs of self-defense.

Think rationally! He heard Lazar's voice in his head. *In danger, focus on the objective.*

The first one dies in a hit-and-run (maybe) and then, two days later—last night—two more, these two fried in the wild. Probably all L Corp and all hastily hushed up. At least one killed with the lightning weapon, the one that got Vlad and his wife.

How did that add up?

Was the lightning killing L Corp? Was *that* the kid with the straw hat? Lazar had connected him to Stasia's death in Brno and Renn had seen him earlier with Volkov in Rome. But it didn't make sense. Were they killing each other now? Who would hush up last night's two deaths without removing the bodies? The whole operation was sloppy. It didn't feel like L Corp—at least, it didn't feel like a Pieter operation, that was sure.

Quickly, Renn had two conclusions:

1) If this was L Corp, it was damage control at a low level, bureaucrats covering their collective asses, meaning they were trying to hide something from those above them, and:

2) Somewhere nearby might be someone with a lightning gun hiding from L Corp.

Renn's imagination fired suddenly with this image. He'd come to Amsterdam because of Billy's newspaper clip, the two men struck by lightning in a snowstorm, without really believing he would find anything that mattered. But now he felt a toehold, a seam in L Corp's oppressive blanket. If this was a seam, maybe he could be the wedge forcing it open.

All he had to do was find someone in Amsterdam, someone hiding whom he knew nothing about. Nothing to it.

His frustrated laugh ended abruptly with his eyes alight, as he took in a sign plastered across the side of the trolley. Pulling the business card from his pocket, he held it up so the torn logo lined up with the one gliding by on the rails—a perfect match. Reading the address below the logo, he turned in a new direction and slipped through the crowd.

~~~~

'Paperless Office'—ha! Katrina Gul lugged her rubbish bin, full of glass cleaner, memos, reprinted Web pages, research papers, doodles, notes, travel reservations, magazines, propositions and bad poetry to the dumpster beside the rear entrance of Zapf! (Was there a point to including the exclamation point as part of the name?). This was her fourth trip today and the place hadn't even emptied yet. She could request a bigger wastebin but she'd never lift it filled.

"Let me help you," said the goateed man in the blue windbreaker, "It looks heavy." He didn't look healthy enough to lift much of anything but he poured the contents inside the bin. While returning it to her cart, the man's hand brushed her shoulder.

A moment later, she was standing among the cubicles in the middle of the office: printouts, piles of backup discs, iPods, laser pointers and entire videogame systems heaped atop confidential memos and reams of code in hieroglyphic streams.

"Let's talk about the man who's missing," Vogel said, startling her. She knew his name but couldn't remember where she'd heard it.

"No one's missing," she said immediately. They were way inside Security and, while Vogel had a badge around his neck, the picture on it looked nothing like him. How had he gotten this far?

"Of course someone is. The man the police came looking for—except they weren't the police, were they?" Katrina's eyes shut down now, betraying no answer but Vogel—she hadn't heard him say his name but knew it somehow—pressed on without doubt. "The police don't show up when someone's missed work for a day or two. They certainly don't sit down with the whole staff and interview everyone—everyone except the only person who knows where he is." He was staring right at her—he was staring right through her, that's how it felt to Katrina. She made sure she felt the sand between her toes of the beach at Scheveningen, running headlong through the dunes in a blustery wind, listening to her mother sing that Beatles song. "That's how L Corp works, not the police."

"Who's L Corp?"

"That's who 'the police' were." His eyes narrowed. "You don't know L Corp?"

Katrina shrugged. "Do they do games? I don't keep up, I just clean."

"Games? They're a NATO security contractor."

Katrina's eyes widened. "What's NATO got to do with anything?"

Vogel looked around. "Aren't you — this place isn't a NATO contractor?"

Katrina's eyes nearly crossed this time. "Zapf!? They do video games." She got to watch *his* face go cockeyed this time.

"De Jogt works here, yes?"

"Of course. You asked about the man who went missing."

"What's his job?"

"Virtual Reality headset," Katrina recited. She had learned the term the day De Jogt let her try on the contraption and she nearly had a seizure. "Optical…Capture…Na-no…"

"Nanotechnology?" Vogel prompted and she nodded, glad for the help. That word always threw her. "And what about Vlad? Saminov?" Katrina went blank and he saw it. "Tall Russian — worked with De Jogt?" And somewhere inside, she felt a presence, something like the one she'd felt when the 'police' were nosing around earlier and Vogel's eyes shrank to slits. "He didn't work here?" he whispered and Katrina went cold.

"You're not supposed to know that," she said, glancing around quickly to make sure no one was within earshot. "How do you—?" but he was off down the hallway, with her rushing behind.

"His cubicle is there," she pointed and he shot past without a look. He passed the security station and the guards didn't even seem to notice him. Then, to her alarm, he blew right through the labs, not even glancing at the one marked 'De Jogt' clear as day. Instead, he kept up a manic pace to the end of the hall and down a flight of stairs, into a warren of narrow hallways and green-painted padlocked steel doors. He moved quickly to one, identical to all the others. "Here!" he said.

Katrina's jaw fell. "He didn't—"

"He didn't tell anyone about the room, I know. This was for after-hours," Vogel said, evidently bored with the subject. "This is where Vlad joined him. And I know the arguments you're going to make about how you can't open it for me."

Katrina watched her hand fitting the key to the lock. "I won't!" she protested while turning it nonetheless. Vogel nodded absently and pulled the door open.

Rows of lockers were shoved rudely against the far wall. A small booth with a square window stood in the corner. The bulk of the room was bare but for a gigantic hunk of rock, several feet deep, the edges heat-blasted and fused smooth, a huge pile of fragments littering the floor. Vogel headed for the booth.

"That is his private—" Katrina began.

Vogel pulled a coil from his pocket and held it out to her. "I know all about it," he said. He walked to the door and just felt the edges. "It's a clean room," he said, as if to himself, pulling the door open. Inside were several serious electron microscopes and a huge box that was never left running when she was in the room. Vogel examined it, turned it on and pressed a button. A series of lights began to run across the top of the display from one end to the other, the machine hummed and an assembly inside a Plexiglas enclosure ran back and forth, back and forth, over and over for about ten minutes. When it stopped, a tray moved from the enclosure to a bay at the end of the machine and a light went on there.

Katrina leaned forward. "Don't move!" Vogel told her and she could see him scanning the tray and then the counter around the machine. He picked up a long tube like a florescent bulb and turned it on, then held it over the tray—and a tiny glint came from the bottom, shining back at them.

"Ah!" Vogel exclaimed. He took a tiny pair of forceps from the counter and a plastic bag from a container next to it, carefully lifted the glinting disk from the tray and placed it in the bag. Then he shooed her back outside.

"I'm right, yes?" he asked. "The 'police' didn't question you?"

"Not me, no," she scoffed. "I just clean up."

Vogel eyes lit up. "Of course. They were important people; they don't waste time on the cleaning woman. Except that it turns out you're the only one who knows what he's doing. You're the only one he let into the room, the only one who saw them at work. And, of course, you're the only one who knows where he went hiding."

"Wha—well, wait—I didn't—"

"He can't be there when you get home tonight, no matter what he said. If he's there, he'll be a corpse." He stared right through her again, she thought of her apartment and, as soon as she did, she heard Vogel repeating the address.

"You leave him alone!" Katrina burst.

"He taught you to block—that was resourceful. Keep at it. But they'll be coming after him. It would be best if you forgot him for a while."

He pressed his finger into her temple and she felt a queasy smile break across her face and then she was dancing in the sand and the weeds, leaping and playing, seven years old and her mother was singing like she'd joined the Beatles.

~~~~

Katrina's building sat in the center of a long block of rowhouses, graffiti splashed across the door, vines creeping the facing to the second story. Bikes stood chained to a steel bar across the front of the place. But the bar on the corner wasn't cheap and the neighbors were expats, professionals and Masters of the Universe affecting a downtown style. It was the kind of neighborhood where people spent a lot of money to look gritty.

Renn held his hand against the front door, trying to sense the occupants inside. He made out two at home in mid-afternoon, one in Katrina's top (third) floor rooms and one directly below, staring out the back window. The presence on the third floor was blocking and Renn decided not to probe—if it was De Jogt, he didn't know how much he'd learned from Vlad. Better to meet face to face.

Renn ran his hand over the magnetic lock, scrambling and opening it instantly. As he vaulted up the inner stairs, he shifted his focus to the woman on the second floor, compelling her to rise and step out into the hallway just as he reached the landing. He passed by her into the apartment, throwing open the side window and clambered onto the fire escape as she headed up the stairs. While she rang the doorbell to the third-floor rooms, Renn approached the third-floor windows from outside. He felt the man in the apartment jump at the sound of the bell, felt his focus turn in that direction. Renn pulled open the window and slid inside.

He was tensed for a hostile reception but that thought quickly vanished. The occupant was De Jogt and he was no threat to anybody. On the contrary—he was sweating, trembling, shrinking away from the ringing door, panicking all on his own.

Renn dismissed the woman from second floor apartment—the bell stopped and he felt her presence receding down the steps.

Close-up, the source of De Jogt's panic became apparent. The man was being torn apart from inside. He was making a valiant attempt at blocking but Renn could hear at least five or six L Corp grunts fighting to squeeze into his head, sending a catalog of terrifying images and enough threats to drown out a New Orleans funeral. The Dutchman hadn't cracked yet but he was close.

If he broke into the conversation in De Jogt's head, L Corp would surely know De Jogt had help. It might make his location easier to pinpoint. But if he took a moment too long, there wouldn't be much De Jogt left to help. Renn reached out a finger to the man's temple and felt the voices disappear.

"That better?" he asked.

De Jogt's face flickered between relief and suspicion. "You're...not him," he said, faltering.

"Who?"

The Dutchman pointed at his forehead. "Him," he repeated—the voice he'd been hearing in his head.

"I'm here to get you away from him."

There was a long lag between Renn offering the answer and De Jogt acknowledging it. The man was shattered. "What happened to me?"

"They were using you—they had you under control at work. And something happened a few days ago."

"Day before yesterday."

"What happened?"

De Jogt struggled to remember, to make sense of what happened, to figure out how to explain what happened. "I went where I wasn't supposed to."

"Okay."

"And I remembered."

"You realized what you'd been doing?"

"Yes. I remembered the voice—actually, I realized it wasn't there anymore...not the same voice as before."

"Really. You'd heard one voice, then suddenly another?"

"A day or two earlier, it changed—and then stopped."

"Hmph! So your usual minder goes off duty—or out of town—and the replacement gets hit by a truck."

"You're the truck?"

"No, literally, he got hit by a truck. And—"

"I went to a place that I didn't remember—"

"And started remembering."

De Jogt nodded.

"And then somebody realized you were off the leash and sent the hounds after you—"

"I didn't want to hurt anybody."

"If you hadn't, you'd be dead or back under control. Period."

"How'd you find me?"

"Katrina knew where you were," Renn answered.

"She wouldn't tell anybody," De Jogt accused and Renn saw the fear in his eyes.

"Yes, I can get into your head—like the man in the straw hat. That's who you're afraid of, yes?" De Jogt nodded vigorously, looking around as if talking about the man would summon him. "Vlad could get into your head too. You remember Vlad?"

"I worked with him but I didn't know him," De Jogt said. "You knew him?"

"A long time ago."

"He warned me—about the voices."

"Vlad figured out what was happening, he'd worked with these people before."

"*With* them?"

Renn nodded. "A long time ago—we both did. And now they're coming after you," Renn said. "We have to get out of here."

"No, no, I can't go anywhere. Not yet."

"Do you have any idea what these people can do to you? Why not?" Renn fumed. He could force the man but, if they were separated, De Jogt would be crippled and helpless.

"Just a few minutes!" De Jogt said, moving deeper into his blocking, a loop of himself as a kid at his mother's funeral. He truly missed the woman—Renn envied him that.

"What's so important?" Renn demanded as the door downstairs banged open and Renn realized their time was up.

"They're here!" he said, grabbing De Jogt under the arm and hauling him onto his feet.

"Not yet! Not yet!" the Dutchman said but Renn had him out onto the fire escape, dragging him upward as he was suddenly inundated by the thoughtstream of the neighborhood. Was there a theater nearby? An auditorium? An office tower? Where did all those chattering minds come from?

De Jogt was falling apart, his defenses crumbling and Renn realized suddenly what he was waiting for.

"You need the postman—I'll take you to him," Renn said as they burst onto the rooftop, vaulted and piled with snow. He dragged De Jogt up and over several more, skittering up and sliding down, before finally hitting a flat roof they could run on.

"They're catching us!" De Jogt said, looking back, pulling a coil out of his pocket and pulling it over his hand.

One look behind and Renn knew he and De Jogt weren't going to outrun their pursuers. They were way too fit and their damn boots gripped in the snow. And, wearing white-noise goggles, he couldn't misdirect them. There were ten more buildings ahead, up and down, before they'd reach the blessed postman doggedly handing out the day's mail.

"Faster!" Renn yelled, a little too loudly, pounding up another slate roof. He took a careful glimpse at the fire escape running down the back into the courtyard in the center of the block and a skylight at the lowest point of the rooftop. As they slid down the other side of the roof, he pointed De Jogt around behind the chimney.

Both men nestled in the snow behind the brick smokeshaft. The Dutchman watched Renn's eyes flutter up under the eyelids — and the skylight popped open, a handful of snow misting into the air around the edge.

A moment later, the shooters came over the rooftop edge and heard a woman's scream through the open rooftop. They jumped immediately down onto the ladder inside and disappeared into the house.

"Come on," Renn said and led De Jogt over to the fire escape. They clattered down to the courtyard, through the back door of a shop and out into insanity.

The biggest street market in Amsterdam! A riot of prawn, herring, salmon, sardines, crab, eels, frites, fancy (and not-so-fancy) watches, hats, fruit shakes, socks and garters, bicycle helmets in every imaginable (and several unimaginable) colors, nuts in big bins, candies in huge bowls, bricks of unwrapped chocolate, leather jackets, jade necklaces, vegetables and fruit, cameras, t-shirts, shifts, camisoles, sausages, bikinis, waffles, sunglasses—sunglasses! Renn grabbed a pair of sunglasses and hats from a booth and slapped them over both their faces.

He hustled De Jogt a few feet into the next store— lithographs of Galapagos turtles, seventeenth-century Amsterdam bankers and skaters, old maps, preserved flowers and narrow sections of lace preserved in plastic sleeves. The postman was busting out of his blue and orange uniform shirt, pushing a cart full of mail.

"Katrina Gul!" Renn demanded, adding the address and apartment. The postman's eyes glazed, he dropped the stack of mail in his hand and dug deep into his cart. Brochures, bills, credit card offers, legal notices flew all over while the proprietors of the shop watched stunned.

"We don't have much time," Renn warned De Jogt.

"I need this!" De Jogt replied. Renn frowned at the postman and he doubled down on the bag, ripping out whole tied bundles at once. Finally, he slit open a bundle and pulled out one limp padded envelope, holding it up for De Jogt to grab.

The Dutchman tore off a corner and turned it over, dropping a tiny plastic disc into his palm. Several more showed inside.

"I made one this morning, at your backroom," Renn said.

"Well, the first thing is to make sure the scumbags don't get them, whoever they are."

"What do they do?" Renn asked.

"They set the sky on fire," De Jogt answered.

Renn grabbed the envelope from De Jogt's hands, walked to the counter and taped the end shut again. He turned to the postman. "Mailing label." The postman handed him one out of his cart. "Mail it somewhere no one will think of, someplace no one could guess." De Jogt scribbled in an address. Renn handed it to the postman along with a Euro note. "Postage. Send it." The postman nodded vigorously as Renn and De Jogt dashed out into the market again.

The crowd should have been thick enough to get lost in. Renn could sense their pursuers just reaching the far corner, having come around the block instead of through it. Half a block's tumult lay between them and Renn saw a tram at the other end. If they could make it there fast enough, it was an easy way out.

That plan came apart in seconds. Three more L Corp goons poured out of a car right in front of the tram and began marching quickly through the crowd right at them.

This was bad. Renn scanned left and right, seeking options.

"How are your legs?" he asked De Jogt.

"Good—why?"

"Because if I get wobbly, you'll have to drag me." His eyes rolled up under the sockets.

A moment later, the place came apart. The fish market suddenly flew into the middle of the street, slimy produce slithering all over. Middle-aged merchants carried thirty-foot area rugs into the crowds and dumped them; Louis Vuitton handbags flew off the racks into the faces and chests of passersby. Four yapping dogs dragged their owners by the leashes into a hopeless tangle, blocking the center aisle. A swarm of parrots and doves erupted from a pet shop, joined by a shower of fireworks from a booth up the way. A brawny man pointed into a cellphone dealer and screamed "Hey! That's my coat! My keys!" and ran into a store to the right, screaming curses at a pair of thieves only he saw.

"This way!" Renn yelled and the pair tore left into a furniture gallery.

The place was packed with dark-wood armoires, heavy mirrored dressers, mounted antelope horns and Bauhaus butcher-block chests. They dashed through a heavy plastic curtain into the back room. While a crowd gathered outside the cellphone store and the L Corp men scrambled to follow the mythical thieves, Renn and De Jogt carried a curlicue-top standing closet out to a van in the back alley.

As they laid the closet onto the rear deck of the van, something crashed behind them. Renn whirled around to see a stack of plates in pieces on the ground, a red-faced worker standing over them.

When he turned back, the van was pulling away, rear doors closing on De Jogt as he was subdued by two L Corp men. Out the back window smirked a young man in a straw hat.

You want to kill me now, don't you? came the voice in his head, the one that had visited him for months now. *Like the guy in the lab you electrocuted?*

I don't want to know you that well, Renn flashed back.

mind games

Baku, Azerbaijan

Baku was a hole.

The area they were in, anyway. The easy phrase would be 'a lunar landscape' but that was being complimentary. Landau tried to ignore the view through the SUV's smoked windows but it only mirrored his anxieties. A desolate plane stretched along the coastline, oil derricks clanking away like nightmare metronomes. A blast of fire hissed up out of an open pipe in the ground as the convoy passed, like a dragon belching after a good drunk.

Landau grimaced. Nothing but bad signs all over. He'd seen the L Corp vans waiting as the plane taxied to the terminal. Waiting for him! That wasn't good. No talk, no introductions, just white-noise glasses and gestures—him into the first van, De Jogt and the guys Landau had recruited for his support team in the second. And now into Hell's Backyard here.

The fields that killed 2 million Russians, Landau knew his history. He'd read a long article, he couldn't remember where, saying that the battle of Stalingrad was fought to keep the Germans from reaching Baku, the richest oil well in the world at the time. A lot of ghosts.

When they rolled off the highway and into the middle of the fields, Landau's mood sank further. There were two more SUV's grouped strategically around a concrete pillbox with slit windows plopped right between two skeletal four-story pyramid derricks. He knew what that meant.

He was not surprised to find Pietr Volkov pacing around inside and the door slamming behind his back as soon as he entered.

"Sit down," Volkov said. It was not a request.

Landau sat.

"Your name is Julian Landau, we recruited you out of Stanford, your psych intakes showed some minor psychotronic ability and difficulty with authority. You graduated training with mediocre results but some talent in field operations so you were given the job of monitoring a potential asset we thought we might make use of someday. *Monitoring*—that was your only job. Am I misstating any of this?"

"Nice to meet you too," Landau said. "I'm sure you're on the money."

"I now find out that, instead, you pulled your asset onto a project of your own, then botched minding him so that he actually caught on to what was going on, whereby you had him killed right in front of a surveillance camera in a NATO safe house, requiring extensive cleanup by the rest of us. At this point, you were suspended from field duties and told to stick to a desk job while awaiting review. However, it turns out you had already pulled a complete outsider with no security clearance whatever into this side project of yours—a video game designer!—attempting to keep him under suggestion twenty-four hours a day all by yourself, which is absurd. You kept him working on this project, which you tested out by killing or maiming homeless people and eventually a sizeable group of African revolutionaries and a few politically sensitive players in local disputes."

"I didn't disrupt anyone L Corp was supporting."

"I'd like to know—in detail—how much you know about who we do and do not support around the world and how you come by this knowledge. While you're at it, you can explain how you decided to take the trip to Africa yourself, while you were supposed to be controlling your man in Amsterdam 24/7."

"It was an important test for the weapon and I was the only one really familiar with it—"

"So you handed off minding the suggestion to a colleague. Two hours after your plane lifted off, your trusted minder walked in front of a truck, your new joe flew the coop, we ended up with a man in the hospital and two more in the morgue, struck by lightning in the middle of a snowstorm. And only when you return are we finally able to track down and kidnap your man in front of numerous witnesses and fly you both here on a corporate jet you—what? Hijacked? Stole? Tell me you charged it to one of our house accounts—nothing would surprise me at this point." Volkov stopped talking finally but his chest was heaving like a marathon runner—Landau had to admit he was a pretty fearsome sight, worked up like this.

"You done now?" Landau said—he had a bad tendency toward flippancy under pressure.

"Not even close," Volkov growled—he really sounded like a wolf in the wild. "This is your chance to keep me from clapping you in cuffs and renditioning you to Yemen for my own amusement."

"I was doing my job! I had good contact with your man Vlad, I was monitoring his every thought twelve hours a day, six days a week—you really should pay more for the hours—"

"You're not helping yourself so far."

"—and sending in my reports daily, just like I'm supposed to. And I kept reporting that this guy was blocked. He knew something really important—a real breakthrough—but he couldn't get to the memory. He kept getting hung up at the same point and—I was taking the mindbender training at the same time—"

"—training you were not authorized for. Training you hacked into, against corporate policy, so you could play us for your own purposes."

"*Play* you? Corporate Policy? You've gotta be kidding me!"

Volkov actually looked taken aback by the kid's nerve.

"You're building a gang of pirates and you're testing us to see if we keep a neat desk? You should give me a medal for initiative, dude! I'm giving you the keys to the kingdom!"

"Which kingdom is that?"

"Which one are you playing for? The whole worldwide security balance-of-power kingdom." Seeing the look on Volkov's face, he hurried on. "Listen to me now, dude—you can kill me later, okay? In the training, there's a module about making people forget and making them remember—and I realized at some point, that was Vlad's problem, somebody had put a lock on some part of his past. He could remember all the routine shit but none of the details—none of the stuff that would let him recreate the work he'd done. Y'know, you're living in some guy's head day and night, you start rooting for him after a while, right?"

"You did more than root for him."

"I *paid attention*. After a while, I noticed a jump in his mindstream—every time he reached a certain thought, his mind would jump to a specific other thought, over and over—and I realized it wasn't a natural jump. Somebody had programmed him to do it, to cover up something important in between. So I managed to break the jump, remove the connection—and the next time, he remembered how to recreate the alloy he'd used in Mother Russia, back in the Project, your old stomping grounds. I'm surprised you didn't find this out way before me."

Volkov ignored the implied challenge. "All this just to make a little coil that shocks the subject to death when you hug them? You took all these chances for *that*? Your irresponsibility is breathtaking—if you think this justifies—"

"The coil's nothing," Landau said sharply. "It's the Tinker Toys, the proof of concept."

"For what?"

"For a hundred Marats—a hundred assassins who can strike down a target at a distance with a lightning bolt out of a clear sky. No authority can prosecute anyone because it was an Act of God— but your enemies can see that they're the ones God's acting against."

"You haven't demonstrated anything like that."

"All the tests were demonstrations of various pieces of the puzzle. Genius takes *time*, dude! I just got the last piece." Landau pulled a tiny glittering circle out of his shirt pocket.

"What is it?"

"It's the gun sight. Nanotechnology—De Jogt's one of the world's geniuses in Virtual Reality headsets. The lens reads your eye's point of focus and sends the lightning from the coil direct to the spot, frying whatever's in the way. If you can see it, you can burn it." He pointed out the window, at the SUV where De Jogt was being held. "That's why we need this guy—you've got to let me at him."

"He's catatonic at the moment."

"Renn's still got a hold on him."

"Of course he has. Max clamped his mind shut the instant you grabbed him back—if we try to force the memory out of him, he'll self-destruct. Which means Max is nearby, somewhere near."

"Find him. Break the clamp."

Volkov laughed. "*You* find him. If Max Renn has a skill, it's elusiveness. When he doesn't want to be found, he could be three feet from you and you won't see him. What's your backup plan?" Landau felt the challenge beneath the question.

"Let De Jogt go."

"What?"

"Release him—and follow him. We need to anyway."

"Why?"

Landau pulled the gunsight from his pocket. "He had one on him. He never makes one of anything. He comes to me with five or six. If we can find the prototype, we can figure out how to reverse-engineer it, even if he doesn't cooperate. When I found one on him, I had my men go back to the market—he and Renn gave an envelope to the postman just before we jumped them."

"Where to?"

"Who knows? Well, actually, the answer is: *he* knows. Let him go and he'll go after the envelope. And wherever he goes, Renn will be there waiting."

"You sound like you're looking forward to that. Don't underestimate Max Renn."

Landau's eyes brightened. "How would you like him—dead or under control? I can give you either one."

Volkov didn't bother hiding his doubts.

"I've done a lot of work on Max Renn. I can hand him to you on a platter. So you'll have a hundred Marats—that's Phase One, Max Renn under your thumb—that's Phase Two." He left the end of the sentence dangling.

"And there's a Phase Three?"

"Of course, that's the best one. Phase Three is, L Corp—through shell corporations in Cyprus—buys a metallurgical firm and De Jogt's videogame company, to launder the work I've done so you can offer it to NATO at a bargain price."

"Why would I do that?"

"To own the back door that's built into it—the back door to the power of the Gods."

Volkov looked almost amused. "You bow to a God, Landau?"

Landau smiled back. "I don't bow to any God—I want to *be* God. The old-fashioned vengeful, deadly, unforgiving God. The

One who wields unlimited destruction, pestilence and famine, fire and brimstone. The One who can light the sky on fire."

sums

Australia

"You're here early."

Duncan was at his desk at 6 am as always. The man either had no life or a life so awful that the office was a refuge—Cornwell didn't want to know which.

"We need to talk," Cornwell said, "off the record first."

"And then?"

"And then I'll do whatever you want."

Duncan put down the report in his hand. "You mean you expect me to *want* to be off the record?"

"I'm giving you the opportunity not to know, if that's what you want."

Duncan's face soured. "Let me guess—this doesn't have anything to do with shipping in the South China Sea, am I correct?"

"Correct."

"Because that is your job, if I remember correctly."

"My job is to inform you of threats to our security wherever I find them," Cornwell said.

"You ever take a vacation?"

"Occasionally."

"When was the last time?"

"I was on vacation September 11th."

"Well," Duncan said drily, "I don't think it was your fault, if that's what you're getting at."

"Whatever—" Cornwell opened a laptop to a photo of a young man with a neatly trimmed beard, straw hat and jeans a size too small, "this little shit is Julian Landau, Yale graduate and current L Corp employee."

"Contractor employee lists are confidential!" Duncan protested without sounding very surprised.

"Fine—I'm telling you. That's pretty confidential."

"How'd you get this information?"

"I have my ways."

"If you're hacking Agency systems, you'll be behind bars—"

"I'm hacking nothing. But I've met people who know and, since they know, I know."

"They'll go to jail with you for sharing classified information."

"They didn't share anything with me. Like I said, I know because they know."

"Bullshit—what does that mean?" Cornwell was relieved it had taken this long to get to this point in the conversation. He'd been totally out of practice reading minds; he'd had to pry Duncan like a tuna can with a rusty opener. But now, after a few months work, he was prepared.

"It means, you're reminding yourself what Gretschmer told you, that I'm a nutcase to be nursed through to retirement, out of courtesy to God knows what. I love that—we regret our decent debts now! And your next thought, of course, is 'How does he know this?' and the usual two-step, wondering who I talked to, who would have shared it with me, as if anybody could tell me what you're thinking *right now*. You're also wondering whether your assistant is wearing a bra today—she isn't. The answer to the next question on your mind is, yes, she would." Duncan was now bright-red, trying to decide if he was angry or insane and not having a good time deciding.

"Listen to me," Cornwell continued. "There are agents around the world who can read minds and force ideas into your mind. We'd fallen out of fashion since the Cold War but someone's pulling together the troops now—they're showing up at the same time and place and not coincidentally, where they can do real damage to world affairs."

"I've read about this," Duncan said. "You took an oath not to—"

"I took an oath not to do this anymore in the service of my country because it was deemed unnecessary. We could bend potential assets with drugs and the guys on top got nervous about the fact that we were getting intelligence they couldn't verify from any other source. Which, if you think about it, is the whole benefit about reading somebody's mind. Idiots!"

"How do I know you're not controlling me now?" Duncan asked.

"Because you're asking me the question," Cornwell answered. He pulled up several more pictures on the laptop. "Here's our contractor again, good ol' Julian Landau, except this shot was taken by a security camera in a park in Amsterdam. The woman in the car with him is Stasia Saminova, Vlad's late wife. They sit next to each other in the car for three and a half minutes, it looks like they're holding hands for a moment, no one says a word, mouths never move, yet she's nodding her head like she understands. Then he touches her temple and walks away and Mrs. Saminova drives off. And the next time anyone sees her, she's on camera in a Brussels safe house, hugging her husband and leaving him dead as a doornail and no one can explain it."

"You don't know it was her—"

"She knows it was her. She knows she killed him but doesn't know how. She talked to a man in the park, she remembers that. He talked to her from *inside* her head and put a device on her hand. She understood it's purpose as soon as he gave it to her—she spent the whole ride to Brussels envisioning the killing in her head, totally unable to resist."

"What's *that* mean?"

"I told you—he made her do it. Irresistible compulsion."

"That's stupid," Duncan said. "You can't hypnotize someone to do anything they wouldn't do on their own."

"Really?!" Cornwell spat. "You're saying this seriously? Check out the Stargate archives, even the declassified stuff. The whole point of paying us out of Defense funds for 18 years was that we made people do things they would never have considered on their own." Cornwell pulled up a newspaper clipping onscreen. "And then there's the special prosecutor in Lima who died suddenly last week at a party, two days before he was supposed to indict his prime minister. His best friend went up and hugged him and he keeled over, dead on the spot, in front of twenty witnesses. Heart attack, they said but he smelled bad, too. Sound like anyone we know?"

"Stop it—"

"The friend turned himself in, confessed to murder though he couldn't explain why or how he did it. They investigated for a week and let him go, despite the media crying for blood and his insisting he was to blame. Zero evidence of foul play, except that the corpse was broiled from within, just like Vlad when I found him in Brussels. The friend committed suicide the day after they released him."

"Okay, that's enough!"

Cornwell stopped stalking. He crossed his arms and nodded. "I would think it would be—more than enough." He clicked open yet another picture on the laptop. "But just in case it isn't, here's Landau's plane tickets in and out of Lima the day the murder took place."

"I said that's enough!" Duncan thundered. "We don't involve ourselves in projects by contractors."

"'Projects?' You think we're killing special prosecutors in Lima now? And we'd farm it out to contractors? Maybe I'm out of touch. Or maybe you're just afraid to ask."

"This is rank speculation on subjects that are way over our clearance!"

"Did you know Vlad Saminov was up to his neck in particle beam research?"

Duncan stopped. "What?"

"Particle beams? If you like old sci-fi movies, you could just call it a ray gun? Lightning with a telescopic sight?" Duncan seemed to have gone blank all of a sudden. "NATO's been trying to develop one since the 40's, spending huge amounts of money and always running up against the same wall—you have to carry around a generator the size of a house to create enough electricity. Saminov insisted he had a way of bypassing that problem, that the

Soviets had made a breakthrough but didn't realize it until it was too late and the country was collapsing." Duncan was staring dumbstruck. "He told me on the phone that a new weapon was being developed 'right under our noses'. He told me that over the phone from the car, just before he died, just before I got railroaded off to sunny Australia by Pietr Volkov, our defense contractor who used to bend minds for the good ol' Soviet Union."

Duncan was staring helplessly now at his desk, at the ceiling, out the window, anywhere other than where he was.

Cornwell leaned across the desk and said quietly, "Don't you think we should at least warn *someone*?"

safe passage

South China Sea

Follow the sounds. Travel til sunrise. I'll meet you there. I swear the note in my pocket buzzed against my leg like an alarm clock.

Where? I wrote but the ink just disappeared into the paper like water in a sponge. Which left me to figure out: Which sounds?

It was evening in Irfunya's hut, the village tucked away to sleep. My ears pricked up for the first thing I heard, which wasn't much. No bird calls in the middle of the sea, just a couple of fish jumping and the waves lapping against the pilings but nothing that would require me to travel till sunrise.

I felt it before I heard it—a buzzing sound, very low, then louder and louder, running along the horizon. Searching, I saw the blinking lights of a slow-moving propeller plane.

I nudged Irfunya on his mat. He waved me off so I nudged him again and then a third time. He opened his eyes glaring at me.

"What?"

"Where's the shuttle go?" We saw it every night moving in the same direction.

"What the fuck?" he grunted and rolled over on his mat.

"No, it's important," I told him and he sat up, resentful.

"Go lotta fucking places," he said and started naming islands I'd never heard of.

"If I was on it till sunrise, where would I end up?" I demanded.

"How I fucking know?" he yelped. "Go to Kota Kinabalu and find out."

"Where's Kota—Kota Kin—"

"Kota Kinabalu! That where it lands! Go there, get on plane and find out. What the fuck! What the fuck!" He went to lie down but I grabbed him by the shoulders.

"How do I get there?"

"Now?"

"Now. I have to go." I waved the note in his face—I'd told him stories about the magical morphing notepaper but he wasn't having any,thanks. "Can we paddle there?"

"Ha! Sure, if you got a fucking year."

Which left us one option.

"Sure, I'll take him," Guntar said and that set off warning bells. Guntar didn't give anything away and his engine didn't turn over without the profit figured beforehand.

Irfunya didn't like it either—he was giving Guntar the evil eye. "You coming back?" he asked me and I felt terrible, like I was deserting him. I hadn't even had the chance to think about it.

"Probably not," I said—it was the truth. As soon as I did, he turned to the room and announced, "I going too! Sick of this place!"

"I thought you liked it here."

"Best place on earth! Don't matter! Get old not moving around!"

"I'm not really sure—"

"Not coming back!" he said, determined now. "Time to go!"

He was bellowing, naturally, because it was his only tone of voice and, within a minute, a whole crowd gathered, most of the village, saying goodbye. Happy goodbyes, no tears. Either they weren't sentimental or maybe they liked him but not all that much. Or maybe it wasn't the first time he'd packed up on short notice. It certainly threw me—I hadn't thought about leaving for good and I certainly hadn't planned on taking him with me.

Guntar immediately got two of his power cruisers ready while everyone else was showing up with food and odd bits of junk as keepsakes. When the festivities ended—and they didn't take long, everyone having toasted and gifted and now standing around looking awkward like *here's your hat, what's your hurry?*, we headed out to sea.

Guntar paid attention in that corner-of-the-eye way he had but that was Guntar, he could make eating breakfast look sneaky so this was birds in the trees for him.

It wasn't until an hour out at sea—too far to swim back, for sure—that he pulled back the throttle all at once and the other boat drew up alongside, with two of his biggest bruisers inside focusing on us over their Kalashnikov's. Guntar put on his biggest smile.

"So," he said, talking directly to me, "what's getting away worth to ya?"

"You don't ask for fucking money!" Irfunya said immediately, stepping between us. "He one of us."

"Who says *you're* one of us, old man?"

"You call me Uncle."

"Not now. We've got a windfall; you can be my mother, it doesn't change that!"

"You're a thief!" Irfunya said.

"I'm a *man!*" Guntar bellowed. "Half the fuckers on those cruise ships you beg from got their shit same way. The world's boats use our water, drain our fishing, dump their shit here like it's a dump. On land, they'd pay to cross the border."

"If we're a *country*," Irfunya needled.

"Hell yeah! I declare myself a fucking country! I declare a tax on all these motherfuckers!" He settled in my face. "The difference between me and them is, I can't afford to work *stupid*! Show me what you got, I take a cut! If we have to strip-search you, we will—Bhota over here has already taken a shine to you. One way or the other, I'm getting my piece before I take you anywhere."

"How do you know I'm trying to get away from anybody?" I said, all nonchalance.

"Because," his face twisted into a nasty smile, "I know who you are."

It's amazing how fast your brain works when you're in the headlights.

He led us below-deck to his mancave up under the bow. It was decorated in Pirate Traditional—the best of what other people threw away or gave up rather than being taken hostage. A sketchy maroon sectional, a cherry sleigh bed, a bison's head (with horns) wobbling in a corner and a wall crammed with not-quite-the-latest-model computers and monitors.

"I've got a half-meter satellite dish on the rear deck," Guntar crowed, not that you could miss it. "She pans 360° from horizon to straight up and holds position in a storm. We get storms out here, bro." He was expansive all of a sudden, on his turf. "That's where I found out about you."

He started clicking away and fired up the Rome clips on YouTube, the scenes I'd checked out in Dubai and more. Irfunya stood paralyzed alongside me, taking it all in.

Guntar twirled around in his chair, a hungry smile on his face. "You're worth a lot of money to *somebody*," he said and I shivered involuntarily.

"I don't think—"

"Don't!" Guntar snapped. "If you were a great thinker, you wouldn't be coming to me for help, would you?" That was hard to argue with.

"Guntar," Irfunya murmured. "Where?"

Irfunya was fixated on the screen, where Max and Volkov squared off for the four thousandth time, a fiery line of energy linking them. Except, I realized, following his eyes, that in this particular clip, the energy surge seemed to be coming from *me*, right off my pointed finger. I remember pointing at the thing, trying to figure it out, but here it looked like it was mine.

Guntar sighed. "Where *what*, Uncle?" That's where I saw my opportunity.

"He wants to know, where's the weapon?"

"In your hand!"

"Yeah? *Where*? Look again!"

Guntar went cross-eyed and rolled back the clip, staring at the monitor like he was going to burn a hole through it. After a pause, he re-racked it again and again, looking for the loophole, the explanation that wasn't there.

"Got no weapon." I told him. "Got *finger*."

"Oh, fuck you!" he burst.

"You think I'm wandering around the South China Sea unarmed? Really?"

And then I held my breath. If Guntar burst out laughing, I was fishfood. Max probably risked this same disbelief every six seconds of his life—but he could back up his threats. Half a minute passed like slow death. Then I wagged my index finger at him and he flinched.

"What does it mean?" Guntar said, looking from the monitor to my finger and back and suddenly he wasn't barking anymore.

"I can't tell you that," was my answer. I learned in the Army, if anything makes you sound authoritative, it's 'I know shit you aren't allowed to know.'

"If you can do all that," he said, voice up an octave, "what are you doing here?"

"Checking you out," I said. The thought hadn't occurred to me until he asked the question but now it seemed absolutely inevitable. His eyes went the size of melons and I could feel the leverage tilting all my way.

"Me?"

"You're running things out here, aren't you?" He couldn't disagree, not after having spent the last few months constantly telling me so. "This is a big fight we're in," I fumbled to fill in the details. "All over the world. We can't watch everything so... so we need people everywhere."

"Watching G8 Security?"

"Think big, Guntar! The people *using* G8 Security! And AT&T, Microsoft, Apple, Fiat, General Dynamics, General Electric, Halliburton, Exxon Mobil, 20th Century Fox, Germany, Russia, Japan and the Pentagon. They've got their own agenda."

"What's their agenda?"

"Not yet," I said, mostly because I hadn't made that part up yet—but also because I had to keep something under my hat, something he could have later if he was a good boy. "You're still on probation."

"Probation?"

Asshole! A second earlier, he was afraid I'd fry him; now he's offended he's not a full partner. "Hell yeah! You think we let some small-time pirate into a major international—"

"*Small-time?*" he thundered, actually scary at that moment. "The South China Sea is the busiest piece of water in the world and I *run* it! I've got a hundred ships—"

"Where?" Irfunya stopped him.

"From here to Hong Kong to Singapore." His face read *Don't fuck with my story, old man.* Naturally, Irfunya ignored him completely.

"What kinda hundred fucking ships you got? Rowboats?"

"A hundred ships is a hundred ships, whattayou care? I did a list one night. US Navy counts its rowboats, I guarantee!" He stared at me defiantly.

I thought about Max, when he was menacing. I went quiet and unblinking and cold. "I apologize for 'small-time'. Bad choice of words. Let's put it this way: we don't take on local partners until we're sure you're the right guy."

"Who else is there out here? Hong Lin? That who you're talkin' to? Now *there's* a pirate! Makes me look like Gandhi! The Chinese like him 'cause he kisses ass."

I had no idea who Hong Lin was but obviously he was the competition—and the Chinese preferred him. "That's the point, isn't it? If we're offering an alternative, it's got to be a better way of life." I was floundering a bit and I couldn't afford to lose the thread. "Uh—Be All You Can Be! Think Different! Just Do It!" He looked confused but he wasn't bailing and that gave me a chance to regroup. "We need you on probation for six months."

"Six months?" he nearly popped a vein.

"You've got potential but you're very raw. You've got a ton of energy but not a lot of strategic judgment."

"That fucking what I tell him," Irfunya said and Guntar told him to shut the fuck up—and there was my out.

"We need actionable intelligence about anything unusual around here we can use. And you've got to show us you can see the big picture, that you've got a better plan than Hong Lin and that you can put a plan into action!"

"And if I do?" he said. "Then what?" The customer was asking me for my best price and when could I deliver?

"Once you're a full-fledged member," I said, "you get whatever you need." I raised my index finger, the finger that flattened Rome, at least in his mind. His face went all giddy for a moment. "But you need a counselor."

"A what?"

"You need a wise voice to lead you to your best judgment and teach patience." I pointed to Irfunya. "This is your Counselor, your chief advisor."

"Him?"

"Me?"

They were a pair of funhouse mirrors; old and young, tall and squat, thin and stout, but the identical expression: You're sticking me with HIM?

"I'm the boss here!" Guntar blustered but he was waiting carefully for my reaction.

"You might the boss *here*—but if you're working with us, you're not The Boss. Get me?"

His face fell a little but he recovered. "Ya—yeah! Sure!"

"You're the boss but he's your right hand. This is part of the bargain. If that changes for any reason, the deal's off. Got me?"

"Yeah, yeah! Got you!"

The two of them were eyeing each other like bad relations. "Make him see the big picture," I told Irfunya. "Show us you can work together." I was almost whispering. "We'll *know* what you're up to."

They nodded like dog figurines in the back window of some old lady's Cadillac.

"Okay, let's get going—I've got a plane to catch."

Guntar was still pacing—he was sweating a bit but he was also doing the sums and I could see they weren't coming out for him.

"Don't take this wrong, okay? I want it, I want it bad," he said, but cautious, more cautious than I'd ever seen him. "We're— we're still pirates, get me? I gotta show results or somebody'll cut me dead in my sleep some night. I gotta show the boys you're not just steaming me. I'm not sayin' you are, y'know, just—"

"No, no, I understand." He was right—and the hook was in; I just needed him to swallow. What did I have to give him? Amazingly, I actually had an answer. I pulled a black rectangle from my right sock. "At the airport, you get this."

"What is it?"

"A credit card."

His eyes nearly crossed. "I got *boxes* of credit cards!"

"Sure you do—with limits and owners cancelling them so they're useless after a couple days. This one has no limit and never runs out."

He gave me the eye bigtime. "Yeah, right."

"This card is issued by a major government to support a false identity. CIA, MI6, SRV—what they used to call KGB. You don't have to know which. For use by major assets working undercover. The bearer is given wide latitude because he's assumed to be in the field with his life on the line and unable to answer questions for months or years at a time." I saw the dawn breaking across his face before I said it out loud. "This is James Bond's fucking AMEX."

He lit up like the Rockefeller Center Christmas tree. The boat swung around South-Southwest at a clip.

The two of them sparred all the way to the airport over their new domain. I felt like the guy who introduced Capone to Meyer Lansky. We saw the tiny control tower, just a glass box on a pedestal, first. The runway ran right up to the shoreline. As we pulled into the marina, Irfunya threw his arms around me and Guntar clapped me on the back.

"Keep him on the straight and narrow," I told Irfunya.

"In his case, that a fucking waste of talent," he said. "I make him useful."

And then I was on the dock and hiking to the terminal, where the old propeller-driven pontoon plane was waiting for passengers.

"Where to?" asked the ticket-seller, who also seemed to be the pilot and the mechanic.

"Where will we be at sunrise?"

"Sunrise? Darwin."

"That's where to," I told him and started pulling bills out of my socks. He took half a sock and waved me toward the open hatch.

redemption

Goa, India

Diya Devangi spread ginger from a shredder into the small bowl with flowers painted around the rim, and squeezed three lemons into the mixture, watching the colors mingle. She added olive oil and lemon juice, salt, pepper and sugar, forming a dark soup at the base and added just enough ground fennel to give it that little bite. The sauce went into a larger bowl filled with thin-sliced cucumbers, cashews and mint from her garden.

The salad was Aryana Singh's favorite since they were girls together, friends from the same block and school, parents of the same circle and caste. Every Sunday of Singh's convalescence, Diya had made her favorite cucumber salad and brought it over to share in the evening, just as the two old friends had in more tranquil times.

Diya pulled plastic wrap tightly over the top of the bowl, washed her hands and hung her striped apron on the hook alongside. It was time to go but she found herself dawdling, searching for reasons not to.

Awful images filled her head—could you have nightmares while awake? In the images, Aryana's face replayed in an awful loop, the surge and the shock endlessly repeating as Diya watched, feeling over and over the sudden blast of heat and the awful pull that wouldn't let go until it hammered Aryana into submission. Unto death. Surely, that was the end, though Diya's mind always skipped away before she could know for certain.

Not wanting to know was a powerful urge, maybe the most powerful there was.

As her hands grasped her blouse, she didn't want to know what she was doing. As she rolled up the sleeve, she pretended to focus on the birds on the branches outside. As she reached for the bundle on the counter, she tried to stop herself, although she knew all too well that it was hopeless. As she unpacked the metal coil and placed it over her hand, she refused to know the inevitable result, what had to come next.

Vacantly, she saw her hand reach for the doorknob, lock the door behind her and start the car. It was someone else doing all this, she thought, not her. She had no control, so therefore she was not doing any of it—that actually made a kind of sense.

But the tears streaming down her cheeks reminded her that she knew all too well.

~~~~

Aryana Singh moved through the crowd like a leper.

Whole families moved away when they saw her coming. In the town she'd grown up, where she was known to most since her childhood or theirs, she'd become a pariah.

At the moment, that was not her concern. Months after the rest of the world, she was finally terrified that she had in fact gone thoroughly stark raving mad.

Goa's streets were India's, a beehive of chatter in a hundred dialects. Her neighbors talked over each other, haggled over goods in stores, apologized excessively and swore oaths by all manner of authority, high and low. Singh was used to that chatter. What was new was the chatter inside her head, where those same neighbors soliloquized to themselves, no mouths moving, thinking their private thoughts while she heard every single one.

Something for the dog, he'll take whatever I bring…

It's her again, hasn't she got someplace else to go?

I didn't water the plants, too late to go back, it's not like they'll die from missing a day…

She knew these people, she recognized their voices in her head and heard their thoughts change as their eyes moved through the crowd.

She'd begun to feel secure again—six months after, she hadn't become paranoid or deranged despite what she'd been through—she had a right to feel proud of herself. It wouldn't have been a surprise if she'd slipped over the edge but she hadn't. She'd offered herself that simple pat-on-the-back a thousand times in recent months, just being kind to herself. But now, her head was bursting with familiar voices that weren't hers and she felt herself teetering on the edge. All her pride seemed vainglorious, her safety, her life, suddenly tenuous.

Even in Rome, it hadn't been like this. There had been many voices but all saying the same thing: *Draw the gun. Draw the gun. You'll know when. Draw the gun.* Over and over to the point that, when a new voice actually told her it *was* time, she was prepared to resist. And, of course, then she'd gotten help.

This time, there was no preparing and no help. This was no chorus of canned orders, this was her familiar world ripped open and naked, the people she knew best ripped wide open and inside-out for her inspection, free of custom, veneer, self-protection, manners and demeanor; fearful and self-doubting, contradictory and spiteful. Just seeing them, their lives laid bare in front of her, made the whole world feel untrustworthy and threatening. Without boundaries, some kind of buffer, people were too much.

Were they looking at her—were they? Were they looking away on purpose? She'd come to the market for...what? It was hard to focus. She stared at herself in a shop window, half-expecting to see her hair gone white. That would have been inevitable in a tale by Hugo or Dumas or Poe and that was the way the moment felt, the kind of drama it called for. Singh cast about in every direction, seeking any avenue that might pull her away from collapse.

And then, bustling across the square, there was Diya, dear Diya, with her usual Sunday bowl and the smile Aryana had counted on since they were children. Diya had comforted her, steadied her, throughout her marriage, after her husband's assassination and her rise to power and now, after her disgrace and retreat to a shaky exile back home.

She rushed toward her eagerly. As she passed the druggist Milal and his friend Jawarlal, chatting over a basket of mangoes, she noticed that she was still picking up their thoughts—the thoughts of everyone in the square but Diya's. Why was she absent? A chill went up Singh's back. The look on Diya's face was conflicted, not welcoming—something was off, wrong. Singh faltered but this was her oldest friend, her most trusted—there could be no doubt, no disloyalty. She picked up her pace.

And a man stepped in front of her, crying "Diya! It's been too long!" and threw his arms around her friend.

And went up in a storm of blinding light and acrid smoke.

Take a right, said a voice in her head. That voice, *his* voice, her protector from Rome. *Turn right into the alley and keep walking, two blocks.*

She froze just long enough to see that Diya was still standing, clutching at the man's shoulders as he collapsed in the center of the square. The rest of the place went crazy, emptying in screams and panic but Diya was unharmed and distinctly relieved at that.

To the right. Go now. Everything depends on it.

Singh turned right, up the alley, pushed by the onrushing crowd, beggars pulling tight the bundles containing their worldly possessions, children clutched in their parent's arms, no thinking now, just *moving*.

Two blocks up, she stepped out of the flow, into the doorway of the tailor shop. No voice told her what to do, she just *knew*. And there he was, straight out of memory, runty and animal, taut and wild-eyed as before.

He touched her forehead and the voices, the babble of thoughts, disappeared.

"You see the danger you're in."

"Diya's trying to kill me? The whole town's in my head? Someone's *doing* this to me? Is it the same people as Rome?"

"Worse. It's the people who want to take the jobs of the people from Rome, the ones who have to prove they're tougher and more ruthless than them."

"Rival spies?"

"No, the next generation of spy entrepreneurs."

Singh blanked.

"Never mind," he said. "For your purposes, it's the same people."

She considered this a moment. "How will I know when they're coming for me?"

"You knew," he said. "You knew it when you saw Diya's face. You can't be loyal now, you can't think of anything or anyone in the way you once did. You have to *know what you know* and act on it at once."

She nodded and sighed. "I understand. I just hope I can defy my instincts."

"I want you to *listen* to your instincts. And I want you to pass up the party conference in two weeks."

"I am the legitimate head of my party. I have been deposed falsely. I have heard my reputation smeared for months. It's time to take back what is mine."

"You'll never get there. These people will never let you. I was lucky to discover this attempt. We won't be that lucky forever."

"Are you telling me to surrender?"

He stared at the floor, out the open doorway, a million miles away and then smiled back at her, a smile more sad and genuine than she'd ever seen from him before.

"I don't know what I want from you, really—except to live to fight another day. To bide your time a bit, pick your battles."

"I thought I was doing exactly that." She stared at Renn's face, at his discomfort with his own answer, at his inability to know how to continue. "I appreciate that you care," Singh said, surprising both of them with her directness.

Renn looked away, wincing and then back to her quickly, as though wanting not to let the moment pass. "I have seriously mixed feelings about caring in general," he said. "Any kind of caring, all kinds of caring."

"It frightens all of us," Singh answered, watching their connection change shape right in front of her. "It's an artificial world—any real feeling is frightening."

She watched him squirm, just another man shrugging off his feelings—what's new? *But this is no ordinary man*, she thought. *He must know better.*

"I was trained to capture thought—facts, secrets—to plant ideas and force actions, usually to the detriment of the person I was contacting," he answered, though she hadn't posed the question aloud. "We were taught—"

"There are more like you?"

"You encountered another in Rome," he said and Singh remembered quite clearly the shock of the taller, broader man alongside the Viewing Box and realizing he was the voice in her head for the last few days. "We were taught to keep our distance, to pull relevant information from the static of voices. Keeping that distance was crucial—those who didn't generally went mad."

There was a light in his eyes that she didn't remember seeing before, a softening and a yearning that made her fear for him instantly.

"I've spent all my life holding people at a distance," he added, pronouncing 'people' like it was the name of a different species, "and now I see myself in them and them in me. We're all stumbling around looking for a reason for our life and knowing there probably isn't one. The things that matter, we know *despite* the facts, not because of them. Whatever we know is never enough, whatever we can do is never enough…"

His voice trailed off and Singh found something in this she recognized.

She led him up the stairs to a landing overlooking the street. Life was already returning to something approaching normalcy— crowds walking cautiously, yammering about the explosion, unnerved but returning to the grateful drudgery of work, picking up groceries for dinner or making arrangements to pick the kids up from school.

"When I became Prime Minister, one of my father's ministers—one I trusted—told me, 'The hardest thing about this job is understanding, no matter how able you are, no matter how hard you try, you will not measurably change most of their lives.'"

"I can hear when they're deluding themselves. I hear them openly at their worst—I heard a man plotting to rape a child a few weeks ago."

"And couldn't do anything."

"I could, this time. But what happens when I can't?"

She listened. "You have to live with it. Which won't be easy, I understand but you can only do what you can."

"That sounds so much better than it feels. What's worse is, doing a good thing and seeing it fade in minutes; do one bad thing and the results linger for years. Gratitude feels like an obligation; pain and fear stay fresh."

"I was responsible for everything," Singh said, "everything we did and didn't do. I saw the poverty every day. I saw the waste. I know what we could do if there were no politics, if there were no interests, if I could just do what I think is right. And, of course, if I did that, I'd find everything that was wrong with what seemed so right, every way individuals could defy and pervert and break down any system we could create. I know that's not quite the same as your—"

"I hear their screams. I feel their pain. I die with them."

Conversation stopped. They stood quietly for a long time, he looking away, she, finally, looking at him. "Alright, it's not the same," she said quietly. "What matters is what we *do*. We don't live alone, none of us. Without others, we possess no real virtues, no real flaws—everything real comes from doing, from seeing how

Ted Krever

we make real choices in the world, when every path entails risk and fear. That's where you discover your real loyalties, your ideals. We are how we treat other people. Other people are family. Other people are home."

"You don't sound much like a politician."

"I'm a political accident—if a zealot hadn't murdered my father, I wouldn't be anywhere near power. And I make pragmatic decisions, I hurt people when I feel I have to. I tell myself someone would be hurt anyway, I'm just choosing who—but the reality is, *I'm* choosing who."

Renn was focused on her now in a way he never had been. It was unnerving, the directness of his gaze. She wondered if the discomfort was not so much about him looking at her—he'd already been inside her mind—but him letting her look back, showing her just that much.

"You need something more from me," she said, "something you're uncomfortable asking."

"I need you to survive. I need to not have to worry about you."

"Meaning?"

"I want you to forget, at least for a little while."

"No."

"Only until I've gotten through this next crisis. If I succeed, hopefully you'll be able to speak out and it'll matter. If I fail, I'll be gone and have no control over you anymore and you'll do what you choose."

"For how long?"

"I don't know, exactly."

"No."

"I can make you forget in a way they'll recognize. They'll know you're no threat to them. They'll leave you alone for a while."

"I'll remember nothing?"

"Yes."

"I have to go to the party conference—that's two weeks. I won't give that up."

"I'll check in and clear you a few days before."

Singh's expression was severe. "No way we can...stay in contact, behind the veil?"

"No. You're blank or you're not. They'll know."

"I'll be distraught. I'll be terrified that I'm going mad, just as they say."

He thought this over for several moments. "I'll monitor you—if you're really on the brink, I'll release you."

"Will you really?"

He sighed now. "I say it, I mean it." He thought a moment. "If something happens to me, the suggestion will die with me, too."

"That won't happen," she said firmly. "You'll release me willingly. That's what real friends do."

He actually laughed at this—surprised by the sound, she realized how rare it was, coming from him. "I don't know how to be a real friend," he said. "I lack an emotional education."

"You'll have to enroll, like the rest of us," she answered. "And pay the tuition. No scholarships. And no grading on a curve."

"You know grading on a curve?"

"We're a corrupt Western-style democracy. I came bundled with all the foreign aid."

They laughed again together and then he swiped a finger across her temple and grabbed her as she went limp. He carried her to the chair at the end of the veranda, intending to set her down. Her neck was warm against his and he lingered a moment before releasing her, remembering Elena's touch, remembering being a younger man, one not so sure of himself but also not so aware of the consequences of every single thing he did.

Finally, he released her into the cushions, retreated down the staircase to the street and lingered until she rose and found her way safely home.

reunion 6
December 2008

Darwin, Australia

I drive Max a long way south out of Darwin in somebody else's car, somebody who pulled his Ford into a steakhouse parking lot and offered me the driver's seat.

"Do you ever think about how these people get home?" I ask as we roll through the suburbs. "The ones who just hand us their cars and walk away smiling? Do you ever wonder how they explain it to their wives? 'Oh, you mean I left this morning with the car and don't know where it is now?'"

"No," Max answers, just like old times.

Except it isn't like old times. We drive connecting roads for about an hour and in that time, all the niceties fade away. First it's roadsigns and identifying markers, then it's lines on the paving and eventually even the paving goes and it's just a beaten-down path in the dust, that part of Australia being expanses of dust or wild eruptions of jungle, depending on the proximity to water.

In the same way, time strips away some of his armor. He's pointing out bits of scenery and pretty animals and what's up with *that*? Since when does Max Renn do pretty animals? Something's brewing, I can see it in the flexing of his hands and neck and the way he's looking all around all the time. Max's senses are everywhere, he doesn't need to look at *anything*—he never used to, anyway.

And then the dirt path pops out of a dense grove into the trailer-park cemetery—half-a-mile of derelict trailer shells and old railroad cars, automobile hoods and roofs, a marble-and-glass dome worthy of a statehouse, a 1950's bus with antelope antlers and a roof turret off a B-24, a yacht with the sails still furled along the masts and an extended family of squawking birds taking up residence and a couple of tanks, the big guns removed but the treads and camo still ready for work.

Just on the other side of this is the trailer-park shopping mall—five Quonset huts in a row, set down on a patch of withering browning grass along the very bottom of Darwin Bay, a view of the skyscrapers rising above the shoulder-height weeds along the water. There's no more than three or four people in sight along the whole strip but the parking lot across the way is filled with cars—apparently, you come to work and don't leave till quitting time. Furniture Liquidators, Estates R Us, Tire

Extravaganza and B2BNT, those are the signs and none of them look like they plan to stay too long in this uplifting location.

"Pull in here and park," Max says, and I take a spot in the second row, facing outward. We can see the road but a row of cars in between keeps anyone out there from getting a good look at us.

"Now what?"

"We wait."

"I thought we were going to rescue Kate."

"That's the plan, assuming she needs rescue," he says, without seeming at all sure about it. He's still flexing and squirming in his seat—this is not the Max I remember. Something's making him real uncomfortable. He was never comfortable—ever—but I never saw him uncomfortable like this either.

There's a long wait, just staring out the windshield, before he talks.

"What do you remember about your family?" he says, and if you'd asked me the ten thousand most likely conversation starters, that wouldn't have been on the list.

"You told me I had a sister in New Jersey," I say. He's still flexing and squirming. "I figure if I had a sister in New Jersey, I'd know it. We drove through Jersey to get to the airport and you never said 'We're passing your sister's house—wave!'" Nothing. He's grimacing to some other conversation in his head.

"Do you remember your family?" he continues, like I didn't say a word.

"I remember Pee Wee and Alex—and Dave," I say and with 'Dave' he comes around a bit, eyes on me finally and trying to focus. "The guys in our house."

"There were a lot of guys in your house." We did have a revolving cast of characters for a while. Dave's halfway house for the veteran infirm of mind and body, ready to graduate the VA Hospital but not quite ready to face the streets just yet.

"It was the same ones for the last six months." Max would visit every once in a while, from his shack farther out into the Everglades, where he didn't have to hear any humans thinking, just alligators and pythons and whooping cranes.

"But that's not family," he says and I sit up.

"They're the family I remember," I say and he tries to decide what he thinks about that. Sometimes he takes me serious for a while and sometimes I'm comic relief, and I'm never really sure which is going on at the moment. "Family's who you come from and they're as far back as I can remember so that's where I come from—since I don't have any sister from New Jersey." Of course, he ignores that again.

"What if you didn't come from anywhere? What if you hated where you came from?" he asks.

"Do you hate where you came from?"

"Not me. Someone else, someone…someone I'm going to have to deal with. Someone who's using me against myself."

"How?"

"I don't know. The way we all use people against themselves, I guess. Find a weakness and push it open, pick at a scab till it bleeds."

"And he's using family against you?"

"He's trying to. Except I don't have a family. They're just a void, a hole."

"Then you start from a hole," I say. "I remembered my mother's voice, heard it in a dream about a month ago, out of nowhere."

"How do you know it was her and not a dream mother?" he asks.

I wouldn't know what a dream mother was.

"I could feel it was her. I knew her, even though I can't tell you her name or remember her face. That's how you know people sometimes, isn't it? You know their innards! What makes them tick, what makes them fight? Even though you don't know their names or faces?"

"Yeah," he nods. "Something like that."

"And I remember Pee Wee and Alex and Dave and I remember Gunner and Munroe and Sully and Robbie from Iraq—and Tauber and Kate and you and that's my family now, all those guys—and Kate."

"Everybody can't be your family."

"Who's everybody? Volkov isn't my family and Marat wasn't my family and the guy who almost kidnapped me on the way here isn't my family. I pick the ones on my side!" I don't know why I'm upset but I don't understand why he's bringing this up either and I don't know why it seems like it bothers him so much. I don't remember ever seeing him get this bothered before, not like this.

It suddenly occurs to me that I know this conversation. This is the conversation you have before you go into battle, when you're thinking maybe you're not going to come out of the battle okay, maybe not going to come out of it at all. We were in Rome overnight planning and plotting and making a big dinner and knowing there was something coming and Max and I never had this conversation, never came close. I don't like it a bit.

"What's the matter?" I ask.

"The main goals here are to get De Jogt and Kate away from Pietr and live to fight another day," he says. "Understand?"

"English is my native language, I understand—why aren't you answering the question?"

"I'm okay," he says but clearly he isn't. "He's coming," he says, looking up all of a sudden and I see a Dodge Charger coming down the road, an obvious rental.

"Who is it?"

"De Jogt."

My eyes go big. "How'd you find him?"

"This is all about a gun sight, a little contact lens that reads where your eye is focusing and sends a lightning bolt to that spot."

"A lightning bolt? Like Marat?" I remember that son-of-a-bitch nearly scorching me six times. Or maybe it was twice but it felt like six times.

"Yeah, except that what Marat did naturally—uniquely—this thing does with technology. So anybody wearing the tech could be Marat."

"Jesus!" I find myself imagining the carnage lightning guns would bring to the Middle East, not to mention tailgating arguments outside 7-11.

"De Jogt's a smart guy," Max says, as the car pulls into the lot a few sections away. "He had to get rid of the prototype, get it away from L Corp when they were following us in Amsterdam. So he mailed it here."

"It's the only one?"

"No, he had one or two on him—they've probably got those already. And I've got one. But those lenses are coated so there's no way to find out how they work. The prototype is the Rosetta Stone—find that one, you can make millions more."

I grab the door handle. "What are we waiting for?" I say but I can already feel the paralysis taking me over, damn Max.

"These are big facilities and we want a tiny piece. Let him lead us to it."

And there he comes, out from between the cars. As soon as he walks through the doors of B2BNT, we're out of the car and following.

It's a huge barn inside, what looks like a mile of stacked shelves, five or six stories high in the middle. The front area contains about twenty cubicles for receiving and checking merchandise coming off a motorized conveyor. The people in front of us hand receipts to the customer counter and get a cubicle number to wait in.

"Where is he?" I say, checking out the cubicles. Nowhere to be seen. Then the next guy at the desk shows a different receipt. A guard steps out from the security desk, gives him a metal swipe and lets him through the desk area and out into the vast array of shelves.

"There you go," Max says. He peels off to the security desk, waves an empty hand in front of the guard and walks right past him. I hear grumbling from the crowd behind us but we're down in the stacks before a protest can develop, with Max peering around. "De Jogt's a good blocker. You go that way," he says, "we meet up at the other end if we don't find him."

I don't go three feet. "There!" I say, not loudly at all but I know Max can read me and he catches right up.

De Jogt sits at a small table beneath a stack of shelves, going through a plastic bin full of smaller plastic boxes. He is totally focused, enough so that we get right up to him before he looks up and shrinks back at the sight of Max.

"You didn't protect me," the Dutchman says immediately. "I did better on my own."

"You did better because they hadn't found you yet," Max answers. "I kept you locked up in Baku so they couldn't learn how to make the lenses—otherwise, do you think you'd still be alive?"

De Jogt returns to his boxes. "Sounds reasonable, doesn't it?" he says but it clearly isn't what he means.

"It's the truth," Max says, closing his eyes and humming mildly—not his wall-shaking *Ohmm* this time. He sticks his hand into the case and comes up with a tiny box.

"That's it!" De Jogt says and grabs for the thing.

Renn pulls it back for just a second and then lets him have it. "We have to keep this away from them," he says. "I'd rather hold...hold..." he stutters, swallowing the ends of the words, sputtering like an engine with a bad cylinder. I'm watching, waiting for him to recover but he goes the other direction instead, wobbling on his feet. His eyes are confused, then desperate. The rest of us are ready to head for the door but when Max takes a step, I see him actually stagger and almost go over onto the floor.

"What's happening?" I yell, like he's gone deaf, too. He's right in front of me but his eyes are miles away and sinking.

And then, as his knees give way and he sinks helplessly to the floor, I see a group in L Corp gear approaching behind him,

led by a grinning, nattily-dressed, smug-as-a-cheerleader Straw
Hat.

~~~~

Somewhere, Off the Coast of Australia

Pietr Volkov's stomach grumbles, watching the helicopter
arch across the afternoon sky. The steel flooring clangs underfoot
as he marches to the helipad on the rear deck.

The oil drilling platform sits twenty-five miles off the coast
of Australia. It's been abandoned for several years; a few dollars in
the right hands have turned on the power again. Construction
crews pore over the decks below, sealing, painting, rigging three
large satellite dishes and rebuilding an inadequate electrical
service to bring the place up to snuff. For now, it is staging,
building a crew but, very soon, it will be a citadel at sea. An L
Corp citadel at sea.

Volkov reaches the pad as the copter touches down. Landau
is out the door before the thing's even settled, as expected—the kid
has to preen, like a peacock. Volkov's acid stomach curdles as a
slightly-built geeky-type follows, meekly, out onto the deck. De
Jogt! *Landau will be insufferable for a week.*

The kid's expression promises more; tantalizingly more.
Volkov doesn't immediately recognize the next man off the copter.

He has to search beyond the facial hair and sunburn to recognize the Soldier.

Gary? Gerry? Whatever. I'll kick Landau up a level or two, Volkov thinks, *throw the arrogant prick an expense account or some toys and watch to see which foot falters.*

With a flourish like a magician's, here comes Landau's posse, hauling a magnetic cage, the one Volkov left behind at the warehouse—and there's no mistaking Renn, no matter that his face is vacant in a way Volkov's never seen before.

Landau's eyes are dancing and no wonder.

"Congratulations," Volkov says with genuine surprise. "That's a clean slate."

"Mm-hmm," Landau purrs, with an expression that says he's already toted up the price tag.

The heliport sits on top of the drilling side of the platform—the offices and crew cabins are on the other side. Volkov leads the whole group across the catwalk to the Crew Module, catching Landau several times almost skipping ahead of him. A narrow metal staircase takes them clanking down to a suite on B Deck, one of the few completed work areas available. The balding, sweaty accountant at the main desk sees Volkov and stiffens.

"Give us a minute," Volkov says while the accountant gets busy organizing the papers on his desk. "*This* minute!" Volkov snarls and the guy bolts out the door.

Landau's men carry Renn's cage into a corner and push De Jogt and the Soldier into chairs by the desks. and then file out into the hall. The room is still cramped as a meatlocker. Slotted vents over a porthole give out on a vista of whitecaps.

"What happened to him?" Volkov asks, eyes on Renn, who does not return his gaze.

"I've put him under," Landau says.

Volkov laughs despite himself. "Nobody puts Max Renn 'under,'" he says. "This is a trick…"

"No trick," Landau says. "I did a lot of work to get him here."

"What sort of work?"

"Oh, we became buddies. We share all kinds of memories, Max and me." To Volkov's disbelieving stare, he explains, "It's all in your e-classes. I figured out his home—the memory he starts from. I sent out images of his bedroom in Novosibirsk, the kitchen, his girlfriend's room—nothing. Know where he felt at home, woke up every time I sent him the image? The lab there in Siberia, the place where they studied him!"

"Where was he hiding?"

"Who cares? I found him. And then it was just a matter of getting him to let me in."

"*Let* you in?"

"I'm not stupid," Landau says. "I've picked up some tricks but I'm not going to force myself on Max Renn. I had to get him to offer himself to me, a little bit at a time, to make it feel inevitable, like he's already told me more than he had, until finally, he really slipped and I found a seam he hadn't plugged, that he didn't know about himself. Once I found that, it was just a matter of time till we'd come up against him in a key moment. We did and I paralyzed him. And here he is."

Volkov's cheeks burn. Landau's smug smile is insufferable.

"Wonderful. Great work," Volkov says finally, searching for a way to take the luster off—and finding one. "So now what do we do with him?"

Landau's face goes blank. "What?"

"What do we do, now that we've got him? Proclaim we've captured the great terrorist and put ourselves out of a job? Idiot! He's our expertise, he's our resume! Without him, our funding dries up, we become just another security contractor."

"But—we've been chasing him!"

"If we'd been chasing him, we'd have *found* him! Did anyone see you take him out of the building?"

"There were people there."

"Which is to say, 'yes.' So now there are witnesses. We'll have to clean up this mess, once I figure out the next step." Landau is taken by surprise, dumbstruck. Volkov, satisfied for the moment to have regained control of the situation, stares long at Renn sitting passively in his cage. "Can you free him up enough to talk— without losing control of him?"

"I think so."

"You *think* so?"

"I haven't tried it so I can't guarantee. But I've got a good grip on him."

Volkov nods. "That's an honest answer. We can do business on that basis. I want to talk to him—let's see what you can do."

Landau stops for a moment, considers this and then shakes his head. "I don't think so," he says. "*I'm* not doing business on that basis."

"What?"

"He's under *my* control," Landau says. "Not yours, not L Corp's—mine."

The bile begins to rise in Volkov's stomach again. "You're taking advantage of our training, which you used without permission—"

"So? *You* control him, then. I'll go fund a mindbender startup and make a pile of money. What are you gonna do with him if I'm not keeping him in check? He's useless to you in a cage."

"He's useless to me with you dictating terms," Volkov says.

"You haven't heard my terms yet. I heard Avery wanted him converted, to get him playing for our team."

"Like that will ever happen."

"So what option does that leave you?"

Volkov hates being questioned, especially by hipster punk trash like this one. It's an itch under the collar, an ache in the teeth. He felt three times that he had Landau under control but the kid keeps kicking the football away. "All I can do is turn him over to the authorities and let them have their show trial."

"Seems like a waste of potential."

"You have a suggestion, just make it!"

"As a matter of fact, dude, I do," Landau needles. Clearly, he knows the 'dude' needles—and clearly, he loves the needle. "I'm your protection, the loose cannon."

"Excuse me?"

"You can't bring him to Avery because you don't have him—*I* do. Which lets you off the hook. But if you're my new best friend, you could go on using him just like you have since Rome—except better."

Volkov's eyes are slits. "Meaning?"

"What have you been doing? 'Ooooh—Booga booga! Terrorist! Scary guy! Vote for who we tell you and run to *Your World* for a security blanket!' Except now, ol' Max'll do exactly what you want, when and where and how you want."

"That is interesting," Volkov admits. It's a merger instead of a competitor. He relaxes a bit.

"But he's my capture, my asset. You want him, you let me in."

"In where?"

"The Inner Circle," Landau says and Volkov stiffens again. "Remember, I hacked your files. I know what you're working on—and what Miriam's working on. I can put two and two together. The next test is, when?—next week? Next month? At that point, L Corp'll be running the table. I want to be in the thick of it. I want points; a share of the booty and the action."

Volkov frowns but Landau doesn't back down. "I'm not gunning for your job, dude. That's Miriam's gig. I *like* being second—I get all the fun and none of the responsibility."

"Don't presume your position—"

"I'm presuming, dude, I'm presuming." Landau pulls out a pistol and holds it to the mesh of the cage, inches from Renn's head. "Otherwise, might as well shoot him dead now, he's useless. Way better dead than at a show trial—someone might believe him. Or—you can deal with me."

"So far, all you've proved is that you can paralyze him. Now prove to me that you can control him."

Landau chirps a smile. "First, we settle the numbers. Then, we'll do a test," he says, "just the three of us."

~~~~

As the helicopter approaches the platform, I'm staring at Max, stuffed coma-like into that magnetic-field cage. I keep waiting for him to wake up and put them all in their place but it keeps not happening—it's surreal to see him helpless. It's like watching your father stumbling-down drunk in church—it's every kind of pain just to watch.

We settle on the helipad, surrounded immediately by twenty shooters in jumpsuits and white-noise goggles. The seawater smashes against huge pylons twenty stories down. A maze of pipes, thin and thick, run uphill five stories at a time, through drilling stations with housings the size of a Hummer, two-story control rooms suspended above the deck, fabrication areas filled with strapped-down spare parts. We cross a long narrow catwalk, just a metal floor, some rails and rivets, to a blocky module with portholes and a staircase scissoring back and forth up the side.

We take the inside stairs, descending through gray-on-gray paint, warning signs everywhere (**NO STEP/ WATCH LIP etc.**), rubber mats on concrete floors and a beaver's-nest tangle of wire and pipes overhead. It's the *Babu* with warning labels. Makes you want to drop and do fifty sit-ups, just to get into the spirit of things.

First we have to listen to Volkov and Straw Hat sparring, then negotiating and then Volkov throws us out, four of his stooges dragging De Jogt and me down the hall into a conference room housing a couple of computer terminals and, all by herself, Kate.

No cage. No handcuffs. No guards. That's unsettling.

And something else—there's something else different about her

, some air that fills the room that doesn't feel familiar.

I swear I remember everything about her *vividly*.

We eye each other for a moment and then embrace.

"Yeah, isn't it?" she says and I have no idea which thought of mine she's responding to. Just looking at her face after all this time, I'm not sure you could say I'm thinking at all. "It's like we barely know each other," she continues, "but...the most intense five days of my life is us."

Five days? Is that all we were together? Is that *possible*? We met in Gettysburg, drove to New York, flew to Rome, then the concert and the boat crossing to Tunisia—Jesus! We're still eyeing each other all awkward, like cousins who still have the hots for each other.

"This is De Jogt," I say. "A civilian. He's what this is all about. "

"Yes," Kate says. "They want the lens. Did they get it?"

"Not yet." He pats his pants pocket. "I have some old ones too—they couldn't pick out the good ones."

"Pull them out," she asks and it's not a request. Kate grabs the pile out of his hand and holds it for about ten seconds. Then she begins picking what seem like identical pieces out of the group. "This one—this—this one" and drops them on the table.

"Damn!" De Jogt says. "How?"

She shrugs. "I can do lots of things without knowing how, exactly. Where's Max?"

"Next door," I tell her. "They're making a deal."

"Who is?"

"Volkov and Straw Hat. Max is in a cage. Straw Hat's got him paralyzed."

She winces at this. She almost looks guilty. What's going on? "How long have you been with him?" she asks.

"Max? Since this morning, though I didn't know it was him for a while." I settle at the table, hit one of the keyboards to see if the screen will light up. It does, with a system that looks vaguely familiar. It looked familiar in the accountant's office too. "Why?"

She taps her forehead. "He's been in here, on and off, the whole six months. Not saying anything to me, just lurking. He knew they'd taken me—Volkov and his people. He knew right away—I could *feel* it." Her face is grim. "These people are—" she shakes her head.

"Evil," De Jogt says and we stare. "They've been inside me, inside my thoughts. I didn't know who they were at the beginning and their gig was interesting, I might have done what they wanted willingly if they'd asked. They didn't bother. They decided on their own to run me like a machine." The look in his eyes is chilling. "That's how I knew whose side I was on, when the time came. Your guy could have run me too—I could feel him in my head—but he talked to me instead."

That's when the door opens and five guards come in and drag him away. They've got the white noise goggles so Kate can't work on their heads. *Live to fight another day*, I hear her voice in my head and remember Max telling me the same thing just before Straw Hat took him down. They drag De Jogt out, kicking and cursing. A bunch more of them stuff the doorway to prevent us following. And then a moment later, Volkov and Straw Hat come barreling in, Volkov stomping right up to Kate.

"Alright—you want to be a healer in the Outback? You want a better world? Go make it. I'll bankroll you."

I'm shooting looks between the two of them. I'm ready to fall over, to tell the truth. Kate—clearly, uncomfortably—is nowhere near as shocked as I am.

"I'll endow enough money," he continues, "for a lavish clinic with a staff of ten for ten years. If you have a modest clinic and invest some of the money wisely—and live sensibly—you might stretch it to fifteen. If you attract investors or charge patients in accordance with their income, maybe your lifetime or more. That's up to you. But if that's what you want to do with your gifts, I'll support you."

"And in return?"

"Go to the Outback and heal. Follow your mission. Become what you're meant to be."

"And stop fighting you."

"I don't see you fighting me. I see you fighting yourself. Yes, of course, if you make trouble for us, all bets are off. But that's my only proviso."

"She just walks away—with half the world's police on the lookout for her?" I barge in. "That's a joke."

Volkov laughs. "My God, Max has the two of you bewitched, hasn't he? That is no problem. That is solved overnight if I wish to solve it—or if Max wishes to solve it, by the way."

"What?"

"Don't you know you have a twin sister? Identical twin, people always said they couldn't tell you apart. Anyone who checks next week will find a birth certificate, school records, a pediatrician, childhood friends and several old boyfriends who remember the twins, with charming and hilarious anecdotes about the times they confused the two of you—the sister who went off to the Outback to do good work and the other, somewhere at large, wanted by the Police for terrorism. That's *if* we come to an agreement." He glances at me. "You can go too," he adds, like I'm going to carry her bags.

"It won't work," I bluff. "Too many people know us. Someone'll see through it." I don't know anybody anymore but it sounds good.

Volkov's expression is way too familiar. I've gotten that face a thousand times from doctors at the VA and girls I took more seriously than they took me. "People *know* Saddam Hussein was involved with 9/11," he says. "People *know* Al Qaeda is coordinating worldwide terrorism against the United States. People *know* Jesus was a Christian. Half the things people *know* are totally wrong and most of them don't matter anyway—it's the basis of our business plan. What matters in your case is that no one will prosecute you or even bring you to trial. I can make that happen. You *know* I can make that happen." He glares at us. "And understand, Max Renn could have made you this same offer—at any time. He doesn't have the staff or the worldwide reach of L Corp but he could accomplish the same thing in a week or two. If he hasn't offered, ask yourself why. Would you rather be tied to a desperate man's futile vendetta—or to an organization that can actually help you?"

I stare at Kate but she isn't returning my looks. Her eyes are withdrawn and there is a tension in her that I don't like at all. "What about Max?" she asks. She's *thinking* about it!

"Max is going to work for us."

"Bullshit!"

"Not of his own free will, I'll admit. Free will is one of those concepts that sounds wonderful but is so inconvenient in other people. Anyway, he's going to be doing public relations for us—and we want to avoid conflicting narratives. We will *pay*, to be precise, to avoid conflicting narratives."

"And he'll be safe?" She *is* taking this seriously!

"We want him jumping around looking healthy and, for that matter, threatening." When this doesn't satisfy her, he adds, "We're going to use him, not hurt him."

I'm not giving Kate the chance to agree. "Okay, she gets her clinic," I say. "What about me?" There has to be some way I can break this up.

"I'm letting you live—consider yourself fortunate," Volkov purrs. "You're no threat."

"I can talk. I can spread a whole lot of information you don't want out there."

"So you're saying I should eliminate you now."

"Kate won't stand for it. She won't work for you if you've killed any of us."

"Marat killed Tauber in Rome and she's considering working with us. People do what's in their self-interest. At least most people do, the sensible ones. The ones that survive." He sighs. "What do you want?" and I have to come up with an answer.

"I want to get paid." He gives me the eyebrow. "I want enough money to not have to think about living where I want, eating what I want or doing what I want."

"I have a partner and we will have a board of directors soon."

"Board—?"

"We're planning an IPO in a year. I have limits. I won't buy you luxury. If you want to be comfortable, we can talk numbers."

I scribble a figure on a pad and shove it across the desk—no time like the present. He cuts it down by two-thirds and shoves it back. I go for half and he nods. "The number's fine but I don't believe you. You're still loyal to Max." Kate's giving me the eye too.

"Of course I am. I always will be. But I've had six months of being hunted, looking over my shoulder every time I'm around people, living off mussels and roots." He's unmoved—I have to do better. "And that won't change. You'll still have to watch me like a hawk for awhile."

"Excuse me?" It's like I've woken him out of a sleep.

"If I ever get a chance to do you harm, to free Max, I'll do it. I'll bide my time and wait for my moment. But I'm not stupid or suicidal. If you're as good as you think you are, maybe that moment never comes. Maybe you get so powerful that even freeing Max wouldn't matter. Maybe I'll get tired of fighting the whole world. Maybe I'll get comfortable drinking piña coladas on the beach." His eyes narrow just enough—he's uncertain. It isn't much but better than a minute ago. Now I've got to turn that worm over. "Meanwhile, how do I know I can trust *you*?"

"What?"

"You're the Evil Empire, right? How are you going to arrange paying me? I've gotta know the details if I'm even going to consider this." This is way over Volkov's head, he doesn't give two shakes about me, all he wants is Kate out of the way. He sure doesn't want to get into a discussion of his cash flow system, so that's right where I'm going. "And Kate too," I continue ranting. "What about *her* money? Where's it locked away? How do we know you'll follow through?"

"We're good for it," Straw Hat says but I'm ignoring him.

"Do I get a check in the mail? How often? Do I have to pay taxes—if I do, the deal's off! If I have a grievance, who do I go to? Where do we put the money where you can't just snatch it away as soon as we're out of your hair? It's not like we can go to court and demand due process."

Volkov's fuming here but Kate's also giving him a defiant look now. He had a cap on the geyser and now it's leaking again. He wants this over with.

"We will open a trust account for each of you," he says in his most authoritative tone, "accruing interest over the years to equal the agreed-upon amount. You'll receive monthly payments in a bank draft to your account on the first of every month."

"I want half the funding in place—in my account with me controlling the funds—before we leave this ship."

"It's a drilling platform."

"I don't care if it's a ballet studio. I want to *know* we're secure before we kiss you goodbye."

"Alright," he sighs. "We're agreed?"

"No, we're agreed when the trust is set up and the money in place."

"That takes time."

"Then no deal. Are you leaving without me?" I ask Kate. She shakes her head and of course, she wouldn't. Even if she was thinking about this seriously, she wouldn't. I round on Volkov. "You're a big cheese—make it happen."

"I'll make it happen," he says. "Is that it?"

"How do I know I can create a secure password here?" and I see his eyes glaze over and know for a fact that he doesn't know shit about computers.

"We have a military-grade Internet service," he says and that only proves it.

"I was in the Army. You could drive a truck through their security. How do I know you haven't got any keyloggers or traps running? I need a root-level list of every program running on your network."

Volkov rolls his eyes. "If I can demonstrate that we're buttoned up, we have a deal?" He shifts back and forth from Kate to me and back. "All of us?"

"Once everything is buttoned up," I say. Volkov motions to somebody in the hall and suddenly he's gone.

The guards in the hall have multiplied to seven now. They lead us back down the hall to the accountant's office from before, a skinny guy in a stained L Corp t-shirt (they got t-shirts?), a few strands of greasy hair swept back across the top of his head. His desk is buried under a mile of paper. When we come in, he's got the in-house phone to his ear, grunting "Yessir! Nosir!" like an automatic weapon. Two guards squeeze into the room with us, the others loiter in the hallway.

"You're both getting trusts—in a hurry?" he says, wiping his forehead and suddenly I hear Kate's voice in my head: *I sure hope you've got a plan.*

You're not taking his offer?

Of course not. I'm teaching him the limits of his charm. What's the game?

Tell you as soon as I know, I flash back and feel my cheeks redden, grateful to know we're still on the same side.

I park myself at the edge of the accountant's desk, where I can get a glimpse of his screen.

The room is bugged—they can hear anything we say, Kate flashes.

Who needs to say anything? I answer.

The guards are tight around us. Mine is clearly preoccupied with Kate's blouse—the middle button is playing peek-a-boo every time she leans forward. I encourage her to keep leaning back and forth.

"I told him we need *secure* accounts," I tell the accountant. "Secure from you. I need a list of everything running on your machine, including root level files. Can you have your sysadmin get me that?"

"I *am* the sysadmin," he huffs. Perfect. "And I'm not giving you root access."

I can't work illusions here - they're wearing the white-noise glasses, Kate flashes and I nod again. *I can destroy a few guns and throw a few of them around but not seven at once.*

"I need to know you're not recording my keystrokes. Call Volkov—he'll tell you to give me what I want." Of course, the son-of-a-bitch does and Volkov replies loudly and rudely, bless him.

Give me a minute, I flash Kate. *I think I can even the odds.*

I turn my chair to the terminal on the back wall, staring at the screen. "I need root access and access to folders, subfolders, all executables; not to make changes, just to know there's nothing nasty lurking in non-standard locations." I'm throwing around all the jargon I can think of in as geeky and passive-aggressive a fashion as I can and it works—I hear the shooters groan with boredom and the sysadmin rolls his eyes and starts printing lists.

I, meanwhile, am studying the screen, which looks awfully familiar.

It looks to be Pac-Man vintage, several screens of big blue boxes with little red and yellow boxes nestled inside and orange and green X's inside them. The next tab reads *INFRA*. Clicking on it gives me another stack of boxes just like the first. This grid is covered with a crazy multicolored patchwork of thick and thin lines criss-crossing in every direction. I hover the mouse over a particularly dense bundle and the letters HVAC appear. A thinner set brings up PLG. Another bundle carries two designations—ELP and GERTS. As soon as I see GERTS, I relax. I don't remember much but I remember GERTS.

Near the bottom of the grid, one box is pulsing white. There are two yellow lines embedded in different edges of the box, one blinking red, one green. I right-click on the green line and a pop-up menu reads:

Current State: Open

Actions:

Lock

Unlock

Emergency Open (NOT recommended)

Close

Emergency Close (NOT recommended)

Seal

Okay, you'll need to take out the guy to your right, I flash Kate and see her nod.

I click **Emergency Close** and we all jump as the hatch door to the hallway throws itself closed and locks with a ringing THUNK! I throw my elbow into my guard's crotch—when he doubles over, I pull his head down hard on the counter and he's out for the count, on the floor lying next to Kate's guard. When did she take him?

"Quick work," I say.

"I might be a little keyed up," she says, looking a little sheepish.

The sysadmin has the phone to his ear but he's staring at us wide-eyed and open-mouthed.

"Maybe I should take out the guy on the other end of his phone?" Kate asks and I realize I can hear the voice yelling on the far end.

"Can you do that?"

Her face is a question mark for a moment—then the yelling stops and the sysadmin hangs up the receiver. "I guess I can," she says. The sysadmin looks like the new puppy at the kill shelter.

The guards outside start pounding on the door.

"Well, you evened the odds in here," Kate says. "Now how the hell do we get out?"

rupture
November 2008

Dresden, Pennsylvania

They had left the horses yoked to the bins in the middle of the grain-heavy fields and disappeared.

To Jaime Montero, they might as well have set the whole town on fire. He had moved, family, two dogs and a canary, to Amish country twelve years earlier to get away from big city life and big city crime. The Dresden police might have to deal with a missing cow or a buggy hijacked by vandals from Harrisburg or Gettysburg—once, there was a theft of some tools, but the Amish had found the thief and dealt with him in their own way. Part of the job, Montero decided early on, was learning when to just stay out of the way.

But when Amish farmers left harvest grain drying in the midday sun, something was seriously wrong.

He made the rounds quickly, circling outward from Stodtsvoll's place to the several adjoining farms and progressively outward. By the time he hit Ten Cows Road, he was calling deputies at home, dragging them away from a day off or in early for the night shift. A panicked confused memory count came up with at least thirty-five men, women and children who should have been working in those empty fields. Horses were now wandering onto the road, clip-clopping politely along the verges eating the long grass and making their way back to their barns. Where were the people?

He made the turn toward Hooper's place, clinging to his last hope. Hooper's was one of the oldest farms in the county, used as a meeting house on special occasions. Hooper was one of the most respected men in the community. He was often the one designated to deal with the police, sometimes to get help, more often to try to ward off Montero's involvement. But special occasions didn't occur suddenly in the midst of work and certainly not during harvest.

Halfway up the hill, Montero made out the figure of a boy in a broad-brimmed hat pushing a hoop through a grove of trees. His heart leapt—was it possible that there was really some sane explanation for this? What could possibly have happened?

As he came over the rise, what he saw was impossible.

The community of respectful, peace-loving Amish, people for whom shunning was major discipline, had taken up positions around the lovely old Hooper farmhouse and were, one by one, throwing flaming torches through the windows or under the porch, fanning the flames with their hats and keeping the children back as they watched the place go up in smoke.

Montero gunned the engine and called the Fire Department, knowing they would never get there in time. The question that rattled him most was: What could old Hooper have possibly done to deserve this? In the Amish world, this was unthinkable. Losing his farm, his home—his community turned against him—he was as good as dead. What could possibly have separated him from the rest so suddenly?

Twenty yards from the house, Montero pulled to the side of the road and stopped, totally lost.

Drifting out of the crowd came old Hooper himself, sage of the community and the seventh generation of his family to live in this house. He took a torch from a neighbor and used it to set alight the rafters over the porch, standing close to admire the flames and watch his whole history turn to ashes.

Montero heard the sirens and saw his deputy's cars coming fast up the road but it wouldn't matter. There could never be an answer to explain this, never.

And there wasn't. After pushing the crowd back, Montero got down to the job of interviewing the members of the mob.

While the roof collapsed and the walls came down, they not only denied they'd had anything to do with a fire, they denied there was one. They stood staring at the fire while denying it existed.

On a nearby hill, two solitary figures stood watching.

"Success," Miriam Fine proclaimed.

"It's a best-case scenario," Jim Avery cautioned. "Impressive, nonetheless."

"Proof of concept," Fine said.

"Maybe," Avery mused, watching the last wall collapse as he returned to the car. "A lot of pieces have to come together. We need a real test—and we don't have lots of time."

reunion 7
December 2008

Somewhere Off the Coast of Australia

Renn finally gets his wish. For once, all is silent. In this moment in time, he is truly alone.

Fragments of sentences play in his head, random syllables and orphaned sounds bubble up out of the void. Surely, there is a world somewhere out there but it seems a long way off now and receding fast.

Every time he'd heard the kid's voice coming to him in his sleep, every time, he'd reminded himself he's just trying to get under my defenses, under my skin. There is little satisfaction now in being right.

By brilliance or dumb luck, the kid had found the memory that powered Renn's blocking, his defenses—the moment in Novosibirsk when Renn had turned Lazar's butcher-boy assistant blue, made him quiver like a D string, his finger locked onto the man's forehead as if Velcro'd. And here now is the inevitable result—Renn on ice, crippled, inert, locked up tight.

For the first time in his life, the only voices he hears are the ones in his own head.

Keep going, you can do it! (What the fuck is 'it'?)

You're a disappointment to (fill in here)...

You're not good enough! It's not enough! (Again, what the fuck is 'it'?)

Don't let anything happen...

I'll show you! You can't stop me!

That last voice, certainly, is his own, the eternal teen-age rebel inside, still giving the finger long after the last meaningful sell-by date. In the other voices, he hears echoes of professors, 'parents', Lazar, even Volkov. The sound of them now just makes Renn feel weary.

I knew the danger; I courted it. I wanted, no, I needed...what did I need? To be known? Whatever it was, I shoved the door open

In truth, the quiet is pleasant. It's tedious hearing the same voices singing the same loops over and over.

Why don't I just give up? Everything I've done has been a disaster—I went to America and hurt the Project, I went to the

Everglades and Dave died, I went to Rome and Tauber died. If I give up, at least I do no harm.

In the distance, Renn feels his cage being carted up stairs and through hallways, bouncing against a doorframe, scraping against a pipe. But he sees nothing detailed, hears nothing specific, knows less than nothing—and he realizes, something inside him likes it that way. Distanced, insulated—safe.

~ ~ ~ ~

The shooters in the hallway are banging their fists against the door and threatening to blow it open. I cycle through the tabs of the computer program, each page showing the same grid with different multicolored lines criss-crossing the boxes.

"What is it?" Kate demands.

"It's infrastructure management for the whole platform," I explain quickly. "Our buddy here (pointing to the accountant) has Admin Access so now I have Admin Access—to everything. I can remotely lock and unlock doors, watch the surveillance cameras, cycle A/C on and off, reroute electricity and disable or purge the plumbing."

Her eyes open wide. "First thing is, get rid of *them!*" she points at the door as the pounding there suddenly and ominously stops. We hear the shooters scuttering across the metal floor like waterbugs, with who knows what nasty plans.

I Shift-click to select all the hallway doors on the floor and flick the **Emergency Open** and **Close** boxes back and forth as fast as I can.

The banging drowns out everything but their howls—the hall is narrow and the heavy doors are wide; anyone nearby gets mashed. After four or five passes, the place goes dead quiet and I stop clicking.

I open the hallway door once more and take a quick look outside. This group of shooters is not going to give us any trouble any more.

"So where's Max?" Kate slams her fist down on the desk. "We need him!" It's exactly what I was thinking.

"Nearby," I say.

"What do you *know*?" she responds immediately. The word rings in the air, the way it does when Max says it to me. 'You have to *know* what you *know*'. It sounded like gibberish when he first said it, but now I understand it's about the things we know that we shouldn't be able to know, the things that come to us without proof or facts or logic, the things that just are.

"He's nearby but he's getting farther away," I say and she nods.

"I'm feeling that too. I've been tapping every back channel he's set up in my brain and I feel him fading fast."

"We *need* him".

She shivers. "I don't understand. Are they drugging him? Where has he gone?"

"He's not gone—he's giving up."

She goes limp. "We've got to reach him, pull him back, before he does," she says. "How do you find something that's totally in the dark?"

A moment later, the world goes dead quiet and dark as the far side of the moon. The clock has stopped and I'm just floating in the middle of nothing. I reach out, the same way I reached for loot on the seafloor—and there's Max. I can feel him nearby, barely there, not fighting, barely existing, just drifting in the endless quiet. It is kind of peaceful, to be honest.

For just a moment, I'm in his space, inside Max's head. I pull out instantly, instinctively, without really understanding why.

I was blocking! That was the problem! The instant I was inside him, I knew I needed to block—and blocking blew me right outside again. What was *that* about?

As I come to, Kate is pulling on my arm like she's pumping water from a well.

"Breathe, dammit!" she yells.

"I *am* breathing!"

"You weren't!"

"I was in-between breaths!"

"For six minutes?"

"It's a hobby."

"What *kind* of hobby? What's it good for?"

"For finding things in the dark!" I say and she goes quiet. "Max is caught. Landau's inside his head, past his blocking. So Max has shut himself down."

"So how do we fix it?"

"How do I know?" Just as I realize she doesn't actually expect me to have an answer, I have the answer. "He needs another block, some place he's been where Landau can't follow."

Kate's eyes widen. "Where would that be?"

"I don't know! When I first met him, he was hiding out, deeper in the Everglades—"

Without transition now, I'm suddenly sliding through tall grass and weeds, scattering long-legged birds and driving through murky water. It doesn't take much to realize my head's returned to the Everglades. But the view is off, somehow.

Kate whiplashes back. "Is that you, broadcasting the swamp?"

"No! It can't be !"

"Why not?"

"Because I've never been an alligator!" That *is* the perspective, I realize, a few inches off the ground. Maybe not even that much. The sun warm on my back, the hissing in my lungs and—I'm sliding, not waddling. Slithering!

And, a moment later, there is Max's voice, clear as glass: *You came for me.*

"We hear you," Kate blurts out loud, surprising herself.

I can't... His voice fades but somehow I can still feel him, he hasn't been cut off, he's having trouble with words. Why? The answer is ridiculous but absolutely obvious in Max Renn's world.

"He's a snake," I tell Kate. "He's having trouble talking because he's a snake. I remember him saying he found their minds way more restful than people."

Kate's eyes light up. I feel her pouring herself into the dream, soaking up the vibrations and riding them.

A moment later, I see bits of the room Max is in, twenty small details, visual grabs coaxing and dragging Max back out into the world.

There's two guards in the interrogation room—and Straw Hat. They've pushed the cage into a corner and the second guard is just now closing the door. I see it swinging closed. What are the numbers on the door? "It's something _23," I tell Kate and she saw it too. I check my screen. A door icon on the Sixth Floor flickers from green to red—623, of course.

"Sixth floor—I'm on it!" Kate dashes out the door; I hear the outside hatch ringing as it closes behind her.

The accountant has been watching all this with eyes the size of melons. Does he hear the voices? Which would be more disturbing, if he did or didn't?

I wave an empty finger at him. "Move over there or I'll use this thing on you!" His eyes widen and he slips over to the chair in the corner. I take his chair, rifling the drawers for guns, letter openers, anything useful as a weapon. All I find is a heavy metal stapler and a hole-punch—I toss those into the far corner. Then I change the sysadmin password and reboot the system platform-wide—at least now, nobody can take it away from me. He's pulled out his phone rebelliously now and is clicking away at the screen.

I suddenly remember the cell phone in my pocket. I pull it out but the battery's dead, which is no shock considering the last time I was near Wi-Fi or a wall outlet was five months ago. When I look up, he's put his phone away and is definitely avoiding eye contact.

"Hand it over," I tell him, brooking no denials. He blinks and offers it up.

I search my wallet, praying I didn't have an attack of neatness recently. Happily, the business card is there. I punch in the phone number and wait, heart pounding. When the man's deep voice answers and we exchange a few sentences, I relax. The cavalry should be on the way soon, as long as we can stay alive until they get here.

That relief doesn't last long.

The loudspeaker system platform-wide erupts with announcements, cryptic codes and locations I've never heard of. *Condition Tango Niner Bravo! Evac Protocol for Delta 6, 4 and Oner!*

Time to take precautions. I rush out to the hall and drag the six knocked-senseless L Corp shooters out onto the landing on the side of the Crew Cube. Then it's back to the office, closing and emergency-locking every hatch on my now-empty floor. No one gets in without my permission or high explosives.

As I return to my seat, I suddenly see myself pounding up a staircase—oh, no, it's Kate, fighting the heaving of the platform, the wind and spray, approaching the third level, sharing her mindstream with me.

Why do I see her from the outside when, surely, it's *her* thoughts I'm monitoring? Somehow, I know the answer—it's the same reason I always see an outside view of myself, one where I always look a bit more Hollywood than I do in the mirror. Is that the Superego? Does that mean I took *Psychology*? I must have been a real disappointment to *that* teacher.

At the same time, somehow—both pictures are vivid but somehow not overlapping—I see Straw Hat and two guards in Max's cell. One guard is my old pal Goldie, the boy with the razor; the other is a new guard, one with a jet-black pony tail. They're arranging equipment around Max's cell on Deck Six. Max is blocking like a snake to make sure Straw Hat—Landau, that's his name—doesn't realizes he's awake while we both carefully examine every detail of the room and the cage, trying to find the way out.

His thinking is slow and muffled. And then I hear his voice again: *This snake thing doesn't work. We need a moment we can both get lost in.* Landau throws a quick glance his way and he jumps back to snakethink.

I start running through memories. *Driving with your eyes closed? That sure is vivid to me.*

I do that all the time, he answers.

Rome? The Viewing Box shattering?

Volkov was there—his memory won't be the same as ours but it's still too close. We need something just the two of us would know understand.

And then it comes to me:

"*Mark Tauber, Savannah Georgia.*" That's when it all started, the moment I started blurting out Dave Monaghan's list of American mindbenders, having no idea who they were. It was the moment we both realized that Dave had dragged me into Max's crazy world, had forced me on him as a central piece of the puzzle. It's was the moment when we both, unwillingly at first, had to work together.

That'll do, he says and the images of his cell suddenly black out. Where'd he go? *Shit! Shit! Shit!*

A second later, Kate's face smashes against a gray wall, machine-gun fire slamming into the staircase four inches away. Three L Corp shooters shoot down from the next platform, calling for backup from the decks above. I hear clanging footfalls on the staircase growing nearer.

Throw them an illusion! Make them see unicorns and aliens!

They're wearing the white-noise goggles—I can't penetrate!

What floor are you on?

Uh, Four! Four!

I cycle the doors on the fourth-floor platform, throwing them open and closed, and watch two of the shooters sail over the railing, their goggles and guns and even a boot flying past Kate and bouncing onto the platform around her.

She banks a shield off the rail at the last shooter above and clips him on the shoulder—he goes flying after the others and she starts up the staircase. A pair of goggles are right in the middle of the second step—she snatches it up and pops it into her breast pocket.

Get Max! she flashes. *We need him!* And suddenly, there's Landau rattling the cage.

"C'mon, Max ol' buddy, up and around! I need you! You're gainfully employed again, like it or not—just like most of the rest of the world."

Mark Tauber, Savannah Georgia—I realize I'm chanting the phrase over and over in my head. It's a bridge somehow between me and Max and, through it, I can feel Max working his legs and arms, barely moving but bringing the feeling back. In his mind, he's staring at me in the boiler room of Dave's house, trying to decide if he trusts me, if he really wants to take me along. But he's seeing me to avoid seeing Landau, who's gazing into the cage, bouncing off Max's blank stare.

"Dude, don't be a stiff!" Landau says. "I'll cut you a piece of the action, okay? I'll be the organ grinder and you can be the monkey!"

I'll show you monkey, you little—

That's what I've been wanting to hear. Let Max come to a boil; then we'll think about letting him out.

I'm cycling screens as fast as I can, juggling Kate's thoughts and Max's in my head without knowing half the time whose thought is whose. Kate's just a few steps from reaching the fourth level—and trouble. The inside staircases from Five to Four are packing up with heavily armed shooters, and a few are trickling down from Four toward Three, to get behind her. They'll have her in a crossfire in a minute.

Shit, Kate! Do you see what I see?

Get me to Six! I've got to get to Six!

I lock all the doors to Three, so those shooters can't get out of the stairwell. They can't get below her anymore.

But that's just defense. To win, you have to *attack*. And my personal motto is: When in doubt, try *everything*.

I lock the doors to *all* the staircases on all three floors, stranding all those shooters between floors. I lock all the doors on both ends of Deck Four, shut down the air conditioning and turn the heat up to 92 degrees.

In the camera view, I see them crowding the doors, pounding, in seconds, not that pounding does a thing to steel plate. The corridor is too short and narrow for them to shoot out the locks. Careful use of explosives is the only other option. They're already pulling C4 and planting it around the hatch.

Kate's carefully approaching Deck Four now—she hears the pounding on the doors; I hear it through her. I can't let those guys out behind her. What *else* have I got?

EFP—AVS—PLG...PLG! Is that Plumbing? I hope so. I block the whole system on Five and Three and purge the contents on both floors—purge them while leaving them nowhere on those floors to go. Which means? Cross my fingers?

The vent indicator goes from red to green and through Kate's ears, I hear this groan and a huge echoing belch and— through Kate's nose (who knew our noses were linked?)—one hell of a stink.

WHAT did you do? she flashes and it really is pretty awful.

I was bad, I return and hear her laughing in my head—that's an odd experience.

"Pull the cage closer," Landau tells Goldie and Ponytail Boy. They pull it forward and Landau reaches out with De Jogt's coil and touches a finger to the bars. The thing sparks and the cage flies backward, slamming against the wall. I can feel the shock and the burn but Max locks himself up, not moving, not reacting. Only his eyes flare but that's enough for Landau.

"That's it—you *listen* when I talk, old man," he gloats. "Let's understand the new order—I can put you under anytime I want. I can *hurt* you and there's nothing you can do about it. I *run* you now."

I feel the anger welling up and I can't tell at first if it's Max who's livid or me—I don't know the boundaries anymore. Kate's pounding up the staircase, rounding Five but it'll be a lopsided battle if Max isn't out of that cage when she reaches Six. He's scanning the cell and so am I, through his eyes—and that's when I notice Goldie plugging the cage into a wall socket. I see the readout on the battery pack showing 'zero'.

See what I'm looking at?

Gotcha.

ELP—wall power outlets. I shut down sockets, one at a time, across the deck. The first thing that goes is a desk lamp. Landau turns, immediately suspicious; a moment later, the room goes black.

THDZZZHHMMMPPPPP!!

There's a flash of light as the cage flies apart and Ponytail Boy cries out, hit by debris. I see a shadow jumping to the light switches, which of course does nothing.

Max is out of the cage now and on the move. Through his eyes, I can see he's low to the floor, focusing on two forms rattling uselessly at the door handle (**EMERGENCY LOCK ON**).

Two short flashes of light, one right after the other and the two silhouettes crumple to the floor.

And then the place blows wide open.

Whiter-than-white, a white that blanks out almost all detail, a white that sears at the eyes—at the root of it stands Landau, hand outstretched, lightning pouring off the coil on his fingers. The bolt passes right over Max's head and bangs into the wall behind. Smoke and bits of sheet rock fill the room. By the time Landau sees him, Max is tearing through the haze and out the broken wall.

He hurtles down the Sixth Floor corridor and bursts out onto the main deck and there's Kate, just gaining the top platform on the far outer edge of the Crew Cube.

Find De Jogt! Max flashes and I go back to shuttling through camera arrays. I don't see the Dutchman anywhere but I do see a whole lot of guards on Five who don't look like they're going anywhere.

Maybe Five? It could be Volkov,.

Before anyone can react, Landau sprints out of the inner staircase and levels a blast that shears off a guardrail and blows over the steel telephone station behind Max.

Get to De Jogt—get him to safety! Max flashes to Kate. *Landau is my problem.*

He takes off at a sprint down the catwalk toward the center section of the platform. *Isn't that the wrong direction?* I think at first and then realize the point is to draw him away from Kate.

Max doesn't get far. ZZZZHHHAAAAFFFF!!! Another blast sizzles right past his head.

"You need to work on your aim!" Max yells and Landau's next blast clips the side of his foot and he goes down hard on the metal deck. The wind's knocked out of him—I find myself huffing and feel my foot screaming, though when I stand on it, it takes the weight.

Max isn't so lucky.

And not just because of the foot—as soon as he hits the floor, I feel Landau slipping inside him, working on his mind, grappling for control. We've been blocking together but now, the connection between us is interrupted, faltering. Max can't finish his thoughts, they wander and garble and fade out, senses overrun.

ZZZAAAAPPPPFFFFF!!!! A bolt flies directly at Kate. She throws up an ion shield and it explodes against the surface, knocking her backward. Startled, she sees a tall dreadlocked dude with a multicolored coat and another coil around his finger come up out of the inner stairway. He shoots another blast but this one's way off-line—she doesn't even bother to respond—but then he lights up a volley of bolts, igniting a whole section of the air around her. He's peppering blasts into the air until the whole section of the sky catches. Kate makes shields as fast as she can but all she has time to do is defend herself.

Landau, on the other hand, shoots with precision— obviously, he's got the good gun sight. He places another blast an inch from Renn's other foot. Max is struggling to stand and the impact throws him over onto the deck again.

"This is stupid," Landau yells. "Nobody wants to kill you, Max. Why make us?"

"That's your best offer—slave?" Max says, dragging himself up and hobbling toward the center platform. "Why would I pick *that*?"

"Because it beats *dead!*" Landau yells, clipping him on the lapel with another blast. Max goes down hard again. I feel the impact and clutch at the searing heat in my shoulder—the accountant looks up at me, alarmed.

"If it's so great, *you* try it!" Max says. He's in trouble and Kate can't help him—her hands are full with the Jamaican, who's bearing down with clusters of lightning. At least she's fighting back. She's producing shields and keeps launching them. Max, on the other hand, just seems to be retreating and taking hits for it. He's made it to a pumping station but limping badly, one arm hanging limp—Landau's picking him apart.

"You can't resist, Max—I found your core memory, the one you *start* from! No substitute is as strong! You can force me to wound you and hurt you but I will regain control and then you'll do whatever I damn well tell you!"

His voice has risen—the kid's maddened by this petty rebellion. I can feel it clearly though I can't be reading Landau so I have no idea where that feeling is coming from.

"You are a *waste*, dude! You've got the power of powers— you can make anybody do anything you want! Women, pretty boys, yachts, mansions, titles, power, flesh—what do you want, Max? What makes you *hungry*? Something's got to mean more to you than *this*, dying a little at a time at the hand of the young gunslinger?"

And suddenly, I see a face I've never seen before, an old photo, black and white, grainy and blurred. A brutish face, three-days beard and a military haircut. A sense of hopelessness settles over me like a heavy quilt. I'm cycling through screens on the computer but I don't know what I'm looking for anymore and what's the point? Everything's hopeless. Landau holds all the cards. There's something about that face that drives me into deeper and darker places.

"The fucking butcher!" Landau cackles and Max shrivels and I realize I'm feeling Max, feeling what *he* feels, the hopelessness Landau's spreading inside him. "Wolf Piecz! The punisher you fried in the lab with a bolt from your finger! I should have known—you told me yourself in Amsterdam. I asked if you were gonna kill me and you said, 'I don't want to know you that well.' Max Renn, the world's greatest mindbender—the closest, most intimate moment of your sorry life, bitch, was the last thoughts of a stranger while you killed him!"

There's not much Max left now. I can feel his resistance fading, retreating into some tiny last-ditch corner. Another blast from Landau shears off a thick iron pipe and sends it crashing four inches from Max, who doesn't even try to get out of the way.

"Dude!" Landau cackles. "That's twisted, even for you!"

Kate has somehow learned how to fashion multiple shields out of one swipe of her hand, blocking whole sections of the air in front of her, giving her time to flick a few back at the Jamaican and the pipes over his head. Not having the good gun sight, he has to defend a whole new section above him. Every time he looks up, Kate sends a few at his feet or banking around the side of his defenses. He's still on the attack but at least she's eating away at him.

I realize, channeling Kate, that she's exhilarated, thrilled at the fight. She'd like it if there were two more of him, now that she's figured out an angle. I remember that feeling, rolling across the desert into Iraq. I also remember what came next—and that makes me fear for Kate.

A moment later, the Jamaican sends a blast that screams wide and ends up in a heat exchanger. The thing bursts right alongside her, sending her flying into a wall of iron pipe. She's dazed, reeling and defenseless.

At the same time, a squad of shooters appears from the drilling side, forming a neat line across the deck:

...*Commander Volkov wants them alive. Use your tranquilizer darts...*

Landau's voice responds: *Surround us but don't interfere. These are my prisoners!*

Those are not my orders, the commander says and his troops take up a clear firing line.

Wait a minute: How am *I* hearing this conversation?

Landau argues with the commander and the Jamaican holds his place, keeping an eye on Kate while awaiting instructions. I'm hearing the whole thing, though the sound is a bit muffled.

We are special agents completing our mission. You are regular troops, don't interfere when we —

We all work for the corporation. I've got my orders like you do.

Don't give me that working-class hero crap! Back off or I'll —

How? How am I hearing this? I'm frantically checking my equipment but a moment later, I *feel* the answer. Kate is rifling her pockets, hearing the same things I am — she plucks the white-noise goggles from the staircase out of her pocket and pops them on. Instantly, the thoughts flashing back and forth between Landau and the Shooter Commander come crystal-clear.

These things aren't just to block us! she flashes. *It's their private communications channel! Inside their defenses! Inside their THOUGHTS!!*

An instant later, the whole squad goes rigid.

A moment after that, the Jamaican jumps sideways as a boulder falls from the sky and crashes into the deck right where he was standing. Suddenly the sky starts raining huge rocks, like refrigerator-sized hail and the Jamaican has to jump around, dodging them and firing wild clusters of bolts to ward off the humongous vultures swooping low between the boulders, pecking at his head.

I click on the deck cameras just to be sure—no boulders, no vultures. *Go Kate!*

The soldiers march to the edge of the deck, throwing their guns and equipment overboard. One officer gets clever and rips the glasses off his head, but this only puts him in the open air and still vulnerable to Kate's illusions. He goes over the side trying to avoid a particularly ugly vulture.

The Jamaican is firing like a demon, but he's got to deal now with the lizards crawling up out of the deck and feasting on his legs. The Jamaican does not like lizards, at least not seven-foot ones with real spiky teeth and purple slashes down the middle of their skulls.

Max has dragged himself to a pumping station, Landau close behind. He's hiding between pipes, moving around equipment. He's got nowhere left to hide.

"What's the point of this, dude? Just give it up! You know how it works, you've done this to people a thousand times in your day."

"Not this."

"I'm sorry, of course not. You wouldn't do this to your poor helpless pinkbrains."

"I don't make anyone into slaves. I'm not a murderer and I'm not a slaver."

"You're not an *anything*!" Landau sneers. "You're not even a fucking mindbender! Dude, you're just a disappointment (Max immediately hears six more voices joining in, all with the same condescending expressions)! You've got all the power but you don't do shit with it! How can you be a mindbender when you feel guilty for stealing a secret or bending some civilian? That's who we *are*!"

"Is that why you do it? Because it's the only way to be who you really are?"

"I do it because I *can*—and because it how you *win*! Winners and Losers! The world is stupid and shallow, dude—it's all about keeping score."

Why are they having a fucking *conversation*? It's like they can't just win—the other guy has to give, has to admit they're right. It's like…family arguments. I don't remember my family but I know that much. And Landau's talking to keep Max distracted until he can seek out and lock down the last section of his brain that's resisting.

"You've got nowhere to go," Landau says. "I've got your root. Game over."

Max doesn't respond. Instead, I hear Kate: *Distract the Jamaican—let me help Max!*

The Jamaican shoots a bolt wildly past Kate—it bores into the deck and it collapses beneath her. She grabs at a beam on the way down, almost knocking herself out but hanging on. Her glasses fly off and clatter onto the deck far below.

The Jamaican wanders to the edge. It's a narrow opening, running right to where Kate clings. If he shoots now, he really can't miss. If he shot totally wide and hit the crane on the far side of the deck, it would still collapse on her.

The crane!

I've never clicked a mouse so fast in my life. I fly through ten pages of identical grid patterns until I find a big square box with a little multi-segment rectangle sticking out the side. The bubble reads MCH and I have no idea what that means but a virtual game controller appears on the bottom of the screen with buttons for moving the arm up down, left and right. It's totally primitive—clearly, just intended to secure the thing in case of storms. But at the moment, it'll do. I gulp hard and start pushing buttons.

The arm flies around like a spastic robot, zips right past the Jamaican and back again. He dodges under a control booth suspended above-deck.

I swing the sucker as hard as I can right back at him—and miss completely. Instead, the arm tears away at the structure over his head and rips it from its moorings. The control room collapses and a huge AC unit on top of it groans and heels forward. The whole section of deck underneath gives way and the Jamaican disappears into it, without catching any rail that I can see.

You need help? I flash to Kate but she's already locked up with Max.

How do I know this? Because the superstructure behind Max and Landau is somehow filling up with a dark starry sky, just a ribbon of sunset orange slicing across the far horizon. In the real world, it's still midmorning, sunny sky—when I look out the porthole, that's what I see. But behind Max and Landau, dark night is coming on fast, a hillside growing out of a blue haze blanketing the platform from end to end.

And Max is suddenly talking back. "So why are we here, both of us? If it's all about keeping score, what's the point? You said yourself, we can have money, power, women, anything we want, right now without anyone's help. I'm a masochist who's hung up on the world's losers, that's my excuse. But what's yours? Why are you still here trying to impress Pietr Volkov?"

"I don't give a shit about him. He's a means to an end."

"So ditch him! You created the lightning gun—they were working for you, Vlad and De Jogt! Why should he share it? Why let him have any control over this thing you did all the sweating for?"

Landau smiles. "Now you're thinking," he says. "Volkov's got connections—Avery's got connections. They make things possible—bigger than these popguns."

"The popguns are pretty impressive."

"You haven't seen their Papa."

The hillside grows out of a deep forest, the high-jutting end of it holding only a few trees and a neat little cabin, windows lit and quavering, either gas lamps or kerosene. Snow starts to fall, big crystalline flakes filling the air around Landau and Max. It's eighty degrees Fahrenheit but only in reality and who cares about that?

"The guns'll be L Corp property," Max parries and Landau turns red.

"I control them!"

"Right, sure," Max says. "Pietr's going to give you ownership of the biggest thing they've got—because why? Because you want to be the big winner? *He* wants to be the big winner! How do you think *that* works out?"

"I'm going to make him bigger!" Landau yells. "I'm going to be his Big Cheese!"

"And there's the point, isn't it?" Max says. "It's not enough to *do* big things—you could do that on your own. But it's not enough. We've got the same weakness—we both want to be known. It isn't real for us unless someone else knows about it. And I suspect that wanting to be known is not a healthy thing for people like us."

"We're not the same!" Landau cries. "I'm taking over the world; you're going to be my slave!"

Landau flashes the butcher's face again but Max doesn't respond at all. I feel Max again inside, draining and filling me up, pulling energy from *Mark Tauber, Savannah Georgia,* the phrase I'm repeating over and over like a mantra. It's my job to keep feeding him that memory. Kate's feeding the dark sky and the cabin and I'm feeding Max's blocking memory and just maybe the three of us might be enough to hold Landau off.

Snow is pelting down everywhere, mounds of it blowing and drifting. Voices echo from the hillside cabin now, angry voices, younger and older, raised and yelling, cutting through the ebbing red along the horizon.

"Fuck you!" Landau says suddenly, breaking away, blinking as though just recognizing the scene around him. "Where do you think—?"

"You told me you killed them, killed your own family, locked the doors and set the place on fire," Max says. "I thought you were boasting, putting me on. But you really did it, didn't you?" A flash of light at the edge of the cabin and suddenly it's burning, the flames crawling the framework of the building, licking at the window casements and doorways.

"Where—? NO!" Landau yells, taking it all in and all at once, I hear the voices—the screams of the people inside as they start to burn. "This is wrong! Stop it!"

Max hobbles out from behind the pipes now, exposing himself, daring Landau to come for him.

"I see myself in people now, I see them in me," he says. "You classify everyone as a winner or a loser, nothing in-between. That's because it's how you see *yourself*—and you're terrified which way the scale's going to tip. The difference between us is, I've got friends who come after me when I'm lost, who find answers when I can't."

Suddenly, the voices are shrieking, the screams from the cabin filling the night sky. Landau looks lightheaded, staggering in spasms, small circles, on the deck, clutching his head in his hands, eyes wide open, though clearly he's straining as desperately as he can to shut them.

"You think I'm weak because I listen to other people's voices, because I can't just shut them down like you do. Shutting out the world isn't strength, it's fear," Max says. "And not of other people. It's fear of what's inside us—of who we've become on our way to being such big winners."

Landau lunges at Max—but, when he gets there, Max isn't there. He's lurched right past him.

"Give it up," Max says. "Live to fight another day."

"I'll kill you!" Landau screams, suddenly a wild animal. "I'll kill EVERYBODY!!" And suddenly the lightning bolts are everywhere, high and low, cutting holes in the deck and blinding, starlike patterns in the sky overhead. Pipes shatter, flying through the snow, the image of the hillside and the burning cabin, lightning criss-crossing the evening sky and shattering the cabin walls, that cabin that won't ever stop burning and that family that won't ever stop screaming in Landau's head. Max, clearly, isn't powering the illusion anymore, it's Landau himself, lost in the memory, drowning in it, finally taking in what he'd held at bay for so long.

Max feints left, Landau lunges that way—but again, Max isn't where he's supposed to be. Max feints right and Landau runs headlong at him, lightning pouring off the coil at point-blank range.

And then somehow Max is behind him. With the strangest expression on his face, aching sadness and pity, he reaches for Landau's temple. The kid seizes up and writhes, stuck to the deck like he's glued to it, attached to Max's finger like it's drilled into his skull, teeth chattering and face going blue, white spidery lines inching down his neck from the spot where Max Renn's finger is frying him.

And then the hatch to the accountant's office opens and I remember all at once where I am. The accountant is nowhere to be seen and I can hear the sea outside—the outer hatch has been opened.

Pietr Volkov walks through the door, pistol in hand and three shooters behind him, dragging De Jogt between them.

Volkov's working hard at my head but I'm maintaining Mark Tauber, Savannah Georgia but good. So he settles for Old Reliable—leveling the pistol at my head. "Time to go on deck," he says coolly.

We climb the inner stairs. Max has pulled Kate up onto the deck, which looks the worse for wear at the moment. Volkov presses the pistol into my temple.

"It's good to know you've adopted the appropriate methods at long last," he tells Max.

"I'm not a murderer," Max says but it doesn't sound the same coming out of his mouth this time.

"We all have our illusions," Volkov says. "Yours was that you would escape. Let's go—"

And then I hear the helicopter blades thumping through the afternoon sky, approaching on the run and a swell rolls through me.

"Attention!" says the deep, familiar voice over a pretty clear loudspeaker. "You are trespassing on Australian government property. All personnel assemble immediately on the foredeck for identification and processing. We are boarding this ship. Any attempt to escape will be apprehended and prosecuted to the fullest extent of the law."

Boots started clattering up and down the stairs, Volkov's getting hailed sixty times a second over the PA. He lurches to a communications station, ready to torch the world on the spot. Take my word for it, I don't get a feeling of accomplishment like this every day.

"This is Pietr Volkov of L Corp, a NATO/SEATO security contractor. We have requisitioned this platform for a project cleared at the highest level. Make no attempt to land. I will provide contacts at US DOD to verify my status and that of this project." He clicks off for barely a second.

"Pietr, old buddy—I thought you wanted to get rid of me!" comes the voice from the copter and now I can't help but grin.

"Who is this?" Volkov demands.

"Scott Cornwell, ol' buddy. Remember me? We played golf a few months ago? I was the ball?"

Volkov's face turns the color of a butcher block table. "Scott," he oozes, "you know my status. I'm virtually a diplomat."

"Pietr—we're a nation of laws. I'll do my best to overlook that."

Now Volkov thunders. "This platform is in international waters! If you attempt to land, you'll be blown out of the water."

"God, you're a hostile fuck!" Cornwell chuckles. "It's Australian government property and nobody there knows anything about you requisitioning it—not to mention wrecking it, from what I can see. But we can discuss that while we evacuate you. Get your staff to the rear platform immediately—we'll take you off first."

Volkov slams the phone into the housing and then nearly rips it out of the wall. "Get my helicopter ready to take off IMMEDIATELY!" he yells. "If another helicopter gets near the pad, shoot them down!" He levels the pistol at me.

"You want to shoot me in front of witnesses?" I tell him. "Scott'll be upset."

Oh, he doesn't like that. I know Cornwell? How can I know Cornwell? Worse, he sees that I brought Cornwell down on him—which means, for some reason he can't fathom, I'm not afraid of being taken by the CIA.

He turns to Goldie. "Get them down to the boats. Get them off here and to headquarters in Darwin. I'm damned if I'm giving Cornwell the pleasure of capturing them."

Volkov stalks off with De Jogt. He's got ten guards with him, all armed to the teeth and the deck is making very nasty groaning noises. "Do you want me to go after him?" Kate asks Max but he doesn't seem to have anything to say. He's retreated inside. I've seen him do that before but this time it doesn't look the same. This time, something hurts.

Goldie and five guards escort us to the water, where a hundred small boats ferry back and forth from the mainland, dropping off supplies and ignoring the carnage above. He takes us to an L Corp ship with a crew of three and puts us onboard with five shooters to keep us manageable. "See you soon," he says in a nasty tone. The crew pushes off and we head out to sea.

I see Cornwell's helicopter pass over us and a stream of others follow. It isn't long before all the boats are turned away and join the procession. Max sits like a statue on the rail, hollow-eyed and motionless.

"Are you getting anything?" I ask Kate and she shakes her head before I've finished the question.

We can't let them take us to Darwin, I flash and she nods like that goes without saying.

A moment later, the shooters throw their guns in a pile and dive over the side into the water. I see the captain's eyes get real agreeable and he turns the ship back out to sea without any instructions that I could hear.

"What happened?"

"I don't have the goggles anymore but I haven't forgotten the frequency they were using," Kate says. "They're really not that smart."

"Where are we going?"

"I just want to get as far away from here as we can get—you have any ideas?"

As it happens, I do. "We can't just drive away from them. We need allies." I watch the sky towards Darwin. "I think the best thing we could do right now is get captured."

thorns
December 2008

Rost Island, Norway

The wildflowers had thorns.

It was the only flaw Katya could find with the place. She'd slept like a baby for the first time in years, delighting upon waking at the sound and smell of the sea, the long grass swaying in the breeze as she set out from the house.

Nils had told her the land would be the first step on her road back and she'd resisted mightily, haughtily. She'd felt exiled, abandoned. But now, trailing the Irish setter between gnarled trees and jumping from rock to rock across an inlet stream, she saw clearly for the first time in a long while.

Peace and Quiet. She couldn't have imagined the possibility a week ago. No photographers would find her here, no journalists asking questions for which she had no answers. On a peninsula jutting into the North Sea, just she and the dog and Nils to follow later in the week—and balmier weather than she had seen in December in many a year—she could start a different life, at least for a while. What was it like to do nothing at all? To just let the hours unfold, like a rock or a bush or some unselfconscious thing? When was the last time she'd asked herself such a question?

The waves were lapping over the dark stones. She skipped a few across the surface of the water and let a few raindrops run down her forehead to the tip of her nose. Darker clouds were moving in, looming behind the little island with its concrete dome. Was it an observatory? She'd seen the glint of a mirror inside that morning, peeking out the bedroom window. Of course, a really good telescope, even half a mile away, could beat hell out of all her daydreams of solitude but they seemed a geeky bunch, puttering back and forth in their little outboard launch every few hours. Not the kind to care about the trials of a Stockholm actress, even one weathering a tabloid breakdown.

The dog raced across the beach, skittering into the water and back, scattering clumps of foam and seaweed in every direction. She settled atop a large boulder, pulled the shawl over her head to keep the sun from burning and laughed a long free cackle at the vain seed inside her that worried about wrinkles while she couldn't imagine ever stepping on a stage again.

But then, maybe she had reached a point where she could imagine imagining.

A moment later, she was flying through the air and crashing down onto a pile of stones. A torrent of wind and rain struck her sideways, drenching her from head to foot. When she regained her feet, welts aching all over her thighs and buttocks, she saw a path slashed clear across the breadth of the beach, a path where the stones were crushed into the coarse sand beneath. She followed the path with her eyes and found herself choking, heart in her throat. At the water's edge lay the body of the dog, almost sheared in half, a line of fire sizzling up the middle of its back — and, out in the sea, on a straight course beyond the dog's body, the observatory or what was left of it, the dome collapsed, mirror shattered, tilting at a crazy angle off its mount, almost invisible for reflecting the sky.

When the authorities arrived half an hour later, Katya was still rooted to the spot, spouting an endless babble to explain how she could possibly have heard nothing, seen nothing, felt only the momentary blast of wind and rain. The interviewers were patient and courteous, reassuring her that, not only would nothing she said ever appear in any public forum, never be heard by anyone outside the scope of the investigation, but that, in fact, she was never to speak a single detail of this to anyone, Nils included. They insisted on reassuring her they would 'replace' the dog.

Not that Katya was reassured in any way. Her head was now filled with far more frightening concerns than she'd ever found on the Stockholm stage.

The End

~~~~

Mindbenders 3: The Big Dream

will follow!

Acknowledgments

To get to this page, I wrote two books, a variety of short stories and an insane number of dead ends. I learned a lot—I sincerely hope never to have to learn so much from any single book ever again.

A host of friends and acquaintances made contributions and suggestions that helped me finally reach this destination. This is only a partial list because I didn't keep notes and it took way too long. So, if I forgot you, my sincere apologies and I will try to correct any omissions in future editions.

Here are the blessed friends I remember right at this moment, in no particular order:

Claire Moed, Samantha Talbot, Elizabeth Lohninger, Joni Wong, Shane Gericke, Tom Monteleone ('make it a bigger world this time'), F. Paul Wilson, Carolla Dibble, Laurie Hardjowirogo, Dianna Dennis, David Leaf, Steve Cosgrove, Margie Nicholson, David Kosky, Maureen Slattery, Marsha Garelick, Sue Leventhal, Barry Nisman, William Papaleo, Joseph Papaleo (father and son, for that matter), Jenny Milchman, Laura Kogel, Tom Smucker and Clare Adams, who offered editorial suggestions along with doing an amazing job of proofreading. If you find any typos here, it's because I didn't transcribe them properly, not because she missed them.

Read a Preview of
'Swindler & Son,'
The new novel by Ted Krever
On Sale December 2018

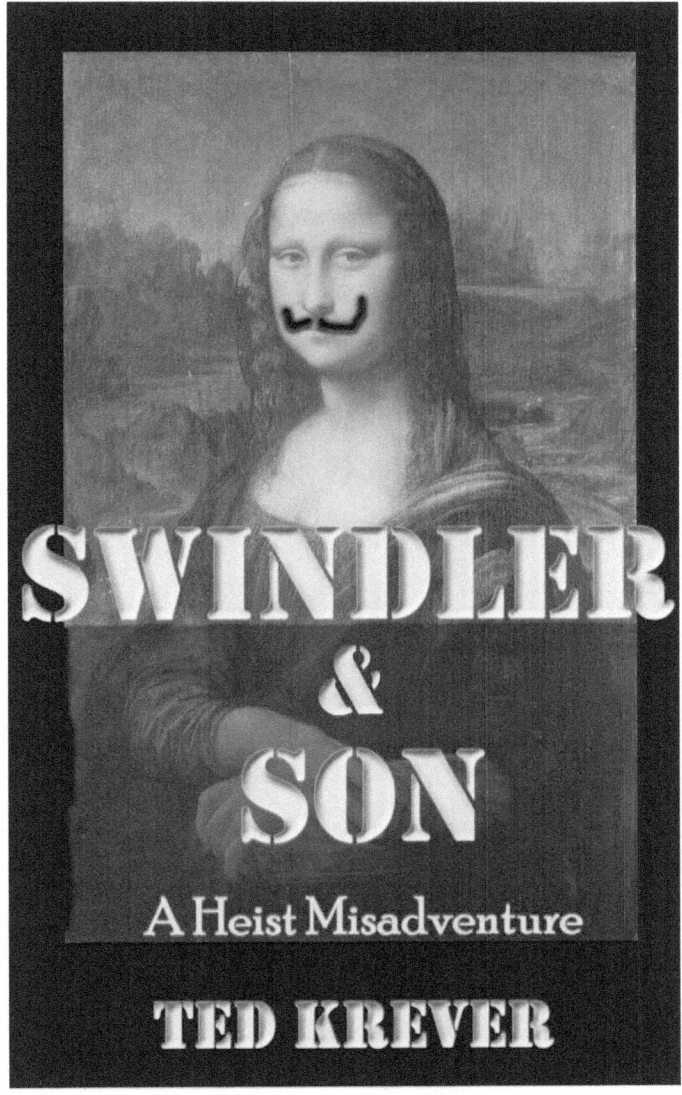

THE START

-So how does it start?

It starts with the sound of my own name spoken aloud.

Call me Nicholas, I'm fine. Nick or Nicky, even better.

But 'Nicholas Marsh' enunciated, first and last, all the way through—when I hear it *that* way, I know I've done something I'm about to pay for.

Hearing it in French, every syllable twisted and slurred and leaking from the earpiece of a Parisian counter-terrorism officer in a Kevlar vest, his back to me and his binoculars trained on my kitchen window—*that's* rock-bottom.

That's how it starts, in the snowy garden of the *Hopital Saint-Louis* in the Tenth Arrondissement, just past sundown on Christmas day, at what I fervently hoped was the end of one of the worst days of my life.

Well, actually, no...

Actually, it started about fifteen minutes earlier, on the other side of the canal, where I was mugged by some twenty-five year-old junkie in a purple-tinted mohawk and a leather jacket.

And several nice tats on his neck that distracted my attention when I should have been focusing on his oncoming fist. He took my wallet and phone and left me aching and dizzy, which is why I wandered groggy several blocks out of my way and approached home through the garden.

I love that garden but none of the official exits land anywhere near my apartment. A few years ago, I found a back door, through the *Musee des Moulages* on the hospital grounds, that let me out near a construction gate right across the street from my building.

I'm just opening that back door when I hear my name and see GIGN, French Special Forces, two officers, huddled like Martians in flak suits, gas masks and sniper rifles, peeking through the construction gate at the wide corner, the entrance to my building and, eight floors above, at the dead coleus drooping from my night table.

Frozen in place, I scan the rooftops and find a squad of dark gray uniforms—and, in case I harbor any last doubts, hear my name one more time from the headset hanging from the blonde officer's right ear. I back instinctively into the doorway, sweating and making twenty-five different plans at the same time.

The bus! They won't be checking the bus on the Boulevard de la Villette, that's an answer. Having any sort of answer helps calms the quiver in my legs, brings them back into something like working order.

This is a mistake—it's got to be. If I'd done something to deserve counter-terrorism, I'd remember it, wouldn't I? More importantly, why in hell didn't somebody tip me off? Who do I know at GIGN?

Out through the door and the museum, retracing my steps, back out the far end of the compound, past the *Chapelle* to the *Rue de la Grange aux Belles*. Up toward the roundabout at a regular clip, walking briskly like a Parisian.

Am I thinking of escape? Hell no, I'm just getting pissed. Why hasn't somebody warned me? Why haven't they given me a chance to buy my way out of this?

Oh sure, GIGN makes it look serious but that just raises the price. I know somebody in every department of government and what they cost. Serious things have been undone before.

By the time the bus makes three stops, I know who to talk to—Beltoise, the second man at the *Surete*. He was at our Christmas party just last night.

I *own* him! At least, I should. If I had a middle-class clientele, if I dealt pot or owned a brothel, I could expect a phone call 24 hours in advance of a raid. It's common courtesy!

He'll be at *D'Azur*, of course, charging his dinner to us as usual.

When I arrive, he's tucked into a dim corner. He rises before I can reach him.

"Why is GIGN all around my apartment? You don't warn me?"

His eyes bulge like marbles. "Where's your phone?"

"Phone? Stolen. I got mugged."

He looks *relieved*. "That's why they're not here yet," he mutters and pulls me into the private room in back.

"Nicky, our past history—and the fact that I like you—is why I'll give you a minute's grace before I call you in." He's serious! His face goes cold—not like he doesn't know me, like he's never *seen* me before. "Normal corruption is one thing—but this?"

Normal corruption? Normal corruption is my *specialty*! He's reducing ten thousand years of civilized give-and-take to a catchphrase. Not to mention, it's fed him quite nicely, thank you, over the years.

I look at his face, at the disappointment and condescension there, and realize what a farce it all is. You treat them like princes but the first time you actually need them to put out...they might as well be in insurance.

Faced with this ingratitude, something inside me just gives up.

"Okay," I tell him. "I surrender."

"What?"

"I'll confess, right now. It's the jet ramps, isn't it?"

He looks confused.

"We have this client, a dictator...you know the old joke about, you're not really a country unless you have your own stamps, your own airline and your own beer? Well, he's got commemorative stamps, a brewery, a Mercedes stretch limo and a portrait of himself as Julius Caesar. But he gets embarrassed when his guests have to descend a staircase off the plane.

"There's a staircase on Air Force One' I tell him and he says, 'They could have a ramp if they wanted one.' So when Kumbatta collapsed, we flew a cargo plane in and liberated a couple of jetramps. The guy was so happy, he painted two Cessna's and proclaimed them the national airline. I don't think we *hurt* anybody."

Beltoise settles into the nearest chair, not saying a word.

"That's not it?"

Silence.

"Okay, Napoleon's penis—that was a good deed, I swear."

"*Excusez moi?*"

"It's your Minister of Defence's fault! Not the present Minister, the old one. He had this...thing about Napoleon's penis, that it should be back in France where it belongs."

"It is in France! Napoleon's body is at Les Invalides!"

"The body, sure, but his penis was removed during the autopsy and it's floated around ever since from collector to collector. It's now owned by a urologist, naturally, in Philadelphia."

"Don't be funny."

"It's true. The BBC measured it a few years ago and found it a bit small. Naturally, that outraged the Minister, who insisted the English don't know how to measure. The urologist's price was just *outrageous* so we found a...more generously-sized one around the same age, for a price the Minister could afford. It made him *happy*."

"You found him another penis?"

"Another *old* penis! You think that was easy? How many three-hundred-year-old penises you think are floating around?"

Beltoise stares at me with—I can't tell if it's respect or concern. The odd thing is, to me, this is actually beginning to feel pretty *righteous*. Confession really *is* good for the soul. "Okay, not the answer. Give me a chance. The eighteen identical one-of-a-kind Moroccan emeralds—"

"No."

"The Van Gogh with the wrong ear missing?"

Beltoise rolls his eyes. "We've never met," he warns, "except for a few state dinners with hundreds of other people I've never met either—but my advice is, you find a quick way out of France now. And don't bother replacing your phone—they'll find you as soon as you do. You understand?"

This is terrifying—Beltoise is a glorified flatfoot with a fancy office. I'm *begging* to be arrested and he's not biting. It's *unnatural*.

"Throw me a bone here," I say. "I don't understand what's happened."

He grimaces. "You know damn well it's the bomb."

"The *BOMB*?"

Of course, I know all about the bomb. I'd arrived back in Paris the day before, just in time for the funerals. Twelve dead, 37 injured, a miracle it wasn't more. A mountain of flowers in plastic sleeves heaped on the rubble, candles arrayed like soldiers in front of the dress shop left somehow intact on the corner.

And a march from the *Place De la Republique* to the *Place de la Nacion*, thousands, orderly and dogged, middle-class families and university students, *Le President* and his rivals, butchers, bakers, artists and computer technicians shuffling through neighborhood streets between broad public squares, solemn and chattering, sombre but fashionable—Paris, formal but somehow intimate. Great buildings and beautiful women dressed in black. Paris is a grand dame, maybe a bit past her prime, but she still knows how to put on a funeral.

'It's an escalation,' they say, the voices that multiply in crowds. Just a few years ago, 'they' were content to shoot up a restaurant or concert hall. Now, somehow, they bring in a bomb the size of a safe to bring down half a block of five-story apartment buildings.

The size of the explosion makes people nervous. Nobody builds a bomb that size to bring down the Rue Breguet. We all sense a grander plan that went awry and the fact that no one claimed responsibility only seems to heighten the tension. You don't even have the consolation of knowing who to be afraid of.

Beltoise, however, has made up his mind.

"It's your shipping certificate!" he yells, no longer caring who hears. "Your company's letterhead! Your *signature* on the bloody thing! You think I will cover for *that*, you're insane!"

I stand frozen for an endless moment, until words I never thought I'd hear myself say come tumbling out of my mouth.

"I didn't do *that*! I'm *innocent*!"

And then, I run.

RUNNING

−You ran?

It's an expression. I know better than to run. I walk at my usual quick pace but not fast enough to attract attention. Okay?

I lose myself in the tangle of back streets, staying off the boulevards, sticking to shorter blocks and parks where I can change direction at will. I stop short in front of angled store windows several times, switch direction several more, take a cab for a short distance and then another to double-back on myself. I'm overdoing it, in truth — if GIGN were really on my tail, they'd just throw on the sirens and take me. Once I'm sure I'm not being followed, I find a thrift shop that's just closing in a church, buy a pair of slacks and a short dark hoodie and wear them out of the store.

−This is tradecraft. Where did you acquire your technique?

Like you don't know. I had a very brief career in — what do you tell strangers at parties? About what you do for a living?

-I don't speak of such things.

We used to call it 'compliance.' I was recruited out of college. They trained me to take in a room or a street, to be invisible when that was useful. Trust no one, calculate the odds, tote up the angles and assume everyone follows their own self-interest.

But they couldn't teach me to be shrewd. I got myself involved in an 'extracurricular' scheme supporting freedom fighters—that is, it became extracurricular once it led to screaming headlines. Next thing I know, I'm getting chewed out in front of a Congressional committee for the exact same things they'd urged us to do in private.

We were thrown out like Big Mac wrappers, three fall guys, small potatoes. A generous severance package—under the table, of course—just go quietly into the night, thank you.

That training comes back to me, now that I'm on the run. Focus! *The bomb! What have I got to do with the fucking bomb?*

I need real information. Somewhere in our files, says Beltoise, is a shipping certificate for a bomb with my signature on it. I can't go home so I almost certainly can't go back to the office. But maybe Harry's apartment is clear.

If this had happened any other time—last week, even!—I could have counted on Harry's counsel, his expertise, his instincts. For fifteen years, he's been there when I needed him.

But that's a huge part of what made this feel like the worst day of my life, even before GIGN's visit. I've no idea if I can count on Harry anymore.

-Explain this please. Who is this Harry and why can't you count on him?

Harry is the majordomo, the ringmaster of our circus, the senior partner in Sandler & Son, affectionately known to staff and select members of the governing elite as Swindler & Son. Everything that isn't about Sara in this story is about Harry.

-And Harry's got problems?

Oh hell no, Harry's got no problems. Harry *is* the problem. Everybody *loves* Harry, *that's* the problem.

And why shouldn't they? Harry makes life a party, a twenty-four-hour Remy Martin and shellfish from the little inlet over *there* and put away your business cards, this isn't some vulgar networking grind, we're here to have *fun!* Remember fun? Harry does.

If you liked the Remy, you must try this cognac—it's Venetian, Dante mentioned it (disparagingly, but he mentioned it) in the *Divine Comedy* and let me introduce you to the Ambassador's wife, she has all the good gossip about the orgies at that other embassy—maybe it was the Czechs but we're not saying. Meanwhile, other groups are discussing 70's film and sex robots and if there's anything else you want to know, the person to speak to is over *there*. The band plays good acoustic jazz, the

Argentine tango couple are giving lessons one-on-one on the terrace and the star of the national football club is kicking balls around with enchanted kids and dazzled grownups on the south lawn.

In Paris, of course. That's our home base. It's one of God's jokes—Harry hated the French so, once we'd been thrown out of every other country in Europe, the only place left to go was Paris. Which, of course, he now loves because how can you not love Paris? It's *Paris*, for God's sake.

And the French love Harry. Big gnarly elegant gay Englishman, what's not to love? He ignores their culture, conducts himself like tenth-generation nobility fallen to trade or maybe a good Savile Row tailor, speaks only enough French to be fed and catered to but laughs and charms so naturally, they can't help themselves. Seduction is the French national pastime; they recognize a Master at work.

I was in Mumbai two years ago, picking up a load of Indian cotton. There was a rash of suicides among cotton farmers in Vidarbha and I was able to pick up several farms' entire crop just by paying off the bank loans. I told myself it was a good deed and a good deal. So I'm in the hotel bar at the end of the day chatting up some girl when a man behind me says, "Oh, you work with Harry Sandler? I was in a steeplechase syndicate with him in Ireland once. Took me for £65,000 quid. Most wonderful time I ever had." He bought us both a drink.

Everybody loves Harry; that's what nearly killed us all. As I watched the Iranian commandos lining up on the deck of the ship three hours ago, in their black stocking caps and their Kalashnikovs aimed at our temples, all I could think was, *Everybody loves Harry*.

Fucking goddamn Harry.

Author Biography

Ted Krever watched the Beatles on Ed Sullivan, went to Woodstock (the good one), and graduated Sarah Lawrence College with a useless degree in creative writing.

He spent several decades creating programs for ABC News, CBS, CNN, A&E, Court TV, MTV News, Discovery People and CBS/48 Hours, and as VP/Production of a short-lived dotcom.

He has driven a 16-wheeler across the Rockies, shot overnight news in NY City, managed a revival-house movie theater and married twice, in a triumph of optimism.

He was once accused of attempting to blow up Ethel Kennedy with a Super-8 projector.

Read more at www.tedkrever.com